BIG GIRL

www.daniellesteelbooks.co.uk

Also by Danielle Steel

* Published outside the UK under the title PASSION'S PROMISE

For more information on Danielle Steel and her books,
see her website at www.daniellesteel.co.uk

DANIELLE STEEL

BIG GIRL

A Novel

CORGI BOOKS

TRANSWORLD PUBLISHERS
61–63 Uxbridge Road, London W5 5SA
A Random House Group Company
www.rbooks.co.uk

BIG GIRL
A CORGI BOOK: 9780552159005

First published in Great Britain
in 2010 by Bantam Press
an imprint of Transworld Publishers
Corgi edition published 2011

Copyright © Danielle Steel 2010

Addresses for Random House Group Ltd companies outside the UK
can be found at: www.randomhouse.co.uk
The Random House Group Ltd Reg. No. 954009

The Random House Group Limited supports The Forest Stewardship Council
(FSC), the leading international forest certification organisation. All our titles that
are printed on Greenpeace approved FSC certified paper carry the FSC logo. Our
paper procurement policy can be found at
www.rbooks.co.uk/environment

Typeset in 11/15.5 Garamond by Falcon Oast Graphic Art Ltd.
Printed in the UK by CPI Cox & Wyman, Reading, RG1 8EX.

2 4 6 8 10 9 7 5 3 1

As always, to my very wonderful children, Trevor, Todd, Beatie, Nick, Sam, Victoria, Vanessa, Maxx, and Zara, who are always there for me, and give me so much joy, caring, love, support, kindness, and just plain old terrific times. In good times and bad, we are there for each other. Thank you for being such *huge* blessings in my life.

With all my love,
Mommy/d.s.

BIG GIRL

Chapter 1

Jim Dawson was handsome from the day he was born. He was an only child, tall for his age, had a perfect physique, and was an exceptional athlete as he grew older, and the hub of his parents' world. They were both in their forties when he was born, and he was a blessing and surprise, after years of trying to have a child. They had given up hope, and then their perfect baby boy appeared. His mother looked at him adoringly as she held him in her arms. His father loved to play ball with him. He was the star of his Little League team, and as he grew older, the girls swooned over him in school. He had dark hair and velvety brown eyes and a pronounced cleft in his chin, like a movie star. He was captain of the football team in college, and no one was surprised when he dated the homecoming queen, a pretty girl whose family had moved to southern California from Atlanta in freshman year. She was petite and slim with hair and eyes as dark as his, and skin like Snow White. She was gentle and soft-spoken and in awe of him. They got engaged the night of graduation and married on Christmas the same year.

Jim had a job in an ad agency by then, and Christine spent the six months after graduation preparing for their wedding. She had gotten her bachelor's degree, but her only real interest during her four years in college was finding a husband and getting married. And they were a dazzling pair with their flawless all-American good looks. They were a perfect complement to each other and reminded all who saw them of a couple on the cover of a magazine.

Christine had wanted to model after they were married, but Jim wouldn't hear of it. He had a good job, and made a good salary, and he didn't want his wife to work. What would people think of him if she did? That he wasn't able to provide for her? He wanted her at home and waiting for him every night, which was what she did. And people who knew them said they were the best-looking couple they had ever seen.

There was never any question about who wore the pants in the family. Jim made the rules, and Christine was comfortable that way. Her own mother had died when she was very young. And Jim's mother, whom Christine called Mother Dawson, sang her son's praises constantly. And Christine readily revered him just as his parents had. He was a good provider, a loving husband, fun to be with, a perfect athlete, and he rose steadily in importance in the ad agency. He was friendly and charming with people, as long as they admired him and didn't criticize him. But most people had no reason to. Jim was a personable young man, he made friends easily, and he put his wife on a pedestal and took good care of her. All he expected of her was to do as he said, worship and adore him, and let him run the show. Her father had had similar ideas, and she'd been perfectly brought up to be the devoted wife of a man like him. Their life was everything she had hoped for, and more. There were no unpleasant surprises with Jim, no strange behavior, no disappointments. He protected her and took care of her, and provided hand-somely. And their relationship worked perfectly for both of them. Each knew their role in the relationship and played by the rules. He was the Adored, and she the Adorer.

They were in no hurry to have children for the first few years, and might have waited longer if people hadn't begun to comment about why they didn't have them. It felt like criticism to Jim, or like the suggestion that maybe they couldn't have them, although they both enjoyed their independence without children to tie them down. Jim took her on weekend trips frequently, they went on fun vacations, and he took her out to dinner once or twice a week, although Christine was a good cook and had learned to make his favorite meals. Neither of them was suffering from the lack of children, although they agreed that they wanted them eventually. But five years after they got married, even Jim's parents were beginning to worry that they might be having the same difficulties that had delayed them from having a family for nearly twenty years. Jim assured them that there were no problems, they were just having fun and were in no hurry to have children. They were twenty-seven years old, and enjoying feeling free and unencumbered.

But the constant inquiries finally got to him, and he told Christine that it was time to start a family. And as she always did, Christine agreed. Whatever Jim thought best seemed right to her too. Christine got pregnant immediately, which was faster than they expected. It was easier than they both had planned, they had assumed it might take six months or a year. And despite her mother-in-law's concerns, the pregnancy was easy for Christine.

When she went into labor, Jim drove her to the

hospital and opted not to be in the delivery room when the baby came, which seemed like the right plan to Christine too. She didn't want him to do anything that would make him ill at ease. He was hoping for a boy, which was her fondest wish too, in order to please him. It didn't even occur to either of them that the baby might be a girl, and they had confidently opted not to fnd out the baby's sex. As virile as he was, Jim expected his first-born to be a son, and Christine decorated the nursery in blue. Both of them were absolutely sure it was a boy.

The baby was in a breech position and had to be delivered by cesarean section, so Christine was still asleep from the anesthetic in the recovery room, when Jim heard the news. And when he saw the baby the nurse presented to him at the nursery window, for a minute, or longer, he thought the baby he was seeing had been switched. The baby had a perfectly round face with chubby cheeks that bore no resemblance to either of them, with a halo of white blond hair. And more shocking than her features or coloring, it was a girl. This was not the baby they had expected, and as she stared at him through the nursery window, all he could think of was that the infant looked like the elderly British monarch Queen Victoria. He said as much to one of the nurses, and she scolded him and said that his daughter was beautiful. Being unfamiliar with the grimaces of newborns, he disagreed. She looked like someone else's child to him, and surely nothing like him or Christine, and he was filled with disappointment as he sat glumly in the waiting room, until they summoned him to Christine. And as soon as she saw the look on his face, she knew that it was a girl and that, in her husband's eyes, she had failed.

'It's a girl?' she whispered, still woozy from the anesthetic, as he nodded speechlessly. How was he going to tell his friends that his son had turned out to be a girl? It was a major blow to his ego and image and something he could not control, which never sat well with him. Jim liked to orchestrate everything, and Christine was always willing to play along.

'Yes, it's a girl,' he finally mustered as a tear squeezed out the corner of Christine's eye. 'She looks like Queen Victoria.' And then he teased Christine a little. 'I don't know who the father is, but she looks like she has blue eyes, and she's blond.' No one on either side of their families was fair, except his own grandmother, which seemed like a stretch to him. But he didn't doubt Christine. This child was obviously some kind of throwback, in their combined gene pool, but she certainly didn't look like she was theirs. The nurses had been saying that she was very cute, but Jim wasn't convinced. And it was several hours before they brought her to Christine, who gazed at her in wonder as she held her and touched her little hands. She was tightly swaddled in a pink blanket. Christine had just been given a shot to keep her milk from coming in, since she had decided not to nurse. Jim didn't want her to, and she had no desire to either. She wanted to get her figure back as quickly as possible, since Jim had always liked her petite, lithe shape and didn't find her attractive while she was pregnant. She had been careful with her weight during the pregnancy. Like Jim, she found it hard to believe that this chubby white blond baby was theirs. She had long, straight sturdy legs like Jim's. But her features didn't look even remotely familiar to either of them. And Mother Dawson was quick to agree with Jim when she saw her, and said she looked like Jim's paternal grandmother, and said she hoped she didn't look like her later. She had been a round, heavyset woman for her entire life, who had been best known for her cooking and sewing skills and not her looks.

By the day after her birth, the shock of her being a female had worn off a little, although Jim's friends at the office had teased him that he would have to try again for a son. And Christine was worried that he was angry at her about it, but he very sweetly reassured her that he was glad that she and the baby were healthy, and they'd make the best of it. The way he said it made Christine feel as though she had come in second best, and Mother Dawson endorsed that idea. It was no secret that Jim had wanted a son and not a daughter, almost as confirmation of his manhood and ability to father a son. And since it had never dawned on either of them that they might produce a daughter, they had no girls' names ready for the chubby blond baby that lay in Christine's arms.

He had been joking about her looking like Queen Victoria, but they both agreed that they liked the name, and Jim took it one step further, and suggested Regina as a middle name. Victoria Regina Dawson, for Queen Victoria. Victoria the Queen. The name seemed strangely apt as they looked at her, and Christine agreed. She wanted her husband to be happy with the choice of name at least, if not the sex. She still felt as though she had failed him by having a girl. But by the time they left the hospital five days later, he seemed to have forgiven her.

Victoria was an easy, happy baby who was good-natured and undemanding. She walked and talked early, and people always commented on what a sweet little girl she was. She remained very fair, and the white blond fuzz she'd had when she was born turned into a crown of blond ringlets. She had big blue eyes, and pale blond hair, and the creamy white complexion that went with it. Some people commented that she looked very English, and then Jim always commented that she'd been named for Queen Victoria, whom she looked like, and then laughed heartily. It became his own favorite joke about the baby, which he was more than willing to share, while Christine tittered demurely. She loved her daughter, but the love of her life had always been her husband, and that hadn't changed. Unlike some women who became totally focused on their children, the central focus of her world was first Jim, and then the baby. Christine was the perfect companion for a narcissist of Jim's proportions. She only had eyes for him. And although he still wanted a son to complete him, and toss a ball with, they were in no hurry to have a second child. Victoria fit easily into their life and caused few disruptions, and they were both afraid that two children, particularly if close together, would be hard to manage, so they were content to have only Victoria for now. Mother Dawson rubbed salt in Jim's wounds by saying it was too bad they hadn't had a son, because then they wouldn't have had to consider having a second child, since only children were always brighter. And of course her son was an only child.

Victoria appeared to be extremely intelligent as she got older. She was chatty and amiable, and had nearly adult conversations with them by the time she was three. She said funny things, and was alert and interested in everything around her. Christine taught her to read when she was four. And when she was five, her father told her she had been named after a queen. Victoria would smile with delight every time he said it. She knew what queens looked like. They were beautiful and wore pretty dresses in all the fairy tales she read. And sometimes they even had magic powers. She knew she had been named after Queen Victoria, but she had no idea what the queen looked like. Her father always told her that she'd been named after the queen because she looked like her. She knew that she was supposed to look like her father's grandmother, but she had never seen a picture of her either, and she wondered if she had been a queen too.

Victoria was still round and chubby when she was six. She had sturdy little legs, and she was often told that she was big for her age. She was in first grade by then, and taller than many of the children. And she was heavier than some of them too. People called her a 'big girl,' which she always took as a compliment. And she was still in first grade when she was looking at a book with her mother one day, and saw the queen she had been named after. Her name was written clearly under her picture. Victoria Regina, just like Victoria's own name.

The queen was holding a pug dog, who looked astonishingly like the monarch herself, and the photograph had been taken late in her life. Victoria sat staring at the page for a long time and didn't say a word.

'Is that her?' she fnally asked her mother, turning her huge blue eyes up to her face. Christine nodded with a smile. After all, it was just a joke. She looked like Jim's grandmother and no one else.

'She was a very important queen in England a long time ago,' Christine explained.

'She's not even wearing a pretty dress, she doesn't have a crown, and her dog is ugly too.' Victoria looked devastated as she said it.

'She was very old by then,' Victoria's mother said, trying to soften the moment. She could see that her daughter was upset, and it tugged at her heart. She knew he meant no harm, but Jim's little joke had momentarily backfired, and Victoria looked stricken. She stared at the picture for ages, and two tears rolled slowly down her cheeks. Christine didn't say a word as they turned the page, and she hoped that Victoria would forget the image she had seen. She never did. And her sense of how her father viewed her, like a queen, was never the same again.

Chapter 2

A year after Victoria saw the photograph of Queen Victoria, which forever changed her image of herself, her parents informed her that she had a baby brother or sister on the way. And Victoria was thrilled. Several of her friends at school had had siblings by then, she was one of the few who didn't, and she loved the idea of a baby to play with, like a real live doll. She was in second grade when they told her the news. And when she heard her parents talking about it late one night, when they thought she was asleep, she heard the frightening words that the new baby was an accident, and she wasn't sure what that meant. She was afraid that it had been injured somehow, and feared it might even be born without arms or legs, or maybe it would never walk when it got older. She didn't know how bad the accident had been, and she didn't want to ask. Her mother had cried about it, and her father sounded worried too. They both said that things were fine the way they were now, with just Victoria. She was an easy child who never bothered them and did as she was told. At seven years old, she gave them no problems, and her father said during the entire pregnancy that he hoped it would be a boy. Her mother seemed to want that too, but this time she decorated the nursery in neutral white instead of blue. She had learned that lesson once before, when Victoria took them by surprise and turned out to be a girl. Mother Dawson predicted that it would be a girl again this time, and Victoria hoped so too. Her parents had once again opted not to find out the sex for sure. Victoria's mother was afraid of a bad surprise, clinging to the hope, for as long as she could, that it might be a boy this time.

Victoria wasn't sure why, but her parents didn't seem as excited about the baby as she was. Her mother complained a lot about how big she was, and her father teased Victoria and said he hoped it wouldn't look like her. He never failed to remind her that she looked like his grandmother. There were few pictures of her, but those that Victoria had finally seen showed a large woman wearing an apron, with seemingly no waist, enormous hips, and a bulbous nose. She wasn't sure which was worse, looking like her paternal great-grandmother, or like the ugly queen whose photograph she had seen posing with her dog. And after seeing the photographs of her great-grandmother, she had become obsessed with the size of her own nose. It was small and round, and she thought it looked like an onion planted in the middle of her face. She hoped for its sake that the new baby hadn't inherited the same nose. But since the baby was an 'accident,' there seemed to be far more serious things to worry about than its nose. Her parents had never explained the accident to her, but she hadn't forgotten the conversation she'd overheard. It made Victoria all the more determined to dedicate herself to the new baby, and do whatever was needed to help with it. She hoped the damage from the accident it had experienced wasn't too great. Maybe it was just a broken arm, or a bump on the head.

Christine's C-section was planned this time, and Victoria's parents had explained to her that her mother would be in the hospital for a week, and she wouldn't be able to see her mother or the baby until they came home from the hospital. They said those were the rules, and she wondered if it was to give them time to fix whatever damage the baby had sustained in the mysterious event that no one seemed to want to discuss or explain.

The day the baby was born, her father came home at six o'clock when Victoria's grandmother was preparing dinner for her. They looked at him expectantly, and his disappointment was evident when he told them it was a girl. And then he smiled and said the baby was beautiful and looked just like him and Christine this time. He seemed enormously relieved, even though it hadn't been a boy. And he said they were calling her Grace, because she was so pretty. Grandmother Dawson smiled too then, proud of her ability to guess the baby's sex. She had been sure it was a girl. Jim said she had dark hair, big brown eyes like both of them, the same white skin as her mother, and perfectly formed tiny pink lips. He said she was so pretty they could have used her for an ad for babies. Her beauty made up for her not being a boy. He made no mention of any injury to the baby, from the accident that Victoria had been worried about for the past eight months, and she was relieved too. She hoped the baby was okay, and she sounded very cute.

They called her mother at the hospital the next day, and she sounded very tired. It made Victoria even more determined to do everything she could to help when they got home.

Grace was even prettier than they'd said when Victoria saw her for the first time. She was absolutely exquisite and perfectly formed. She looked like a baby in a picture book, or an ad, as her father had said. Grandmother Dawson clucked over her immediately, and took the bundle from Christine's arms as Jim helped her into a chair, and Victoria tried to get an even better look. She was aching to hold the baby, kiss her cheeks, coo over her, and touch her tiny toes. She wasn't jealous of her for an instant, only happy and proud.

'She's gorgeous, isn't she?' Jim said proudly to his mother, who instantly agreed. There was no mention made of his paternal grandmother this time, and no need to. Baby Grace looked like a porcelain doll, and they all agreed that she was the prettiest baby they had ever seen. She looked nothing like her older sister who had big blue eyes and wheat-colored hair. It was hard to imagine that the two were even sisters, or that Victoria actually belonged in this family, with all of them so dark while she was so fair. And her pudgy body looked nothing like them either. No one compared this baby to Queen Victoria, or mentioned her round nose. She had the nose of a pixie or a cameo, just like Christine's. It was clear from the moment she was born that Grace was one of them, while Victoria appeared to have been dropped on their doorstep by someone else. Grace was perfect, and all Victoria felt was love as she looked at her with adoration in her grandmother's arms. She couldn't wait for them to set her down so she could pick her up herself. This long-awaited baby sister was hers. She had begun to love her long before she was born. And now she was here at last.

Jim couldn't resist teasing his older daughter, as he always did. He was that kind of guy, and loved making jokes at the expense of someone else. His friends thought he was very funny, and he had no qualms about who he made the butt of his jokes. He turned to Victoria with a wry grin, as she gazed lovingly at the baby.

'I guess you were our little tester cake,' he said, ruffling her hair affectionately. 'This time we got the recipe just right,' he commented happily, as Grandmother Dawson explained that a tester cake was what you made to check the combination of ingredients and the heat of the oven. It never came out right the first time, she said, so you threw the tester cake away and tried again. It made Victoria suddenly terrified that because Grace had come out so perfectly, maybe they would throw her away. But no one said anything about it, as her mother, grandmother, and new baby sister went upstairs. Victoria followed them with a look of awe. She stood at a discreet distance and watched everything they did. She wanted to learn how to do it all herself. She was sure her mother would let her, once her grandmother went home. She had asked before Grace came, and her mother said she would.

They changed the baby into a tiny pink nightgown, wrapped her in a blanket, and Christine gave her the bottle of formula they'd given her at the hospital. And then she burped her and laid her down in the bassinet. It was the first chance Victoria had gotten to take a good long look at the new arrival. She really was the most beautiful baby Victoria had ever seen, but even if she hadn't been, even if she had had their great-grandmother's nose, or looked like Queen Victoria too, she would have loved her anyway. She already did. Her beauty didn't matter to Victoria at all, only to her family.

While her mother and grandmother were talking, Victoria cautiously stuck her finger into the bassinet right into the baby's hand, and the baby looked up at her, and curled her tiny fingers around Victoria's finger. It was the most exciting moment of Victoria's life so far, and she instantly felt the bond between the two of them, and knew it would only get stronger and last forever. She made a silent vow to take care of her all her life and never let anyone hurt her or make her cry. She wanted baby Grace's life to be perfect, and was willing to do whatever she had to to ensure that. Grace closed her eyes then and went to sleep, as Victoria stood and watched her. She was so glad there had been no damage from the accident, and Grace was here at last.

She thought of what her father had said then about her being the tester cake, and wondered if it was true. Maybe they had only had her to make sure they got it right with Grace. And if that was true, they certainly had. She was the sweetest thing Victoria had ever seen, and her parents and grandmother said so too. For one tiny instant, Victoria wished that someone else had been the tester cake, and they had felt about her the way they obviously did about Grace. She wished that she was a victory and not a failure of the recipe or the oven temperature. And whatever their intentions had been in having her first, she just hoped they never decided to throw her away. All she wanted now was to share the rest of her life with Grace, and be the best big sister in the world. And she was glad for the baby that she hadn't gotten their great-grandmother's nose too.

She went downstairs to have lunch with her parents and grandmother then, while the baby slept peacefully upstairs, having just been fed and changed. Her mother had told her that she would sleep a lot for the first few weeks. At lunch, her mother talked about getting her figure back as quickly as she could, and Jim poured champagne for the adults, and smiled at Victoria. There was always something faintly ironic about the way he looked at her, as though they shared a joke, or as though she was the joke. Victoria was never quite sure which it was, but she liked it when he smiled at her. And now she was happy to have Grace. She was the baby sister she had dreamed of all her life, someone to love, and who would love her just as much as she loved her.

Chapter 3

Victoria's mother taught her to do everything for the baby. By the time Grace was three months old, Victoria could change a diaper, bathe her, dress her, play with her for hours, and feed her. The two were inseparable. And it gave Christine a much-needed break on busy days. Victoria helping her mother with the baby gave Christine time to play bridge with her friends, take golf lessons, and see her trainer four times a week. She had forgotten how much work babies were. And Victoria loved to help her. The moment she came home from school, she washed her hands, picked her sister up, and took care of whatever she needed. It was Victoria who won Grace's first smile, and it was obvious that the baby adored her, just as Victoria was crazy about Grace.

Grace remained a picture-perfect baby. By the time she was a year old, whenever Christine took the girls to the supermarket with her, someone stopped her. Living in Los Angeles, there were often movie scouts in ordinary places. They solicited Christine for movies, TV shows, commercials, print ads, and working in advertising; Jim had been offered his share of those opportunities too, whenever he showed her picture. Victoria would watch in fascination as people approached them and tried to get her mother to let them use Grace in every kind of ad, TV show, or movie, and Christine always graciously said no. She and Jim had no desire to exploit their baby, but they were always flattered by the offers and told friends about them later. Watching the exchanges, and hearing about them afterward always made Victoria feel invisible. It was as though she didn't exist when the scouts talked to her mother. The only child they saw was Grace. Victoria didn't mind it, but sometimes she wondered what it would be like to be on TV or in a movie. It was fun that Grace was so pretty, and Victoria loved dressing her up, like a doll, with ribbons in her curly dark hair. She was a beautiful baby and turned into an equally lovely looking toddler. And Victoria nearly melted the first time her baby sister said her name. Grace chortled happily whenever she saw her, and was fiercely attached to her older sister.

When Grace was two and Victoria was nine, their grandmother Dawson died, after a brief illness, which left Christine with no help with the baby except for what Victoria did to assist her. The only babysitter they had ever used was Jim's mother, so after her mother-in-law's passing, Christine had to find a babysitter they could rely on when they went out in the evenings. Thereafter there was a parade of teenage girls who came to use the phone, watch TV, and let Victoria take care of the baby, which both sisters preferred anyway. Victoria got more and more responsible as she got older, and Grace got more beautiful with each passing year. She had a sunny disposition and laughed and smiled constantly, mostly at the urging of her older sister, who was the only person in the family who could make her laugh through her tears or stop a tantrum. Christine was far less adept with her than her older daughter. Christine was only too happy to let her take care of Grace. And by then, her father still regularly teased her about being their 'tester cake.' Victoria knew exactly what that meant, that Grace was beautiful and she wasn't, and they had gotten it right the second time around. She had explained that to a friend once, who had looked horrified by the explanation, much more so than Victoria, who was used to the term by now. Her father didn't hesitate to use it. Christine had objected to it once or twice, and Jim assured her that Victoria knew he was just teasing. But in fact Victoria believed him. She was convinced by then that she was the mistake, and Grace their ultimate achievement. That impression was reinforced by each person who admired Grace. Victoria's sense of being invisible became deeply entrenched. Once people had commented on how adorable and beautiful Gracie was, they had no idea what to say about Victoria, so they said nothing and ignored her.

Victoria wasn't ugly, but she was plain. She had sweet, natural fair looks, and straight blond hair that her mother put in braids, as compared to Grace's halo of dark ringlets. Victoria's hair had gotten straight as she got older. She had big innocent blue eyes the color of a summer sky, but Grace and her parents' dark ones always seemed more exotic and more striking to her. And their eye color was all the same, as was their hair. Hers was different. And both her parents and Grace had thin frames, her father was tall, and her mother and the baby were delicate and fine-boned and had small frames. Grace and her parents were a reflection of each other. Victoria was different. She had a square look to her, a bigger frame, and broad shoulders for a child. She looked healthy, with rosy cheeks and prominent cheekbones.

The one remarkable feature about her was that she had long legs, like a young colt. Her legs always seemed too long and thin for her squat body, as her grandmother had put it. She had a short torso that made her legs seem even longer. Despite her wider frame, she was nonetheless quick and graceful. And even as a child, she was big for her age, not enough to be called fat, but there was nothing slight about her. Her father always made an issue that she was too heavy for him to pick her up, while he tossed Grace in the air like a feather. Christine had a tendency to be underweight even after her babies, and in great shape thanks to her trainer and exercise classes. And Jim was tall and lean, and Grace was never a really chubby baby.

What Victoria was more than anything was different from the rest of them. Enough so for everyone to notice. And more than once, people had asked her parents within her hearing if she was adopted. She felt like one of those picture cards they held up at school that showed an apple, an orange, a banana, and a pair of galoshes, while the teacher asked which one was different. In her family, Victoria was always the galoshes. It was a strange feeling she'd had all her life, of being different, and not fitting in. At least if one of her parents had looked like her, she would have felt as though she belonged. But as it was, she didn't, she was the one person out of sync, and no one had ever called her a beauty, as they did Gracie. Gracie was picture perfect and Victoria was the unattractive older sister, who didn't match the rest of them.

And Victoria had a healthy appetite, which kept her body broader than it might have been otherwise. She ate big portions at every meal, and always cleaned her plate. She liked cakes and candy and ice cream and bread, particularly when it was fresh out of the oven. She ate a big lunch at school. She could never resist a dish of french fries, or a hot dog bun, or a hot fudge sundae. Jim liked to eat well too, but he was a big man, and never gained weight. Christine existed mostly on broiled fish, steamed vegetables, and salads, all of which Victoria hated. She preferred cheeseburgers, spaghetti and meatballs, and, even as a child, often helped herself to seconds, despite her father frowning at her, or even laughing about it and making fun of her. No one in her family ever seemed to gain weight except her. And she never skipped a meal. Feeling full gave her a sense of comfort.

'You're going to regret that appetite one day, young lady,' her father always warned her. 'You don't want to be overweight by the time you go to college.' College seemed like a lifetime away, and the mashed potatoes were sitting right in front of her, next to the platter of fried chicken.

But Christine was always careful what she fed the baby. She explained that Grace had a different frame and was built like her, although Victoria sneaked her lollipops and candy, and Grace loved it. She would scream with delight when she saw a Tootsie Roll Pop emerge for her from Victoria's pocket. And even when Victoria only had one, she gave it to her sister.

Victoria had never been popular in school, and her parents very seldom let her have friends over, so her social life was limited. Her mother said that two children making a mess of the house was enough for her to deal with. And she never liked any of Victoria's friends when she met them. She always found fault with them for one reason or another, so Victoria stopped asking to invite them. As a result, no one invited Victoria over after school, since she never reciprocated. And she wanted to get home to help with the baby. She had friends at school, but her friendships didn't extend past school hours. The drama of her early school years was being the only child in fourth grade who didn't get a valentine. She had come home in tears, and her mother told her not to be silly. Gracie had been her valentine, and the next year Victoria told herself she didn't care, and braced herself for disappointment. She actually got one that year from a girl who was as tall as she was. All the boys were shorter. The other girl was a beanpole, and actually much taller than Victoria, who was wider.

And the next drama she faced was growing breasts when she was eleven. She did everything she could to hide them, and wore baggy sweatshirts over everything she owned, lumberjack shirts eventually, and everything two sizes larger. But they continued growing, much to Victoria's chagrin. And by seventh grade she had the body of a woman. She thought of her great-grandmother often, with her wide hips and thick waist, large breasts and full figure. Victoria was praying she never got as big as her great-grandmother had been. The only thing different about her were the long thin legs that never seemed to stop growing longer. Victoria didn't know it, but they were her best feature. Her parents' friends always referred to her as a 'big girl,' and she was never sure what part of her they were referring to, her long legs, big breasts, or ever-widening body. And before she could figure out which part of her they were looking at, they turned their attention to the elflike Gracie. Victoria felt like a monster beside her, or a giant. And with her height, and her womanly body, she looked much older than her years. Her art teacher in eighth grade called her Rubenesque, and she didn't dare ask him what it meant, and didn't want to know. She was sure it was just a more artistic way of calling her big, which was a term she had come to hate. She didn't want to be big. She wanted to be small, like her mother and sister. She was five feet seven when she stopped growing in eighth grade, which wasn't enormous, but it was taller than most of her female classmates, and all of the boys at that age. She felt like a freak.

She was in seventh grade when Gracie started kindergarten, and she took her to her classroom. Her mother had dropped them both off at school, and Victoria had the pleasure of taking Grace to meet her teacher and watched her walk into the room with caution and turn to blow a kiss to her big sister. She watched over her all year at recreation, and took her home after afternoon day care. And the same was true in eighth grade, when Gracie was in first grade. But in the fall Victoria would be entering high school, at a different school, in another location, and she would no longer be there for Gracie, or see her if she walked past her classroom during the day. And she was going to miss her. And so was Gracie, who relied on her older sister and loved seeing her peek into her classroom throughout the day. Both girls cried on Victoria's last day in eighth grade, and Gracie said she didn't want to come back to school without Victoria in the fall. But Victoria said she had to. Eighth grade was the end of an era for Victoria, and one she had cherished.

It always made her happy knowing Gracie was nearby.

The summer before Victoria entered high school she went on her first diet. She had seen an ad for an herbal tea in the back of a magazine, and sent away for it with her allowance. The ad said that it was guaranteed to make her lose ten pounds, and she wanted to enter high school looking thinner and more sophisticated than she had in middle school. With puberty and a richer figure, she had put on roughly ten pounds over what she was supposed to weigh, according to their doctor. The herbal tea worked better than expected and made her desperately ill for several weeks. Grace said she was green and looked really sick, and asked why she was drinking tea that smelled so bad. Her parents had no idea what was wrong with her, since she didn't tell them what she'd done. The evil brew had given her severe dysentery, and she didn't leave the house for several weeks, and said she had the flu. Her mother told her father that it was typical pre-high school nerves. But in the end, just by making her so ill, the herbal tea caused her to lose eight pounds, and Victoria liked the way she looked as a result.

The Dawsons lived on the border of Beverly Hills in a nice residential neighborhood. They had the house they'd lived in since before Victoria was born, and Jim was the head of the ad agency by then. He had a satisfying career, and Christine kept busy with her two girls. It seemed like the perfect family to them, and they didn't want more children. They were forty-two years old, had been married for twenty years, and had a manageable life. They were happy they hadn't had more kids, and were pleased with the two they had. Jim liked to say that Grace was their beauty, and Victoria had the brains. There was room for both in the world. He wanted Victoria to go to a good college and have a meaningful career. 'You'll need to rely on your brains,' he assured her, as though she had nothing else to offer the world.

'You'll need more than that,' Christine had said. It worried her sometimes that Victoria was so smart. 'Men don't always like smart girls,' she said, looking worried. 'You have to look attractive too.' She had been nagging her about her weight in the past year, and was pleased about the eight pounds she'd lost, with no idea of what Victoria had done to herself for the past month to shed the weight. She wanted Victoria to be thin too, not just smart. They were much less worried about Gracie, who with her charm and beauty, even at seven, looked as though she could conquer the world. Jim was her willing slave.

The family went to Santa Barbara for two weeks at the end of summer, before Victoria started high school, and they all had a good time. Jim had rented a house in

Montecito, as he had before, and they went to the beach every day. He commented on Victoria's figure, and after that she wore a shirt over her bathing suit and refused to take it off. He had observed how big her bust was, and had then mitigated it by saying she had killer legs. He referred far more often to her body than he did to her excellent grades. He expected that of her, but always made it clear that he was disappointed by her looks, as though she had failed somehow, and it was a reflection on him. She had heard it all before, many times. He and her mother went for long walks on the beach every day, while she helped Gracie build sand castles with flowers and rocks and Popsicle sticks on them. Gracie loved doing it with her, which made Victoria happy. Her father's comments about her looks always made her sad. And her mother pretended not to hear, never reassured her, and never came to her defense. Victoria knew instinctively that her mother was disappointed by her looks too.

There was a boy Victoria liked in Montecito that summer, in a house across the street. Jake was the same age she was, and he was going to Cait in southern California in the fall. He asked if he could write to her from boarding school, and she said he could, and gave him her address in L.A. They talked late into the night about how nervous they were about high school. Victoria admitted to him in the darkness, as they shared a stolen bottle of beer, from his parents' bar, and a cigarette, that she had never been popular before. He couldn't see why. He thought she was a really smart, fun girl. He liked talking to her and thought she was a nice person. She'd never had beer before, nor smoked, and she threw up when she went home. But no one noticed. Her parents were in bed, and Gracie was fast asleep in the next room. And Jake left the next day. They were going to visit his grandparents in Lake Tahoe before he started school. Victoria had no grandparents anymore, which she thought was a blessing sometimes, since she only had her parents to comment on her looks. Her mother thought she should cut her hair and start an exercise program in the fall. She wanted her to do gymnastics or ballet, without realizing how uncomfortable Victoria was about appearing in front of other girls in a leotard. Victoria would have died first. She'd rather keep the figure she had than lose it that way. It had been easier just making herself sick with the nasty herbal tea.

It was boring for her in Montecito when Jake left. She wondered if she'd hear from him once he started school. For the rest of the time in Montecito, she played with Grace. Victoria didn't mind that her sister was seven years younger, she always had fun with her. And her parents always told their friends that the seven-year age difference between them really worked. Victoria had never been jealous of her baby sister for a minute, and was a totally reliable babysitter now that she was fourteen. They left Gracie with her older sister whenever they went out, which they did with increasing frequency as the girls got older.

They had one big scare during the trip, when Grace ventured too far out at the water's edge one afternoon, at low tide. Victoria had been with her and went back to their towel for a minute to get more sunscreen to put on her sister. And then the tide came in, and the current in the water got strong. A wave knocked Gracie over, and within an instant she disappeared as she was sucked out into the ocean and tossed under a wave. Victoria saw it happen and screamed as she raced to the water, dove into the wave, and came up spluttering with a grip on Grace's arm as another wave hit them both. By then, their parents had seen it too, and Jim was running toward the water, with Christine right behind him. He rushed into the surf, and grabbed both girls with his powerful arms and pulled them out, as Christine stood watching in silent horror, frozen to the spot. Jim turned to Gracie first.

'Don't ever do that again! Don't play in the water alone!'

And then he turned to Victoria with a fierce look in his eye. 'How could you leave her alone like that?' Victoria was crying, shaken by what had happened, with her wet shirt glued to her body over her bathing suit.

'I went to get sunscreen for her, so she didn't burn,' she said between sobs. Christine said nothing and put a towel around Grace, whose lips were blue. She had been in the water for too long before the tide began to turn.

'She almost drowned!' her father shouted at her, shaking with fear and fury. He rarely got angry at his children, but he was shaken by the close call, as they all were. He never said a word about Victoria rushing in to get her, and pulling her out of the surf right before he arrived. He was too upset by what had almost happened, and Victoria was too. Grace had taken refuge in her mother's arms, who was holding her tight in the towel. Her dark ringlets were wet and plastered to her head.

'I'm sorry, Daddy,' Victoria said softly.

He turned his back and walked away as her mother comforted her younger sister, and Victoria wiped the tears from her eyes with the back of her hand. 'I'm sorry, Mom,' she said softly, and Christine nodded and handed her a towel to cover herself up. The message in her gesture was clear.

High school was easier than Victoria had expected in some ways. The classes were well organized, she liked most of the teachers, and the subjects were more interesting than they'd been in middle school. Academically, she loved the school, and was excited by the work. Socially, she felt like a fish out of water, and was shocked by the other girls when she saw them on the first day. They looked a lot racier than anyone she'd gone to school with so far. Some wore provocative clothes and looked older than their years. All the girls wore makeup, and many of them looked much too thin. Anorexia and bulimia had clearly entered their lives. Victoria felt like a moose on the first day, and all she wanted was to look 'cool' like everyone else. She carefully observed the outfits that they favored, many of which would have looked terrible on her, although the miniskirts they wore would have looked great. Victoria had opted for jeans and a loose shirt to hide her shape. Her long blond hair was hanging down her back, her face looked freshly scrubbed, and she wore high-top sneakers she and her mother had bought the day before. Once again she was out of step. She had worn the wrong thing, and looked different from the other girls.

The ones she saw congregating outside school when she arrived looked like they were entering a fashion contest of some kind. They appeared to be eighteen years old, and some of them obviously were. But even the girls her own age seemed much older than their years. And all she could see at first was a flock of thin, sexy girls. She wanted to cry.

'Good luck,' her mother said when she dropped her off, smiling at her. 'Have a great first day.' Victoria wanted to hide in the car. She had her schedule clutched in her trembling hand and a map of the school. She hoped she could find her way without asking directions. She was afraid she might burst into tears as raw terror clutched her heart. 'You'll be fine,' Christine said as Victoria slipped out of the car, and tried to look casual as she hurried up the stairs past the other girls, without meeting their eyes or stopping to say hello. They looked like an army of 'cool' girls, and she felt anything but 'cool.'

She saw some of them in the cafeteria at lunch that day, and steered a wide berth around them. She helped herself to a bag of potato chips, a hero sandwich, yogurt, and a package of chocolate chip cookies for later, and sat at a table by herself, until another girl sat down. She was taller than Victoria, and rail thin. She looked as though she could have played basketball against most of the guys, and asked Victoria permission to sit down.

'Mind if I sit here?'

'No, that's fine,' Victoria said, opening the potato chips. The other girl had two sandwiches on her tray, but she looked like nothing she ate would show. Other than her long brown hair, she almost looked like a boy. She wasn't wearing makeup either, and she was wearing jeans and Converse too.

'Freshman?' the other girl asked as she unwrapped her first sandwich, and Victoria nodded, feeling paralyzed by shyness. 'I'm Connie. I'm captain of the girls' basketball team, as you may have guessed. I'm six-two. I'm a junior. Welcome to high school. How's it been so far?'

'Okay,' Victoria said, trying to look unimpressed. She didn't want to tell her that she was scared out of her mind and felt like a freak. She wondered if Connie had too at fourteen. She looked extremely relaxed and comfortable with who she was now, but she was also sitting with a freshman, which made Victoria wonder if she had any friends. And if she did, where were they? She looked taller than almost every boy in the room.

'I reached my full height at twelve,' she said conversationally. 'My brother is six-six and plays for UCLA on a basketball scholarship. Do you play any sports?'

'Some volleyball, not much.' She had always been more academic than athletic.

'We have some great teams here. Maybe you want to try out for basketball too. We have a lot of girls your height,' she added, and Victoria almost said, 'But not my weight.' She was fiercely aware of how everyone looked, and looking at them on the way in, she felt twice their size. She felt less out of place with this girl, who at least did not look anorexic or dress as though she were going on a date. She seemed friendly and nice. 'It takes a while to get the hang of high school,' Connie reassured her. 'I felt really strange the first day I got here. All the boys I saw were half my size. And the girls were a lot prettier than I was. But there's something for everyone here, jocks, fashionistas, beauty queens, there's a gay/lesbian club, you'll figure it all out after a while and make friends.' Victoria was suddenly glad that Connie had sat down with her. She felt like she at least had one new friend. Connie had finished both her sandwiches by then, and Victoria was embarrassed to realize that she was so nervous, all she had eaten were the chips and the cookies. She decided to eat the yogurt and save the rest. 'Where do you live?' Connie asked with interest.

'L.A.'

'I drive in from Orange County every day. I live with my dad. My mom died last year.'

'I'm sorry,' Victoria said, immediately sympathetic. Connie stood to her full height, and Victoria felt like a dwarf next to her. She handed Victoria a piece of paper with her phone number on it, and Victoria thanked her and slipped it into her pocket.

'Call me if I can help with anything. The first few days are always tough. It'll get better after that. And don't forget to try out for the team.' Victoria couldn't see herself doing it, but she was grateful for the friendly reception from this girl, who had gone out of her way to make her feel at ease. Victoria no longer believed that it was an accident that she had sat down at her table. As they chatted, a good-looking boy walked by and smiled at Connie.

'Hey, Connie,' he said, whizzing by with his books in his hand, 'signing up recruits for the team?'

'You bet.' She laughed at him. 'He's captain of the swimming team,' she said when he was gone. 'You might like that too. Check it out.'

'I'd probably drown,' Victoria said, looking sheepish. 'I'm not a great swimmer.'

'You don't have to be at first. You learn. That's what coaches are for. I swam for the team freshman year, but I don't like to get up that early. Practice is at six A.M., some-times five before a meet.'

'I think I'll pass,' Victoria said with a grin, but she liked knowing she had options. This was a whole new world. And everyone looked like they liked it here, and had found their own niche. She just hoped that she'd find hers, whatever it was. Connie told her that there were sign-up sheets on the main bulletin board outside the cafeteria, for all the clubs. She pointed it out on their way out, and Victoria stopped to look. A chess club, a poker club, a film club, foreign language clubs, a Gothic club, a horror movie club, a literary club, a Latin club, a romance-novel book club, an archaeology club, a ski club, a tennis club, a travel club. There were dozens of clubs listed. The two that interested Victoria most were film and Latin. But she was too shy to put her name on either list. She had taken Latin in middle school the year before and liked it. And she thought the film club might be fun. And neither of them required taking her clothes off or wearing a uniform that would make her look gross. She wouldn't have joined the swim club for that reason, although she was actually a decent swimmer, better than she had admitted to Connie, and she didn't relish the idea of basketball shorts either. She thought the ski club might be fun too. She went skiing every year with her parents.

Her father had been a champion skier in his youth, and her mother was pretty good too. And Gracie had been in ski school since she was three, and so had Victoria before her.

'See you around,' Connie said as she sauntered off on her giraffe-like legs.

'Thank you!' Victoria called after her, and then hurried to her next class.

She was in good spirits when her mother picked her up outside at three.

'How was it?' her mother asked pleasantly, relieved to see that Victoria looked happy. It obviously hadn't been as scary as she'd feared.

'Pretty good,' Victoria said, looking pleased. 'I like my classes. It's sooooo much better than middle school. I had biology and chem this morning, English lit and Spanish this afternoon. The Spanish teacher is a little weird, he won't let you speak English in his class, but the others were all pretty nice. And I checked out the clubs, I might do ski and film, and maybe Latin.'

'Sounds like a reasonable first day,' Christine said as they drove toward her old school to pick Grace up after day care. As they parked in front of the school, Victoria suddenly felt as though she had matured a thousand years since June. She felt so grown up now being in high school, and it wasn't bad at all. Gracie was in tears when Victoria ran inside to pick her up.

'What happened?' Victoria asked her as she scooped her up into her arms. She was so small at seven that Victoria could carry her easily.

'I had a *horrible* day. David threw a lizard at me, Lizzie took my peanut butter sandwich, and Janie hit me!' she said with a look of outrage. 'I cried all day,' she added for good measure.

'So would I if all those things happened to me,' Victoria assured her as she walked her to the car.

'I want you to come back,' she said, pouting at her older sister. 'It's no fun here without you.'

'I wish I could,' Victoria said, but suddenly not so sure. High school had looked okay to her that day, better than she'd thought it would. It had definite possibilities, and she wanted to explore them now. Maybe there was hope that she'd fit in after all. 'I miss you too.' It was sad to realize that they'd never be in the same school again. The age difference between them was too great.

Victoria put her in the backseat, and Grace reported her miseries to her mother, who was instantly sympathetic. Victoria couldn't help noticing, as she always did, that their mother had never been as tender with her as she was with Grace. Their relationship was different and simpler for her mother. The fact that Gracie looked like them made it easier for their parents to relate to her. Gracie was one of 'them,' and Victoria was always the stranger in their midst. Victoria wondered if Christine also hadn't known how to be a mother yet when she was born and had learned with Gracie, or maybe she just felt more in common with her. It was impossible to know, but whatever it was, Christine had always been more matter of fact with her, more critical and distant, and demanded more of her, just as her father did. And in his eyes, Gracie could do no wrong. Maybe they had both just softened with age. But her being a reflection of them seemed to be part of it. They'd been in their twenties when Victoria was born, and were in their forties now. Maybe that made a difference, or maybe they just didn't like her as much. Grace hadn't been named after an ugly queen, even as a joke.

Her father asked her about school that night, and she reported on her classes, and mentioned the clubs again. He thought her choices were all good, particularly Latin, although he thought the ski club would be fun and a good way to meet boys. Her mother thought Latin sounded too brainy and she should join something more sociable, in order to make friends. They were both aware that Victoria had had very few friends in middle school.

But in high school she could meet people, and by junior year she'd be driving and wouldn't need them to chauffeur her at all. They could hardly wait, and Victoria liked the idea too. She didn't want her father making sarcastic remarks about her to her friends, as he did whenever he gave them a ride somewhere, even if he thought his comments were funny. She never did.

She signed up for the three clubs that interested her the next day, but none of the sports teams. She decided to fulfill her athletic requirement with just Phys Ed, although she could have taken ballet too, which would have been her worst nightmare come true, leaping across the gym in a leotard and a tutu. She shuddered at the thought when the assistant PE teacher suggested it to her.

It took her a while, but in time Victoria made friends. She dropped out of the film club eventually because she didn't like the movies they picked to watch. She went on one of the ski club trips to Bear Valley, but the kids that went were stuck-up and never talked to her. She signed up for the travel club instead. And she loved the Latin club, although it was all girls, and she took Latin all of freshman year. She met people, but it wasn't easy making friends in high school either. A lot of the girls seemed to be in airtight little groups and looked like beauty queens, and that wasn't her style. The academic girls were as shy as she was and hard to meet. Connie proved to be a good friend for two years until she got a scholarship to Duke, and left when she graduated. But by then, Victoria was comfortable at the school. She heard from Jake at Cait once in a while too, but they never got together again. They always said they would and never did.

She had her first date during sophomore year when a boy from her Spanish class invited her to the junior prom, which was a big deal. Connie said he was a great guy, and he was until he got drunk in the bathroom with some other boys and got kicked out of the prom, and she had to call her father for a ride home.

She got her first car the summer before junior year, and had taken driver's ed the year before, and had her learner's permit so she was all set. From then on, she drove herself to school. It was an old Honda her father had bought for her, and she was excited about it.

It wasn't something she talked about to anyone, but by junior year her body had gotten bigger than it was before. She had gained ten pounds over the summer. She had a summer job at an ice cream store, and ate ice cream on all her breaks. Her mother was upset about it and said it was the wrong job for her. It was too much temptation for Victoria, as proved by the weight she gained.

'You look more like your great-grandmother every day'

was all her father said, but it made the point. She brought home ice cream cakes shaped like clowns for Gracie every day. She loved them and no matter how many she ate, she never gained a pound. She was nine by then, and Victoria was sixteen.

But the main benefit of her summer job was that she earned enough money for a trip to New York with the travel club during Christmas break, and it changed her life. She had never been to such an exciting city and liked it much better than L.A. They stayed at a Marriott hotel near Times Square, and they walked for miles. They went to the theater, opera, and ballet, rode the subway, went to the top of the Empire State Building, visited the Metropolitan Museum, the Museum of Modern Art, and the United Nations, and Victoria had never had so much fun in her life. They even had a snowstorm while she was there, and when she got back to L.A., she was dazed. New York was the best place she'd ever been, and she wanted to live there one day. She said she might even go to college there if she could get into New York University or Barnard, which might be a stretch despite her grades. But she floated on the experience for months.

She met her first serious high school boyfriend right after New Year's. Mike was in the travel club too, but had missed the trip. He was planning to go to London,

Athens, and Rome with the club during the summer. Her parents wouldn't let her go – they said she was too young, although she'd be turning seventeen. Mike was a senior, and his parents were divorced, so his father had signed the permission slip. Victoria thought he was very grown up and worldly and fell madly in love. For the first time in her life, he made her feel pretty. He said he loved her looks. He was going to Southern Methodist University in the fall, and they spent a lot of time together, although her parents didn't approve. They thought he wasn't smart enough for her. Victoria didn't care. He liked her, and he made her happy. They spent a lot of time making out in his car, but she wouldn't go all the way. She was too scared to take that leap. She said she wasn't ready. And in April he dropped her for a girl who would. He took the new girl to senior prom, and Victoria sat home nursing a broken heart. He was the only boy who'd asked her out all year.

She never had many dates or a lot of friends. And she spent the summer on the South Beach Diet. She was diligent about it and lost seven pounds. But as soon as she got off the diet, she gained it back plus three more pounds. She wanted to lose the weight for senior year, and her PE teacher had told her she was fifteen pounds overweight. She lost five pounds at the beginning of senior year, by eating smaller portions and fewer calories, and promised herself she'd lose more before graduation. And she would have if she hadn't gotten mono in November, had to stay home for three weeks, and ate ice cream because it made her throat feel better. The fates had conspired against her. She was the only girl in her class who gained eight pounds while she had mono. Her size was a battle she couldn't seem to win. But she was determined to beat it this time, and swam every day during Christmas vacation and for a month after. And she jogged around the track every morning before school. Her mother was proud of her when she lost ten pounds.

She was determined to lose the other eight pounds, until her father looked at her one morning and asked her when she was going to start working out to lose some weight. He hadn't even noticed the ten pounds she had lost. And after that she gave up swimming and jogging and went back to eating ice cream after school and potato chips at lunch, and bigger portions, which satisfied her. What difference did it make? No one noticed it, and no one asked her out. Her father offered to take her to his gym, and she said she had too much work at school, which was true.

She was working hard to keep up her grades, and had applied to seven schools: New York University, Barnard,

Boston University, Northwestern, George Washington in Washington, D.C., the University of New Hampshire, and Trinity. Everything she had applied to was either in the Midwest or the East. She had applied to no schools in California, and her parents were upset about it. She wasn't sure why, but she knew she had to leave. She had felt different for too long, and although she knew she would miss them, and especially Gracie, she wanted a new life. This was her chance, and she was going to grab it while she could. She was tired of competing and going to school with girls who looked like starlets and models and hoped to be that one day. Her father had wanted her to apply to USC and UCLA, and she refused. She knew it would just be more of the same. She wanted to go to school with real people, who weren't obsessed with how they looked. She wanted to go to college with people who cared about what they thought, like her.

She didn't get into either of her first-choice schools in New York, nor Boston University, which she would have liked, nor GW. Her choices in the end were Northwestern, New Hampshire, or Trinity. She liked Trinity a lot but wanted a bigger school, and there was good skiing in New Hampshire, but she chose Northwestern, which felt right to her. The greatest thing it had going for it was that it was far away, and it was a great school. Her parents said they were proud of her, although they were distressed that she was leaving California and couldn't understand why she would. They had no concept of how out of place and unwelcome they had made her feel for so long. Gracie was like their only child, and she felt like the family stray dog. She didn't even look like them, and she couldn't take it anymore. Maybe she'd come back to Los Angeles after school, but for now she knew she had to get away.

She was one of the top three students in her class, and had been asked to give a speech after the valedictorian, which stunned the audience with the seriousness and value of what she said. She talked about how different she had felt all her life, how out of step, and how hard she had tried to conform. She said she had never been an athlete, nor wanted to be. She wasn't 'cool,' she wasn't popular, she didn't wear the same clothes as all the other girls during freshman year. She didn't wear makeup till sophomore year, and still didn't wear it every day. She had loved Latin class even though it made everyone think she was a geek. She went down the list of all the things that had made her different, without saying that she felt even more out of place in her own home.

And then she thanked the school for helping her to be who she was, and find her way. She said that now they were all going out into a world where they would *all* be different, where no one would fit in, where they had to be themselves to succeed, and follow their own paths. She wished her classmates luck on their journey to find themselves, and herself as well, and she said that once they all found themselves, discovered who they were, and became who they were meant to be, she hoped they'd meet again one day. 'And until then, my friends,' she said, as tears rolled down her classmates' and their parents' cheeks, 'Godspeed.' It made a lot of her fellow students wish they had known her better. The speech impressed her parents too with its eloquence. And it brought home the realization that she was leaving soon, and it softened both of them as they congratulated her on the speech. Christine realized that she was losing her, and she might never live at home again. Her father was suddenly very quiet too when they met up with her after the ceremony and they had all tossed their caps into the air, after saving the tassels to put away with their diplomas. Her father clapped Victoria lightly on the back.

'Great speech,' he complimented her. 'It'll make all the weirdos in your class feel good,' he added sincerely as she looked at him with wide-open eyes. Sometimes she wondered if he was just stupid, or maybe mean. He never failed to miss the point. She could see that now.

'Yeah, like me, Dad,' she said quietly. 'I'm one of them. The weirdos and the freaks. My point was that it's okay to be different, and from now on we'd better be, if we're going to make something of ourselves. It's the one thing I learned in school. Different is okay.'

'Not too different, I hope,' he said, looking nervous. Jim Dawson had conformed all his life, and he cared a lot about what people thought of him. He had never had an original thought in his life. He was a company man through and through. And he didn't agree with Victoria's philosophy, although he admired the speech and how well she had delivered it. He could see in her ability when she did it that she had inherited something from him. He was known for his excellent speeches too. But Jim never liked to stand out or be different. That had never been okay with him. Victoria was well aware of it, which was why she had never in her entire life felt at ease with them, and she felt even less so now, because she was different from her parents in so many ways. And it was why she was starting the most important adventure of her life, and leaving home to do it. She was willing to push herself out of her comfort zone if it meant finding herself at last, and the place where she belonged. All she knew now was that it wasn't here, with them. No matter how hard she had tried, she just wasn't like them.

She realized too that Gracie was growing up as one of them, and she did fit in. Perfectly. She and her parents were like clones. Victoria hoped that one day her younger sister would spread her wings and fly. And for now, Victoria had to do it. She could hardly wait, even if it terrified her at times. She was scared to death of leaving home, but excited too. The girl they had said looked like Queen Victoria all her life was taking off. She smiled as she left her school for the last time, and whispered to herself, 'Watch out, world! Here I come!'

Chapter 4

Victoria's summer at home before she started college was bittersweet in many ways. Her parents were nicer to her than they had been in years, although her father introduced her to a business associate as his tester cake. But he also said he was proud of her, more than once, which surprised Victoria, since she never really thought he was. And her mother seemed sad to see her go, although she never openly said it to Victoria. It made Victoria feel as though they had all missed the boat. Her childhood and high school years were over, and she wondered why they had wasted so much time and concentrated on all the wrong things: her looks, her friends or lack of them, her weight was their main focus, along with her resemblance to her great-grandmother, whom no one knew or cared about, just because their noses were the same. Why did they care so much about the wrong things? Why hadn't they been closer to her, more loving, given her more support? And now there was no time left to build the bridge between them that should have existed all along and never had. They were strangers to each other, and she couldn't imagine it being any different later on. She was leaving home, and might never live with them again.

She still wanted to move to New York after college, it was her dream. She would come home for holidays, see them on Christmas and Thanksgiving and when they visited her, if they did, and there was no time left to put in the bank the love they should have been saving all along. She thought they loved her, they were her parents, and she had lived with them for eighteen years, but her father had made fun of her all her life, and her mother had been disappointed that she wasn't prettier, complained that she was too smart, and told her men didn't like smart women. Her whole childhood with them had been a curse. And now that she was leaving, they said they were going to miss her. But when they said it, she couldn't help wondering why they hadn't paid more attention to her while she was there. It was already too late. Did they really love her? She was never sure. They loved Gracie. But what about her?

And the one she hated most to leave was Gracie, the little angel in her life, who had dropped from the skies when she was seven and loved her unconditionally ever since, just as Victoria loved her. She couldn't bear to leave her and not see her every day, but she knew she had no choice. Gracie was eleven now, and had already come to understand how different Victoria was from the rest of them, and how mean their father was at times. She hated it when he said things to Victoria that hurt, or made fun of her, or pointed out how much she didn't look like them. In Gracie's eyes, Victoria was beautiful, and she didn't care how fat or thin she was. Gracie thought she was the prettiest girl in the world and she loved her more than anyone.

Victoria dreaded leaving her, and cherished every day they spent together. She took her out for lunch, to the beach, had picnics with her, took her to Disneyland, and spent as much time with her as she could. They were lying on the beach one afternoon in Malibu, next to each other, looking up at the sun, when Gracie turned to her and asked a question that Victoria had asked herself as a child too.

'Do you think maybe you were adopted and they never told you?' Gracie asked her with an innocent look as her older sister smiled. She was wearing a loose T-shirt over her bathing suit, as she always did, to conceal what was beneath it.

'I used to think I was when I was a kid,' Victoria admitted, 'because I look so different from them. But I don't think I am. I guess I'm just some weird throwback to another generation, like Dad's grandmother or who-ever. I think I'm their kid, even though we don't have much in common.' She didn't look like Gracie either, but they were soul mates and had been for all of Grace's short life, and they both knew it. Victoria just hoped Gracie didn't grow up to be like them. She didn't see how she could, but they had a powerful influence on her, and once Victoria was gone, they would hold on to her even more tightly, and mold her to their own images.

'I'm glad you're my sister,' Gracie said sadly. 'I wish you weren't going away to college, and that you had stayed here.'

'I do too, when I think about leaving you. But I'll come home for Thanksgiving and Christmas, and you can come to visit me.'

'It won't be the same,' Gracie said as a tear sneaked down her cheek, and they both knew it was true.

The whole family looked like they were in mourning when Victoria packed her bags for college. And the night before she left, her father took them all out to dinner at the Beverly Hills Hotel, and they had a good time together. There were no jokes that night at anyone's expense. And the next day, all three of them took her to the airport, and the moment they got out of the car, Gracie burst into tears and threw her arms around Victoria's waist.

Her father checked in her luggage, while the two girls stood crying on the sidewalk, and Christine looked at her daughter unhappily.

'I wish you wouldn't go,' she said softly. She would have liked to try again if she had the chance. She could feel Victoria slipping through her fingers forever. She had never really thought about what this day would feel like. The pain of it took her by surprise now.

'I'll be home soon,' Victoria said, and hugged her, still crying, and then she hugged her little sister again. 'I'll call you tonight,' she promised her, 'as soon as I get to my room.' Gracie nodded and couldn't stop crying, and even her father's eyes were damp when he said goodbye to her in a choked voice.

'Take care of yourself. Call if you need anything. And if you hate it, you can always transfer to a school out here.' He hoped she would. It was as though her leaving California for college were a rejection of him. They had wanted her to stay in L.A., or close to it, which wasn't what Victoria wanted or needed.

After kissing them all again, Victoria went through security, and waved for as long as she could see them. They didn't leave the airport until she had disappeared from sight. The last she saw of her family was Gracie leaving the airport, walking between her parents. They all looked the same, with their dark hair and slim bodies. Her mother was holding Gracie's hand, and Victoria could see that her sister was still crying.

She boarded the flight to Chicago, thinking about all of them, and as the plane took off, she looked out the window at the city she was fleeing, to find the tools she needed for a new life somewhere else.

She didn't know where that would be, but the one thing she did know was that it couldn't be here, or with them.

Victoria's years in college were exactly what she hoped they would be. The school was even better than she had dreamed or expected. It was big and sprawling, and the classes she took and did well at were her ticket to freedom. She wanted to acquire the skills she needed to have a job and a life someplace other than L.A. She missed Gracie, and sometimes even her parents, but when she thought of living with her parents, every fiber of her being told her that she could never live with them again.

And she loved her frequent visits to Chicago and discovering everything she could about the city. It was lively and sophisticated, and she thoroughly enjoyed it, despite the brutally cold weather.

She went home for Thanksgiving freshman year, and saw instantly that Grace had grown taller, and prettier, if that was even possible. Her mother had finally relented and let her do a commercial for Gap Kids. Grace's photograph was suddenly everywhere, and she could have had a career as a model, but her father wanted a better life for her. And he swore that he'd never let a child of his go to college so far from home again. He told Grace that she'd have to go to UCLA, Pepperdine, Pomona, Scripps, Pitzer, or USC. He was not going to let her leave L.A. In his own way, he genuinely missed Victoria. He didn't have much to say when she called, except that he hoped she'd come home soon, and then he passed the phone to her mother, who asked what she was doing and if she'd lost any weight. It was the question Victoria hated most because she hadn't. And then she dieted frantically for two weeks before she went home.

And when she got back to L.A. for Christmas vacation, her mother noticed that she had lost a little weight. She had been working out at the gym at school, but she admitted that she hadn't had any dates. She was working too hard at school to even care. She told them she had decided to get a teaching degree, and her father instantly disapproved. It gave them a new topic to disagree on, and distracted them from her weight and lack of dates.

'You'll never make decent money as a teacher. You should major in communications, and work in advertising or PR. I can get you a job.' She knew he meant well, but it wasn't what she wanted to do. She liked the idea of teaching, and working with kids. She changed the subject and they talked about how cold it was in the Midwest – she hadn't even been able to imagine it until she was there. It had been well below zero for the whole week before she came home. And she was enjoying going to hockey games. She wasn't crazy about her roommate, but she was determined to make the best of it. And she had met some people in her dorm. But mostly, she was trying to get accustomed to the school, and to being away from home. She said she missed decent food, and this time no one commented when she took three helpings of pot roast. And she was happy taking time off from going to the gym while she was home. She appreciated the weather in L.A. as she never had before.

Her father gave her a new computer for Christmas, and her mother gave her a down coat. Gracie had made her a montage of photographs of them, starting when she was born, on a bulletin board to hang up in her dorm room. And when she left after Christmas, Victoria wasn't sure if she was coming home for spring break. She said she might travel somewhere with friends. In fact, she wanted to go to New York and try to line up a summer job, but she didn't mention it to them. Her father said that if she didn't come home in March, they would come to see her after that, and take her to Chicago for the weekend. And it was even harder leaving Gracie that time. The two sisters genuinely missed each other, and her parents said they missed her too.

Second semester of freshman year was hard for Victoria too. The midwestern winter was dreary and cold, she was lonely, she hadn't met many people, she had no close friends yet, and she caught a bad case of flu in January. When she did, she lost the thread of going to the gym again and started living on fast food. By the end of second semester, she had gained the dreaded freshman fifteen, and none of the clothes she had brought with her fit anymore. She felt huge, and was twenty-five pounds overweight. She had no choice but to start working out again, and she swam every day. She managed to lose ten pounds of the extra weight fairly quickly, with a purging diet, and some pills one of her dorm mates had given her that made her desperately sick. But she could get into her clothes again, and she was thinking about going to Weight Watchers to lose the other fifteen, but she always had an excuse not to. She was busy, it was cold, she had a paper due. It was a constant battle with her weight. And even without her mother hounding her, and her father making fun of her, she was unhappy about her size, and she didn't have a date all year.

She went to New York as she hoped to over spring break, and managed to get a job as a receptionist at a law firm for the summer. The pay was decent, and she could hardly wait. She didn't tell her family about it till May, and Gracie called her sobbing on the phone. She had just turned twelve, and Victoria nineteen.

'I want you to come home! I don't want you to go to New York.'

'I'm coming home in August before I go back to school,' she promised, but Gracie was sad that she wasn't coming home till then. She had just done another ad, for a national campaign. Her parents were putting the money away in trust for her, and she liked the modeling and thought it was fun. But she missed her sister. Life at home wasn't nearly as much fun without her.

They had also met Victoria in Chicago, as they'd promised, for a long weekend in April, and it had snowed. It had been a seemingly endless winter, and when Victoria finally finished her exams, she was excited to fly out of Chicago on Memorial Day weekend. She was starting work in New York the day after Memorial Day.

She had bought some skirts and blouses and summer dresses that were appropriate for her job at the law firm. And she had gotten her weight back in control again by not eating any desserts or bread or pasta. It was a low-carb diet that seemed to be working. It was heading in the right direction at least, and she hadn't eaten ice cream in a month. Her mother would have been proud of her. It had also occurred to her that while her mother complained about what she ate, she had always kept a hefty supply of ice cream in the freezer. And she had served all the fattening things Victoria liked to eat. She had always put temptation in Victoria's way. At least now she could only blame herself for what she ate, Victoria told herself. And she was trying to be diligent and sensible about it, without going on any crazy diets, or borrowing someone else's pills. She hadn't had time to go to Weight Watchers yet, but she had promised herself that she would walk to work every day in New York. She was going to be working on Park Avenue and East 53rd Street, and staying at a small residential hotel in Gramercy Park, which was a thirty-block hike to work, a mile and a half. Three miles if she walked both ways.

Victoria liked her summer job. The people at the law firm were nice to her. She was competent, responsible, and efficient. Mostly, she answered the phones, handed envelopes to messengers, or accepted them for the lawyers in the firm. She directed clients to attorneys' offices, took messages, and greeted people at the front desk. It was an easy but busy job, and most days she wound up staying late. And by the time she left, in the torrid summer heat, she was too tired to walk home, so she took the subway back to Gramercy Park. But she managed to walk to work on the days she wasn't late, at least some of the time. When it took longer than she'd planned to get dressed or do her hair, she'd have to take the subway to work, so she wouldn't be late.

Victoria was considerably younger than most of the secretaries at the law firm, so she didn't make any friends. People were busy and didn't have time to socialize and chat. She spoke to a few people in the employee dining room at lunchtime, but they were always in a hurry and had things to do. And she didn't know a soul in New York. She didn't mind. On weekends she went for long walks in Central Park, or listened to concerts, lying on a blanket on the grass. She went to all the museums, walked around the Cloisters, explored SoHo, Chelsea, and the Village, and wandered around the campus of NYU. She still would have liked to transfer there, but she thought she would lose credits and didn't know if she had the grades. She was planning to stick it out at Northwestern for the next three years, or finish sooner if she could by going to summer school, and then move to New York and find a job. She knew after living in the city for a month that this was where she wanted to work, without any doubt. Sometimes during her lunch hours she looked up lists of New York schools. She was determined to teach at one of the private schools. And nothing was going to sway her from her plan.

When she finished her job at the law firm, she flew to L.A. for the last three weeks of her summer vacation, and Gracie threw herself into her sister's arms the minute she walked through the door. Victoria was surprised to see that the house looked smaller, her parents older, and Gracie suddenly looked more grown up than she had four months before. But she looked nothing like Victoria had looked at the same age, with her rapidly maturing body, full figure, and big breasts. Gracie was tiny like their mother, with the same lithe figure and narrow heart-shaped face. But despite her skinny body, she still looked more mature. And on Victoria's first night back, Grace admitted that she had a crush on a boy. She had met him at the swim and tennis club that their mother took her to every day. He was fourteen. And Victoria was too embarrassed to admit to her or her parents that she hadn't had a date in over a year. When they pressed her about it repeatedly, thinking she was being coy, she finally invented a mythical boy she had gone out with at Northwestern. She said he was a hockey player and was studying to be an engineer. Her father informed her immediately that all engineers were bores. But at least they thought she had a date. She said he had spent the summer with his family in Maine. They seemed relieved to hear that she had gone out with someone, and she said she hadn't gone out with anyone in New York. But dating someone at school made her sound more normal than the reality of the nights she had spent studying alone in the dorm.

Her mother pulled her aside and told her she might have gained a little weight in New York, and when they went to the club so Gracie could see her 'boyfriend,' Victoria stayed in her shirt and shorts, instead of putting on a swimsuit, which was what she always did when she gained weight. And she and Grace had an ice cream nearly every day on the way home. But she never touched the Häagen-Dazs her mother had stocked in the fridge. She didn't want them to see her eat it.

The weeks in California flew by, and they were sad again to see her leave. Gracie was more composed this time, but it was hard knowing they wouldn't see Victoria again for three months until Thanksgiving. But she would be busy with a heavy workload at school, and Gracie was going into seventh grade. It was difficult for Victoria to believe that Gracie would be in high school in two years.

Victoria's roommate sophomore year was a nervous-looking girl from New York. She had an obvious eating disorder and was frighteningly thin. She admitted after a few days that she had been in a hospital all summer, and Victoria watched her get thinner every day. Her parents called her constantly to check on her, and she said she had a boyfriend in New York. She looked miserable at school, and Victoria tried to ignore the atmosphere of stress she created. She was a crisis in full bloom. Just looking at her made Victoria want to eat more. And by the time Victoria went back to L.A. for Thanksgiving, her roommate had decided to leave school and go back to New York. It was a relief to know that she wouldn't be there when Victoria got back. It was hard to live with the tension she exuded in the room.

It was between Thanksgiving and Christmas that Victoria met the first boy who had interested her since she'd been there. He was in pre-law, in his junior year, and he was in an English lit class with her. He was a tall, good-looking boy with freckles and red hair, from Louisville, Kentucky, and she loved to listen to his drawl when he talked. They were in a study group together, and he invited her out to coffee afterward. His father owned several race horses, and his mother lived in Paris. He was planning to spend Christmas with her there. He was fluent in French, and had lived in London and Hong Kong. Everything about him seemed exotic to Victoria, and he was a kind, gentle person.

They talked about their families, and he said his life had been pretty upside down since his parents' divorce, and his mother constantly moved from one place to another around the world. She had married someone after his father and was divorced again. He thought Victoria's life sounded a lot more stable than his own, and it was, but she didn't consider her childhood a happy one either. She had been an outsider in her own home all her life. And he had been a newcomer wherever he was. He had gone to five schools after eighth grade. And his father had just married a twenty-three-year-old girl. He was twenty-one. He admitted to Victoria that his stepmother had come on to him, and he had almost slept with her. They had both been drunk, and by some miracle of good judgment, he had managed not to give in to temptation, but he was nervous about seeing her again. He had decided to spend Christmas with his mother in Paris instead, although she had a new French boyfriend he wasn't crazy about either.

He was very funny about his stories, but there was something almost tragic about the tales he told about a lost boy caught between crazy, irresponsible parents. He said he was living proof that people with too much money screwed up their kids. He had been seeing a shrink since he was twelve. His name was Beau, and despite some romantic moments and a little heavy petting on the night before she left, they hadn't slept with each other when she went to L.A. for Christmas. He promised to call her from Paris. And he seemed wonderfully romantic and exotic to her. She was fascinated by him. And this time when her parents asked who she was dating, she could say a junior in pre-law. It would sound respectable to them, although she couldn't imagine her father or mother liking him. He was much too offbeat for them.

Beau called her over the holidays and had gone to Gstaad with his mother and her friend. He sounded bored and a little lost. And he texted her constantly with things that made her laugh. Gracie wanted to know if he was handsome but said she didn't like red hair.

And this time Victoria watched her diet. She passed on desserts even though her father expressed surprise when his 'big girl' said no. It was impossible to shake his view of her as someone who ate all the wrong things and was always overweight.

Victoria lost five pounds during her ten days in L.A. And she and Beau got back to Northwestern within hours of each other on the same day. She had thought of nothing but him over the holiday, and she wondered how long it would take for them to wind up in bed. She was glad that she had saved herself for him. Beau would be her first, and she could easily imagine him being gentle and sensual in bed. They were kissing and laughing and cuddling when he came to her dorm room, and he said he was so jet-lagged that nothing happened that night. Nor for the next many weeks. They were with each other constantly, they studied in the library together, and since she no longer had a roommate, sometimes he fell asleep on the other bed. They spent a lot of time kissing and fondling, and he loved her breasts, but it never went past that point. He told her she should wear miniskirts because she had the best legs he had ever seen. He appeared to be totally enthralled with her, and for the first time in her life, Victoria was seriously losing weight.

She wanted to look great for him. And she was feeling good about herself.

They had snowball fights and went ice skating, they went to hockey games, restaurants, and bars. He introduced her to his friends. They went everywhere together and always had a terrific time. But no matter how close they got to it, they never made love. She wasn't sure why, and she was afraid to ask. She wondered if he thought she was too fat, or if he respected her too much, or if maybe he was afraid, or if his near miss with his twenty-three-year-old stepmother had traumatized him, or his parents' divorce. Something was holding him back, and Victoria had no idea what it was. He obviously wanted her, and their makeout sessions grew more and more passionate, but their hunger for each other was never consummated, and it was driving Victoria insane. They were down to their underwear one night in her dorm room, and then he held her in his arms and lay there silently without moving for a long time, and then he got out of bed.

'What's wrong?' she asked him quietly, sure that it was something about her. Something wrong with her. Maybe her weight. All her feelings of not being good enough came back to her in a rush as he sat down on the edge of her bed.

'I'm falling in love with you,' he said miserably, as he dropped his head into his hands.

'So am I with you. What's wrong with that?' She was smiling at him.

'I can't do this to you,' he said softly, and she touched his red hair falling over his eyes. He looked like Huck Finn or Tom Sawyer. He was a boy.

'Yes, you can. It's okay.' She tried to reassure him, as they sat there in their underwear.

'No, it's not. I can't . . . you don't understand. This is the first time this has ever happened to me . . . with a woman . . . I'm gay . . . and no matter how much I think I love you now, sooner or later I'm going to end up with a man again. I don't want to do that to you, no matter how much I want you now. It won't last with us.'

For a long moment, she didn't know what to say. This was way beyond her realm of experience, and more complicated than any relationship she had imagined with him. And he was being fair. He knew that sooner or later he'd want a man again. He always had.

'I never should have started it, but I fell in love with you the day we met.'

'Then why can't this work?' she asked softly, grateful for his honesty, but it hurt nonetheless.

'Because it won't. This isn't who I am. This is some

kind of wild, delicious fantasy. But it's not real for me. It could never be. I was wrong to think it could. You'll get hurt. I don't want to do that to you. We have to stop,' he said, looking at her with his big green eyes. 'Let's at least be friends.' But she didn't want to be his friend. She was falling for him, and her body was crying out for him, and had been for a month. He looked painfully confused and guilty for what he'd almost done, and the charade he'd played out for a month. 'I thought it could work, but it can't. The first time I see a guy I want, I'll be gone. That's not good enough for you, Victoria. You deserve so much more.'

'Why does it have to be so complicated? If you're falling in love with me, then why wouldn't it work?' She was near tears, of disappointment and frustration.

'Because you're not a man. I think you're some kind of ultimate female fantasy for me, with your luscious body and big breasts. You're what I think I should want, but in reality I don't. I want a man.' He was being as honest with her as he could be, and his referring to her 'luscious' body was the nicest thing anyone had ever said to her. But no matter how luscious her body or how big her breasts, he didn't want her after all. It was rejection exquisitely packaged, but rejection nonetheless. 'I'd better go,' he said, slipping back into his clothes as she watched. He was dressed again in a flash and stood looking at her lying on her bed. She hadn't moved, or said another word. 'I'll call you tomorrow,' he said, and she wondered if he would, and if he did, what would he say? He had said it all tonight. She didn't want to only be friends. She thought they had more than that together. For a while he had seemed totally infatuated with her.

'I guess I should have told you in the beginning. But I wanted it to work, and I didn't want to scare you off.'

She nodded, unable to find the right words, and she didn't want to cry. It would have been so humiliating now, as she lay on her bed in her bra and thong. He looked at her for a moment from the doorway, and then he was gone, and she climbed under the covers and cried. It was frustrating and depressing all at once, but she also knew he was right. It would have been even worse if she'd slept with him, and wanted something she couldn't have. It was better this way. But she felt horrible and rejected nonetheless.

She was awake for hours, thinking about the time they'd spent together and the confidences they'd shared, the endless makeout sessions that went nowhere but titillated them both, as they were wrapped in each other's arms, aroused. It all seemed so pointless now. She turned off the light and finally went to sleep. He didn't call her in the morning, but Gracie did instead. Victoria's heart felt like a brick in her chest when she thought of the night before.

'How's Beau?' Gracie asked in her cheerful twelve-year-old voice.

'We broke up,' Victoria said, sounding almost as bad as she felt.

'Oh . . . that's too bad . . . he sounded nice.'

'He was. He is.'

'Did you have a fight? Maybe he'll come back.' She wanted to sound hopeful for her older sister. She hated it when Victoria was sad.

'No, he won't. It's okay. So how are things with you?' Victoria said, steering her off the subject, and Gracie gave her the full report on the boys in seventh grade, and then they finally hung up, and Victoria could mourn the loss in peace. Beau didn't call her that day, or for the next several days, and then she realized she would have to see him in class. She was panicked over it, and then screwed up her courage and went to class, where the teacher casually mentioned that Beau had dropped out of English lit. And Victoria felt her heart sink again. She barely knew him, but it was a loss anyway. And as she left the classroom afterward, she wondered if she'd ever see him again. Maybe not. And when she looked up, she saw him standing farther down the hallway, watching her, and slowly he approached as she stood still and waited. He touched her face gently with one hand and looked like he wanted to kiss her, but he didn't.

'I'm sorry,' he said, and looked as though he meant it. 'I'm sorry I was so stupid and selfish. I thought it would be easier for both of us if I dropped the class. If it's any consolation, this isn't easy for me either. I just didn't want to make a bigger mess later on.'

'It's okay,' she said softly, and smiled at him. 'It's okay. I love you, for whatever that means to you now.'

'A lot,' he said, and brushed her cheek with his lips, and then he was gone. And Victoria walked back to the dorm alone. It was snowing and bitter cold, as she walked along the frozen road, thinking about Beau, and hoping their paths wouldn't cross again. It was so cold, she didn't even feel the tears rolling slowly down her cheeks. All she could do now was put him out of her mind, and try to overcome her own feelings of failure. Whatever his reasons, he hadn't wanted her. And the feeling of not being wanted or loved was all too familiar to her. The experience with Beau was a confirmation of everything she had feared all her life.

Chapter 5

Victoria's last two years in college raced by. She took a summer job in New York again at the end of sophomore year. She was a receptionist in a modeling agency this time, and it was as wild as her previous job at the law firm had been sedate. And she had a great time. She befriended some of the models, who were the same age as she, and the people who did the bookings were fun to be with too. All of them thought she was crazy when she said she wanted to teach school, and she had to admit that working at a modeling agency was a lot more exciting.

Two of the models invited her to live with them, and she gave up her dreary room at the hotel. And despite the parties they went to, the hours they kept, the clothes they wore, and the men they went out with, she was impressed by how hard they worked. The girls who were successful worked like dogs, and were diligent about the modeling jobs they did. They went crazy after hours, but the good ones were on time for every shoot, and worked tirelessly until the work was done, sometimes on twelve- or fourteen-hour shoots. It wasn't as much fun as it looked.

And Victoria was always stunned by how thin they were. The two girls she lived with in Tribeca almost never ate. It made her feel guilty for all that she did, and she tried to follow their example, but she was starving by dinnertime. Her roommates either didn't eat at all or ate aggressively dietetic food, and very little of it. They seemed to exist on next to nothing, and had tried every kind of purge and colonic to keep their weight down. Victoria had a different constitution than they did. She couldn't survive on the tiny amounts they consumed. But she followed their more reasonable diet tips as best she could, avoiding carbs and eating much smaller portions, and she looked good when she went back to L.A. for a month before she went back to school. She had hated to leave New York, and had had a ball. The head of the agency had told her that if she ever wanted a job with them, they would hire her anytime. And Gracie loved hearing the stories she told when she got home. She was going into eighth grade that year, and Victoria her junior year. She was halfway through college and still had her sights set on a teaching job in New York. More than ever, it was where she knew she wanted to be. Her parents had lost hope of ever getting her to move back home. And Gracie knew it too.

The two sisters spent a wonderful month together until Victoria went back to school. Gracie had gotten prettier than ever that year, and she had none of the awkwardness of most girls her age. She was lean and graceful, was taking ballet, and had flawless skin. And her parents still let her do a modeling job every now and then. Gracie readily admitted she hated school. She had a booming social life, a horde of friends, and half a dozen boys calling her all the time on the cell phone her parents had finally given her. It was a far cry from Victoria's monastic life at school, although things got slightly better for her during junior year.

She dated two boys one after the other, although neither seriously, but she got to go out on most weekends, which was a vast improvement over the first two years. She finally lost her virginity to one of the boys she dated, although she didn't love him. And she never ran into Beau again. She wasn't even sure if he was still at school. She saw some of his friends once in a while, from the distance, but she never spoke to them. It had been an odd experience and still upset her when she thought about it. He had been like a beautiful dream. The boys she went out with after that were much more real. One was a hockey player, like the boy she had invented in freshman year. And he liked Victoria more than she liked him. He had grown up in Boston, and he was a little rough around the edges, and had a tendency to drink too much and get belligerent, so she stopped seeing him. And the one she went out with after him, and ultimately slept with, was pleasant but boring. He was studying biochemistry and nuclear physics, and she didn't have much to say to him. The only thing they liked about each other was having sex. So she concentrated on her studies, and eventually stopped seeing the physicist, after a few months.

Victoria stayed at Northwestern for summer school at the end of junior year. She wanted to lighten her load for senior year and focus on student teaching. It was hard to believe how fast the time had gone. She only had one year left before she graduated, and she wanted to concentrate on getting a job in New York for the following year. She started sending out letters in the fall. She had a list of private schools where she was hoping to teach once she got her credentials. She knew the pay wasn't as good as it was in the public schools, but she thought it would be right for her. By Christmas she had sent out letters to nine schools. She was even willing to do substitute teaching at several schools, if she had to wait for a full-time position to open up.

The answers came back like gumballs out of a machine in January. She was turned down by eight schools. Only one school hadn't answered, and she wasn't optimistic when she hadn't heard from them by spring break. She was thinking about calling the modeling agency where she'd worked to see if she could work for them for a year, until a position opened up in one of the schools. It would be better pay anyway than teaching school, and maybe she could room with some of the models again.

And then the last answer came. She sat staring at the envelope the way she had when her college acceptances came. She had opened them gingerly one by one, trying to guess what was in the envelope. And she thought it more than unlikely that she would be offered a job by this school. It was one of the more elite private schools in New York, and she couldn't imagine them hiring a teacher fresh out of college. She helped herself to a candy bar she had stashed in her desk, and came back to tear open the envelope. She unfolded the single page, and braced herself to be rejected again. *Dear Miss Dawson, thank you for your inquiry, but we regret that at this time* . . . she formulated their answer in her head, and then stared at the letter in disbelief. They hadn't offered her a job, but they were inviting her to come to New York for an interview. They explained that one of their English teachers would be taking an extended maternity leave in the fall, so while they didn't have a long-term position to offer her, it was possible that they might be able to hire her for a year, if the interview went well. She couldn't believe her eyes, as she let out a whoop and danced around the room, still holding the candy bar. They had asked her to advise them if she would be able to come to New York for a meeting with them in the next two weeks.

She rushed to her computer and formulated a letter, telling them that she'd be delighted to come to New York. She printed out the letter, signed it, stuck it in an envelope, and put on her coat to run to the mailbox. She had given them her cell phone number and e-mail address as well. She could hardly wait to go to New York. If she got this job, it was her dream come true. This was what she wanted. New York, not L.A. She had spent four years at Northwestern dreaming of going to New York. She was thankful for the teacher who was going on maternity leave and hoped she'd get the job. Just hearing from them was cause for celebration, and she went out and got a pizza after she dropped the letter in the mailbox, and then wondered if she should have called instead.

But they had her phone number now, so they could set up the meeting, and she could be on a plane to New York the next day. She took the pizza back to her dorm room, and sat smiling at their letter. Just having a shot at a teaching position in a private school in New York was the happiest day of her life.

They called her back three days later on her cell phone, and gave her an appointment for the following Monday. She promised to be there, and then decided to spend the weekend before in New York. It occurred to her that the appointment she had just made with them was on Valentine's Day, an ignominious day for her ever since fourth grade. But if she got the job, it would change her opinion of Valentine's Day forever. She hoped it was an omen of some kind. She booked the reservation as soon as she hung up, and then lay on her bed in her dorm room, smiling, trying to figure out what she'd wear to the interview. Maybe a skirt and sweater with high heels, or slacks and a sweater and flats. She didn't know how fancy she should look for a job at a private school in New York, and she had no one to ask. She'd have to wing it and just guess. It was all she could do to keep from running up and down the hall screaming with excitement. Instead, she just lay on her bed, grinning like a Cheshire cat.

Chapter 6

The Madison School on East 76th Street, near the East River, was one of the most exclusive private schools in New York. It went from ninth through twelfth grades, and was a preparatory school for college. The school was expensive, had an excellent reputation, was coed, and its students were from among the elite in New York, with a handful of scholarship students who were lucky enough to qualify. Once accepted, the students had every possible academic and extracurricular opportunity. They got into the best colleges in the country, and it was considered one of the finest private high schools in New York. It was heavily endowed so their science and computer labs had state-of-the-art equipment that competed with any college. Its language department was exceptional, offering

Mandarin, Russian, and Japanese as well as all the European languages, and its English department was outstanding. Several of their students had become successful writers later on. And their teaching staff was exceptional as well, with degrees from important universities. And typical of most private schools, the teachers were severely underpaid. But the opportunity to work there was considered a real prize. Just getting an interview was a major coup for Victoria, and getting the job, even temporarily for a year, was beyond her wildest dreams. If she had to choose one school she would have given anything to teach at, this was it.

She took a flight after her last class before the weekend, and arrived in New York late Friday night. It was snowing, all the flights had been delayed by several hours, and they closed the airport right after she landed; she was grateful they hadn't been rerouted somewhere else. And people outside the airport were fighting for cabs. She had booked a room at the hotel where she'd stayed before, in Gramercy Park. It was two A.M. when she finally got there, and they had saved a small ugly room for her, but the price was one she could afford. She rapidly got into her nightgown, without bothering to unpack, brushed her teeth, got into bed, and slept until noon the next day.

When she woke up, the sun was shining brightly on

two feet of snow, which had continued to fall throughout the night. The city looked like a postcard. And children outside her window were being pulled on sleds by their mothers; others were having snowball fights, ducking for cover behind cars buried in snow that would take their owners hours or days to dig out of. Snowplows were attempting to clear the streets and spreading salt on the ground. Victoria thought it was a perfect winter day in New York, and fortunately had brought a pair of the snow boots she wore almost every day at Northwestern, so she was prepared. And at one o'clock she set off on foot toward the subway, which she had taken every day to work when she lived there. She got off at East 77th Street and walked east toward the river. She wanted to look at the school before she did anything else.

It was a large, beautifully maintained building with several entrances, and could have been an embassy, or an important home of some kind. It had been recently remodeled and was in pristine condition. A discreet bronze plaque over the entrance said only 'The Madison School.' She knew that just under four hundred students were enrolled. A rooftop garden provided open-air space during lunch and recreation. And they had recently built a state-of-the-art gym for all sports activities in what had once been a parking lot across the street. The school offered every possible amenity and opportunity. It stood solid and silent on the snowy sunny afternoon, while a lone janitor cleared a path through the snow outside the school. Victoria smiled at him as she stood looking up at the school, and he returned the smile. She couldn't even imagine being lucky enough to work there in her favorite city in the world. As she stood looking at it, she was wearing the thick white down coat her mother had given her, and felt like a snowman herself. The coat was unflattering but warm. She felt like the Michelin Man or the Pillsbury Doughboy when she wore it, but it had served her well, and was the warmest coat she owned for the arctic temperatures at school. And she was wearing a white wool hat pulled down to her eyes as a wisp of her blond hair peeked out over her brow.

Victoria stood for ages looking up at the school, and then she turned and walked away and went back to the subway to go to Midtown. She wanted to go shopping for something to wear on Monday. She wasn't happy with the outfits she had brought with her, and one of them was too tight. She wanted to look perfect when she interviewed for the job, and she knew how unlikely it was that they would hire her fresh out of school, and they must have had many other applicants, but her grades and recommendations were good, and she had all the excitement and enthusiasm of youth for her first teaching job. She hadn't told her parents that she had come, because her father still wanted her to look for something in another field, with better pay and more possibilities for advancement in the future. Her dream of a teaching career didn't meet their standards as something they could brag about or that would enhance their image. 'My daughter is a teacher' did nothing for them, but working at the Madison School in New York meant everything to Victoria. It had been her first choice when she sent out inquiries to the best private schools in New York, and met all her criteria for dream job, no matter how low the pay. She would manage to live on it somehow if she even got the chance.

Victoria walked back through the snow to the subway, got off at East 59th Street, took the escalator upstairs to Bloomingdale's, and began looking for something she could wear. The clothes she liked frequently didn't come in her size. She was wearing a size fourteen at the moment, although they were a little tight. She sometimes let herself get heavier, without meaning to, in the winter, and then had to wear her size sixteens. The pressure of wearing fewer clothes, showing her body in bathing suits and shorts, and not being able to hide everything under a coat usually helped her bring her size down in summer. She wished she had been more disciplined about it recently. She had already promised herself to lose weight by graduation, and particularly now if she got this job in New York. She didn't want to be at her biggest when she started her first teaching job.

After endless discouraging searching and some truly upsetting try-ons, she found a pair of gray slacks and a long dark blue blazer to wear with a pale blue turtleneck sweater the same color as her eyes. She bought a pair of high-heeled boots that added a younger look to the outfit. It looked dignified, respectable, not too dressy, and just elegant enough to make her look serious about the job. It was the look she assumed would be worn by teachers at that school. And she was happy with the outfit, when she got back on the subway with her shopping bags and rode back downtown to her hotel. The streets were still snarled by snowplows, buried cars, and tall mounds of shoveled snow everywhere. The city was a mess. But Victoria was in great spirits with her purchases. She was going to wear a pair of small pearl earrings her mother had given her. And the well-cut navy blazer hid a multitude of sins. The outfit looked young, professional, and trim.

The morning of the interview Victoria woke up with a knot in her stomach. She washed and blow-dried her hair, then brushed it into a sleek ponytail and tied it with a black satin ribbon. She dressed carefully, put on the big down coat, and went out into the February sunshine. The weather had warmed up and was turning the snow to slush with ice rivers in the gutters. She had to be careful not to get splashed with it by passing cars as she made her way to the subway. She thought of taking a cab, but she knew the subway was faster. And she reached the school ten minutes before her nine o'clock interview, in time to see hundreds of young people filtering into the school. Almost all were wearing jeans, and a few of the girls wore miniskirts and boots despite the cold weather. They were talking and laughing, with a wild assortment of hairdos and hair colors, carrying their books. They looked like kids in any other high school, not the offspring of the elite. And the two teachers standing at the main entrance as they filtered in were dressed the same way the kids were, in jeans and down jackets, running shoes or boots. There was a nice informal feeling to the group, and wholesome too. The two monitors were a man and a woman. The female teacher wore her long hair in a braid; the male teacher's head was shaved. Victoria noticed that he had a small bird tattooed on the back of his head. They were chatting animatedly as they followed the last stragglers inside, and Victoria walked in right behind them, wearing her new outfit and hoping she would make a good impression. Her appointment was with Eric Walker, the headmaster, and they had mentioned that they would want her to meet with the dean of students too. She gave the receptionist her name, and waited on a chair in the lobby. Five minutes later a man in his mid forties came out to greet her, in jeans, a black sweater, a tweed jacket, and hiking boots. He smiled warmly at Victoria and invited her into his office, and waved at a battered leather chair on the other side of his desk.

'Thank you for coming in from Northwestern,' he said, as she took off her bulky coat so he could see her new blazer. She hoped he wouldn't decide she was too uptight for the school, which turned out to be much more casual than she had expected. 'I was afraid you might not be able to get in, with the snowstorm,' he said pleasantly. 'Happy Valentine's Day, by the way. We were having a dance on Saturday, but we had to cancel. The kids from the suburbs and Connecticut couldn't have gotten in. About a fifth of our students commute to school. We had to reschedule for next weekend.' He had her CV on his desk, Victoria noticed, and was fully prepared for the meeting. She saw that he had the transcript of her grades that she had sent him too. She had Googled him and knew that he had gone to Yale, and had a master's and Ph.D. from Harvard. He was Dr. Walker, although he didn't use the title on his correspondence to her. His credentials were impressive. And he had published two books on secondary education for laymen, and a guide for parents and students on the college application process. She felt insignificant in his presence, but he had a warm friendly demeanor, and turned his full attention to her.

'So, Victoria,' he said, leaning back in his own ancient leather chair, behind a handsome English partner's desk he said had been his father's. The things in his office looked expensive and well worn to the point of battered. And there were bookcases crammed full of books. 'What makes you think you want to be a teacher? And why here? Wouldn't you rather be back in L.A., where you won't have to shovel snow to get to school?' He smiled as he said it, and so did she. She liked him, and wanted to impress him, and she wasn't sure how to do it. All she had brought with her were enthusiasm and truth.

'I love kids. I've always wanted to be a teacher "when I grew up." I just knew it was right for me. I'm not interested in business, or getting up the corporate ladder, although that's what my parents think I should do, and what they respect. I think that if I make a difference in a young person's life, it would be much better and more meaningful than anything else I could do.' She could see in his eyes that it was the right answer, and she was pleased. And she meant it.

'Even if it means you're miserably paid, and make less money than everyone else you know?'

'Yes, even if I'm miserably paid. I don't care. I don't need a lot to live on.' He didn't ask her if her parents were going to help her – that wasn't his problem.

'You'd make a lot more money working for the public school system,' he said honestly, and she knew that too.

'I don't want to do that. And I don't want to go back to L.A. I've wanted to live in New York since high school. I would have gone to college here if I'd been accepted at NYU or Barnard. I know this is right for me. And Madison was my first-choice school.'

'Why? Rich kids are no easier to teach than others. They're smart kids, and they're exposed to a lot of things. No matter what their grades are, and we have our weak students too, they're savvy, and you can't bullshit them. They know it if you don't know your stuff, and they'll call you on it. They're more confident and bolder than kids with fewer advantages, and that can be tough for a teacher. And the parents can be tough here. They're very demanding, and they want the best that we can give them. And we're fully committed to doing just that. Does it bother you that you'd only be four or five years older than some of your students? The opening we have will involve juniors and seniors, and we might have you cover an English class for sophomores as well. They can be a handful, especially in this school where some of them are mature for their age. These kids have a lot of exposure to a very sophisticated lifestyle with all that that entails. Do you think you're up to it?' he asked her candidly, and Victoria nodded at him with a serious look in her big blue eyes.

'I think I am, Dr. Walker. I think I could handle it. I'm certain of it, if you give me the chance.'

'The teacher you'll be replacing will only be out for a year. I can't promise you anything after that, no matter how well you perform here. So this isn't a long-term commitment on our part, but only for a year. After that, we'd have to see what would come up, if anyone else is leaving or going out on leave. So if you want a long-term commitment, you should probably look somewhere else.' She couldn't say that all her other options had turned her down.

'I'd be thrilled with a year,' she said honestly. She didn't know it, but they had already checked her references with the modeling agency and the law firm, and were impressed by how good they were, in terms of her reliability, her conscientiousness, her professionalism and honesty. She had also completed her student teaching assignments, and the references on them had been excellent too. All Eric Walker needed to decide now was if she was the right teacher for their school. She seemed like a bright, sweet girl. And he was touched by how much she wanted the job.

After he spent forty-five minutes with her, Eric Walker passed her on to his assistant, and she gave Victoria a tour of the school. It was an impressive building with well-kept classrooms, full of alert students using brand-new, very expensive equipment. It was an atmosphere that any teacher would have given anything to teach in, and they all looked like bright, alert, interested, good kids to her. And then she met with the dean of students, who told her something about their student body, and the type of situations she'd face. They were the same as high school students anywhere, except with more money and opportunities, and in some cases very complicated family situations. But difficult home lives were not exclusive to the very rich, nor the poor.

At the end of the second interview, they thanked her for coming, told her they were seeing several other candidates, and would let her know. And after thanking them too, Victoria then found herself out on the street, looking up at the school, praying she would get the job.

She had no idea if she would, and they had been so pleasant to her that it was hard to tell if they were just very polite or enthused about her. She didn't know. She walked west all the way to Fifth Avenue, and then north five blocks, to the Metropolitan Museum, where she saw a new wing of the Egyptian exhibit, and then had lunch in the cafeteria alone, before treating herself to a cab back to her hotel.

She sat in the backseat watching New York slide by and people swarm around like ants in the streets. All she could hope was that she would be part of it one day. She expected to hear back from Madison in a few weeks. And she realized that if she didn't get the job, she would have to start interviewing at other schools, in Chicago, and maybe even L.A., although the last thing she wanted to do was go home. But if nothing else turned up, she might not have any other choice. She dreaded the thought of living in L.A. again, and even worse, the possibility of living at home, and facing all the same problems she'd always had there. Living with her parents would be too depressing.

She packed her bag and took a cab to the airport. She had an hour to spare before her flight, and she was so anxious after the interview, wondering whether she had done well or not, that she went to the restaurant nearest her gate and ordered a cheeseburger and a hot fudge sundae, and devoured both. She felt stupid once she had. She hadn't needed it, or the french fries that came with it. But she had been starving and nervous, and the meal she'd eaten offered some comfort and relief from her terrors. What if she didn't get the job? She told herself that if she didn't, she'd find something else. But the Madison School was the one she wanted most, if they would just give her a chance. She knew how unlikely that was, fresh out of school.

When they called her flight, she got up, picked up her hand luggage, and headed for the gate. All she could do now was wait and go back to Northwestern. All things considered, for once it hadn't been a bad Valentine's Day. And it would be the best one of all if she actually got the job in the end. She was still nervous about it, when she got on the plane, even after the cheeseburger and hot fudge sundae. They hadn't helped. And she reminded herself as she put on her seatbelt that she would have to be serious about her diet again, and start jogging. Graduation was only three months away. But when she was offered a bag of nuts and another of pretzels, she couldn't refuse. She ate them absentmindedly as she thought about her interview, hoping she hadn't blown it in some way, and praying she'd get the job.

Chapter 7

Eric Walker, the head of the Madison School, made the call to Victoria himself in the first week of March. He said it had been a tough choice between her and several other teachers, but he was happy to tell her that she had the job, and she was thrilled. He said a contract had been sent to her by mail.

She was going to be the youngest member of the English department, and she would teach four classes, to sophomores, juniors, and seniors. She had to report for teachers' meetings on September 1st, and school would start the following week. In exactly six months, she was going to be teaching at the Madison School in New York. She could hardly believe it. And unable to keep the good news to herself, she called her parents that night.

'I was afraid you'd do something like that,' her father said with a disapproving tone. He actually sounded disappointed in her, as though she'd been arrested for taking her clothes off in a supermarket and was in jail. As in *why did you go and do a dumb thing like that?* 'You're never going to make a penny as a teacher, Victoria. You need to get a *real* job, in advertising or PR, or something in the communications field. There are lots of things you can do. You can work in the PR office of any major company. You can go to work at McDonald's and make more than you will as a teacher. It's a total waste of time. And why New York? Why not here?' He didn't even ask what kind of school it was, and gave her no credit for landing her first job, in a first-rate school, against stiff competition. All he had to say was that it was the wrong job in the wrong city, and she'd always be poor. But teaching was her chosen career, and it was one of the country's best private schools.

'I'm sorry, Dad,' she said, apologizing for it, as though she had done something wrong. 'It's a really great school.'

'Really? How much are they paying you?' he asked bluntly. She didn't want to lie to him, so she told him the truth. And she knew too that it was going to be hard to live on, but it was worth the sacrifices to her, and she wasn't planning to take anything from him. 'That's pathetic,' he said, sounding disgusted, and handed the phone to her mother, who sounded worried the minute she got on the phone.

'What happened, dear?' her mother asked.

'Nothing. I just got a terrific job, teaching at a wonderful school in New York. Dad just thinks they're not paying me enough, that's all. But it's a real coup that they hired me at all.'

'It's such a shame that you want to be a teacher,' her mother said, echoing the party line, and managing to convey to Victoria, just as she always had, that she had failed, and was a disappointment to them. They took the fun out of everything for her, and always had, and any sense of accomplishment over what she had achieved. 'You could make so much money doing something else.'

'I think I'll really like the job, Mom. I love the school,' she said, sounding young and hopeful, and trying to hold on to the excitement and enthusiasm and pride she had felt before she called.

'I suppose that's nice, dear. But you can't be a teacher forever. At some point you'll have to get a real job.' When did teaching become not a 'real' job? It was all about money to them, and how much you made. 'Your sister just made fifty thousand dollars for a two-day shoot for a national campaign,' her mother said. It was more than

Victoria was going to make in a year. And Grace just did it for fun, and the college fund their parents had set up for her. To Gracie, modeling was like a game, for which she was highly paid, and she only did it occasionally. Victoria was going to be working hard for the money she made. The discrepancy and dichotomy were shocking to her. But it was no secret that teaching was not a highly paid job, and she had known that when she chose it as a career. She didn't have the modeling opportunities that Gracie did anyway. They were not an option for her. And teaching was her vocation, not just her work. She hoped that she'd be good at it. 'Where are you going to live?' her mother asked her, sounding worried about that too. 'Can you afford an apartment on a teacher's salary? New York is a very expensive city.'

'I'll get something with roommates. I'll go back there in August and get settled before I start work.'

'When are you coming home?'

'Right after graduation. I want to spend this summer with you.' She wasn't planning to get a summer job this year. She wanted to take some short trips with Gracie, and spend time with them, before she officially moved to New York. She might never live in L.A. again, or have as much time to spend with them, although she would have summers off if she continued to teach. But she might have to take summer jobs to supplement her income. This was her last summer to be home and not working, and her parents were fine with it.

Victoria didn't go home for spring break – she took a job waiting on tables in a diner just off campus, to make some money to sock away. She was going to need every penny she could save for New York. But the meals they gave her for free at the diner got her off her diet again. She lived on meat loaf and mashed potatoes with gravy, and lemon meringue and apple pie à la mode for two weeks. It was tough to resist, especially the blueberry pancakes for breakfast at six A.M. when she started work. Her dream of losing weight by graduation was fading fast. And it was depressing always being on a diet, some new exercise program, and spending life on a treadmill to atone for her sins.

After killing herself at the gym all through April, and watching what she ate, she finally lost ten pounds. She was proud of herself. And she went to rent her cap and gown on the first of May. There was an endless line where they were handing them out, and when she finally got to the head of the line, the man assigning them looked at her to guess her correct size.

'Big girl, huh?' he said with a broad grin, and she had to fight back tears. She didn't answer, and didn't comment when he handed her an extra large that she didn't need. But she was tall enough to wear it, so she didn't complain. It was huge on her at least. She was planning to wear a short red skirt, high-heeled sandals, and a white blouse under it at graduation. The skirt was short, but no one would see it until she took the gown off. She loved the color, and her legs looked great.

She packed up all her things and sent them home two days before graduation, the day before her parents arrived. Gracie was coming with them, of course. And she was more beautiful than ever when Victoria saw her, wearing a white T-shirt and short shorts. She was fifteen now and, despite her diminutive size, looked eighteen. She could still do ads for children's clothes and often did. Victoria felt like an elephant standing next to her and her mother, but she loved Gracie anyway. The two sisters almost squeezed the air out of each other when they hugged, after they met her at the dorm.

They took Victoria out for dinner that night, at a really nice restaurant that night, where several of the other graduates were having dinner too. Victoria had asked about bringing a few of her friends along, but her father had said they'd rather have dinner alone with her. And he felt the same about their celebratory lunch the next day too. He said they wanted Victoria to themselves, but what he was really saying, as he always did, was that he was not interested in meeting her friends. It was nothing new to Victoria. But she was happy to be with them anyway. And Gracie was constantly cuddling up to her. The two sisters were always inseparable when they were together. And Grace was starting to think about college too. She wanted to go to USC. And their parents were pleased because it was close to home. Her father said she was a real southern California girl, which made Victoria sound like a traitor for going to college in the Midwest, instead of congratulating her for her sense of adventure and going to a hard school.

The graduation ceremony of the Weinberg College of Arts and Sciences at Northwestern the next day was fraught with pomp, ceremony, and emotion. Christine was already crying when the procession began, and Jim was looking unusually proud with a damp eye as his daughter walked by him in her cap and gown, and Gracie snapped a picture and Victoria grinned, while trying to look solemn.

Just over a thousand students got their diplomas that day from Weinberg, in alphabetical order. Victoria shook hands with the dean who handed it to her. And she screamed as loud as everyone two hours later, when they threw their caps in the air and embraced each other. She had been solitary for much of her time at Northwestern, but she had nonetheless made some friends, and they had exchanged e-mail addresses and cell phone numbers, and they promised to stay in touch, even if that seemed unlikely. And then suddenly they were out in the world, as graduates, ready to take their place in their chosen careers.

Victoria had dinner with her family again that night at Jilly's Café, and it felt like a real celebration, as other graduates did the same at nearby tables. The next morning she and her family flew back to L.A. together. Victoria had spent the night at the Hotel Orrington with them, sharing a room with Gracie, as she had to give up her dorm room right after graduation. The two girls chatted late into the night, until they fell asleep next to each other. They were looking forward to spending the next three months together. Victoria hadn't told anyone, but she was planning to spend the summer following a serious weight-loss program so she could look her best when she started teaching at Madison in September. Her father had commented, when she took her gown off after graduation to return it, that she looked bigger than ever. As usual, he had said it with a broad smile. And then he complimented her on her long legs as he always did, but the first comment was far more powerful than the second. She never heard the compliment once he hit her with the insult.

She sat between her father and Grace on the flight home, and her mother was across the aisle reading a magazine. The two girls had wanted to sit together. They didn't even look related. And as she got older, Gracie was more and more the image of her mother. Victoria at every age was the image of no one.

Her father leaned over to speak to Victoria right after takeoff. She and Gracie had been talking softly, and were thinking of watching a movie.

'You know, you've got the time to look for a decent job when you get back to L.A. You can always tell that school in New York that you've changed your mind. Think about it,' he said in a conspiratorial tone.

'I like the job in New York, Dad,' Victoria insisted. 'It's a great school, and if I back out now, my name would be dirt forever in the teaching community. I want the job.'

'You don't want to be poor for the rest of your life, do you?' he said with a look of contempt. 'You can't afford to be a teacher, and I'm not going to subsidize you forever,' he commented bluntly.

'I'm not expecting you to, or even now, Dad. Other people live on teachers' salaries. So can I.'

'Why should you have to? I can line up some

interviews for you next week.' He was dismissing her entire achievement in landing the job in New York. To him, it wasn't even a job. He kept telling her to get a 'real' job for decent money.

'Thank you for the offer,' she said politely, 'but I want to stick with what I've got for now. I can always figure it out later if I really can't live on it. But I can always take a summer job and save the money.'

'That's pathetic. It may seem all right to you at twenty-two, but trust me, it won't when you're thirty or forty. You can interview at the ad agency if you want to.'

'I don't want to work in advertising,' she said firmly. 'I want to be a teacher.' It was the thousandth time she'd said it to him. He shrugged in answer and looked annoyed, and after that she and Gracie put their head-phones on and watched the movie. She was relieved not to have to talk to him about it anymore. Her parents were only interested in two things about her, her weight and how much money she was going to make at her job. And the third topic they brought up from time to time was her absence of a love life, which in both their opinions was a result of the first subject, her weight and size. Her father said, whenever the subject came up, that if she'd lose some weight, she'd find a boyfriend. She knew that wasn't necessarily the case, since plenty of girls who had perfect figures and were half her size couldn't find a boyfriend. And other girls who were overweight were happily married, engaged, or had significant others. Romance, she knew, wasn't directly tied to your weight, there were a lot of other factors. And her lack of self-esteem and their constantly picking on her and criticizing her didn't help her with that problem. They were never proud of her or satisfied with what she was doing, although both of her parents had said they were proud when she graduated from Northwestern. They just wished it had been UCLA or USC, and that she had found a different job than the one in New York, preferably one in L.A. in a different line of work. Whatever she did was never right or enough for them. And they never seemed to realize how painful their constant criticism was for her, or that it was why she no longer wanted to live in L.A. She wanted to put a whole country between them. That way she only had to see them at Thanksgiving and Christmas, and maybe one day she wouldn't go home for those either. But for now, she wanted to be with Gracie. Once Gracie left home, Victoria wasn't sure when she'd go home or how often. They had succeeded in driving her away and didn't even know it.

She and Gracie got in the back of the car on the way home from the airport. Their parents were talking in the front seat about what they were going to do for dinner. Jim offered to barbecue some steaks in the backyard, and he turned toward the backseat and winked at his older daughter. 'I don't need to ask you, I know you're hungry. What about you, G, how do steaks sound for dinner?' he asked Gracie. Victoria stared out the window, looking like she'd been punched in the stomach. That was the reputation she had here, and the image they had of her, the one who was always hungry.

'Steaks sound fine, Dad,' Gracie said vaguely. 'We can order Chinese if you don't feel like making barbecue, or Victoria and I can go out for dinner if you and Mom are tired.' They both would have preferred it but didn't want to insult their parents. And Jim insisted that he was happy to barbecue, as long as he and Victoria wouldn't be the only ones eating. It was the second shot he had taken at her in five minutes. It was going to be a long summer if this was how it started. It was a reminder to her that nothing had changed. Four years away at college, and a diploma, and they still treated her like the resident uncontrollable eater.

They sat in the backyard that night and ate dinner. Christine decided to skip the steak and just ate salad. She said she'd eaten too much on the plane, and Grace and Victoria ate the steaks their father had made. Grace helped herself to a baked potato, but Victoria didn't, and just put salad on her plate with the steak.

'Are you sick?' her father said with a straight face. 'I've never seen you turn down a potato.'

'I'm fine, Dad,' Victoria said quietly. She didn't enjoy the comment, and she had decided to start her latest diet the moment she got home. She stuck to it, even though they offered her ice cream for dessert, and would have commented on that too if she'd said yes.

After dinner the two girls sat in Gracie's room, listening to music. Although Gracie's taste was younger and wilder, they shared lots of things in common. Victoria was happy to be at home with her.

They spent a lot of time together that summer, once Grace got out of school, a few weeks after Victoria's graduation. The family went to Santa Barbara for the long weekend of Memorial Day. And after they got back, Victoria drove Gracie everywhere. She became her personal chauffeur and companion, and the girls were inseparable for two months. Victoria saw some of her old school friends who had come back to L.A. after graduation, or stayed to go to school there. She didn't have a lot of close friends, but it was nice to see familiar faces, particularly before she moved away. Two were going on to graduate school, and she thought she'd like to do that one day herself, but at NYU or Columbia. She saw several of the boys she'd known at school, who'd never paid particular attention to her. One of them asked her out for dinner and a movie, but they didn't have much to say to each other. He had gone into real estate and was obsessed with money. He wasn't impressed with her choice of a teaching career either. The only one who seemed to admire it was her younger sister, who thought it was noble. Everyone else thought she was foolish and reminded her that she'd be poor forever.

For Victoria, being at home for the summer was a chance to stock up on memories she would cherish forever. She and Gracie shared their dreams and fears and hopes, and their private peeves about their parents. Gracie thought they babied her too much, and she hated the way they bragged about her. Victoria's main regret was that they didn't. Their experiences in the same family were diametrically different. It was hard to believe they had the same parents. And although Gracie was the person responsible for making Victoria invisible to them and redundant, Victoria never held it against her, and she loved Grace for the little girl she was and had been, the baby who had come to her like an angel when she was seven.

And for Grace the summer they shared after Victoria's

graduation was a last chance to hang on to her big sister. They had breakfast together every morning. They laughed a lot. Victoria took Gracie out with her friends to the swim club. She played tennis with them, and they beat her every time, because they moved faster than she did. She helped Gracie shop for new clothes for school, and they decided what was hip and what wasn't. They read fashion magazines together and commented on the new styles. They went to Malibu and other beaches, and sometimes they just lay in the backyard and said nothing, knowing that they were close and loving every minute of it.

It was an easy summer for Christine, since Victoria did everything for Gracie, which gave her all the free time she wanted – not to be with her daughters, but to play bridge with her friends, which was still her favorite pastime. And in spite of her protests, her father set up several interviews for Victoria to find a 'better' job than the one she had waiting for her in New York. Victoria thanked him and discreetly canceled them all. She didn't want to waste anyone's time, nor her own. Her father was angry about it, and told her again that she was making all the wrong decisions about her future and would never amount to anything as a teacher. She was used to hearing things like that from him, and it didn't sway her. She was the child they had never been proud of and had either ignored or made fun of.

She confessed to Gracie one day that summer that if she had the money, she would love to have a nose job, and maybe she would sometime. She said that she liked Gracie's nose, and wanted one like it, or a 'cute' nose of her own. Gracie was touched when she said it, and she told Victoria that she was beautiful anyway, even with her own nose. She didn't need a new one. Gracie thought she was perfect just the way she was. It was the unconditional love that they had given each other all their lives and that Victoria thrived on, and so did Gracie. Their parents' love was always conditional, depending on how they looked and if their achievements were valid according to their parents' standards, and if they made their parents look good in the process. Gracie had basked in their praise all her life, because she was an accessory that enhanced them. And because Victoria was different and didn't fit in, she had been emotionally starved by them, but not by Gracie. Grace had always lavished love on her and worshipped Victoria in every way. And Victoria adored her, wanted to protect her sister, and didn't want her to turn out like her parents. She wished she could take Gracie with her. They both dreaded the day she would leave for New York.

Grace helped Victoria pick new items for her wardrobe that would look appropriate to her students when she taught high school. She had stuck to her guns and her diet this time, and could just get into a size twelve by the beginning of August. It was tight, but it fit. She had dropped several pounds over the summer, although her father asked her regularly if she didn't want to lose some weight before she left for New York. He didn't notice a single pound she lost; nor did her mother, who was always distressed about her daughter's size, no matter what it was. The label they had put on her as a child was stuck there forever, like a tattoo. She was a 'big girl,' which was their way of calling her a fat girl. She knew that if she weighed a hundred pounds and were disappearing, they would still see her as a 'big girl.' They were the mirror of her inadequacies and her failings, and never of her victories. The only victories they saw were Grace's. That was just the way they were.

The family went to Lake Tahoe together for a week before Victoria had to leave. They had a good time. The house their father had rented for them was very pretty. And both girls water-skied in the freezing lake, while their father steered the boat. The best part about her taking a teaching job, Gracie said, was that they would still be able to go on summer vacations together, and

Victoria promised to have her come and visit in New York. She could even visit the school where she'd be teaching, and maybe sit in on one of her classes if they let her. She hoped they would.

And finally the day arrived for Victoria to leave. It was a day that she and Grace had dreaded, for all the good-byes they didn't want to say. They were both strangely silent on the way to the airport. They had stayed awake all the night before, and lay in one bed so they could talk. Victoria told Gracie she could move into her room, because she liked it better, but Gracie didn't want to take her room away. She wanted her to have a place to come home to. They stood hugging each other for a long time at the airport, as tears streamed down their cheeks. Despite their many assurances to each other over the summer, they both knew that it would never be the same again. Victoria was going to a grown-up life in another city, and they had agreed that it was better for her. The one thing they both were certain would never change was how much they loved each other. The rest would be different from now on. It had to be. From the moment Victoria set foot on the plane, she would be a grown-up. And when she came home, it would only be to visit. There was nothing left for her here except painful memories and her sister Grace. Her parents had abandoned her emotionally the day she was born, when she didn't look the way they'd planned, or anything like them. It had been unacceptable to them, and a crime they could never quite forgive her, and didn't even try. Instead they made fun of her and diminished and dismissed her. They always made her feel unwanted and not really good enough for them.

'Take care of yourself, dear, and let us know how you are,' her mother said, hugging her loosely, as she always did, as though Victoria were too big for her to get her arms around, or as though her proportions might be contagious. There was too little of Christine internally for her to give much to anyone else, except Jim. She gave him all she had, and always shortchanged her girls, even Grace. She was only too happy to let Victoria stand in for her with Grace.

'I'll find you a job when you give up teaching,' her father said as he hugged her. 'It won't take long,' he confirmed with a grin. 'You'll get tired of starving.' Despite the words, he pressed a check into her hand. It was for a thousand dollars. It was a generous gift, and she was glad to have it. It would help with her rent or the deposit for an apartment that she had yet to find.

She and Grace hugged one last time, and then she had to wrench herself away and go through the security line.

When she turned back to wave, she and Gracie were both crying, and her father had his arm around their mother's shoulders. Gracie was standing alone, and the look that passed between the two girls from the distance said it all. Victoria knew that they would be allies forever. She touched her heart, blew Grace a kiss, and then she was gone, to her new life. She knew that her life in L.A. was only her history now.

Chapter 8

It took Victoria two weeks to find an apartment once she got to New York, and by the end of the first week, she was beginning to panic. She couldn't stay at a hotel forever, although the check from her father helped. She had saved the money from her past summer jobs, and the one she'd had at spring break, and she would have her salary to live on. She called the school to see if any of the teachers was looking for a roommate, but they told her no one was. She called the modeling agency where she had worked, and one of the booking agents told her that he had a friend who was looking for a roommate, and by sheer luck it was in the East 80s, which was close enough to the school to work for her. He gave her the friend's number, and she called immediately. There were already three people living in the apartment, and they were looking for a fourth. They told her that the room they were looking to fill was small, and two of them were men and one was a woman, and the price was within her budget. She made an appointment to go over that evening when they got home from work. Miraculously, it was six blocks from the school where she was going to teach. But she didn't want to get too excited until she saw it. It sounded too good to be true.

When she got there, it was an old prewar building in decent condition, although it looked like it had seen better days. It was on East 82nd Street, near the river. The front door was locked, and she had to be buzzed in, and then she rode the elevator upstairs. The hallway was dark but clean, and a young woman let her into the apartment. She was wearing workout clothes and said she was leaving for the gym. She was in good shape and looked to be about thirty. She said her name was Bunny, for Bernice, which she hated, and she worked in an art gallery uptown. Both men had come home to meet her too. Bill had gone to college with Bunny at Tulane and was an analyst on Wall Street. He said he was recently engaged and would be moving out in the next year. He said he usually stayed at his girlfriend's apartment, especially on weekends. The other man, Harlan, was gay and recently out of school, and worked for the Metropolitan Museum in the Costume Institute. All of them seemed serious, all were pleasant and well spoken, and she told them she would be teaching at the Madison School. Bill offered Victoria a glass of wine, and a few minutes later Bunny left for the gym. She had an incredible figure, and the two men were nice looking. Harlan had a great sense of humor and a southern drawl and reminded her of Beau, whom she had never seen again after their aborted near-affair. Harlan was born in Mississippi. She told them she came from L.A., and was desperate to find a place to live before she started work the following week.

The apartment was big and sunny, with a double living room, a small den, a dining room, a kitchen that had seen better days, and four modest-size bedrooms, and it was under rent control. The bedroom they showed her was small, as they had warned her, but the other rooms were pleasant and spacious, and they said they had no problem with it if she wanted to entertain, although most of them didn't, and they said they went out a lot. None of them were from New York, and the room they showed her had no furniture in it. Harlan suggested she go to IKEA, which was what he had done. He'd been living there for a year. And because the apartment was under rent control, the rent they had suggested to her was one

Victoria could easily afford, even on her salary, and it was a safe neighborhood, with shops and restaurants nearby. It was an ideal young people's apartment, and they said that everyone in the building was either very young or very old and had been there forever. It was perfect for Victoria, and when she asked if she could rent it, both men approved. Bunny had already given them her okay before she left for the gym. And the booking agent at the modeling agency who had recommended her had told them what a great girl she was and what a nice person. She was in, and smiled broadly as she shook hands with the two men. They required no security deposit, and told her she could move in immediately. As soon as she bought a bed, she could stay there. Harlan told her about a firm you could call, give them your credit card number, and they would deliver a mattress the same afternoon. Welcome to New York!

Victoria gave them a check for the first month's rent, they gave her a set of keys, and when she left to go back to her hotel, her head was spinning. She had a job, an apartment, and a new life. All she had to do now was buy furniture for her bedroom, and she could move in. She called her parents that night to tell them, and Gracie was delighted for her. Her father questioned her intently about where it was, and what sort of people her roommates were. Her mother wasn't thrilled to hear that two of them were men. Victoria reassured her by saying that one was engaged and the other one wasn't interested in women, and all three of her new roommates seemed like terrific people. Her parents sounded cautious about it. They would have much preferred her living alone than among strangers, but they knew she couldn't afford it, and her father didn't want to pay rent for her in New York. It was time for her to make her way in the world.

The next day she rented a van and went to IKEA. She bought all the basics she needed for her bedroom, and was amazed by how little it cost her. She bought two lamps, a rug, curtains, two wall mirrors, bedding, a comfortable chair, two night tables, a nice-looking chest of drawers, and a small mirrored armoire, since the room only had one closet, and she hoped her things would all fit. The bad news was that all the furniture had to be assembled, but Harlan had told her that the handyman in the building would do it if she gave him a decent tip.

They helped her load it into the van at IKEA, and an hour later she was at the apartment and unloading her furniture with the help of the superintendent. It took another hour to get it all upstairs, and just as Harlan had said, the handyman came up with his tool box and started assembling the pieces that needed it. She called the company that delivered mattresses and box springs, and they arrived even before the handyman had finished. And by six o'clock when Bunny came home from work, Victoria was sitting in the middle of her new room, admiring how it looked. She had chosen white furniture and white lace curtains, with a blue and white rug, and it all had an airy California feeling to it. She had even bought a blue-and-white-striped bedspread and matching cushions. And there was a comfortable blue armchair in the corner of the room, where she could read if she didn't want to sit in the living room. And earlier she had bought a small TV that she could watch from her bed. Her father's check had gone a long way to helping her with her purchases. She looked ecstatic as she sat on the bed and grinned when Bunny walked in.

'Well, don't you look like a happy camper,' Bunny said, smiling at her. 'I like your stuff.'

'Yeah, me too,' Victoria said happily. This was her first real apartment. All she'd had till then were dorm rooms, and this was considerably bigger, although it wasn't huge by any means. And she shared a bathroom with Bunny. The two men shared the other bathroom, and she had already noticed that Bunny's bathroom was immaculate and she was meticulously neat. The setup was ideal.

'Are you staying here tonight?' Bunny asked with

interest. 'I'm home if you want help unpacking.' Victoria had spent all afternoon putting things together, and she had sheets to sleep there that night, and a stack of brand-new towels that she wanted to run through the washing machine in the basement laundry room.

'I've got to pick up my stuff at the hotel.' She had checked out that morning so she could save the money and had stored her bags with the porter. 'I'll go get it in a little while and come back later.' The men came home then and admired her new room. It looked fresh and clean and modern, and Harlan said it looked like a Malibu beach house. She had even bought a framed photograph of a long sandy beach and blue water that looked peaceful to her and hung it on one wall. There was a smell of new furniture in the room, which had recently been painted. She could see the street from her windows, and the neighboring rooftops. The building was on the north side of the street and faced south, so she knew it would be sunny.

Her new roommates all told her they would be home that night and were planning to cook dinner if she wanted to join them, so she left shortly afterward to pick her things up at the hotel, return the van, and be back in time for dinner.

The apartment was full of good cooking smells when

she got back, and all three of them were apparently great cooks. Bill's fiancée, Julie, had joined them by then, and the four of them were in the kitchen, laughing and drinking wine, when Victoria walked in with four suitcases. She had brought her entire winter wardrobe with her, in case she needed it before she went home again at Thanksgiving. Bunny said that was a good thing since it could get cold in October.

Victoria had stopped to buy a bottle of wine for them and set it on the kitchen table. It was Spanish wine, and they all said they liked it, and opened it immediately. They had already killed the first bottle, which was easily done when shared by four people. Victoria had been tempted to buy ice cream on her way home, but she didn't. Moving was a little stressful, but so far everything had gone well.

The five of them sat down to dinner at ten o'clock, when everyone was hungry. They came and went in and out of the kitchen until then. Bunny was doing most of the cooking that night, and both men went to the gym before dinner. They all were diligent about their workouts, and Bill's fiancée Julie had a gorgeous body. She worked for a cosmetics company, and all of them thought it was great that Victoria was teaching school, and very brave since her students would be almost as old as she was.

'Kids terrify me,' Bunny confessed. 'Whenever they come into the gallery, I run and hide. They always break something, and then I get in trouble.' She said that she had been a fine arts major and had a boyfriend in Boston who was going to law school at BU and came down to see her on weekends, or she went to see him.

They all seemed to have their lives in perfect order. Over dinner, Harlan said that he had broken up with his partner six months before, and then moved into the apartment, and was taking a break from romance. He said he wasn't dating, and Victoria admitted that she wasn't either. None of her romances had ever worked out so far, and she didn't like her father's theory that it was because of her weight and looks. She felt as though she was cursed. Her father thought she wasn't pretty enough, and her mother thought she was too smart for most men and would put them off. She was either too ugly or too smart, but in any case, no one had fallen head over heels for her, and she hadn't either. All she'd had till then were what she would have qualified as crushes, except for the ill-fated false start with Beau, and the brief affair with the physics major, and some dates that had gone nowhere. She was hoping her luck would improve in New York. And it had – she had found a great apartment and three terrific roommates. She really liked them. The dinner they served was delicious. Bunny had made paella with fresh seafood in it, which seemed perfect on a hot summer day, and she had made sangria that they drank after the wine. She served cold gazpacho first, before the paella. And for dessert she produced half a gallon of 'cookies and cream' ice cream, which was unfortunately one of Victoria's favorites, and once it was sitting on the table, she couldn't resist it.

'This is like serving heroin to an addict,' Victoria complained, helping herself to a full bowl as the carton was passed around the table. Before that, they had all cleaned their plates. The paella had been delicious. And so was the ice cream.

'I love ice cream too,' Harlan confessed, but didn't look it. He looked as though he hadn't eaten in ten years, and was six-three, which allowed him a lot of leeway. But Victoria hadn't had ice cream in ages, so she decided to indulge and treat herself. They were celebrating, after all. And later she silently congratulated herself for not having a second helping, although the first portion had been large. Between the five of them, they finished the ice cream. Julie put away a healthy amount too, but none of the others looked as though they had an issue with food. All of them were slim people, and very trim and toned. They all said they were religious about the gym, and both

Bill and Bunny said it helped them with stress. Harlan said he hated working out but felt an obligation to stay in shape. And Bunny said they'd been thinking of collectively buying a treadmill so they didn't have to go to the gym every day. Victoria said it sounded like a great idea. She couldn't avoid it if it was sitting right in the apartment. They were a busy, lively group, full of projects, plans, and ideas. And Victoria was looking forward to living with them. It was going to be a happier circumstance for her than living alone in a tiny apartment. This way she could have more space, and company whenever she wanted. And when she didn't, she could go to her room, which was peaceful and pretty now, thanks to IKEA. She was thrilled with what she'd gotten, and how it had all come together. It had been a great idea, and she thanked Harlan for suggesting it.

'Anytime,' he said, smiling at her. 'I used to do window dressing on the side. I did stores all over SoHo, and the windows at Chanel. I want to be an interior designer when I grow up. But right now I'm busy at the Costume Institute. But I always have other ideas and projects.' He seemed like a very creative person, and Victoria liked the way he dressed.

Sitting around with them in the kitchen made her hope that maybe, living with them and going to the gym as often as they did, she could keep her weight under control. She knew her weight was constantly fluctuating and always higher than it should be, but she had a feeling they would be a good influence on her, if she stayed away from desserts. All her new roommates were slim. She had envied people like them all her life. She was naturally a big girl, thanks to her paternal great-grandmother, and her breasts made her seem top heavy. She had an hourglass figure that would have worked well in another era. She often wondered if her great-grandmother had had long thin legs like hers. You couldn't tell in photographs, because they had worn long skirts in those days. Now that Victoria had lost weight over the summer, she could wear shorter skirts again. But she knew she'd never get there by eating ice cream. She felt guilty about the Ben and Jerry's cookies and cream she had just consumed. She'd have to find a gym tomorrow, or go jogging. Maybe Bunny could take her to hers. Victoria suddenly felt overwhelmed by all she had to do here. And in a few days she'd be starting school, as a teacher this time, not a student. It was very exciting!

They all went back to their own rooms around one A.M., after lengthy conversations. Julie spent the night with Bill. And as Victoria settled into her new queen-size bed, she nestled under the covers and lay there smiling.

Everything about this room felt good and looked just the way she wanted it to. It was her own cozy little world in the new life she was building for herself. It was just the beginning. Soon she would have a new job, new friends, new students, and one day maybe even a boyfriend. It was hard to imagine. Finding the apartment had been a first step, and now suddenly she was a New Yorker.

She missed Gracie as she fell asleep that night, and thought about calling her, but she was too sleepy, and she had talked to her that morning, while she was shopping at IKEA. Gracie had been so happy for her, and Victoria had promised to send her photographs of the apartment and her room. She drifted off to sleep thinking about her sister and when she would come to visit. And in Victoria's dream they went shopping together, and she was suddenly much thinner, almost as though she had a new body to go with her new life. The salesgirl brought her a dress in a size fourteen, and Victoria told her she wore a size eight now, and everyone in the store applauded.

Chapter 9

Victoria had two days of meetings before the first day of school. She met the other teachers and tried to remember their departments and subjects and which age level they taught. She had a chance to study the books she'd be using, all of which had been selected by the teacher she was replacing for a year. She had even outlined the syllabus for her, which Victoria had been worried about for days. This was going to be much easier than she thought, and she chatted easily with the other teachers and introduced herself. The English department was one of the biggest, and there were eight teachers, all of them considerably older than she was, and most of them women, although three were men. She noticed that all of the male teachers who worked at Madison were either gay or married, but she hadn't come here to find a boyfriend, she chided herself, she had come to teach.

And at night after the meetings, she studied the books and the syllabus again, and made notes to herself about homework assignments and quizzes she wanted to give the kids, but first she wanted to get to know them, and get a sense of who they were. She was going to be teaching four classes, one sophomore, one junior, and two senior, and she had been warned at Northwestern during her student teaching that seniors were always tough. They were chomping at the bit to leave school and get on with their lives in college, and by the second half of the year, when they had gotten their college acceptance letters, it was almost impossible to get their attention and make them work. It was going to be a challenging year for her, and she could hardly wait to sink her teeth into it. She hardly slept at all the night before school started.

On the first day of school, Victoria was up at six A.M. She made a healthy breakfast of eggs, toast, cereal, and orange juice, and made a pot of coffee for her roommates to drink as well. She was dressed and at the breakfast table by seven, and back in her bedroom, making some notes again by seven-thirty. And at a quarter to eight, she was out the door, and walking to school. She arrived promptly at eight A.M., and the students were due at eight-thirty.

She went straight to her classroom, and paced nervously around the room and then stood looking out the window. She was expecting twenty-four students that morning. There were desks for all of them and a few spares, and a big desk for her at the front of the room. It was a class on English composition, and she had writing assignments to give them. She knew it would be hard to get their attention after their summer vacations. And the kids she would be teaching that day were in the home stretch. They were seniors, and they'd be visiting colleges and doing their applications all through the fall. And she'd have to write recommendations for them. That made her an important element in their lives, and gave her a direct impact on their future, so they had to be serious and diligent in her class. She knew their names, and now she would see the faces that went with them. She was staring into space, looking out the window, when she heard a voice behind her.

'Ready for the onslaught?' She turned and saw a gray-haired woman. She was wearing jeans, a faded T-shirt with the name of a band on it, and sandals. She looked like she was still on vacation and it was a warm day in New York. She smiled when Victoria turned around with a startled look. Victoria had worn a short black cotton skirt, a loose white linen top, and flat shoes. The baggy top hid a multitude of sins, and the reasonably short skirt showed off her legs. But she wasn't looking to seduce them, only teach them.

'Hi,' Victoria said with a look of surprise. She had seen the other woman at the teachers' meetings, but hadn't met her and couldn't remember what department she was in, and didn't want to ask her.

'I'm social studies. I have the classroom next to you, so if they start a gang war, I can help you. My name is Helen.' She was smiling as she came to shake Victoria's hand. She looked to be around Victoria's mother's age, somewhere in her mid to late forties. Victoria's mother had just turned fifty. 'I've been here for twenty-two years, so if you need a cheat sheet or a guide, just ask me. They're good people here, except the kids and their parents. Some of them anyway. Some of them are great kids, in spite of the privileged circumstances they live in.' As she said it, a shrill bell rang, and a few minutes later they could hear footsteps pounding up the stairs. It sounded like everyone was running.

'Thank you,' Victoria said, not sure what else to say. The statement she had made about the students and their parents was pretty damning, and an odd position to take for a woman who worked in a school full of rich kids.

'I love my students, but sometimes it's hard to get

them to deal with reality. How real is it when your parents have a boat, a plane, and a house in the Hamptons, and you spend every summer in the South of France? That's the way it is for these kids. What the rest of the world deals with is pretty remote to them. It's up to us to introduce them to the real world. And sometimes it's not easy. Sooner or later you can get there, with most of them. But not very often with their parents. They're past it, they don't want to know how the other half lives. I guess they figure it's not their problem. But the kids have a right to know and make choices.' Victoria didn't disagree with her, and she hadn't thought a lot about the lifestyles of these kids and how it would affect their view of the world. But Helen sounded faintly bitter about it and resentful of the kids. And Victoria wondered if she was jealous of the privileged lives they led. And as she thought it, the first student walked into the class-room, and Helen went back to her own.

The first student was a girl called Becki. She had blond hair to her waist, and was wearing a pink T-shirt, white jeans, and expensive Italian sandals. And she had the most beautiful face and body Victoria had ever seen. She took a seat in the middle of the classroom, which meant she wasn't anxious to participate, but she wasn't one of the shirkers in the back row either. She smiled at Victoria as she sat down. She had a casual air about her and looked as though she thought she owned the world. She had the cockiness of seniors Victoria had seen before. There were only four years separating the two young women, and Victoria felt a tremor sensing Becki's self-confidence, but she reminded herself that she was the boss here. And they didn't know exactly how young she was. She realized that she was going to have to earn their respect.

As she thought about it, four boys bolted through the door, almost at the same time, and sat down. They all looked at Becki, and obviously knew her, and glanced in Victoria's direction with mild curiosity. A flock of girls entered the room then, laughing and talking. They said hi to Becki, ignored the boys, glanced at Victoria, and took seats in a block at the back of the room. That meant to Victoria that they wanted to keep talking and exchange notes, or maybe even text each other throughout the class. She would have to keep an eye on them. More girls then, more boys, a few stragglers who came in alone, and several in groups. And finally, after a full ten minutes, her first class had arrived. Victoria greeted them with a big smile and told them her name. She wrote it on the black-board and then she turned to them.

'I'd like you all to introduce yourselves so I can put the faces with the names.' She pointed to a girl in the front row, to her extreme left as she faced them. 'Let's go all around the room.' And they did. They each said their name as she looked at the list she had on her desk for that class. 'Who knows where they want to apply to college?' Less than half the hands in the room went up. 'How about telling us?' She pointed to a boy in the back row who already looked bored. She didn't know it yet, but he had been Becki's boyfriend the year before, and they broke up before the summer. Now both of them were unattached. Becki had just gotten back from her father's villa in the South of France. And like many of the students at Madison, her parents were divorced.

The boy Victoria had asked about the colleges he was applying to reeled off a list. Harvard, Princeton, Yale, Stanford, Duke, Dartmouth, and maybe MIT. He had every top school on that list, and she wondered if he was telling the truth or pulling her leg. She didn't know the cast of characters yet at all. But she would.

'What happened to the circus college in Miami?' she asked him with a blank expression, and everyone laughed. 'That might be fun.'

'I want to take chemical engineering, with a minor in physics, or maybe the other way around.'

'How are your grades in English?' she asked him. He was the kind of boy who would think an English comp class was a drag. But it was a required course, even for him.

'Not so good,' he admitted sheepishly in answer to her question. 'I'm stronger in science.'

'What about you?' she asked the others. 'How are you at English comp?' It was a reasonable question, and they were honest with her. Some said they sucked and others said they were good at it, and there was no way for her to know the truth, particularly not this soon.

'Well, if you want to get into those colleges, and I assume that several of you do, then you're going to need decent grades in English. So let's work on it together this year. I'm here to improve your writing skills. It should help you with the essay on your college app, and I'll be happy to assist any of you with those applications, if you like.' It was an interesting spin on the purpose of the class, and the point hadn't been lost on them. They sat up and listened to her more closely for what came next.

She talked about the value of being able to write clearly and coherently, not in flowery prose, but to be able to write an interesting story with a beginning, a middle, and an end. 'I think we ought to have some fun this year too. Writing doesn't have to be dreary. And for some people, I know it's hard.' She glanced at the boy who wanted to go to MIT – English comp was clearly not his thing. 'You can add some humor to what you write, or write it tongue-in-cheek. You can write social commentary on the state of the world, or a story that you invent from beginning to end. But whatever you write, make it simple and clear, and make it something special that others will want to read. So in that vein, I'm going to ask you to write something that we'll all enjoy reading.' As she said it, she turned around and wrote on the blackboard that ran the length of one wall of the room, behind her desk. She wrote in a clear hand that they could all read easily: 'My summer vacation.' And as she did, everyone groaned, and she turned around to face them again. 'There's a twist to it, a little spin. I don't want to hear about the summer vacation you did have, which might be as boring as mine with my family in L.A. I want you to write about the summer vacation you wish you'd had. And when you're finished writing it, I want to wish I had that vacation too. And I want you to make me understand why. Why was that the vacation you wanted to have, or wished you had? You can write it as an essay in first person, or as a story in third. And I want some really great stuff. I know you can do it if you try.' She smiled broadly at them then, and said something they didn't expect. 'Class dismissed.' For a moment they looked at her, a little stunned, and then they let out a whoop and got up, and started shuffling out of the room. She tapped her desk once, and told them that the assignment was due the next time the class met, in three days. With that, they groaned again, and she got more specific. 'And it doesn't have to be long,' she said as they beamed.

'I wish I'd spent my summer vacation in a bordello in Morocco,' one boy said, and everybody laughed at his irreverence. Making fun of a teacher was something kids always enjoyed at every age. It was a thought Victoria couldn't imagine the boy saying, but she didn't react. Kids that age liked to shock adults. She gave no indication that he had.

'That would work,' Victoria said calmly, 'as long as I believe you. If I don't, you're out of luck. That's the hitch. Make me believe you, make me care, make me fall in love with the characters, or with you. That's the whole point of writing, to convince the reader that what you've written for them is real. And in order to do that, you have to believe it too. Have fun,' she said, as the rest of the students left the room.

Victoria had a break between classes then, and sat at her desk making a few notes, when Helen, the teacher from the next classroom, walked back in. She seemed to be interested in everything Victoria did. Carla Bernini, the teacher on maternity leave, was her best friend, and

Victoria wondered if she was defending her buddy's turf, or at least keeping an eye on it for her.

'How did it go?' she asked as she sat down in one of the chairs.

'Pretty well, I think,' Victoria said honestly. 'They didn't throw things at me, or hit me with any bottle rockets. No stink bombs. And I kept it short, which always helps.' She had done that with her student teaching too. You couldn't sit around forever, talking about writing. You just had to do it, no matter how hard and daunting it was. 'The assignment I gave them was easy. It'll show me what they can do.'

'It must be difficult stepping into someone else's shoes,' Helen said randomly, and Victoria shrugged.

'I try not to think about it. We each have our own style.'

'What's yours?' Helen asked with interest, as though she were interviewing her.

'I don't know yet. Today is my first day. I graduated in May.'

'Zow! That's got to be pretty unnerving. Aren't you a big brave girl.' Her tone reminded Victoria of her father, but she didn't care. She knew she had done a good job. And Helen could challenge her all she wanted, for whatever reason. Victoria knew she would have to prove herself to the teachers too, not just the students. But so far she thought it had gone well.

Victoria's next class came in an hour later, and this time several of them were seriously late. They were seniors too.

The assignment she gave them was different than the first one.

The topic this time was what I want to be when I grow up, and why. 'I want you to put some serious thought into it. And I want to respect and admire you when I'm through reading. It's okay to make me laugh. Keep it light, unless you want to be an undertaker or embalmer. But short of that, I want to laugh.' And then the second class left too. She had held her own with both groups. And she had met all her seniors now. They seemed like good kids and hadn't given her a hard time. But she knew they could if they wanted to, and she was very young. They didn't have any particular allegiance to her yet, but she knew it was too soon. She hoped they would in time. And she knew that the level of their respect depended on her. It was her job to make them care.

Helen stayed and talked to her for a few minutes, and then they both packed up their things and left their classrooms. Victoria checked her mailbox on the way out, and then sat in the teachers' lounge poring over a stack of memos from the headmaster and the dean of students. There were several announcements, mostly about policy changes that impacted the school. She went to an English department meeting that afternoon, and when she left the building, it took her ten minutes to walk home. She loved living so close. She wanted to walk to work every day.

When Victoria got to the apartment, everyone asked how her day had gone. They were all there.

'It was actually terrific,' Victoria said happily. And Gracie called her and asked her the same question an hour later, and she gave her the same answer. Essentially, it had gone really well, and she liked the kids. They might have been around the world with their parents, and had every lesson known to man, yet there was something innocent and endearing about them. And she wanted them to learn to think intelligently, use good judgment, and wind up with the life they wanted, whatever and wherever that was. Her job, as she understood it, in this school or any other, was to open the door into the world for them. And she wanted to open many, many doors. They had begun.

Chapter 10

Victoria met her junior and sophomore students on the second and third days of school, and she was surprised to find them much harder to deal with than the seniors. The juniors were stressed about the heavy workload they'd have that year, which would count more than any other year in their applications to colleges, and they were afraid she'd give them too much homework. And the sophomores were unfriendly and almost belligerent, and there was no harder group to teach than fifteen-year-old girls. It was everyone's least favorite age, and Victoria's too, with the exception of her sister Grace, who seemed nicer than most girls her age. There was a nasty quality to them, and Victoria heard two of the girls talking about her size as they left the class. They talked just loud enough for her to hear them, and she had to remind herself that they were just bratty kids, but their comments cut through her like a knife. One of the girls had referred to her as 'fat'; the other one said she looked like a tank in the dress she'd worn. She took it off that night and put it in a pile to give away. She knew she wouldn't feel comfortable wearing it again. And when she went out to the kitchen in her apartment that night, she finished off someone's pint of Ben and Jerry's, in a flavor she didn't even like.

'Bad day?' Harlan asked as he walked in and made himself a cup of tea, and offered one to her.

'Yeah, sort of. Sophomore girls can be pretty nasty. I met my sophomore class for the first time today.' She looked seriously unhappy as she sat in the kitchen and sipped her tea, eating the brownies she had bought on the way home.

'It must be tough being so young, and teaching high school students who're almost as old as you are,' he said sympathetically.

'I guess so. The seniors were pretty good actually. The younger ones were the worst so far. They're just bitchy. And the juniors are always scared to death, because it's the most important year before college, so they're under a lot of pressure, from us and their parents.'

'I wouldn't want your job,' he said, grinning ruefully. 'Kids can be so tough. Standing up in front of thirty of them would do me in.'

'I don't have a lot of experience with it yet,' Victoria admitted, 'but I think I'm going to love it. My student teaching was fun, but I was assigned to freshman kids. This is pretty different, and these are very high-end kids. They're a lot more sophisticated than the ones I did my student teaching with in Chicago. These guys are going to keep me on my toes. I just want to keep my class interesting for them. Kids that age can be very unforgiving.'

'They sound dangerous to me,' he said and pretended to shudder, and Victoria laughed.

'They're not as bad as that,' she defended them. 'They're just kids.'

But the next day when she met with her seniors again, she was inclined to agree with Harlan. She was expecting both groups to hand in their writing assignments. Less than half of each class had done them. When she first realized it, Victoria looked disappointed.

'Is there some reason why you didn't?' she asked Becki Adams.

'I had too much work to do for my other classes,' Becki said with a shrug, while the girl sitting next to her laughed.

'May I remind you that this is a required English class? Your English grade this term will depend on what you do here.'

'Yeah, whatever,' Becki said, turning to the girl next to her to say something in a whisper. And she glanced up at Victoria as she did, which made her feel they were talking about her. She tried to regain her composure, collected the papers that had been done, and thanked the students who had completed the assignment.

'For those who didn't,' Victoria said calmly, 'you have till Monday. And from now on, I expect you to turn your assignments in on time.' It threw off the assignment she had planned to give them to do over the weekend. But less than half the class had done the work.

She discussed the power of the essay then, and handed out some examples, explaining why they worked, and pointing out the strengths of each piece. And this time the entire group ignored her. Two girls in the back row were wearing iPods, three of the boys were laughing at a private joke, several of the girls were passing notes, and Becki pulled out her BlackBerry and sent texts. Victoria felt like she'd been slapped and wasn't sure what to do. They were five years younger than she was and behaving like total brats.

'Are we having a problem here?' she finally said quietly.

'Are you under the impression that you don't have to pay attention to this class? Or even be polite? Do you care about your grades at all? I know you're seniors, and your junior transcript goes on your college apps, but if you flunk this class, it's not going to look so great and may keep you out of the college of your choice.'

'You're just a temp till Mrs. Bernini gets back,' a boy in the back row called out.

'Mrs. Bernini isn't coming back this year. That could be bad news for both of us, or good news if you decide to make the best of it. It's up to you. If you'd rather fail this class, that's your choice. You can explain it to the dean. And your parents. It's very simple actually – you do the work, you get the grades. You don't bother, and don't turn your assignments in, you fail the class. I'm sure Mrs. Bernini saw it the same way,' Victoria said, as she walked past Becki and took her BlackBerry away.

'You can't do that! I was texting my mom!' she complained with an angry look.

'Do it after class. If there's an emergency, go to the office. Don't text in my class. That goes for you too,' she said, pointing to a girl in the second row, who had actually been exchanging text messages with Becki. 'Let's get this straight, no BlackBerrys, no cell phones, and no iPods in my class. No texting. We're here to work on English composition.' They didn't look impressed, and while she was talking to them, the bell rang, and they all stood up. No one waited for her to dismiss the class. She was seriously disheartened as they left the room, and she put the assignments that had been turned in into her briefcase. And she was even more depressed when her second class of seniors came in, and were equally disruptive. She had been identified as the teacher to play with, be rude to, and ignore.

It was as though a memo had gone out to all seniors to jerk her around. She was near tears when Helen came into her classroom after the kids left. Victoria was gathering up her things and looked upset.

'Bad day?' she asked, looking sympathetic. Until then Victoria wasn't sure if she and Helen were allies, but she looked friendly when she walked in.

'Not so great actually,' Victoria admitted as she picked up her briefcase with a sigh.

'You've got to get them in control fast before they beat you up. Seniors can be nasty if they get out of hand. Juniors are always stressed out of their minds, and sophomores are just kids. Freshmen are babies and scared to death the first half of the year. They're easy.' She had it down pat, and Victoria smiled.

'Too bad Mrs. Bernini didn't teach freshmen. And I've got a double dose of seniors with two classes.'

'They'll eat you for breakfast if you let them,' Helen warned her. 'You have to kick ass. Don't be too nice, and don't try to be their friend. Especially as young as you are. The kids at Madison can be great, and most of them are smart, but a lot of them are very manipulative and think they own the world. They'll clean the floor with you if you don't watch out, and so will their parents. Don't take any shit from them. Trust me. You need to be tough.' Helen looked serious as she said it.

'I guess you're right. Less than half of them did the assignment and they sat around the class texting, writing messages, and listening to iPods. They couldn't have cared less.' Helen knew how hard that was for a young teacher, and had been there herself.

'You've gotta be tough,' she said again, as she followed Victoria out of her classroom and headed back to her own. 'Give them big assignments, challenge them, give them an F when they don't turn in an assignment. Kick them out if they're not paying attention or doing the work. Confiscate their stuff. It'll wake them up.' Victoria nodded. She hated to be that way, but she suspected Helen was right. 'And forget the little creeps over the weekend. Do something nice for yourself,' she said in a motherly tone. 'And first thing Monday morning, kick their asses. Mark my words, they'll sit up and take notice.'

'Thanks,' Victoria said, and smiled at her again. 'Have a nice weekend.' She appreciated Helen's advice, and it made her like her better than she had at first.

'You too!' Helen said, and went back into her classroom to pick up her things.

Victoria walked home from school with a heavy heart. She felt like an utter failure with her two senior classes, and the juniors and sophomores hadn't gone well either. It almost made her wonder why she had wanted to be a teacher. She had been all idealistic and starry-eyed, and she wasn't doing them any good. The end of the week had gone badly, and she was afraid that she wouldn't be able to control them, as Helen suggested, and it would get worse. Thinking about it, she stopped to get something for dinner, and she wound up buying three slices of pizza and three pints of Häagen-Dazs ice cream in different flavors, and a bag of Oreo cookies. She knew it wasn't the answer, but it was comfort food for her. When she got home, she put the pizza in the oven, and opened the pint of chocolate ice cream first. She was more than halfway through it when Bunny came home from the gym. Victoria had been planning to go with her all week but hadn't had time, while she worked on her plans for her classes. And she was too tired at night. Bunny didn't comment when she saw her eating the ice cream, but Victoria felt guilty immediately, put the lid back on, and put it back in the freezer with the rest.

'How was your week?' Bunny asked kindly. She thought Victoria looked upset.

'Hard. The kids are tough, and I'm new.'

'I'm sorry. Do something fun this weekend. The weather is going to be great. I'm going up to Boston, Bill is at Julie's, and I think Harlan is going to Fire Island. You'll have the apartment to yourself.' That wasn't entirely good news to Victoria, who was feeling lonely, homesick, and depressed. She missed Grace.

After Bunny left to catch her flight to Boston, Victoria ate the pizza and then called home to talk to Grace. Her mother answered and asked how she was. Victoria said she was fine, and then her father got on the phone.

'Ready to throw in the towel and come home?' he asked with a hearty laugh. She wouldn't have admitted it to him, but she almost was. She had felt completely inadequate in the classroom and like an utter failure. What he said jolted her back into reality. She wasn't about to give up.

'Not yet, Dad,' she said, trying to sound happier than she felt. And then Gracie got on the phone, and Victoria almost burst into tears. She really missed her and was suddenly lonely in the empty apartment in a new city with no friends.

They talked for a long time. Gracie told her what she was doing in school, they chatted about her teachers and her classes, and there was a new boy she said she liked. He was a junior. There was always a new boy in Gracie's life, and never one in her sister's. Victoria hadn't felt this miserable in a long time, and she was feeling sorry for herself. But she didn't say anything to Gracie about what a mess the week had been. After they hung up, Victoria took out the vanilla ice cream, opened it, walked into her room, turned on the TV, and got into her bed with her clothes on. She put on a movie channel, and finished the ice cream as she watched a movie, and then felt guilty when she looked at the empty ice cream carton next to her bed. It had been her dinner. And she could almost feel her hips growing as she lay there. She was utterly disgusted with herself. She put her pajamas on shortly after, got back in bed, and pulled the covers over her head. She didn't wake up until the next morning.

To atone for her sins of the night before, she went for a long walk in Central Park on Saturday, and jogged partway around the reservoir. The weather was gorgeous, and she noticed couples strolling all around her, and she felt sad not to have a man in her life. Looking around, she felt as though everyone else did, and she was the odd person out, and always had been. She was crying when she jogged to the edge of the park, and then walked home in her T-shirt and gym shorts and running shoes. And she promised herself she wouldn't eat any more ice cream that night. It was a promise she intended to keep. And as she sat home alone in the empty apartment and watched another movie, she didn't eat the ice cream. She ate the bag of Oreo cookies instead.

She spent Sunday correcting the assignments that some of the seniors had done. She was surprised by how good they were, and how creative. A few of her students had real talent, and the essays they'd written were very sophisticated. She was impressed, and said so when she faced her first class on Monday morning. They had slouched in and sprawled in their seats with obvious uninterest. There were at least a dozen BlackBerrys evident on their desks. She walked around the room and picked them up one by one, and put them on her own desk. Their owners reacted immediately and she assured them they could have them back after class. Several of the BlackBerrys were already vibrating with messages on her desk.

She praised them then for their essays, and they were

pleased, and then she collected the rest. All but two students had done them. The two who hadn't were tall, good-looking boys, who appeared cocky and cynical when they said they hadn't done the assignment, again.

'Is there a problem? The dog ate your homework?' Victoria asked calmly.

'No,' a boy named Mike MacDuff said to her. 'We were out in the Hamptons and I played tennis all day Saturday, and golf with my dad on Sunday. And I had a date Saturday night.'

'I'm thrilled for you, Mike. I've never been to the Hamptons, but I hear it's great out there. I'm glad you had such a nice weekend. That'll be an F on your assignment.' And with that, she turned her attention to the rest of the class and handed out copies of a short story she wanted them to look at, while Mike scowled at her. The boy sitting next to him looked uncomfortable, and had figured out that he was getting an F too.

She helped them dissect the short story, and showed them why it worked. It was a good story, and they seemed to enjoy it, they paid closer attention to her this time, and she felt better about the class. Even Becki had contributed some remarks about the story. And Victoria asked them to write a short story as their assignment. Mike stopped at her desk on the way out, and in a gruff voice he asked whether, if he did the assignment he'd missed, she'd drop the F for his failure to write it.

'Not this time, Mike,' she said pleasantly, feeling like a monster, but she remembered Helen's warning on Friday not to let them get away with anything. She had to make an example of Mike and the other boy who hadn't bothered to do the first assignment.

'That sucks!' he said loudly as he strode out of the room and slammed the door on the way out. Victoria looked undisturbed, and got ready for the second class, which started a few minutes later.

They were tougher than the first group. And there was a girl in the class who was determined to take Victoria on and humiliate her. She made several comments about women who were overweight before Victoria started talking. She pretended not to have heard the girl's remarks. Her name was Sally Fritz. She had dark red hair and freckles, and a tattoo of a star on the back of one hand.

'Where did you go to school anyway?' she asked Victoria rudely as she started to teach the class. She had totally interrupted what Victoria was saying.

'Northwestern. Are you thinking of applying?'

'Hell, no,' Sally said loudly. 'It's too cold there.'

'Yes, it is, but I loved it. It's a good school, once you get used to the weather.'

'I'm applying to California and Texas.'

Victoria nodded. 'I'm from L.A. There are some terrific schools in California,' she said pleasantly.

'My brother went to Stanford,' Sally volunteered as though they weren't in class, and she didn't care if they were. She was very brash. Victoria went on with the class then, and shared the same short story with them that she had gone over with the first class that morning. This group was livelier and more critical of the piece, which made for some interesting discussions around the room, and they got into it, in spite of their intention of torturing her and being difficult. She swept them all into the analysis of the story and a lively exchange, and some of them were still talking about it when they left the room, and Victoria looked pleased. She didn't mind being challenged by her students, or even argued with if they had valid points. The goal of her teaching was to make them question what they knew and thought they believed in. The short story she had exposed them to had done that. It had been a victory for her. And she stopped in to see Helen on her way to the teachers' lounge to correct papers.

'Thanks for the tip the other day,' she said shyly. 'It helped.'

'To kick their asses?'

Victoria laughed in answer. 'I don't think I did that. But I gave two F's in my first class for failure to hand in the assignment.' It was a lot tougher than she thought she would be in the second week of school.

'That's a start.' Helen grinned at her. 'I'm proud of you. It'll wake up the others.'

'I think it did. And I'm confiscating iPods and BlackBerrys whenever I see them.'

'They hate that,' Helen confirmed. 'They'd much rather send text messages to their friends than listen to you, or me, for that matter.' The two women laughed. 'Did you have a nice weekend?'

'Nice enough. I went to the park on Saturday, and corrected papers on Sunday.' And ate two pints of ice cream, pizza, and an entire bag of cookies. But she didn't say it. She knew it was a measure of how discouraged she was. She always ate more when she was unhappy, even though she promised herself she wouldn't. She could see an imminent return to her size fourteen and sixteen wardrobe in her future. She had brought all four sizes with her. She wanted to avoid winding up a sixteen, which could easily happen at the rate she was eating. She knew she had to start dieting again. It was a constant merry-go-round she could never seem to get off. With no friends, no boyfriend, and no social life, feeling unsure of herself in her job, she was at high risk for putting on weight in New York, despite her good resolutions not to. They never lasted. At the first sign of a crisis, she dove into a pint of ice cream, a bag of cookies, or a pizza. And she had done all three that weekend, which had set off an alarm in her head to be careful before it got out of hand.

Helen could sense that she was lonely, and she seemed very young and innocent to her, and like a nice girl. 'Maybe we can go to a movie next weekend. Or a concert in the park,' she offered.

'I'd like that,' Victoria said, looking happy. She felt like the new kid on the block, and she was. And she was the youngest teacher in the school. Helen was twice her age, but she liked Victoria. She thought she was bright, and Helen could tell she was trying, and was dedicated to teaching. She was naïve, but Helen thought she would learn the ropes in time. It was challenging for everyone in the beginning, especially teaching older kids. High school students were the toughest. But Victoria looked like she could handle it if she kept the kids in control. 'Are you going to the lounge?' she asked Helen hopefully.

'I've got another class. I'll catch you later.' Victoria nodded, and walked down the hall to the lounge. It was deserted. Everyone had gone to lunch, and she was trying not to. She had brought an apple in her briefcase and had vowed to be good. She sat munching it as she read the papers. And once again, they were surprisingly good. She had some very bright students. She just hoped she was bright enough to teach them and hold their interest for the entire year. She was feeling very unsure of herself. Now that she was faced with a classroom full of real people, this was much harder than she had anticipated, and it was going to take more than just discipline to keep them in line. Helen had given her some helpful hints, and Carla Bernini had set up the syllabus before going on maternity leave, but Victoria knew that she had to infuse her classes with life and excitement in order to keep the kids hooked. And she was scared to death that she wasn't good enough to do it and would fail. She wanted to be good at it more than anything. She didn't care how little the job paid, this was her vocation, and she wanted to be a great teacher, the kind kids remembered for years. She had no idea if she could do it, but she was trying her best. And this was only the beginning. The school year had just started.

For the next two weeks, Victoria fought to keep her students' attention. She confiscated cell phones and BlackBerrys, she gave them tough assignments, and one day when her sophomore class was too restless, she took them for a walk around the neighborhood, and made them write about it. She tried to come up with every creative idea she could, and to get to know every one of her students in all four classes, and she began to get the feeling after two months that some of them liked her. She racked her brain on the weekends searching for ideas for them, new books to read, and new projects. And sometimes she surprised them with unexpected quizzes and assignments. There was nothing dull about her classes. And by late November, she felt like she was beginning to get somewhere with them and win their respect. Not all of her students liked her, but at least they were paying attention and responding to her. By the time she got on the plane to go home for the Thanksgiving holiday, she had a feeling of accomplishment, until she saw her father. He looked at her with surprise when he met her at the airport with her mother and Grace, who hurled herself into Victoria's arms with glee, as her big sister kissed her.

'Wow! The ice cream must be good in New York,' he commented, grinning broadly, and her mother looked pained, not at his comment but at Victoria's appearance. She had gained back everything she lost, while correcting papers at night and on weekends and working on her classes. She had been living on Chinese takeout, and double chocolate milk shakes. The diet she kept meaning to start just hadn't happened. Her whole focus had been on her classes and her students and not on herself. And she kept eating all the wrong foods to give herself energy, comfort, and strength.

'I guess so, Dad,' Victoria said vaguely.

'Why don't you steam fish and vegetables, dear?' her mother said. Victoria marveled that after not seeing her for almost three months, her weight was all they could think about. Gracie just looked at her and beamed. She didn't care what size Victoria was, she just loved her. The two sisters walked off arm in arm toward the baggage claim, happy to be back together.

On Thanksgiving day, Victoria helped her mother cook the turkey, and she enjoyed the day and the meal with them, miraculously without negative comments from her father. The weather was balmy and warm, and they sat in the backyard afterward, and her mother asked her about her teaching.

'Do you like it?' She was still puzzled why her daughter would want to be a teacher.

'I love it.' She grinned at her sister then. 'And my sophomore students are horrible. They're all little monsters like you. I confiscate their iPods all the time, so they'll listen to me.'

'Why don't you make them write lyrics?' Gracie

suggested as her older sister looked at her in amazement. 'That's what my teacher did, and we loved it.'

'That's brilliant!' Victoria could hardly wait to try it on them. She had been planning to have her juniors and seniors write poetry in the weeks before Christmas. But lyrics for the sophomores was a great idea. 'Thank you, Gracie.'

'Just ask me about the sophomores,' she said proudly, since she was one herself.

Her father managed to stay off the subject of her weight for the rest of the visit, and her mother discreetly said that she should go to Overeaters Anonymous, which really hurt Victoria's feelings, but other than that, it was a warm, comfortable weekend, especially with Gracie. And they all drove her back to the airport on Sunday. She was planning to come back in four weeks to spend Christmas with them, so this time their goodbyes weren't tearful. She was going to spend the whole vacation with them, since they had two weeks off school. And on the plane on the way back to New York, she thought again about Gracie's suggestion to have the sophomores write lyrics.

She presented the idea to her sophomore class on Wednesday morning, and they looked ecstatic. It was something they could really wrap their minds around, and for once they looked enthusiastic about an assignment. Her juniors and seniors were less thrilled with the poetry they had to write, and she was starting to help some of them with their essays for their college applications. She had her hands full.

The lyrics the sophomores wrote for her were terrific. One boy brought a guitar in, and they tried to put music to some of his words. The assignment was a huge success, and they asked if they could extend the project until Christmas vacation, and she agreed. And she gave most of them excellent grades for what they did. She had never given so many As. And the poetry assignments were surprisingly good too. By Christmas vacation, Victoria felt as though she had won their confidence, and all of them were behaving better in her classroom. Helen had noticed it too. The students looked happy and enthusiastic now when they left her room.

'What did you do to them? Give them drugs?'

'I took my fifteen-year-old sister's suggestion. I've had the sophomores writing lyrics,' Victoria said proudly, and Helen was impressed by her creativity.

'That's pure genius. I wish I could do that in my class.'

'I stole the idea from my sister's teacher. But it worked. And the older kids have been writing poetry. A few of them really have talent.'

'So do you,' Helen said with a look of admiration.

'You're a damn good teacher. I hope you know that. And I'm happy that you're learning to control the class. It's better for them, and you. Even at their age, they need boundaries, discipline, and structure.'

'I've been working on it,' Victoria said honestly, 'but sometimes I think I really screw up. There's a lot more creativity to teaching than I originally thought.'

'We all screw up,' Helen said candidly. 'That doesn't make you a bad teacher. You keep trying and you find what works till you win them over. That's the best you can do.'

'I love what I'm doing,' she said happily, 'even if they drive me crazy sometimes. But they don't seem as cocky lately. One of the kids even wants to go to Northwestern because I said I loved the school.' Helen was smiling at her as she listened. She could see Victoria's passion for her profession in her eyes, and it warmed Helen's heart.

'I hope Eric is smart enough to hire you permanently after Carla comes back. He'll be crazy if he loses you,' Helen said warmly.

'I'm just grateful to be here. We'll see what happens about next year.' She knew that contracts would be offered in March and April, and she didn't know if they'd have an opening for her. She hoped so, but nothing was sure. For now, it was working, for her and the kids and the school. Eric Walker, the headmaster, had been hearing good things about her from the students. And two of the parents had commented that they liked her assignments. She really inspired the kids, and when necessary she pushed them. She thought outside the box, and wasn't afraid to try new things. She was exactly the kind of teacher they wanted.

And she had stopped eating quite as voraciously after Thanksgiving. Her father's comment, and her mother's suggesting Overeaters Anonymous, had slowed her down a little. She hadn't started any crazy new diets yet, and she was planning to do that over Christmas. She had thought about going to Weight Watchers, but she told herself she didn't have time. But for now she had eased up on the ice cream and pizza. And she was buying salads and cooked chicken breasts to eat in the kitchen with the others when she got home, and she made sure she had fruit for an afternoon snack. She still hadn't developed a social life, other than the occasional movie date with Helen, but she enjoyed her roommates. She saw more of Harlan than anyone, because Bill was always with Julie, and Bunny had been going to Boston almost every weekend to be with her boyfriend. She was thinking of moving to be with him. But Harlan was around almost as much as she was. He was single and unattached too. And he worked as hard as she did. When he came home at night, he was exhausted and happy to crash in front of the TV in his room, and meet her for a snack in the kitchen.

'So where are you going for Christmas?' she asked him one night over a cup of tea.

'I've been invited to South Beach. I'm not sure if I'm going. Miami isn't really my scene.' He was a serious man who worked diligently at the museum. She knew he wasn't close to his family, and wasn't planning to go back to Mississippi for the holidays. He said his parents were still upset that he was gay, and he wasn't welcome, which she thought was sad for him.

'I'm going back to L.A. to see my parents and sister,' Victoria said pensively, thinking that her parents had never fully accepted her either. She had been a misfit and an outcast in their midst all her life. Even her size upset them and made her look different. Her mother would have preferred to die than be the size she was, and would never have let that happen. And her father still couldn't resist remarks at her expense, with no awareness of how hurtful they were to her. She never believed that his cruelty was on purpose.

'Do you miss them when you're here?' Harlan asked, curious about her family.

'Sometimes. They're familiar. Mostly I miss my little

sister. She's always been my baby.' Victoria smiled at Harlan as he poured them both another cup of tea.

'I have an older brother who hates me. Being gay was not the thing to be in Tupelo, Mississippi, when I was growing up, and it still isn't. He and his friends used to beat me up all the time. I didn't even know why till I was fifteen and figured out why they did it. Up until then, I thought I was just different. After that, I knew. I left the minute I turned eighteen, and came to college up here. I think they were as relieved as I was. I only go back once every few years, when I run out of excuses.' It sounded sad to her and very lonely. But her life at home would have been too, without Gracie.

'I'm the odd man out in my family too,' she admitted. 'They're all thin people with brown eyes and dark hair. I'm the family freak. My father always gives me a hard time about my weight. My mother leaves clippings on my desk about new diets.'

'That's mean,' Harlan said sadly, although he had noticed the things and quantities she ate when she was tired or depressed. He thought she had a pretty face and great legs, despite the generous middle. But in spite of it, she was a good-looking woman. He was surprised that she wasn't dating. 'Some parents do so much damage,' he said thoughtfully. 'It makes me glad I'll never have kids. I wouldn't want to do to anyone what they did to me. My brother is a real jerk. He works in a bank and he's dull as dishwater. He's married and has two kids. He thinks being gay is like a disease. He keeps hoping I'll get over it, like amnesia, and remember that I'm straight, which would be less embarrassing for him.' Harlan laughed as he said it. He was twenty-six years old and comfortable about who he was. He was hoping to become a curator at the Met eventually, even though the salary wasn't great. But he was very dedicated to his work, just as Victoria was to teaching. 'Will Christmas be fun in L.A.?' he asked with a wistful expression, and she nodded. It would be because of Gracie.

'I loved it when my sister was little, and she still believed in Santa Claus. We still put out cookies for him, and carrots and salt for the reindeer.' He smiled when she said it.

'Do you have plans for New Year's Eve?' he asked with interest, trying to imagine her life there. She never said much about her parents, only her little sister.

'Not really. I usually stay home with my sister. One of these days she'll be old enough to have a serious date, and then I'll really be up shit creek.'

'Maybe we can do something if we're both back here,' he said, and she liked the idea. 'We can go to Times

Square and watch the ball drop with all the tourists and hookers.' They both laughed at the image.

'I might come home from L.A. in time to do that,' Victoria said thoughtfully. 'I go back to school a few days later. I'll see what's happening out there.'

'Text me and let me know what you're doing,' he said, and she nodded, and they put their cups in the dishwasher.

Victoria left little gifts on each of their beds for all three of her roommates when she went to L.A., and she had presents for Gracie and her parents in her suitcase. She was happy to go home and be with her family and especially to see Gracie. When they got home from the airport, they all decorated the tree and drank delicious rum punch. It was pungent and burned her tongue a little, but she liked it, and her head spun slightly when she went to bed. It felt good to be home, and Gracie slipped into bed next to her, and they giggled and talked until they fell asleep. And both her parents seemed in good spirits. Her father said he had landed an important new client for the agency, and her mother had just won a bridge tournament. And Gracie was thrilled to be on vacation and have Victoria home for the holidays. She was happy to be there.

Everything went smoothly on Christmas, and her

parents and Gracie liked their presents. Her father gave her a long gold necklace, because he didn't have to worry if it fit, he said. And her mother gave her a cashmere sweater and two books on exercise and a new diet. Neither of them noticed that she had lost weight since Thanksgiving. Gracie did and complimented her, but her praise was never as potent as their parents' insults.

And two days after Christmas, Gracie got invited to a party on New Year's Eve, given at the home of one of her friends in Beverly Hills. Victoria had nothing to do. The people she knew were all working in other cities, and two of them who still lived in L.A. had gone skiing. All Victoria did over the holidays was spend time with Grace. And Gracie offered to stay home with her on New Year's Eve.

'Don't be silly – you should be with your friends. I was thinking of going back to New York then anyway.'

'For a date?' Gracie looked at her with interest. This was the first she had heard of it.

'No, just one of my roommates. I don't know if he'll be there, but we were talking about doing something on New Year's Eve.'

'Does he like you?' Gracie asked with a mischievous look, and Victoria laughed at the question.

'Not like that. But he's a good friend, and we have

181

fun together. He works at the Metropolitan Museum.'

'How boring,' Gracie said, and rolled her eyes. She was disappointed that he didn't sound more promising. She could see that Victoria didn't consider him an option as a romance.

In the end, Victoria left L.A. the morning of New Year's Eve. Gracie was going to the party at her friends', and her parents had been invited out to dinner. She would have been alone at the house, so she decided to go back to New York. She needed to get ready for school anyway. And she texted Harlan, hoping he would be back in New York. Her father drove her to the airport, while Gracie and their mother were getting their hair done. Victoria and Gracie had said goodbye that morning.

'Do you think you'll come back after you finish the year in New York?' her father asked her on the way to the airport.

'I don't know yet, Dad.' She didn't want to tell him that she didn't think so and was happy there. She didn't have a wide circle of friends yet, but she liked her room-mates, her apartment, and her job. It was a start.

'You would do so much better in another field,' he repeated for the thousandth time.

'I like teaching,' she said quietly.

And then he laughed and glanced at her. 'At least I

know you'll never starve.' She marveled at the fact that he never missed an opportunity to take a dig at her or cut her down. It was an important part of why she was in New York. She said nothing to him after that, and sat quietly as they drove to LAX. And as he always did, he helped her with her bags and tipped the porter for her. And then he turned to hug her, as though he had never made the comment in the car. He never got it.

'Thanks for everything, Dad.'

'Take care of yourself,' he said, and sounded sincere.

'You too.' She hugged him, and then walked into the security lines. She boarded the plane and just as she did, she saw that she had a text from Harlan.

'I'll be back in New York by six o'clock,' he had texted her. She was landing at nine P.M., local time.

'I'll be at the apartment by ten,' she texted back.

'Times Square?' was his response.

'Okay.'

'It's a date.' She smiled as she turned her phone off. At least it was nice to know that she'd have something to do on New Year's Eve, and someone to spend it with. She had lunch on the plane, watched a movie, and slept for the last two hours of the flight. It was snowing when she landed in New York, tiny gentle flurries that made it look like a Christmas card as she rode into the city in a cab.

She was excited to be back, although always sad to leave Gracie, and she had promised to let her come to visit for spring break. And her parents had said they might come with her. Victoria hoped not.

Harlan was waiting for her at the apartment, with a tan, fresh from Miami. He said he didn't like the gay scene there, it was too glitzy and superficial, and he was happy to be back too.

'So how was L.A.?' he asked her as she walked into the apartment.

'Okay. I had fun with my sister.' She smiled back, and he opened a bottle of champagne and handed her a glass.

'Did your parents behave?'

'No better or worse than usual. I had a good time with my sister, but I'm happy to be back.'

'Me too.' He grinned and took a sip of the champagne. 'You'd better wear your snow boots for Times Square.'

'Are we still going?' The snow was swirling outside, but it was a gentle snow that hung in the air before it fell to the ground.

'Hell, yes. I wouldn't miss it for the world. We have to watch the big ball fall. We can come back and get warm afterward.' She laughed and finished her glass of champagne.

They left the apartment in a cab at eleven-thirty, and

got to Times Square ten minutes before midnight. There was a huge crowd watching the giant mirrored ball, and Victoria smiled at Harlan as the snow fell on their hair and lashes. It felt like the perfect way to spend the night. And then on the stroke of midnight, the mirrored ball plummeted, and everybody cheered. They stood there laughing and hugging, and he kissed her on the cheek.

'Happy New Year, Victoria,' he said, smiling happily. He loved being with her.

'Happy New Year,' she said as they hugged and looked up at the sky like two children, watching the snow come down. It looked like a stage set, and the moment felt perfect to both of them. They were young, and it was New Year's Eve in New York. For now anyway, it didn't get better than that. And it felt good to both of them to spend the evening with a friend. They stood there until their hair and coats were covered with snow, and then they walked a few blocks along Times Square among the bright lights and people, and hailed a cab to go home. It had been a perfect evening for both of them.

Chapter 11

Victoria's senior students were tense in January. They had two weeks after vacation to finish their college applications, and many of them hadn't done it, and needed help. She stayed after school every day to advise them on their essays, and they were grateful for her excellent guidance and advice. It brought her closer to the students she worked with, and some of them talked about their hopes and plans, their families, their lives at home, their dreams. Even Becki Adams asked for help, and several of the boys. A few of them admitted that they needed scholarships, but most of the kids at Madison had no worries about money. And all of them were relieved when they finished their applications and mailed them off. They wouldn't hear back until March or April, and now all they had to do was finish the school year without flunking out or getting into trouble.

On the last two days in January, Victoria attended an education conference at the Javits Center with several other teachers. There were a number of panels they could sign up for, group discussions, and lectures by well-known educators. She found it very interesting, and was grateful the school had let her participate. She had just left a lecture on early identification and warning signs of adolescent suicidality, by a child psychiatrist, when she collided with a man who wasn't looking where he was going and nearly knocked her down. He apologized profusely and helped her pick up the pamphlets and brochures that he had knocked out of her hand, and when he stood up, she was startled by how handsome he was.

'Sorry, I didn't mean to knock you down,' he said pleasantly with a dazzling smile. It was hard not to stare at him, and she noticed several other women looking at him too. 'Great lecture, wasn't it?' he said with a friendly smile. The lecture had opened a whole new line of thought for her. She had never worried that any of her students might be suicidal or secretly troubled, but she realized now that it was a real concern.

'Yes, it was,' she agreed.

'I teach juniors and seniors, and it sounds like they're the most at risk.'

'So do I,' she said, as they drifted in the same direction toward a buffet that had been set up for their breaks. It had been a fascinating conference so far.

'Where do you teach?' He seemed perfectly comfortable chatting with her, and he was inclined to continue as they both stopped at the buffet.

'The Madison School,' she said proudly, smiling at him.

'I've heard of it. Fancy kids, eh? I teach public school. That's a whole other world.'

They went on chatting for a few minutes, and he introduced her to Ardith Lucas, a woman he knew who joined them, and then he invited Victoria to sit at a table with them. Everyone was jockeying for seats before they went to the next panel or lecture. And there were several tables set up around the room with free literature and books they could buy. He had a bag full, and Victoria had already collected the stack of brochures of most interest to her, which she'd dropped and he'd helped her pick up. He said his name was John Kelly, and he looked a few years older than she. Ardith was considerably older and said she couldn't wait to retire. She said she had done her time as a teacher for forty years and was longing to be free. Victoria and John were just starting out.

The three of them talked all through lunch. John was dazzlingly good looking, extremely nice, and very bright. And after lunch he jotted down his phone number and e-mail for her, and said he'd love to get together sometime. She didn't get the feeling he was asking for a date, but wanted to be friends, and she had a feeling he was gay. She gave him her information too. She didn't know if she'd hear from him again, forgot about it, and a week later she was surprised when he called and invited her to lunch on a Saturday.

There was a new Impressionist exhibit at the Metropolitan Museum, and they both wanted to see it. She met him in the lobby, and they went through the exhibit, enjoying it together, and then went to the cafeteria for lunch. She was having a very nice time with him, and then mentioned that one of her roommates worked at the Costume Institute and was setting up a new exhibit that day. And after lunch they decided to drop by and see Harlan. He looked surprised to see Victoria, and was impressed by her new friend. It was impossible not to notice John's blond good looks, and his extremely athletic body, and when she saw them look at each other, her earlier impression of John was confirmed. The two men were drawn to each other like magnets.

Harlan gave them a private tour of the Costume Institute, and when they left, John looked as though he hated to leave. And as they walked down the steps of the museum, he commented on what a terrific guy Harlan was, and Victoria agreed. She felt like Cupid suddenly, and loved the idea of introducing them. And on the spur of the moment, she invited John to dinner at the apartment on Sunday night. He looked very happy to accept, and then he took a bus downtown to where he lived, and Victoria walked home.

Harlan didn't come home till eight o'clock that night, after setting up the exhibit, and he wandered into her room when he got in. She was lying in bed watching TV.

'What was that vision of gorgeousness you brought to the Costume Institute today? I nearly fainted when you walked in. How do you know him?'

Victoria laughed at the look on his face. 'I met him at a teachers' conference last week. He nearly knocked me down, literally.'

'Lucky you. He seems like a really great guy.'

'Yes, I think so too,' she said, smiling at Harlan, 'and I think he plays on your team.'

'So why did he ask you out?' Harlan looked suspicious, and was worried he might be straight.

'To be friends, I think. Believe me, he doesn't look at

me the way he looked at you.' Men never did, not in her experience at least. 'And by the way, I invited him to dinner tomorrow night.' She laughed out loud at the look on Harlan's face. He looked as though she had just told him he'd won the lottery.

'Is he coming?'

'Yes. And you'd better cook dinner. If I do, I'll poison us all, unless we order pizza.'

'I'd love to,' Harlan said happily, and went back to his room, looking like he was floating on a cloud. He had never seen anyone as handsome as John. Harlan was a good-looking man too, and Victoria thought they looked like a good match. She wondered if some premonition or instinct had led her to introduce them to each other. It had been a spur-of-the-moment idea but now seemed like divine inspiration to her, and to Harlan as well.

He was a very proficient cook, and spent the whole next day in the kitchen, after buying a leg of lamb, potatoes, string beans, and chocolate cake at a nearby bakery. And by dinnertime, the smells emanating from the kitchen were delicious. John Kelly arrived right on time. He had brought a small bouquet of flowers and a bottle of red wine. He handed the flowers to Victoria, and the wine to Harlan, who opened it and poured them each a glass, and then they went to sit in the living room.

And the two men got on like a house on fire. They never stopped talking until dinner, which was an hour later. And Harlan had set the table nicely with place mats and linen napkins, and candles on the table in the dining room. He had gone all out. And by the end of dinner, Victoria felt as though she were intruding on a date, and left them alone. She said she had papers to grade before school the next day. She closed the door softly, after telling Harlan she'd help him do the dishes later, and she turned on her TV and lay down on her bed. She was dozing when John knocked on her door to say goodbye and thank her. And when she heard the front door close, she went out to the kitchen to help Harlan clean up.

'So, how was it?' Victoria asked him with a smile.

'Wow!' Harlan said, smiling broadly. 'He's the most terrific man I've ever met.' He was twenty-eight-years-old and seemed extremely grounded, serious, and responsible and was fun to talk to as well. Harlan said he'd had a great time.

'He likes you too,' Victoria commented as she rinsed the dishes Harlan handed her.

'How do you know?'

'Anyone can see that,' she reassured him. 'His face lit up every time you looked at each other.'

'I could have talked to him all night,' he said dreamily.

'Did he ask you out?' she asked, enjoying the romance starting right beneath her eyes, and she loved the idea that she had introduced them.

'Not yet. He said he'd call me tomorrow. I hope he does.'

'I'm sure he will.'

'We have the same birthday,' Harlan said as she laughed.

'That must be a sign. Okay, now you owe me big time. If you two wind up together, I want a street named after me or something.'

'If I end up with him, you can have all my autographed baseball cards from when I was a kid, and my grand-mother's silver.'

'I just want you to be happy,' she said kindly.

'Thanks, Victoria. He seems like such a great guy.'

'So are you,' she said warmly.

'I never feel that way about myself. I always feel like everyone is better than I am, smarter, nicer, better look-ing, cooler.' He looked nervous as he said it.

'So do I,' she said sadly. She knew the feeling, and why she had it. It came from years of her parents telling her how inadequate she was, and her father letting her know that he thought she was fat and ugly. It had undermined her confidence and self-esteem since birth. And it was a cross she had to bear now. Deep down, she always believed that he was right.

'I guess our parents do that to us early on,' Harlan said quietly. 'I don't think he's had an easy time of it either. His mother committed suicide when he was a kid, and his father won't see him because he's gay. But he seems pretty healthy and normal in spite of that. He just got out of a relationship he's been in for five years. His partner cheated on him, so they broke up.' Victoria was happy for Harlan and hoped that something came of it for both of them. He thanked her profusely again, and then they turned off the lights and went to their rooms. It had been a delicious dinner and a lovely night. And she had enjoyed talking to both men, although not as much as they had enjoyed talking to each other.

She left early the next morning, and didn't see Harlan that day, or the next. It was Wednesday when she ran into him in the kitchen when they both got home from work. She was afraid to ask if he had heard from John, in case he hadn't, but he volunteered the information very quickly.

'I had dinner with him last night,' he said, beaming.

'How was it?'

'Amazing. I know it's too soon to say it, but I'm in love.'

'Just go slow, and see how it goes.' Harlan nodded but didn't look capable of following her advice.

She met John again in their kitchen that weekend. He and Harlan were cooking dinner, and John had brought over his wok and offered to leave it with him. They invited Victoria for dinner, but she said she had other plans, and went to a movie by herself so they could be alone. And they were out when she got back. She didn't know where they'd gone, and she didn't need to know. This was their story now, and their life. She just hoped it would turn out to be a loving relationship for both of them, and it looked that way for now. They appeared to be off to a terrific start. She smiled to herself as she thought about it and went to her room. As usual on the weekends, everyone was out. It reminded her that she hadn't had a date since she'd been in New York. No one had asked her out since the summer before in L.A., at least six months.

She didn't go anywhere where she was likely to meet men, except the teachers' conference where she'd met John. Other than that, she didn't go to a gym or belong to a club. She didn't go to bars. There were no single, straight, age-appropriate teachers at her school. No one had introduced her to anyone, and she hadn't met anyone on her own. She thought it would have been nice if she had, but so far all she had to fill her life was her work. And this time it was Harlan's turn, and John's. She was happy for them. And she knew that sooner or later she would meet someone. At twenty-two, it was unlikely that she would be alone for the rest of her life, no matter how overweight her father thought she was. She remembered her grandmother's old saying that there was a lid for every pot. She hoped that Harlan had found his. And with luck, she hoped that one day, she'd find hers.

Chapter 12

In March her parents and Gracie came to visit Victoria in New York during Gracie's spring break. They stayed for a week, and the two sisters had a ball, while their parents visited friends and kept busy on their own. And several times they had dinner together. Victoria picked the restaurants from a guide someone had given her, and they enjoyed them all. And Gracie loved being in New York with her. She stayed at the apartment with Victoria, and their parents stayed at the Carlyle, which was just down the street from the school where Victoria taught. The school was on spring break too so she had lots of time to spend with them. They came to her apartment several times, and met her roommates. Her father liked Bill, and thought Bunny was beautiful, but neither of her parents was enthused about

Harlan. Later, over dinner, Jim made several negative comments about his being gay, and Victoria sprang to his defense.

By the time they left, Gracie was convinced that she wanted to move to New York too, and even go to college there if she could get in. Her grades were not as strong as Victoria's had been, and for the moment Victoria doubted that she'd get into NYU or Barnard. Still, there were several other great schools in New York. Victoria was sad to see her leave at the end of a week that had been fun for both of them.

Two weeks after they'd been there, Eric Walker called her into his office, and she felt like a kid who had done something wrong. She wondered if someone had reported her, or one of the parents had complained. She knew that several of the parents thought that she gave too much homework, and had called to negotiate with her. She was non-negotiable. Her students had to do the work she gave. Helen had taught her well, and her motto was 'Be tough.' Victoria was never as tough as Helen was, but she made her students toe the line, and they had come to respect her for it in the past six months. She no longer had problems with any of them in class, thanks to Helen's good advice.

'How do you think your classes are going, Victoria?'

the headmaster asked her with a pleasant expression. He didn't look angry or upset, and she couldn't imagine why she was there. Maybe he was just touching base. The school year was coming to a close, and her time at Madison would be up in June.

'I think they're going well,' she said. She sincerely believed they were, and hoped she was right. She didn't want to end her time there in disgrace. She knew that if they didn't hire her for the coming year, she would have to start looking for a new school soon. But she was going to hate leaving the job she had. Madison was just her kind of school, and she loved how bright the kids were. She was going to miss them all.

'As you know, Carla Bernini is coming back to school in the fall.' He went on, 'We'll be happy to have her back, but you've done a great job, Victoria. The kids all love you, and they rave about your classes.' And he'd had good feedback from the parents too, despite her fears about the homework. 'I actually asked you to come in today, because we've had a change of plans. Fred Forsatch is going on sabbatical next year. He wants to take classes at Oxford and spend some time in Europe. Normally, we'd need to replace him.' He was their Spanish teacher. 'But Meg Phillips has a double major, and she'd like to take over his classes for next year, which leaves us with another year to fill in the English department. She only teaches seniors, as you know, and I hear you have a real gift with them. I was wondering if you'd like to take her spot next year, until Fred comes back. It means you could stay with us for another year, and who knows after that. How does that sound to you?' Her eyes were wide as she listened to him, and it was the best news she had had since he'd offered her the job a year before. She was thrilled.

'Oh my God, are you kidding? I'd love it! Are you serious?' She sounded like one of her students, and he laughed.

'No, I'm not kidding. Yes, I'm serious. And yes, I am offering you a job for next year.' He was pleased that she was so enthusiastic about it. It was exactly what he had hoped to hear. They chatted for a few more minutes, and then she went back to the teachers' lounge and told everyone there.

She thanked the Spanish teacher profusely when she saw him later that afternoon. He laughed when he saw how happy she was. And he was just as pleased at the prospect of being in Europe for a year. It was something he had wanted to do for a long time.

Victoria floated all the way home, she told her roommates when they came in, and they cheered. When she called her parents that night to tell them the news, their reaction was more or less what she had expected, but she wanted to tell them anyway. She still felt obliged to report on her life to them, despite their predictably disappointing reactions, and this time was no different.

'You're just deferring getting a real job, Victoria. You can't live on that salary forever,' her father said, but actually she was living on it. She hadn't asked him for help since she left home. She was careful about what she spent, and she still had some savings left. The small rent she paid kept her budget in good shape most of the time.

'This is a real job, Dad,' she insisted, knowing it was pointless trying to convince him. 'I love my job, the kids, and the school.'

'You could be making three or four times what they pay you, at any ad agency out here, or just about any company that would hire you.' He sounded disapproving, and he was not impressed that the best private school in New York had offered to hire her for a second year, and was pleased with her performance.

'It's not about the money,' Victoria said, sounding disappointed. 'I'm good at what I do.'

'Anyone can teach, Victoria. All you do is babysit those rich kids anyway.' In a single sentence he had dismissed her abilities and her career. And what he said wasn't true, she knew. Anyone couldn't teach. It was a very specific skill, and she had talent at it. Not everyone was able to do what she did. But it meant absolutely nothing to her parents. She didn't speak to her mother since she was out playing bridge, but Victoria knew she wouldn't have been impressed. She never was, and she took her cues from her husband. She echoed every opinion he had, on every subject. 'I'd like you to give this some serious thought before you sign that contract,' he urged her, and she sighed.

'I already have. This is what I want, and where I want to be.'

'Your sister will be very upset that you're not coming home,' he said, playing the guilt card. But Victoria had already warned her during spring break that she might stay another year if she got the chance, and Gracie had understood. She also knew first hand why Victoria was unhappy at home. Their parents never missed a chance to make her feel bad. It always made Gracie feel guilty that they were so nice to her, and never had been to their older daughter. Gracie had observed it all her life. It was no wonder that she had thought Victoria was adopted, when they were younger. It was hard to believe that they would be so critical and uncharitable with their own child, but they were. Nothing she did impressed them, or was ever good enough, and this was no different. Her father was annoyed, not proud of her. And as usual, only Gracie celebrated for her and with her when she called her about the job.

Harlan and John were excited about it for her too. They both gave her a big hug to congratulate her. John was a regular feature at the apartment now, and had been for two months. And the relationship was getting solid. And Bill and Bunny liked him too.

She had dinner with John and Harlan that night, and she told them about her father's reaction, and said that it was nothing new, and typical of him.

'You should go to a shrink and talk about it,' John said quietly, and Victoria looked shocked. She didn't have any mental problems, didn't suffer from depression, and she had always managed her problems on her own.

'I don't think I need to do that,' she said, looking horrified and a little hurt. 'I do just fine.'

'Of course you do,' John said easily, and he believed her. 'But people like that are very toxic in our lives, especially our parents. If they've been saying things like that to you all your life, you owe it to yourself to get rid of the messages they've left in your brain and your heart. That can really hold you back and hurt you in the long run.' She had told Harlan about being named after Queen Victoria, and why, and he agreed with John. 'You might find it very helpful.' And they were also both convinced that her weight problem was due to the constant put-downs of her father. It seemed obvious to them. And her mother sounded no better, from what Victoria said about her. Harlan hated the stories she told about her parents and her childhood, and the emotional abuse she had endured for years. They hadn't abused her with fists, but with words.

'I'll think about it,' she said softly, and put it out of her head as soon as she could. The thought of going to a therapist was really upsetting to her. And it didn't surprise either of them that without thinking, she helped herself to a bowl of ice cream after dinner, although neither of them was eating dessert. Neither of them insisted about the shrink, and Harlan didn't bring it up again.

And before the summer, Victoria lined up a summer job for June and July so she didn't have to go home. She took a job for very little pay tutoring underprivileged kids at a shelter where they lived while waiting to go into foster care. It sounded depressing to Harlan when she told him, but she was excited about it. She was starting there the day after Madison closed for the summer.

Gracie had a summer job that year too. It was her first one, at sixteen, and she'd be working at the desk of the swim and tennis club they belonged to. She was thrilled about it, and their parents sounded pleased. They thought Victoria's job sounded unpleasant, and her mother told her to wash her hands a lot or she might catch a disease from the kids she tutored. She thanked her for the advice and was annoyed that the job she was doing didn't impress them, nor did her work as a teacher, but Gracie working at the desk in a tennis club was cause for celebration and endless praise. It didn't make her angry at Gracie, only at them.

Before she started work, Gracie was coming to visit Victoria in New York.

This time Gracie came alone without their parents, and they had even more fun than they had had in March. She kept herself busy in the daytime, going to galleries and museums and going shopping, and Victoria took her out to movies and restaurants at night. They even went to a Broadway play.

And as usual Victoria was planning to go home in August. It was the longest time she spent with them now every year. But this time she only intended to stay for two weeks, which was more than long enough for her. And once there, as usual, her father criticized her frequently about her job, and her mother nagged her constantly about her weight, which had gone up again after a brief dip in the spring. Before she left New York, Victoria had gone on a cabbage diet, which helped her lose weight. The diet was miserable, but it worked, and then a short time afterward she gained all the weight back again. It was a battle she just couldn't seem to win. It was discouraging.

When she got back to New York, she was disheartened by the things her parents had said, and the weight she had put back on, and she thought about Harlan's suggestion that she see a shrink. And in a dark mood one day right before school started, she called a name he had given her. It was a woman he had met, and he said that a friend of his had gone to her and liked her a lot. Before Victoria could change her mind, she called her and made an appointment for the following week. And she agonized about it as soon as she did. It seemed like a crazy thing to do, and she thought about canceling, but didn't have the courage to do that either. She felt stuck. And she ate half a cheesecake alone in the kitchen the night before she went. What if the woman discovered that she was crazy, or that her parents were right about her and she was a total failure as a human being? What kept her from canceling the appointment was the hope that they were wrong.

When Victoria went to the appointment with the psychiatrist, she was literally shaking, and had felt sick to her stomach all day. She couldn't remember why she had made the appointment and wished she hadn't, and her mouth was so dry when she sat down that she felt like her tongue was stuck to the roof of her mouth.

Dr. Watson looked sensible and pleasant. She was in her early forties, and she was wearing a well-cut navy blue suit. She had a good haircut, wore makeup, and looked more stylish than Victoria had expected, and she had a warm smile that started in her eyes. She asked Victoria a few details about where she had grown up, where she had gone to school, and college, how many siblings she had, and if her parents were still married or divorced. They were all easy questions to answer, especially the one about Gracie. Victoria lit up like a light-bulb when she answered the question about having a sibling, and then described her and how beautiful she was. She told the doctor then about how different she herself looked from all of them and had thought she was adopted as a child, and her sister had thought so too.

'What made you think something like that?' the doctor asked casually, sitting across from Victoria as they sat in comfortable chairs. There was no couch in her office, only a box of Kleenex, which seemed ominous to Victoria and made her wonder if people cried often when they were there.

'I was always so different from them,' Victoria

explained. 'I don't look like them in any way. They all have dark hair. I'm fair. My parents and sister have dark brown eyes. Mine are blue. I am a big person. All three of them are thin. Not only do I put on weight easily, I overeat when I'm upset. I've always had a problem with . . . with my weight. Even our noses aren't the same, but I look like my great-grandmother.' And then she blurted out something she didn't expect to say. 'I've felt like an outsider with them all my life. My father named me after Queen Victoria because he said I looked like her. I always thought she was beautiful because she was a queen. And then I saw a photograph of her when I was six, and realized what my father meant. He meant I was fat and ugly just like her.'

'What did you do then, once you knew that?' the doctor asked quietly with a sympathetic expression.

'I cried. It almost broke my heart. I always believed he thought I was beautiful until then. And from then on I knew the truth. He used to laugh about it, and when my sister was born when I was seven, he said I had been their tester cake, to check the recipe, throw the tester cake away, and they got it right the second time. Gracie was always the perfect child, and she looks just like them. I didn't. I was the tester cake they wanted to throw away. She was the prize.'

'How did that make you feel?' The cool quiet gaze stayed focused on Victoria's face. Victoria didn't even know that there were tears rolling down her cheeks.

'It felt terrible, about me, but I loved my baby sister so much I didn't care. But I've always known what they thought of me. I'm never good enough, no matter what I do. And maybe they're right. I mean, look at me, I'm fat. And every time I lose weight, I gain it right back again. My mother gets upset every time she looks at me and tells me I should be on a diet or going to the gym. My father hands me the mashed potatoes and then makes fun of me when I eat them.' What she was saying would have horrified anyone, but nothing showed on the psychiatrist's face. She just listened sympathetically with an occasional murmuring sound.

'Why do you think they say those things to you? Do you think it's about them or about you? Doesn't it say more about them as people? Would you say things like that to your child?'

'Never. Maybe they just wanted me to be better than I am. The only thing they think is beautiful about me are my legs. My father says I have killer legs.'

'What about inside? What about the kind of person you are? You sound like a good person to me.'

'I think I am . . . I hope I am . . . I try very hard to do

the right things. Except about eating. But I mean to other people. I've always taken good care of my sister.' Victoria sounded sad as she said it.

'I believe that, and that you do the right things,' Dr. Watson said, looking warm for the first time. 'How about your parents? Do you think they do the right things, for you for instance?'

'Not really ... sometimes ... they paid for my education. And we've never been deprived. My father just says things that hurt me. He hates how I look, and he thinks my job isn't good enough.'

'And what does your mother do then?'

'She's always on his side. I think he was always more important to her than my sister and I were. He's everything in my mother's life. And my sister was an accident. I didn't know what that meant till I was about fifteen. I heard them say it before she was born, and I thought she was going to arrive all banged up. And of course she didn't. She was the most gorgeous baby I've ever seen. She's been in commercials and ad campaigns a few times.'

The portrait of her family that Victoria painted was totally clear, not only to the psychiatrist, but to herself as she listened to what she said. It was the portrait of a text-book narcissist and his enabling wife, who had been unthinkably cruel to their oldest child, rejecting and ridiculing her all her life, for not being an appropriate accessory to them. And her younger sister had fit the bill for them perfectly. The only surprise was that Victoria had never hated her little sister, but loved her as much as she did. It was proof of her loving nature and generous heart. She took pleasure in how beautiful Grace was. And she had accepted the horrible things her parents had said about her as gospel. She had been shackled by their cruelty all her life. Victoria was embarrassed by some of the things she had said, but they were all true, and had the ring of truth to the psychiatrist as well. She didn't doubt them for a minute.

And then she glanced at a clock just beyond Victoria's shoulder and asked her if she would like to come back the following week. And before she could stop herself, Victoria nodded and then said that she would have to come in the afternoon after school since she was a teacher, which the psychiatrist said was fine. She gave her an appointment and handed her a card with the time written on it, and smiled.

'I think we did some good work today, Victoria. I hope you think so too.'

'We did?' She looked surprised. She had been entirely open and honest with her. And she felt suddenly disloyal to her parents for the things she had said. But she hadn't lied. They had said all those things to her over the years. Maybe they hadn't meant them to be as cruel as they sounded. And what if they did? What did that mean, about her and about them? It was a mystery to her now, which would have to wait another week to be solved, until she met with the shrink again. But she didn't feel crazy when she left, as she had feared. She felt saner than she ever had, and painfully lucid about her parents.

Dr. Watson escorted her out, and when Victoria stepped out into the sunlight, she felt dazed for a minute and blinded by the light. The doctor closed the door softly behind her, and Victoria slowly walked away. She had a feeling that she had opened a door that afternoon and let the light into the dark corners of her heart. And whatever happened now, she knew she couldn't close that door again. And thinking about it, she cried with relief as she walked all the way home.

Chapter 13

For Victoria's second year at the Madison School, she got a very respectable raise. It wasn't an amount that impressed her father, but it gave her a little more leeway in how she lived. And now she only taught seniors, which was her favorite group anyway. Juniors were much more intense and stressed out, and sophomores were immature and harder to direct. They were still babies in many ways, testing their limits and often rude. Seniors were in the home stretch, and had begun to acquire a certain poise and sense of humor about life. And they were enjoying their last year at home as kids. It made them much more fun to be with. Nostalgia began to set in during their last months in high school. Victoria enjoyed being part of it and sharing their final year with them. They were almost cooked.

Carla Bernini came back to school after her year-long maternity leave and was impressed by all that Victoria had accomplished with her students, and had a deep respect for her, however young. And they became good friends. She brought her baby to school once in a while to visit, and Victoria thought he was really cute. He was a bouncing happy baby, who reminded her of Grace at the same age.

And she was continuing to see Dr. Watson at her office once a week. She thought it was making subtle changes in how she looked at life, saw herself, and viewed her life-long experiences with her parents. They had been toxic and hurtful to her all her life. She was beginning to face that now. And she had taken some positive steps since she had started therapy. She was dieting again and had joined a gym. Sometimes the sessions of remembering the things her parents had done and said left her so raw that all she could do was come home and drown herself in comfort foods. Ice cream was always her drug of choice, and sometimes her best friend. But the next day she would eat very little and spend extra time at the gym to atone for her sins. Dr. Watson had recommended a nutritionist who'd given Victoria good advice about planning her meals. Victoria had also tried a hypnotist, which she hadn't liked and which had no effect.

Most of all she enjoyed her job and the kids she taught. She was learning a lot, about teaching, and about life. And she had more confidence in herself since starting to see the shrink, even if she hadn't conquered her eating issues yet. She hoped she would one day, even if she knew she would never look like Gracie or her mother. Since working with the shrink, she was happier with herself.

She was in a good place when school started, and a new chemistry teacher came on board to replace one who had retired. He seemed like a good guy, and had pleasant looks. He wasn't movie star handsome, but he had a gentle, kind manner, and was friendly to teachers and kids. Everybody liked him, and he had made a real effort to get to know them all. He sat down next to Victoria in the teachers' lounge one day. She was eating a salad from a nearby deli, and trying to correct the last of some papers she wanted to return to the students that day. She still had some spare time before her next class, when he unwrapped a sub sandwich at the table, sitting next to her. She couldn't help noticing that it smelled delicious, and she felt like a rabbit eating her salad. She had sprinkled the lettuce leaves with lemon, instead of the generous portion of ranch dressing she would have preferred. She was trying to be good, and had an appointment with her shrink the next day.

'Hi, I don't think we've met. I'm Jack Bailey,' he introduced himself between bites of the sandwich. He had salt and pepper hair, although he was in his early thirties, and a beard, all of which gave him a mature appearance to the kids. He was easy to take seriously, and Victoria smiled at him and introduced herself as she munched her lettuce.

'I know who you are,' he said, smiling at her. 'Every senior in this school loves you. You're a tough act to follow when they come to me after your class. They have so much more fun with you. I don't know how you come up with some of your ideas. You're a star here.' It was a nice thing to say, and she was pleased.

'They're not always so crazy about me,' she assured him. 'Especially when I give them surprise quizzes.'

'I could never decide if I wanted to be a physicist or a poet when I was growing up. I think you made the better choice.'

'I'm not a poet either,' she said simply, 'just a teacher. How are you enjoying the school?'

'I love it. I taught in a small rural school in Oklahoma last year. The kids are a lot more sophisticated here.' And she knew he was too. She had heard that he had graduated from MIT. 'I'm having a lot of fun discovering New York. I'm originally from Texas. I lived in Boston for a couple of years after I graduated, then migrated to Oklahoma. I love being in this city,' he said warmly, as he finished his sandwich.

'Me too. I'm from L.A. I've been here for a year. There's still a lot I want to do and see.'

'Maybe we should do that together,' he said with a hopeful look, and for a moment she felt a flutter. She wasn't sure if he was serious about the suggestion, or just being friendly. She would have loved to go out with someone like him. She'd had a few dates in the past few months, including someone she'd gone to high school with in L.A., and all of them were duds. Her dating life was still almost nonexistent, and Jack was the only really eligible man at school. All of the single female teachers had been talking about him since he arrived, and referred to him as a 'hunk.' Victoria was well aware of that as they were speaking.

'That would be fun,' she said casually in case he hadn't really meant it.

'Do you like theater?' he asked as they both stood up. He was considerably taller than she was, well over six feet.

'Very much. I can't really afford it,' she said honestly, 'but I go once in a while, just to treat myself.'

'There's an off-off-Broadway play I've been meaning to see. It's a little dark, but I hear it's great. I've met the playwright. Maybe we could go this weekend, if you're free.' She didn't want to tell him that she was free for the rest of her life, particularly for him. She was flattered by his interest.

'That sounds great,' she said, smiling warmly, sure that he wouldn't follow up on the invitation. She was used to men being friendly to her, and never calling her after that. And she had very few opportunities to meet single men. She lived and worked among women, kids, and gay and married men. An eligible bachelor was a rarity in her world. Her shrink had been encouraging her to get out and meet more people, not just men. Her world was limited to and defined by school.

'I'll send you an e-mail,' he promised as they both left the teachers' lounge and went back to work. They were teaching classes at the same time. He waved and disappeared in the opposite direction, to where the science labs were, and she drifted past Helen's classroom on the way to her own. She was talking to Carla Bernini, and both women looked up and smiled as she walked by. She stopped in the doorway for a minute.

'Hi, you guys.' She loved the camaraderie they all shared. Both women were older than she was, but working at a school was frequently like being part of a family, with a lot of older siblings who were her fellow teachers, and younger ones who were the students. They were all in this together.

'Rumor has it that you had lunch with the hunk in the lounge,' Carla said with a broad grin, and Victoria smiled, looking sheepish.

'Are you kidding? We sat at the same table. Leave the poor guy alone. Half the school is after him. He was just being polite. Do you two have radar, or are you bugging the teachers' lounge?' All three women laughed. They knew only too well that all schools were gossip mills, where teachers talked about each other as well as the students, and what was happening in their lives, and everyone knew everything that went on.

'He's cute,' Carla volunteered, and Helen agreed, as Victoria rolled her eyes.

'Believe me, he's not after me. I'm sure he has better fish to fry.' And it was common knowledge that the hot new French teacher was after him. What chance would she have?

'He'd be lucky to have you,' Carla said warmly. She had become very fond of their youngest colleague, and she had a lot of respect for Victoria as a teacher, even though she still had a lot to learn. But she had done very well in her first year.

'Thanks for the vote of confidence,' Victoria said

again, and walked on to her classroom. It was amazing to her how fast news traveled in a high school. Faster than the speed of sound. She wondered if he would actually send her an e-mail. She doubted it, but he'd been nice to talk to over lunch. She didn't expect anything to come of it, and said as much to her shrink the next day.

'Why not?' her doctor asked her. 'Why do you think he won't follow through on what he said?'

'Because it was no big deal, just casual conversation over lunch. He probably didn't mean it.'

'What if he did? What would that say to you?'

'I guess that he likes me, or maybe he's just lonely.'

'So you think you're only worthy as a stopgap for lonely guys? What if he actually likes you?'

'I think he was just being polite,' Victoria said firmly. She'd been disappointed before by men who she thought were interested in her and never called her.

'What makes you think that?' her psychiatrist said with quiet interest. 'Do you think you deserve a nice man to go out with?' There was a long silence while Victoria pondered the question.

'I don't know. I'm overweight. I'm not as pretty as my sister. I hate my nose. And my mother says men don't like smart women.' The psychiatrist smiled at her answer, and Victoria laughed nervously at her own response.

'Well, we can agree that you're smart. That's a good beginning. And I don't agree with your mother. Smart men like smart women. The superficial ones may not, and may be threatened by them. But you wouldn't want one of those men. Your nose looks fine to me. And weight is not a character flaw, it's something you can change. A man who really likes you and cares about you won't care about your weight one way or another. You're a very attractive woman, Victoria, and any man would be lucky to have you.' It was nice to hear, but Victoria didn't entirely believe her. The evidence in the other side of the scale had been too heavy for too long – the insults of her father, the constant dismissal of her parents, her own sense of failure. 'Let's see if he calls you. But even if he doesn't, all that means is that he has other interests. It doesn't mean that no man will ever want you.' She was twenty-three-years-old, and so far no male she'd ever known had fallen seriously in love with her. She had been passed over and ignored for years, except by friends. She felt like a shapeless, sexless, totally undesirable object. And it was going to take hard work and dedication to turn that around. It was why she was here. To change the image her parents had given her of herself. And she said she was willing to do whatever it took, even if the process was painful for her. Living with her own sense of defeat was worse. It had been her parents' legacy to her, to make her feel unlovable, because they didn't love her. It had started the day she was born. She had twenty-three years of their negative messages about her to cancel out now, one by one. And finally she was ready to face it.

Victoria felt a little discouraged after the session. It was hard digging through her past at times, pulling all those ugly memories out into the open and looking long and hard at them. She was still feeling down about it when she got home. She hated remembering those things, and all the times her father had hurt her feelings and her mother had turned a deaf ear and blind eye and never come to her defense. Her own mother. The only one who ever had was Gracie.

And what did that say about her? That her own mother didn't love her? Nor her father. And the only one who could was a child, who didn't know any better. It told her that no intelligent adult could love her, not even her parents. And she had to learn to remind herself now that it was a flaw in their psychological makeup, not her own.

She turned on her computer when she got home and checked her e-mail. She had one from Gracie, telling her what was happening at school, and about a drama with a new boy she had a crush on. At sixteen she had more boys

circling her at one time than Victoria had had in a lifetime, even if they were just kids. The voice on her
computer said she had mail as she finished reading
Gracie's message with a grin. And then she switched over
to see who it was. She didn't recognize the e-mail address
at first, and as she read it again, it clicked for her immediately: Jack Bailey. The new chemistry teacher at
lunch in the student lounge. She opened his e-mail
quickly, trying not to feel anxious. It could have been
something about school or one of the students they
shared, and she sat staring at the e-mail after she read it.

*Hi. Nice seeing you at lunch yesterday, and having
time to chat. I managed to get two tickets to the play I
mentioned to you. Any chance you'd like to join me on
Saturday? Dinner before or after? Potluck at nearby
diner, provided by starving chem teacher. Let me know
if you're free and it's of interest. See you around school.*
Jack.

Victoria sat staring at it endlessly, wondering what it
meant. Friendship? A date? Someone who had no friends
in New York and was just lonely? Did he like her? She felt
like Gracie with her high school romances as she tried to
read between the lines. It made her nervous, and maybe

it was just what it appeared to be. Dinner and a play on a Saturday night, offered by a nice guy. They could figure out the rest later, if they wanted to go out again. She couldn't wait to tell Harlan about it when he got home.

'That's what they call dating, Victoria. A guy asks you out. He offers to feed you, possibly entertainment, in this case a play. And if you both have fun, you do it again. What did you answer?' He asked with interest, but he was happy for her. She looked excited.

'Nothing. I wasn't sure what to say. How do you know it's a date?'

'Time of day. Offer of food. Entertainment provided. Saturday night. Your sexes, your ages, career in common. You're both single. I'd say it's a pretty safe bet that this is a date.' He was laughing at her, and she looked nervous.

'Maybe he just wants to be friends.'

'Maybe. But plenty of romances start as friendships. Since you both work at a fancy school, I don't think he's an ax murderer. He doesn't appear to have any serious addictions, or substance abuse issues. He probably hasn't been recently arrested. I think you'd probably be safe for dinner and a play. If not, you can always carry Mace.' She grinned at the suggestion.

'Besides, this isn't just his show, you know. You might

decide *you* don't like *him*.' He wanted her to know that she had decision-making power here too.

'Why would I do that? He's smart, he's nice looking. He went to MIT. He's got a lot more going for him than I do. He could go out with anyone he wanted.'

'Yes, and so could you. And besides, he asked *you*. Let's keep the playing field level here. You have just as much free choice here as he does. No one died and made him king.' It was good advice, and she knew it, and it was a reality check for her. She felt so inadequate and unlovable most of the time, she knew now, that she forgot that she had a voice in this too. The decision was not only just his. 'And don't forget the lamb chop factor,' Harlan said with a serious air, as he made them both a cup of tea.

'What's that?' Victoria asked with a puzzled expression.

'You meet a guy who is so gorgeous it knocks you flat on your ass, and you can hardly breathe when you see him. He's brilliant, charming, and funny, as well as the best-looking guy you've ever seen. Maybe he even drives a Ferrari. Then you see him eat a lamb chop, like he was born in a stable and eats like a pig in a trough, and you never want to see him again.' Victoria burst out laughing at what he said.

'Can't you teach him table manners?' she asked innocently.

Harlan shook his head with a determined look. 'Never. It's too embarrassing. And so is introducing a guy like that to your friends, while he sits at the table, slobbering over his lamb chop, slurping his soup, and licking his fingers. Forget the guys who eat like Tom Jones. You can check him out at the diner,' he said seriously, while Victoria grinned.

'Okay. I'll order lamb chops and offer him one.'

'Trust me. It's the ultimate test. You can live with almost anything else.' They were both laughing by then, and he was teasing her, but there was a small degree of truth to what he said. It was hard to predict in the beginning what would totally melt your heart about someone, or turn you off forever. Guys who tipped badly or left no tip at all, were rude to waiters, or crude, had always been a turn-off for her. She had never considered lamb chops before. 'So what are you going to do now?' Harlan asked her. 'I suggest you accept his invitation. I can't remember the last time you had a date, and you probably can't either.'

'Yes, I can,' she said defensively. 'I went on a date in L.A. this summer. He was someone I was in eighth grade with, and I ran into him at our swim club.'

'So? You didn't mention him before.'

'He was incredibly boring. He sells real estate for his

mother, and he spent the whole dinner talking about his low back pain, his migraines, and his hereditary bunions. It was a pretty boring evening.'

'Jesus, you wonder how a guy like that ever gets laid. He must not get a lot of second dates.' They were both laughing at her description. 'I hope you didn't sleep with him.'

'No,' she said primly, 'he had a headache. And so did I by dessert. I ate dinner and left. He called a couple of times after that, and I lied and told him I'd gone back to New York. Fortunately, I didn't run into him again.'

'In light of that experience, I think you ought to go out with the chemistry teacher. If he's not signing up for bunion surgery and doesn't get a migraine at dinner, you'll be way ahead of the game.'

'I think you're right,' she said, and went to answer Jack Bailey's e-mail. She told him she accepted with pleasure and it sounded like fun. She offered to pay her share, since they were both poverty-stricken teachers. He e-mailed that it wasn't necessary, as long as she didn't mind dinner at the diner, and told her he'd pick her up on Saturday. It was done. All she had to do now, she realized as she went to tell Harlan, was figure out what to wear.

'A very, very, very short skirt,' he answered without

hesitation. 'With legs like yours, you should only wear miniskirts. I wish I had those legs,' he teased her, but what he said was true. She had long, beautiful, graceful legs that drew all attention away from her thicker middle. And he thought she had a pretty face, in a wholesome, blond, all-American way. She was a very decent-looking woman, and an extremely nice one, with a bright, lively, sharp mind and a good sense of humor. What more could a man want? He hoped the date worked out for her. Particularly since he had been happy for the last eight months with John Kelly, thanks to her. They were a perfect combination, and it had become a serious affair. They were starting to talk about moving in together. And they loved taking Victoria out to dinner with them. Harlan had become her best friend in New York, and her only real confidant other than her sister. And he gave excellent advice.

When Jack arrived promptly at seven o'clock on Saturday night, the apartment was empty. All the others were out for the evening, and he walked around the apartment, admiring how pleasant it was, and how spacious.

'Wow, I live in a shoebox compared to you,' he said enviously.

'It's rent-controlled. I was lucky, and I live here with

three other people. I found it as soon as I moved to New York.'

'You really lucked out.'

She offered him a glass of wine, and a few minutes later they left for dinner. They took the subway to the diner in the Village, and he said the play was starting at nine o'clock, so they had just enough time for dinner.

She had taken Harlan's advice, and he had checked her over before he went out to meet John. She was wearing a short black skirt, a white T-shirt, and a denim jacket, with high-heeled sandals that showed off her legs. And she looked very pretty. She wore a little makeup and her long blond hair down. Harlan had said it was the perfect outfit for a first date. Sexy, young, simple, and it didn't look like she was trying too hard. He had said solemnly definitely no cleavage on a first date, although she had plenty of it. He told her to save it for later, and she hadn't been planning to show it off anyway. She was happy in the loose T-shirt. And she and Jack chatted constantly on the way downtown. He was fun to be with and had a good sense of humor. He made her laugh at the description of the schools he'd worked in. And it was obvious that he genuinely liked kids. It was equally so that he liked her.

She contemplated the menu with a frown when they got to the diner. She always had a weakness for meat loaf

and mashed potatoes, which reminded her of her grandmother's cooking, which had been the best thing about
her, but she didn't want to overdo it and eat too much.
The fried chicken sounded good too. She finally decided
on sliced turkey breast and ordered string beans. And the
food was good. She almost burst out laughing when Jack
ordered lamb chops and a baked potato. He ate them
with a knife and fork. No sign of Tom Jones. She could
tell Harlan that he had passed the test. And she hoped
that she had too. They shared a piece of homemade apple
pie à la mode for dessert. When they finished their meal,
he said, 'I like a woman who has a healthy appetite,' and
told her that the last girl he had gone out with was
anorexic, and it had driven him crazy. She never ate, and
was apparently severely neurotic in other ways. He didn't
see anything wrong with Victoria enjoying her food.

They both liked the play, and talked about it all the
way back to her place on the subway. It was depressing,
but beautifully acted and well written. She'd had a really
great evening with him, and she thanked him as they
stood outside her building in the warm night air.

She didn't invite him to come upstairs at the end of the
evening, it was too soon. But it definitely felt like a date
to her. Jack looked happy too and said he'd like to go out
with her again. She thanked him, and he hugged her, and

there was a spring in her step and a smile on her face when she walked into the empty apartment. For a minute she was sorry she hadn't invited him upstairs for a drink, but decided it was better this way. And much to her surprise, he called her the next day.

He said there was an art show downtown that he was going to and wanted to know if she'd like to join him. She did, they met downtown, and had dinner together again. By the time she got back to school on Monday morning, they had had two dates, and she couldn't wait to tell her shrink. It felt like a real victory to her, a huge compliment, and they seemed to be compatible in many ways. They ran into each other in the teachers' lounge at lunchtime, and she appreciated that he was discreet and didn't refer to seeing her on the weekend. She didn't want the whole school knowing that they'd gone out with each other outside school, especially for a proper 'date.' He was casual and friendly, but nothing more, and then he called her that night to invite her out on Friday for dinner and a movie. She was really excited when she told her roommates about it over dinner in the kitchen.

'It sounds like we have a live one here,' Harlan said, grinning at her. 'And he passed the lamb chop test. Shit, Victoria, you're in business.' She laughed and felt silly, and almost helped herself to a second piece of garlic bread to celebrate. John was a terrific cook, but she stopped herself. She really wanted to lose some weight, and she had good reason to do it now. She had a date!

Their movie date on Friday was as much fun as the other two had been. And they met again on Sunday, for a walk in the park, and he held hands with her as they strolled along. They bought ice cream from a man with a hand truck rolling through the park, but she forced herself to throw it away before she finished. She had lost two pounds that week, and had been doing sit-ups every night in front of the TV. Even her shrink was excited about her budding romance, although Victoria hadn't slept with him yet. He hadn't tried, and she didn't want to do that too soon. She wanted to be sure how she felt about him before she did, and that they had something real between them. She didn't just want sex. She wanted a relationship, and Jack was beginning to seem like the perfect candidate for it, after four dates. They went back to her apartment on Sunday afternoon, and he met Bunny and Harlan, and was very nice to both of them. And they both liked him.

October was the most exciting, hopeful month she'd had in years as she and Jack continued to see each other every weekend, and on the third weekend they went out, he kissed her. They talked about it, and both agreed that they wanted to wait a little while before they took the relationship to another level. They both wanted to be cautious and mature and get to know each other better before they took a major leap. It made her feel safe and comfortable with him, and not pushed beyond her limits. He was respectful of her, and every time they saw each other, they got closer and had a wonderful time. Victoria's shrink fully approved.

Victoria had told him a little about her parents, though not a great deal. She hadn't told him about the tester cake remark, or being named after Queen Victoria, but she did say that they had never praised her, and were critical of her choice of career.

'We have that in common,' Jack said to her. 'My mother always wanted me to be a doctor, because her father was. My father still wants me to be a lawyer like him. I love being a teacher, and they warn me constantly that I'll never make a decent living or be able to support a wife and kids. But other people do it, and this is what I want to do. When I went to MIT, my father thought I should at least be an engineer.'

'My father says the same thing, minus being able to support a wife and kids. I guess no one congratulates anyone for becoming a teacher. It seems like an important job to me. We have a pretty major influence on kids.'

'I know. People get paid five million bucks for hitting a baseball out of the park. But educating young people isn't worth a damn thing to anyone, except to us. It's a little sick.' They both agreed. They agreed on almost everything. And in early November things were heating up between them. They had been dating for just over a month, seeing each other once or twice a weekend, and Victoria could sense that they were going to sleep with each other soon. They were working up to it. She felt totally at ease with him, and was falling in love. He was a terrific guy, straightforward, honest, intelligent, warm, funny. He was everything she had ever dreamed of in a man, and as Gracie would have said, she thought he was cute. She had told her younger sister all about him, and she was thrilled, although Victoria had said nothing to her parents, and had warned Gracie not to either. She didn't want to deal with their negative comments, or their predictions of doom. It was still inconceivable to them that any man would fall in love with her. But she could tell that Jack thought she was pretty, and the warmth they shared in their relationship made Victoria bloom like a garden in spring. She looked relaxed, more sure of herself, and constantly happy. Dr. Watson was concerned – she didn't want her self-esteem to come from a man, rather than be generated from within. But Jack was certainly helping how she felt about herself. And she had dropped ten pounds, by watching her portions and what she ate. She remembered the nutritionist's warning not to skip meals, and to eat healthy food. This time there were no crash diets, no herbal teas, no purges. She was just happy, and everything else fell into place accordingly. They were both talking about their plans to go home for Thanksgiving, and were considering coming back to New York during the weekend, so they could spend part of the holiday together.

She was thinking about it one evening, when she walked into the kitchen and saw John and Harlan deep in thought and earnest conversation. They both looked unhappy, and she quickly found an excuse to leave the kitchen. She didn't want to intrude. They seemed as though they had a problem. And Harlan stopped her just before she went back to her room with a cup of tea.

'Got a minute?' he asked her as she hesitated. She could see that John was upset. She wondered if they were having an argument and hoped it wasn't serious. Their relationship had been so good until then, for almost a year now. She would hate it if they broke up, and she knew Harlan would be distraught.

'Sure,' Victoria said in answer to his question, with no idea how she could help them, but willing to try. Harlan waved at a chair at the kitchen table, as John let out a sigh. 'Looks like you guys are having a problem,' she said sympathetically, as her heart went out to both of them.

'Yeah, kind of,' John admitted. 'It's kind of a moral dilemma.'

'Between the two of you?' She looked surprised. She couldn't imagine either of them cheating on the other. And she was certain that Harlan was faithful, and assumed that John was too. They were just that kind of people, with good values, morality, and a lot of integrity, and besides, they loved each other.

'No, it's about a friend,' Harlan answered. 'I hate meddling in other people's business. I always wondered what I would do if I found out something that would hurt someone I love, but thought that they should know. It's a situation I've never wanted to be in.'

'And you are now?' Victoria asked innocently, and they both nodded at the same time. John sighed again, and this time he spoke up. He knew it was too hard for Harlan to do it, and he was the one who had the information first hand. They'd been talking about it for two weeks, and had hoped it would work itself out. But it hadn't. It had gotten worse. And neither of them wanted to see Victoria heading for a wall. They loved her too much as their friend, and almost like a sister.

'I don't know all of the details. But it's about Jack. Your Jack. Life is really weird at times, but I've been talking to a teacher I work with at my school. I've never liked her, and she's kind of a bitch. She's very full of herself, and she's always working some guy. She's been talking a lot lately about some teacher she's having an affair with. He works at another school. She sees him every weekend, but apparently only one night, and she's pissed about it. They see each other one night and one afternoon, and she thinks he's cheating on her, although he says he isn't. Other than that, she thinks he's a great guy, and she says he's crazy about her. They're planning to spend Thanksgiving together instead of going to their families, and he told her he would go see them on Saturday after Thanksgiving for the weekend. And then, I don't know, but it rang a bell for me. I asked her what this guy's last name is, and where he teaches. I never bothered to ask her before, because I really don't give a damn. She says his name is Jack Bailey, and he teaches chem at Madison.' John turned sad eyes toward Victoria, and she looked like she was going to faint or burst into tears. 'It sounds like your guy is riding two horses, or trying to. I wanted to say something before you got in any deeper. It sounds like he's splitting every weekend, and now Thanksgiving, between the two of you, which is a shit thing to do, if he hasn't told you that's what he's doing and you haven't agreed to it. And honestly, this girl is really a bitch. She's just not a decent person. I don't know what he's doing with her, when he has you.' It made both John and Harlan feel sick, for her, and now she looked it too. She started to cry as they sat at the kitchen table, and Harlan handed her a tissue. They felt terrible telling her but thought that she should know what she was dealing with, and whom.

'What am I going to do?' she asked them through her tears.

'I think you have to talk to him about it,' John said simply. 'You have a right to know what he's doing. He's seeing a lot of you. And apparently of her too, every weekend. And she says she's been sleeping with him for two months.' He didn't add salt to the wound by telling Victoria that the other woman claimed he was great in bed. She didn't need to hear that too, particularly since she hadn't slept with him yet herself, but they all knew that she would soon. She had kind of guessed that it would happen naturally over Thanksgiving, and with all her roommates away, she'd been planning to invite him to stay at the apartment, when they got back from their holiday with their families. Although she knew now that he'd been planning to spend it with the other woman, and lying to her about where he was spending the weekend. He was lucky it was a big city and he hadn't run into either of them when he was with the other. But it was a small world anyway, and by sheer coincidence he was seeing a woman who worked with one of her best friends. The possibility of that happening was slim, but it had happened. Providence had intervened.

'What do I say to him? Do you think it's true?' She was hoping it wasn't, but John was honest with her again, however painful.

'Yes, I do. She's a slut, but there's no reason for her to lie or make this up. I think he's the one who's not being honest. And it's a rotten thing to do to you, even if you're not sleeping with him yet. You've been dating him for almost as long as she has. It sounds like he's playing you both.' Victoria felt sick as she listened, and sat frozen in her seat. She felt cold suddenly, and the boys saw her shiver.

'Do you think he'll tell me the truth now?' she asked miserably.

'Probably. He's been pretty much caught red-handed. It would be interesting to hear what he does say, and how he explains it. This will be a tough one to justify or clean up.'

'I never asked him if he was seeing someone else,'

Victoria said honestly. 'I didn't think I had to. I assumed he wasn't.'

'It's a good question to ask,' Harlan added sadly. 'Some people don't 'fess up unless you ask. But by this point, seeing each other every weekend and building a relationship, he should have told you whether you asked or not.' She nodded and thanked John for the information, although she hated hearing it, and he looked miserable for having told her. But they all knew it was right. She had to know. She sat with them in the kitchen for a long time, mulling it over, rehashing what they knew, and was confused, hurt, and angry about it. She managed to avoid Jack at school all the next day. She didn't feel ready to confront him. And that night he called her.

'Where were you today? I looked for you all over and couldn't find you,' he said, sounding as affectionate as ever. It was Thursday, and they were supposed to have dinner together the next day. She tried to keep her voice normal, but it was hard. She didn't want to confront him about what she'd heard until they were face to face. This was not a conversation she wanted to have with him over the phone. She had felt sick about it all day, and hadn't slept the night before. It was hard to believe that someone she cared about so much and had been so open with, and trusted so much, had been so dishonest with her. It had been a heart-wrenching revelation. All her fears came back to her that she wasn't good enough to be loved. She hoped he had some reasonable explanation for it. But she couldn't imagine one. She was willing to listen to what he had to say, and wanted to hear it, but the evidence John had presented to her was pretty damning.

She told Jack she had been busy all that day, meeting with students and their parents about the college process, and she invited him to come to the apartment for a drink before dinner the following night. He said it sounded like a great idea, and he was as warm as ever. She had never pressed him about spending both nights of the weekend together, and never wanted to be pushy, but she decided to try it now and see what he would say in response.

'Maybe we can do something Saturday night too. There are some really great new movies out,' she said innocently.

'Maybe we can do that Sunday afternoon,' he said with a tone of regret. 'I have to correct exams all day Saturday and Saturday night. I'm way behind on it now.' There was her answer. She could have Friday night and Sunday afternoon, but not Saturday or Saturday night. And with a sinking heart and a knot in her stomach the size of her head, she knew that what John had told her was true. She hadn't doubted it, but hoped he was wrong somehow. Apparently, he wasn't.

She was distracted and nervous at school all day Friday and saw Jack in the teachers' lounge briefly at lunchtime. She nearly ran out the door, and told him she was late for a student meeting. And he arrived at her apartment right on time on Friday night. He looked as appealing and as relaxed as ever. There was a quality about him that made him look honest and sincere. He exuded integrity in a way that suggested that he was a person you could trust. And she had, whole-heartedly. Apparently, he was not what he appeared. It was a bitter pill for her to swallow. They were alone in the apartment. Everyone was out on Friday night. And Harlan and John knew what she'd be doing. She had told them. They were at John's place to give her space but had told her they were available if she needed them.

She had no idea how to start the conversation as she poured him a glass of wine with trembling hands. She had worn slacks and an old sweater. Suddenly she didn't feel beautiful, as she often did when she was with him. She felt ugly, and unloved, and betrayed now. It was a terrible feeling. She hadn't bothered to wash her hair or wear makeup. The notion of competing with the other woman was foreign to her. Her spirit and her confidence in herself had folded like a house of cards. He was proving her father right, she wasn't worthy of being loved. Someone else was.

Jack was looking at her carefully as he held his glass of wine. He could see that she was upset, and had no idea what it was about.

'Something wrong?' he asked innocently.

Her hand was shaking as she set down her glass, and her stomach did a roll. 'Maybe,' she said softly and raised her eyes to his. 'You tell me. I never mentioned it before. Harlan's boyfriend John works at the Aguillera School in the Bronx. Apparently a friend of yours does too. I guess you know who she is better than I do. She says she's been having an affair with you for two months, and she sees you every weekend. I guess that makes me pretty stupid, and you dishonest, or something like that. So what's the deal, Jack? What's the story?' She looked him dead in the eye, and he stared at her for a minute, set down his glass, and walked across the room to look out the window, and then he turned toward her again, and she could see that he was furious. He had been caught.

'You have no right to snoop around about me,' he started on the offensive, but it got him nowhere. She didn't buy it.

'I didn't. It fell into my lap, and I guess I'm lucky John

told me. She's been bragging about you. It's a small world, Jack, even in a city the size of New York. How long were you planning to do double duty, and why didn't you tell me about it?'

'You never asked me. I never lied to you,' he said angrily. 'I never told you we were exclusive. If you wanted to know that, you should have asked me.'

'You don't think you should have volunteered that by now? We've been seeing each other every weekend for almost two months. Apparently the same amount of time you've been involved with her. What does she think is going on?'

'I never told her I was exclusive with her either,' he said, looking angry. 'And it's none of your business anyway. I haven't slept with you, Victoria. I don't owe you anything, except pleasant company when we go out, and a nice evening.'

'Is that how it works? Those aren't the rules I play by. If I'd been seeing someone else, sexually or not, I would have told you. I would have felt I owed you that, just so you don't get confused or hurt. I had a right to know, Jack. Just as a human being and someone you supposedly cared about, I deserved that. This wasn't just about dinner. We were trying it out as a relationship. And I guess you're doing the same with her. And who else is there? Do you have slots open during the week too? It sounds like you've been a pretty busy guy, and not an honest one. It was a shitty thing to do, Jack, and you know it.' There were tears in her eyes when she said it.

'Yeah, whatever,' he said, nasty with her for the first time, and he looked cold now. He didn't like being called on the carpet, or being accountable for his behavior. He wanted to do whatever he wanted, no matter who got hurt, as long as it wasn't him. He wasn't the man she'd thought him, not by a long shot. Lamb chops hadn't been a problem, but his integrity was. He had none. The fact that she never asked was no excuse for him leading her on. 'I don't owe you any explanations,' he said, standing and looking down at her unkindly. 'This is dating, that's all it is, and if you don't like the heat, get out of the kitchen. Or in this case, I will. Thanks for the wine,' he said, strode to the door, and slammed it behind him. That was it. Two months with a guy she liked and had believed in, and he had cheated on her, lied, and had no regret whatsoever. He didn't give a damn about her. That much was evident. Victoria sat in her chair shaking after he left, but proud of herself for having confronted him. It had been ugly and painful, and she told herself that she was better off finding it out now, but she felt like someone had died when she walked back into her bedroom, lay down on the bed, and sobbed into her pillows. She hated what he had done, but worse yet, she felt terrible about herself. All she could think as she remembered the look in his eyes before he left was that if she had been worthy, he would have loved her. And he didn't.

Chapter 14

Victoria still felt shattered over the disappointment with Jack Bailey when she left for L.A. for Thanksgiving. It was good to see Gracie, and share the holiday with her family, but she was feeling terrible about herself. Gracie could see it, and was sad for her. She could tell how upset she was by what she was eating. All her parents noticed was that she had gained weight, and Victoria went back to New York on Saturday. She couldn't take it any longer.

She called Dr. Watson on Monday morning after Thanksgiving and went in to see her. They had been talking about Jack for the past several weeks. No matter how Victoria turned it around, she still felt somehow to blame, and that if she were truly lovable and worthy of being loved, Jack would have behaved differently.

'It's not about who you are,' her psychiatrist said kindly, again, 'it's about who he is. His lack of integrity, his dishonesty. This wasn't your failure, it was his.' Victoria knew it intellectually, but she couldn't get it emotionally. For her, it always went back to whether she was lovable or not. And if her parents hadn't loved her, who would? And the same principles applied to them. Their failure to love her as she was spoke volumes about who they were, but it still made her feel terrible about herself. And she tried to fill the void with gallons of ice cream when she went home to L.A. over Christmas. She was still depressed and couldn't seem to turn it around. Her parents knew nothing about the relationship with Jack.

She had never shared it with them, and she knew that if she had, they would only have found a way to blame her when it failed. Of course he couldn't love her if she was too fat, and the other woman in his life was probably thin. And in some part of her psyche, Victoria believed that too. She had never had the courage to ask John what the other woman looked like. She believed her parents' subliminal and overt messages. Men only loved girls who looked like Gracie. And no man wanted an intelligent woman. She didn't look like Gracie, and she was a bright girl. So who would want her? She was still seriously depressed when she went back to New York on New Year's Eve. She spent midnight on the plane and when the captain announced Happy New Year at midnight, Victoria pulled a blanket over her head and cried.

It had been agony seeing Jack at school between Thanksgiving and Christmas. She never ate lunch in the teachers' lounge anymore. She stayed in her classroom, or went for walks outside, along the East River. It was a serious reminder of why it wasn't smart to get romantically involved with someone at work. Picking up the pieces later was a mess. And there were whispers among teachers and students that they had been dating and she had gotten dumped. It was humiliating beyond belief. Victoria did all she could to disappear, although it was Jack who should have been ashamed. And she heard just before Christmas that he was dating the French teacher who had been chasing him since the first day of school. She felt sorry for her, since she assumed he was still seeing the woman at John's school, and not being any more honest with the French teacher than he had been with her. Or maybe the French teacher was smarter and knew the right questions to ask, like 'Are we exclusive?' Or maybe he would have lied. In any case, it wasn't Victoria's problem anymore. Jack Bailey was no longer in her life. It was a dream that had almost happened, and had fallen apart before it did. More than anything, for Victoria, it was a loss of hope. Helen and Carla tried to comfort her as gently as they could, but she avoided them too. She didn't want to discuss it with anyone, in school or out. She didn't talk to John and Harlan about it either now. It was done. But they could see how badly it had impacted her.

She was grateful for the distraction when she went on a college tour with Gracie in January, over a long weekend. They went to visit three schools in the East, but Gracie was determined to stay on the West Coast. She was a California girl, but they both enjoyed the trip anyway. It was a wonderful chance to be together. And Gracie didn't say anything when Victoria ate a huge steak and baked potato with sour cream, followed by a hot fudge sundae for dessert when they went out to dinner. She knew how sad she was over Jack. And Victoria was well aware herself that even her baggiest pants had gotten tight since Thanksgiving. She knew she had to do something about it, but she wasn't ready to yet. She wasn't ready to give up what her shrink called 'the bottle under the bed,' which in her case was fattening foods. In the long run, the result of eating them only made her feel worse, like an alcoholic, but they offered comfort for a minute.

One of the highlights of Gracie's visit to her sister was spending a day with Victoria at school. She sat in on her classes, and she had fun talking to the other students. And it gave her students further insight into Victoria to meet her younger sister. Gracie was a big hit in the classroom, spoke up easily, and was the instant focus of all the boys, who wanted her e-mail, and to know if she was on Facebook, which she was. She handed her e-mail address out like candy, and they grabbed it. Victoria was relieved that Gracie left before she turned her classes upside down. She was more beautiful than ever at nearly eighteen, which suddenly made Victoria feel old as well as huge. It depressed her to think that she would be turning twenty-five in a few months. A quarter of a century. And what did she have to show for it? All she could focus on was that she had no man in her life and was still battling her weight. She had a job and a sister she loved and nothing else. She had no boyfriend, and had never had a serious one, and her social life consisted of Harlan and John. It didn't seem like enough at her age. And Dr. Watson broadsided her the next time they met, when Victoria told her about the college tour she'd taken with Gracie and how much fun it was for her.

'I want to raise a question for you to think about,' her psychiatrist said quietly. Victoria had come to rely on her in the past year and a half and value what she said. 'Do you think it's possible that you keep the weight on so you don't have to compete with your beautiful younger sister? You take yourself out of the running, by hiding behind your own body. Maybe you're afraid that if you lost the weight, you still couldn't compete, or don't want to.'

Victoria brushed off what she said and summarily dismissed it. 'I don't have to compete, nor should I, with a seventeen-year-old girl. She's a kid. I'm an adult.'

'You're both women, in a family where your parents pitted you against each other, and told you that you weren't good enough, and she was, from the day she was born. That's a heavy weight for both of you, and more so for you. So you withdrew from the competition.' It was an interesting point that Victoria didn't want to hear.

'I was big before she was born,' Victoria insisted.

'Big compared to your sister. Don't confuse the issue. But being overweight is different.' The psychiatrist was suggesting that it was a protective covering she wore, a camouflage suit that kept people from seeing her as a woman, even though she was a pretty girl. But not as beautiful as Gracie. So she checked out of the competition and disappeared into a body that made her invisible to most young men, except ultimately the right one. But her psychiatrist hoped that she would take the weight off before that, only because it made her unhappy.

'Are you saying I don't love my sister?' Victoria asked, looking angry for a moment.

'No,' her doctor said quietly, 'I'm saying you don't love yourself.' Victoria fell silent for a long moment, as tears ran freely down her cheeks. She had learned long since what the tissue box was for and why people used it as often as they did.

In the spring of Victoria's second year at Madison, they offered her a permanent job in the English department. And she was relieved to hear that Jack Bailey's contract wasn't being renewed. The rumor was that he'd been told 'it wasn't a good fit.' But his heated affair with the French teacher had turned ugly, and they'd been seen fighting in the halls, and the passionate Parisian had hit him right in school. And after that, Jack had gotten involved with one of the students' mothers, which was a well-known taboo in the school. Victoria was relieved that he was leaving. It was painful every time she ran into him in the halls, and a reminder to her that somehow she had been inadequate and not enough for him to love her, and he had been dishonest and a jerk.

She was thrilled to have the job for good and not have to worry about it every year. Now she had a home at Madison and could settle in with a sense of security about her work. Helen and Carla had been thrilled when she told them and took her out for lunch. And she celebrated the news that night with Harlan and John. Bill had moved out by then, to live with Julie, and John had taken over his old room and was using it as an office, and they were sharing Harlan's room. John was a good addition to the group and Bunny liked him too. She was spending more and more time in Boston, and Victoria had a feeling she'd be moving soon too, and possibly getting married. As single people, it was a fluid community, but she, John, and Harlan weren't going anywhere. She didn't even bother to call her parents about the job, although she told Gracie, who was two months away from graduation and was ecstatic over being accepted at USC. And she was planning to live in the dorms. Their parents would have an empty nest at last. They weren't happy about it, but she was adamant, and their parents always gave in to *her*. It struck Victoria that they were more upset about Gracie moving to the dorms than about her own move three thousand miles away. Whatever happened, Gracie was always the apple of her father's eye and his baby, and Victoria was their tester cake. They hadn't thrown her away, but they might as well. Their lack of affection and approval for her had done just as much damage. And for Victoria, it was the reality of her relationship with them.

Chapter 15

Gracie's graduation was a gala celebration. Whereas Victoria's graduation, even from college, had been dealt with quietly, their parents allowed Gracie to invite a hundred kids to a barbecue in the backyard, with her father at the grill, making chicken, steaks, burgers, and hot dogs. And there was catering staff in T-shirts and jeans. The kids had a ball. Victoria flew out for the party and the graduation the next day. Gracie looked adorable in her cap and gown. And their father actually cried when she got her diploma. Victoria couldn't remember his ever doing that for her, probably because he hadn't. And their mother was undone. It was an extremely emotional event. And the two sisters embraced afterward and cried too.

'I can't stand it!' Victoria laughed through her tears as she hugged her. 'My baby has grown up! How dare you go to college! I hate this!'

She wished too that Gracie had tried harder to get into a school in New York, instead of staying in L.A. She would have loved to have her closer, so she had family in New York. But she would also have liked to see her little sister get away from their parents' stifling influence. They hovered over her, and her father was a powerful force in her life, and tried to form her every opinion. Victoria had never been able to tolerate it, but Gracie bought into a lot of it, their lifestyle, their opinions, their politics, their philosophies about life. There was much she agreed with and even admired about them. But Gracie had had a very different set of parents than Victoria did. Gracie had parents who worshipped and adored her, and supported her every move and decision. That was heady stuff. And she had no reason to rebel against them, or even separate from them. She did everything their father thought she should. He was her idol. And Victoria had had parents who ignored her, ridiculed her, and never approved of a single move she made. Victoria had had good reason to move far away. And Gracie had just as many compelling reasons to stay close to home. It was incredible to realize how different their experiences and lives had been with the same parents. It was like night and day, positive and negative. Sometimes Victoria had to remind herself of how much easier Grace's life had been, and how much kinder they had been to her, to explain to herself why Gracie didn't want to separate from them. It had been a big decision for Gracie to live in the dorm rather than stay at home. That felt like a major move to her, although it seemed like a tiny one to her older sister and not big enough. Victoria still believed that they were toxic people, and her father a narcissist, and she would have liked to see her sister get more breathing space from their parents, but she didn't want it. In fact, Gracie would have fought to stay close to them.

Victoria's graduation gift to her was a big one. She was careful with her money, and saved whatever she could. She wasn't extravagant despite living in New York. And she offered to take Gracie to Europe as a graduation present. They had gone with their parents when they were much younger, but their parents hadn't been interested in traveling in years. So Victoria was taking Grace to Paris, London, and Venice in June, and Rome if they had time. Grace was so excited she couldn't stand it, and so was Victoria. They were planning to be gone for three weeks, with four or five days in each city. With Victoria's new job at Madison, she had gotten a raise that allowed her not to work this summer. After going to Europe with Gracie in June, she was planning a trip to Maine with Harlan and John in August.

Gracie had a million plans of her own before she started college in late August. Victoria realized, as Gracie did, that now things were going to change for all of them. She had grown up, Victoria lived far away. Their parents had a chance to be more independent and do things on their own. They would all get together for holidays, but in between they all had their own lives to lead. Except for Victoria, who had a job, but not a life. She was still trying to carve one out for herself. At twenty-five, she still felt as though she had a long way to go. She wondered sometimes if she'd ever get there, and had started referring to herself jokingly as Gracie's spinster sister. It felt at times as though that was going to be her lot in life.

Gracie, on the other hand, had a dozen boys chasing after her at all times, some of whom she liked, some of whom she didn't, and one or two of whom she was always crazy about and couldn't decide between the two. Finding boys had never been her problem. And Victoria was proving her parents right at every turn. She wasn't pretty enough to find a man, according to her father, and much too fat to attract one. And according to her mother, she was too intelligent to keep one. Either way, she had no one.

They left for Paris the day after school closed for Victoria in New York. Gracie flew to New York with two suitcases filled with summer clothes, and the girls left for the airport early the next morning. Victoria had one suitcase, and she checked their luggage in at the airport, while Gracie talked to her friends on her cell phone. Victoria felt a little like a tour guide on a high school trip, but she was really looking forward to traveling with her sister. They boarded the plane in high spirits, and Gracie was still texting frantically when the flight attendant told her to turn off her phone. Victoria was holding on to their passports. Sometimes she felt more like Gracie's mother than her sister.

They talked, ate, slept, and watched two movies on the six-hour flight to Paris. It was over before they knew it, as they landed at Charles de Gaulle airport at ten o'clock at night. It was four in the afternoon for them, and they had slept on the plane, so neither of them was tired, and they were excited to look around as they drove into the city in a cab. Victoria was using a chunk of her savings to pay for the trip, and their father had sent her a nice check to help her, which she was grateful for.

At Victoria's request in broken French, the cabdriver drove them through the Place Vendôme, past the Hotel Ritz, into the excitement and beauty of the Place de la

Concorde, with all the lights on the fountains, and then they drove up the Champs-Élysées toward the Arc de Triomphe. They turned onto the broad avenue just as the Eiffel Tower exploded in sparkling lights, which it did for ten minutes on the hour. They were both on sensory overload from the beauty of it all, as Gracie looked around in awe. And there was an enormous French flag fluttering in the breeze below the Arc.

'Omigod,' Gracie said, looking at her sister, 'I'm never going home.' Victoria smiled, and they held hands as the driver spun them through the free-form traffic around the Arc de Triomphe, and they headed back down the Champs-Élysées again, toward the Seine, saw the view of the Invalides, which housed Napoleon's tomb, and sped across the Pont Alexandre III, onto the Left Bank. They were staying at a tiny hotel Victoria had heard about, on the rue Jacob. They were planning to travel as inexpensively as possible, stay in small hotels, eat in bistros, and go to galleries and museums. They were on a tight budget for a trip both girls knew they would remember all their lives. It was an incredible gift from Victoria to her sister.

They had onion soup that night at a tiny bistro around the corner from their hotel. After dinner they walked around the Left Bank, and then came back to their hotel and went upstairs and talked until they fell asleep. Gracie had been getting text messages from her friends at home from the moment she turned her phone on at the airport, and they continued long into the night.

The two girls had croissants and café au lait in the lobby of the hotel the next morning, and then they set out on foot to go to the Rodin Museum on the rue de Varenne, and from there to the Boulevard Saint-Germain, bustling with activity, where they had coffee at the venerable old artists' restaurant, Aux Deux Magots. And after that they went to the Louvre and spent the afternoon there seeing famous treasures.

Gracie wanted to see the Picasso Museum, which they did the next day. They had dinner in the Place des Vosges, which was one of the oldest sections of the city, in the Marais. And after that they rode on a Bateau Mouche, all lit up on the Seine.

They saw an exhibit at the Grand Palais, walked in the Bois de Boulogne, visited the lobby of the Hotel Ritz, and walked down the rue de la Paix. They both felt as though they had walked all over Paris in the five days they were there. They had seen everything they wanted to by the time they left for London, and they were just as energetic there. They went to the Tate Gallery, the Victoria and Albert Museum, and Madame Tussaud's

Wax Museum in the first two days. They saw the crown jewels in the Tower of London, the changing of the guard at Buckingham Palace, visited the stables and went to Westminster Abbey, and walked down the grandeur of New Bond Street, looking into all the expensive shops they couldn't afford. Victoria had treated herself to an expensive handbag at Printemps in Paris, and Gracie went wild with T-shirts and funny jeans in the King's Road in London, but they had both been very well behaved, and spent their money wisely. At night they had dinner in small restaurants, and they stopped at sandwich shops in the daytime. They managed to do and see everything, and their parents checked on their progress daily, mostly, Victoria knew, because Gracie was with her, and they said they missed her.

They had been gone for almost two weeks when they flew from London to Venice, and their pace slowed dramatically once they were there. Their arrival at the Grand Canal was breathtaking, and Victoria paid for a gondola ride to their hotel, while Gracie lay happily in the boat and looked like a princess. The moment they arrived in Italy, every man in the street was looking at her, and when they walked around Venice, several times Victoria noticed men following them and staring at her younger sister.

They walked through the Piazza San Marco, and bought gelato, went into the church itself, and wandered endlessly for hours along the narrow winding streets, in and out of churches, and when they finally stopped for lunch, Victoria ordered an enormous bowl of pasta and ate it all. Gracie had picked at hers and said it was delicious. She was too excited to eat much, and it was hot. They hadn't stopped moving for a minute. And they both agreed afterward that Venice was their favorite city. They did more walking, eating, and relaxing there, moving at a slower pace, and they spent hours at outdoor cafés just watching people. Gracie insisted on buying a tiny cameo brooch for their mother, which wouldn't even have occurred to Victoria, but she had to admit that it was very pretty, and a very sweet gesture. They bought a tie for their father at Prada, and silly souvenirs for themselves. There was a gold bracelet that Victoria fell in love with in a shop near the Piazza San Marco, but she decided she couldn't afford it, and Gracie bought a music box shaped like a gondola that played an Italian song neither of them knew.

Their days and nights in Venice were absolutely perfect. They visited the Doge's Palace, and every major church in their guidebook. They took a gondola ride under the Bridge of Sighs, and hugged as they glided underneath it, which supposedly meant they would be together forever, although the promise was only meant for lovers. But Gracie insisted it applied to them too. And for their one elegant evening, they went to Harry's Bar, where they ate another enormous meal. The food in Venice was fantastic, and Victoria ate risotto or pasta with delicious sauces at every meal and tiramisu for dessert. This wasn't about comfort food, it was about exquisite Italian cuisine, but its effect on her body was the same.

They both hated to leave and fly to Rome for the last leg of the trip. They did more walking, shopping, and visiting churches and monuments there. They visited the Sistine Chapel, took a tour of the Catacombs, and wandered around the Colosseum. And they were both exhausted but happy by the end of the trip. It had been as unforgettable as Victoria had hoped, and a moment in their lives and a memory that she knew both of them would cherish forever. They had just tossed a coin in the Fountain of Trevi and found their way to an outdoor café on the Via Veneto, when their father called them. He couldn't wait for them to come home, and Gracie sounded excited to see him too. They were planning to fly from Rome to New York. Gracie was going to spend two days with her sister in New York, and then fly back to

L.A. on her own. Victoria had promised to come out to help her settle into the dorm in August, but she had no plans to spend time in L.A. this year. Her life was in New York now, and she knew that Gracie would be busy with her friends before they all went their separate ways for college. It was a relief for Victoria not to spend two or three weeks living with her parents. She wanted time to relax in New York.

On the flight from Rome to New York, they talked about everything they'd done and seen. And Victoria was relieved that there hadn't been a single bad moment on the trip. Gracie had been a pleasure to be with. And although their views of their parents were very different, Victoria was careful not to dwell on it. They talked about other things. And Gracie had thanked her profusely for the incredible trip. They were halfway to New York when Gracie handed her a small package wrapped in Italian gift paper, with a little green ribbon. She looked mysterious and excited when she gave it to her big sister, and thanked her again for the fabulous trip. She said it was the best graduation present in the world.

Victoria opened the package carefully, and felt something heavy inside it. It was in a soft black velvet pouch, and when she opened it, she saw the beautiful gold bracelet she had fallen in love with in Venice, and had decided not to buy herself.

'Oh my God! Gracie, that's crazy!' The generosity of the gift took her breath away, and Gracie put it on Victoria's wrist.

'I bought it with my allowance and the money Dad gave me for the trip,' her sister told her proudly.

'I'm never taking it off,' Victoria said as she leaned over and kissed her.

'I've never had such a great time in my life,' Gracie said happily, 'and I probably never will again. I'm sad that it's over.'

'Me too,' Victoria admitted to her. 'Maybe we can do it again sometime, when you graduate from college.' She smiled wistfully. That seemed like a lifetime away right now, but Victoria knew how fast the years would fly by from now on. It seemed like only yesterday when she had graduated from high school, and now she was twenty-five and her college graduation was three years behind her. And she knew it would happen just as fast for her younger sister.

They talked for a long time on the flight, and then finally drifted off to sleep. They both woke up as they were landing in New York. It was sad to think that the trip was over. The time together had been magical, and they looked at each other and smiled nostalgically as they landed. They were both thinking that they wished they could start the trip all over again.

It took them an hour to get their bags and get through customs, and another hour to get into the city in a cab. By the time they pulled up in front of Victoria's building, Rome, Venice, London, and Paris felt like they were a lifetime away.

'I want to go back!' Gracie said mournfully as Victoria let them both into the apartment. It was a weekend, and everyone was away, and they had the place to themselves.

'So do I,' Victoria said as she read a note from Harlan, welcoming her home. He had left some groceries in the fridge so she could cook Gracie breakfast. And Victoria put their bags in her bedroom. It felt strange coming home.

They went to bed early that night, after calling their parents to say that they had arrived safely. Gracie was always good about that, and didn't want them to worry. She had never gone through a rebellious phase and sometimes Victoria wished she had. It might have been healthier than being so close to their parents. She hoped that now Gracie would find some independence in college, but she had a feeling they'd be wanting her to come home all the time. It made Victoria glad that she had gone to Northwestern, but they had never been as attached to her. And Gracie was their baby.

The next morning Victoria made French toast for breakfast, then they took the subway to SoHo, and walked around among the street vendors, shoppers, and tourists. The streets were jammed, and they had lunch at a little sidewalk café. But it was nothing like Europe, and they both agreed that they wished they were back in Venice. It had been the high point of their trip. And Victoria was proudly wearing the beautiful gold bracelet Gracie had given her.

They spent Sunday at a concert in Central Park, and had dinner after Gracie packed again. Victoria had already put all her things away. And the two girls sat talking at the kitchen table late into the night. The others weren't due back till Monday, and the following weekend was the Fourth of July weekend. Gracie had a million plans in L.A., and Victoria had none in New York. Harlan and John were going to Fire Island, and Bunny to Cape Cod.

Victoria took her sister to the airport the next morning, and both girls cried. It was the end of a beautiful trip, a wonderful shared time, and Victoria felt as though someone had torn her heart out after Gracie left, and she took the shuttle back into the city. Gracie texted Victoria before the flight took off. 'Best vacation of my whole life, and you're the best sister. I love you forever. G.' There were tears in Victoria's eyes when she read the message, and when she got back to her apartment, she called Dr. Watson. She was glad to hear that the doctor had an opening that afternoon.

Victoria was happy to see her, and told her about the trip. She commented on how easy Gracie had been, how much fun they had had, she showed her the bracelet on her arm, and laughed when she told her about the men who had followed Gracie around in Italy.

'And what about you?' the doctor asked her quietly. 'Who followed you around?'

'Are you kidding? Given the choice between me and Gracie, who do you think they'd follow?'

'You're a good-looking woman too,' Dr. Watson confirmed. She could hear how much Victoria had done for her younger sister, and hoped that she had gotten enough emotional sustenance for herself in return.

'Gracie is gorgeous. But I worry about how close she is to my parents,' Victoria admitted to her doctor. 'I don't think it's healthy. They're nicer to her than they ever were to me, but they stifle her, they treat her like a possession. My father fills her head with all his ideas. She needs her own.'

'She's young. She'll get there,' the shrink said philosophically. 'Or maybe she won't. She may be more like them than you think. That may be comfortable for her.'

'I hope not,' Victoria said, and the psychiatrist agreed, but also knew that it didn't always work out that way. And not everyone was as brave as Victoria, breaking free and moving to New York.

'And what about you? Where are you heading these days, Victoria? What are your goals?'

She laughed at the question. She often laughed when she really wanted to cry. It was less scary that way. 'Get skinny and have a life. Meet a man who loves me, and whom I love too.' She had gained weight on the trip, and wanted to lose it over the rest of the summer.

'What are you doing to make that happen?' the psychiatrist asked quietly about the man Victoria hoped to meet.

'Nothing right now. I just got back this weekend. It's not that easy to meet people. Everyone I know is married, in a relationship, or gay.'

'Maybe you need to branch out a little bit, and try some new things. Where are you these days about your weight?' She was usually either on a diet or in deep despair.

'I ate a lot of pasta in Italy and croissants in Paris. I

guess I have to pay the piper now.' She had bought a book about the latest popular diet before she left on the trip and hadn't read it yet. 'It's always a fight.' Something was stopping her from losing the weight she wanted to. And yet she was always sure that on the other side of the weight rainbow stood the man of her dreams.

'You know, you might find someone one of these days who loves you just the way you are. You don't have to go on a crash diet to find someone. Keeping trim is good for your health. But your love life doesn't have to depend on it.'

'No one is going to love me if I'm fat,' she said glumly. It was the message her father had given her for years, almost in the form of a curse.

'That's not true,' the psychiatrist said calmly. 'Someone who loves you will love you fat, thin, or any shape.' Victoria didn't answer, and it was obvious she didn't believe what Dr. Watson had said. She knew better. There were no men pounding down her door, stopping her on the street to beg for her phone number, or asking her for dates. 'You can always go back to the nutritionist. That worked for you pretty well.' And they had discussed Weight Watchers many times, but she never got there. She said she was too busy.

'Yeah, I guess I'll call her in a few weeks.' She wanted

to settle in first. But she wanted to lose some weight before she went back to school. She was in her bigger clothes again after the trip. She talked about her trip again then, and the hour was over. As she walked outside, she had the feeling again that she was stuck. Her life was going nowhere. And she bought herself an ice cream cone on the way home, and told herself what difference did it make anyway. She would start dieting seriously tomorrow.

Harlan and John were home when she got in, and so was Bunny. They were happy to see her, and they had dinner together that night when Bunny got back from the gym. John had made a big bowl of pasta and lobster salad, both of which were irresistible. Harlan could see that she had gained weight, but he didn't say anything. They were just happy to be together again, and Bunny told her she was engaged and showed them her ring. She was getting married the following spring. It didn't come as a surprise to any of them, and Victoria was happy for her.

Gracie had texted her earlier to let her know that she had gotten home, and she called Victoria that night before she went to bed. She said their parents had taken her out to dinner, and she was going to Malibu with friends the next day. She had a busy summer ahead. And

Victoria went to sleep dreaming of Venice, sitting in the gondola next to Gracie under the Bridge of Sighs. And then she dreamed of the risotto milanese they'd eaten at Harry's Bar.

The rest of the summer went by too quickly. Victoria spent the Fourth of July weekend at a bed and breakfast in the Hamptons with Helen and a group of single female teachers from Madison. She went to Maine with Harlan and John in August. There were some blisteringly hot days in New York where she did nothing but lie around. It was too hot to go jogging, so she went to the gym once in a while. It was a token effort, but she wasn't in the mood. She was sad after Gracie left following their trip. They'd had such a good time together. Victoria really missed her, and was lonely without her. She went to one Overeaters Anonymous meeting, and never went back.

And as she had promised, she flew out to California for the weekend to help Gracie settle into her dorm room at USC. It was a day of chaos, bittersweet memories, and tears of hello and goodbye. Victoria helped her unpack, while their father set up her stereo and computer, and their mother neatly folded underwear into a drawer.

Gracie had two roommates in a tiny room, and it was

a major feat getting everyone's things put away in lockers, a single closet, and three chests of drawers, with three desks and three computers crowding the room. And all three sets of parents and Victoria were trying to help their girls. By late afternoon, they had done everything they could, and Gracie walked outside with them. She looked as though she was about to panic, and her father looked like he was about to cry. And Victoria had a heavy heart. Gracie really was grown up now, and they had to open the door to the cage and let her fly. Her parents were far more reluctant to do that, and it wasn't easy for Victoria either.

They were standing outside the door of the dorm, talking, when a tall, good-looking boy with a tennis racket in his hand sauntered by. He stopped the moment he saw Gracie, as though he had been struck by lightning and couldn't move another step. Victoria smiled at the look on his face. She had seen boys react to her sister that way before.

'Freshman?' he asked her. He could tell from the hall where he was standing, and she nodded. She had the same look in her eyes that he did, and Victoria almost laughed. It would be just too simple if Gracie found the man of the moment the day she moved into the dorm. How easy was that?

'Junior? Senior?' she inquired with a hopeful look, and he grinned.

'Business school,' he answered with a broad smile, which meant he was at least four years older than she was, and probably more like five or six. 'Hi,' he said then, glancing at all of them. 'I'm Harry Wilkes.' They had all heard of Wilkes Hall and wondered if he was of the family that had donated it. He shook hands with her parents and Victoria and then smiled dazzlingly at Gracie and asked if she'd like to play tennis at six o'clock. She beamed and said she would. He promised to come back for her then and then jogged off.

'Well, that was easy,' Victoria commented as he left. 'Tennis anyone? You really don't know how lucky you are.'

'Yes, I do,' she said with a dreamy look. 'He's really cute.' And then as though she had been taken over by an alien being from outer space, she spoke to Victoria in an undertone: 'I'm going to marry him one day.'

'Why don't you check him out at tennis first?' Victoria had seen all the boys who had come and gone in her high school days. This was only the beginning of four years of college. She just hoped Gracie didn't follow in their mother's footsteps and spend all four years looking for a husband, instead of having fun. There was no reason to even think of marriage at her age.

'No. Seriously. I am. I just felt it when he said hello to me,' Gracie said with a serious look that made Victoria want to throw water on her to wake her up.

'Hello. This is college. Four years of fun, things to learn, and great guys. Let's not get married the first day.'

'Leave it to your sister to find the richest kid on campus,' their father said proudly, assuming he was the Wilkes of Wilkes Hall. 'He looked pretty taken with her.'

'So was half of Italy in June. Let's not lose our heads here,' Victoria said, trying to be the voice of reason, but no one was listening to her. His name had done it for her father. His looks had done it for Gracie. And the word *marriage* did it for their mother. Poor Harry Wilkes was a goner, Victoria thought to herself, if the three of them got hold of him. 'Listen, you,' she said to her little sister, 'try not to get engaged before I come back for Thanksgiving.' She gave her a big hug then, and the two sisters held each other, wishing they could stop time and freeze this moment forever. 'I love you,' Victoria whispered into her dark curly hair. Gracie looked like a child in her sister's arms, and Gracie looked up at her with tears on her lashes.

'I love you too. I really meant what I said before. I just got this weird feeling about him.'

'Oh shut up,' Victoria said, laughing, and gave her a

sisterly shove. 'Have fun at tennis. Call and tell me how it was.' Victoria wasn't leaving for New York till the morning. There was nothing to stay for once Gracie left the house, nothing to keep Victoria there. There hadn't been in years.

The three of them walked back to the enormous parking lot and found her father's car. Victoria got into the backseat, and they rode in silence all the way home, each of them lost in thought, thinking how fast it had all gone. One minute Gracie was a baby, a toddler careening around the room at full speed, Victoria was taking her to first grade and kissing her goodbye, then suddenly she was a teenager, and now this. And they all knew with sadness and certainty that the next four years would wing past them just as fast.

Chapter 16

Their collective fear that Gracie's college years would rush by too quickly proved to be true. It happened in the blink of an eye, and the next thing they all knew, she was graduating from USC. She was in a cap and gown, and her parents and older sister saw her hat fly high in the air again. It was over. Four years of college. She had a bachelor's degree in English and communications, and hadn't figured out how to use it yet. She wanted to work for a magazine or a newspaper, but hadn't started interviewing yet. She was taking the summer off and planned to look for a job in September. And she had their father's blessing. She was going to Europe with friends in July, to Spain and Italy, and her boyfriend was going with them, and then the two of them were meeting up with his parents in the South of France. Her prediction on her first day at USC had almost materialized. They weren't married, but Harry Wilkes had been her boyfriend for all four years of college, and Gracie's father heartily approved. They were indeed the family that had donated the hall of the same name. Harry had graduated from business school the year before, and he was working for his father in an investment banking firm. He was solid as a rock, her father liked to say, and a very good catch. He was with them along with half a dozen of her friends when they went to lunch after graduation, and Victoria noticed them talking conspiratorially at the other end of the table, and then he kissed her and she smiled.

Victoria liked Harry, although she thought him a little too controlling, and she wished her younger sister had been more adventurous while she was in college. She had been with Harry constantly. She had left the dorms in junior year to live in an apartment with him off campus, and they were still living together now. Victoria thought she was too young to be so settled so early and limited to one boy. And he reminded her a little of her father, which made her nervous too. Harry had opinions about everything, and Gracie endorsed all of them, with no differences of her own. Victoria didn't want her turning into their mother one day. A shadow of her husband, put on earth to enhance him and make him feel good about himself. What about her?

But there was no denying that Gracie was happy with Harry. And Victoria had been shocked when her parents made no objection to the two of them living together. She was sure they wouldn't have done the same for her. And when she had mentioned it to her father, he told her not to be so uptight and old-fashioned, but part of that was because Harry's family had so much money. Victoria was sure that they wouldn't have been as easy-going if Harry Wilkes were poor. She had said as much to Helen, and Harlan and John, whenever she talked to them about it. She worried about Gracie a lot. She was always fearful that Gracie had been brainwashed by their parents into pursuing all the wrong ideals.

The luncheon celebration had started late after graduation and went on until four in the afternoon. They finally left the table, and Gracie went to return her rented cap and gown. She handed Victoria her diploma for safe-keeping, and said Harry was going to drive her home. They were going out with friends that night. Harry was driving the Ferrari his parents had given him when he graduated from business school. Victoria saw them kiss as soon as they walked away, and it seemed only yesterday that he had been standing holding a tennis racket outside her dorm the day she moved in as a freshman.

'I must be getting old,' Victoria said to her father as they got in his car and drove away. She was turning twenty-nine. 'She was five years old about five minutes ago. How did we get here?'

'Damned if I know. I feel the same way about you.' He even managed to look sentimental as he said it, which surprised Victoria.

During Gracie's four years in college, Victoria had gone out with a few men she'd met here and there, an attorney, a teacher, a stockbroker, a journalist. But none of them had mattered to her, and the relationships had only lasted a few weeks or months. She was the head of the English department at Madison now, and still living in the same apartment. She shared it with only Harlan and John. They each used a second bedroom as a study. Bunny had gotten married three years before and had two children. She had just moved to Washington, D.C., with her husband and babies. He had a State Department job, which they all suspected was really CIA, and she was a stay-at-home mom. Harlan was still working at the Costume Institute, and John was teaching at the same school in the Bronx. And she had stopped seeing Dr. Watson two years before. There was nothing more to say to her. They had covered the same territory many times, and they agreed. There were no mysteries left to discover. Her parents had given her a raw deal and poured all their love into her sister, and had never had any for her, even before Gracie was born. In plain talk, she'd been screwed, but she loved her sister dearly anyway. And she had very little feeling for her parents, neither anger nor affection. They were selfish, self-centered people who should never have had children at all, or not her anyway. Gracie suited them. She didn't. And Victoria was doing fine in spite of it. Victoria felt that Dr. Watson had helped her a great deal. She still had the same parents, and a problem with her weight, but she was dealing with both more successfully than before.

She still hadn't found the man of her dreams and maybe she never would, but she loved her job, she was still teaching seniors, and her weight still fluctuated up and down. Her eating habits depended on the weather, her job, the state of her love life or lack of it, or her mood. At the moment she was heavier than she liked. She hadn't had a date in about a year, but she always insisted that her weight had nothing to do with her love life and the two weren't related. Harlan was always vocal about disagreeing with her, and pointed out that she gained weight, and ate more, when she was lonely and miserable. They had put a treadmill in the living room, and a rowing machine, both of which she had contributed to, and she never used them. Harlan and John always did.

Victoria was going back to New York the morning after Gracie's graduation, and she had dinner with her parents at home that night. It was a sacrifice she made at least once in every trip. Her father was talking about retiring early in a few years. Her mother was still a fanatical bridge player. And Victoria had less and less to say to them every year. Her father's jokes about her weight weren't amusing, and now he had added to them comments about the fact that she wasn't married, didn't have a boyfriend, and wasn't likely to have kids. He tied it all to her weight. She didn't argue about it with him anymore, or try to defend herself or explain. She just let the comments and wisecracks go by without answering them. They never changed. And he still thought her job was a total waste of time.

At dinner, he talked about getting Gracie a job as a copywriter at his ad agency, after she came home from Europe. Victoria was helping her mother load the dishwasher after dinner when Gracie came home unexpectedly. Since she was living with Harry, she didn't drop by very often, and they were all surprised to see her, and pleased. Her cheeks were pink and her eyes were sparkling as she stood in the kitchen and looked at them.

And Victoria had a sudden flutter in her stomach as Gracie blurted out the words she feared.

'I'm *engaged!*' There was a deadly silence in the room for a fraction of a second, and then her father let out a whoop and spun her around in his arms as he had when she was a child.

'Bravo! Well done! Where's Harry? I want to congratulate him too!'

'He dropped me off. He went to tell his parents,' she said happily, as Victoria went back to the dishes without a word. And their mother was clucking and flapping and hugged her daughter. And with that, Gracie stuck out her small hand, and they could see a large round diamond ring on her finger. It was really happening. It was true.

'This is just like your father and me,' her mother said excitedly. 'We got engaged the night we graduated. And married at Christmas.' They all knew. 'When's the wedding?' she asked, as though she wanted to start planning it right away. They didn't question for a minute what she was doing, or if she was too young, for obvious reasons relating to Harry. They thought it was a great idea, and a major coup for their daughter to marry a Wilkes. It was all about their egos, not what might be best for Gracie. Victoria finally turned around then, and looked at her younger sister with worried eyes.

'Don't you think you're too young?' she asked honestly. Gracie was just twenty-two, and Harry was twenty-seven, which was still young in Victoria's opinion.

'We've been dating for four years,' Gracie said as though that made it all right, but it didn't to her sister. It made it worse. She never gave herself a chance to grow on her own, develop her own opinions, or meet other boys in college, or even date them.

'Some of my high school kids have dated people for four years. They're not old enough to get married either. I'm worried about you,' she said honestly. 'You're twenty-two years old. You need a real job, a career, some independence, and your own life before you settle down and get married. What's the rush?' For a minute she was terrified that she might be pregnant, but she didn't think she was. Gracie had announced that she was going to marry him the first day they met. And now it had happened. He was her dream come true. This was what Gracie wanted, and she looked angry at Victoria for the questions she was asking and the obvious lack of enthusiasm she showed.

'Can't you be happy for me?' she asked petulantly. 'Does everything have to be the way you think it should be? I'm happy. I love Harry. I don't care about a career. I don't have a vocation like you. I just want to be Harry's wife!' It didn't seem like enough to Victoria, but maybe Gracie was right. And who was she to decide?

'I'm sorry,' she said sadly. They hadn't had an argument in years. And the last one had been about their parents, when Gracie had hotly defended them to her sister, and Victoria told her how wrong she was. She had finally backed down, because her sister was too young to understand, and was one of them anyway. And this time she felt the same way. Victoria was the one who was different again, who wasn't happy for her and dared to say it, who didn't fit in. 'I just want you to be happy, and have the best life you can. And I think you're very young.'

'It looks like she's going to have a good life to me,' her father said, pointing at the ring. Seeing him do that made Victoria feel sick. And she knew she wasn't jealous. But having a daughter who was married to a rich man was going to be a perfect complement to her father's narcissism. With the ring on her finger, Gracie had become a trophy, proof of his success as a father, that he had raised a daughter who could marry a rich man. Victoria hated what it meant. And Gracie didn't see it. She was too wrapped up in her own life, and too afraid to go out in the real world, get a job, meet new people, make something of herself. So she was marrying Harry instead. And just as Victoria thought it, Harry walked into the kitchen, beaming, and Gracie jumped into his arms. It was easy to see how happy she was, and no one wanted to deny that to her. Their father clapped Harry on the back, and their mother went to get a bottle of champagne, which Jim opened immediately, and poured a glass for each of them, as Victoria looked at them and smiled nostalgically. The milestones were moving faster now. Graduation from high school, college, and now she was engaged. It was a lot to digest all at once. And putting her objections aside, Victoria walked across the room and hugged Harry, for her sister's sake, as Gracie looked at her, relieved. She didn't want anyone interfering with what she was doing, trying to stop her, or challenging her. This was her dream.

'So when's the big day? Have you set the date?' her father asked, after they toasted the couple and each took a sip of champagne.

Harry and Gracie were beaming at each other again, and Harry answered for her, which was one of the things Victoria didn't like about him. Gracie had a voice too, and she wanted her to use it. She hoped the wedding wouldn't be too soon.

'June,' Harry said, smiling at his tiny bride. 'We have a lot to organize before then. Gracie is going to be busy planning the wedding.' He glanced from his future mother-in-law to his future sister-in-law, as though he expected them to drop everything and get to work on the wedding too. 'We're figuring on four or five hundred people,' he said blithely, without consulting the bride's parents to ask if that was okay. He hadn't asked for her hand either. He had proposed, but he also had known that Jim Dawson would approve. Grace's mother looked like she was going to faint when she heard the number of guests at the wedding. But Jim looked pleased as he opened another bottle of champagne and poured another round.

'You ladies can figure all of that out,' he said, smiling first at Harry and then at his wife and daughters. 'All I have to do is pay the bills.' Victoria stood watching her father, thinking that he was a sellout, but this was the kind of match he wanted for his daughter, without questioning if she was too young or if it might be a mistake. And Victoria knew that if she said anything to them, she would then be accused of being the overweight older daughter who didn't have a boyfriend and couldn't find a husband, who was jealous of her beautiful younger sister and wanted to stand in her way.

They finished the second bottle of champagne, and everyone hugged the young couple again. Harry said his parents wanted to have dinner with them sometime soon. And Victoria got a chance to hug her sister again.

'I love you. I'm sorry if I upset you.'

'It's okay,' Gracie whispered. 'I just want you to be happy for me.' Victoria nodded. She didn't know what to say. And then the newly engaged couple went on their way. They were meeting friends and going to a party, and Gracie wanted to show off her ring. Victoria heard her BlackBerry come to life after they left, and checked it. It was from her sister. 'I love you. Be happy for me.' Victoria answered just as quickly with the only response she could give her. Her response said, 'I love you too.'

'Well, you've got a year to plan the wedding,' Jim said to Christine as soon as Grace and Harry left. 'That'll keep you busy. You may even have to take some time off from bridge.' As he said it, Victoria got another text. It was from Gracie again.

'Maid of honor?' it said, and Victoria smiled. They were going to rope her into this one way or another, but she wouldn't have dreamed of denying her sister, or herself, that honor, if she was going through with this.

'Yes. Thank you. Of course!' she answered Gracie by text. So she was the maid of honor, and her baby sister was getting married. It had been quite a day!

Chapter 17

As soon as Victoria flew back to New York, two days after Gracie's graduation, she called Dr. Watson. Her psychiatrist was still in the same place, with the same number, and called Victoria back on her cell phone that night. And she asked how she had been. She said she was fine and was anxious to see her, so Dr. Watson managed to squeeze her in the next day. She noticed when Victoria walked in that she looked slightly more grown up but essentially the same. She hadn't changed. Victoria was wearing black jeans, a white T-shirt, and sandals. It was a hot New York summer day. And her weight was about the same as it had been the last time they met. No better and no worse.

'Is everything all right?' the psychiatrist asked her,

sounding concerned. 'You sounded like it was urgent.'

'I think it is. I think I'm having some kind of wake-up call or identity crisis or something.' She had been upset since graduation day. It was hard enough watching Gracie graduate, without having her get engaged on the same day. 'My little sister got engaged a few days ago. She's twenty-two years old. She got engaged on her graduation day from college, just like my parents. They think it's fine since the man she's marrying, or wants to, has tons of money. I think they're all crazy. She's twenty-two years old. She won't have a job, he doesn't want her to. She wanted to work in journalism, now she doesn't care. And she's going to end up just like my mother, being a backdrop for him, and seconding all his opinions, of which her fiancé has many, just like my father. She's going to lose herself married to this guy, and the thought of it is making me crazy for her. And all she wants to do is get married. I think she's too young. Or maybe I'm just jealous because I have no life. All I have is a job I love. That's it. And if I say anything about thinking she shouldn't get married, to her or my parents, they'll think it's sour grapes.' The story poured out of her like marbles rolling down a hill.

'Is it sour grapes?' the shrink asked her bluntly.

'I don't know.' Victoria was always honest with her.

'What do you want, Victoria?' the doctor pressed her. She knew it was time to do that now. Victoria was ready. 'Not for her. For yourself.'

'I don't know,' she said again, but the doctor knew better.

'Yes, you do. Stop worrying about your sister. Think of yourself. Why are you back here? What do you want?' Tears filled Victoria's eyes as she listened to the question. She did know. She was just afraid to say it, or admit it to herself.

'I want a life,' she said softly. 'I want a man in my life. I want what my sister wants. The difference is I'm old enough to have it, and I never will.' Her voice suddenly grew stronger, and she felt braver. 'I want a life, a man, and I want to lose twenty-five pounds by next June, or at least twenty.' It was clear.

'What's happening in June?' The doctor looked puzzled.

'Her wedding. I'm the maid of honor. I don't want everyone to feel sorry for me because I'm a loser. Her fat spinster older sister. That's not who I want to be at her wedding.'

'Okay. That's fair. We've got a year to work on it. That sounds reasonable to me,' the psychiatrist said, smiling at her. 'There are three projects here. "A life," you said, and you have to define what that means to you. A man. And your weight. We've got work to do.'

'Okay,' Victoria said with a quaver in her voice. It was an emotional moment for her. She had had an epiphany. She was tired of not having what she wanted, and not even admitting it to herself because she thought she didn't deserve it, because her parents had told her so. 'I'm ready.'

'I think you are,' the doctor said, looking pleased, as she glanced at the clock behind Victoria's shoulder. 'See you next week?' Victoria nodded, suddenly aware of all that she had to do. This was bigger than a wedding. She had to go on a serious weight-loss program, and do whatever she had to do to keep it off this time. She had to make an effort to get out in the world and meet men, and dress for the part. And open her life to other opportunities, people, places, things, everything she had been longing for but never had had the courage to do. This was scarier than when she'd moved to New York, and harder to organize than any wedding. But she knew she had to do it. When Gracie got married, Victoria would be thirty. By then she wanted her dream too, not just Gracie's.

She walked back from the doctor's office feeling empowered. She walked into the apartment, went straight to the kitchen, and started cleaning out the fridge. She started with the freezer and threw all the frozen pizzas and eight pints of ice cream into the garbage. As she was doing it, Harlan and John walked in. John was working at the museum with him that summer, during summer break from school.

'Oh shit, this looks serious,' Harlan said, looking at her in amazement. The chocolate candy she'd brought home from a school party went next, and a cheesecake she had left in the fridge half eaten. 'Is there a message here, or are you just doing spring cleaning?'

'I'm losing twenty-five pounds by June, and keeping them off this time.'

'Is there some reason for this resolution?' he asked cautiously, as John reached into the fridge and took out two beers. He opened them and handed one to Harlan and took a swig of his own. It tasted good. But beer wasn't her thing. She preferred wine, which was fattening too. 'A new guy maybe?' Harlan asked her, looking hopeful.

'That too. I just haven't met him yet.' She turned to face them as she closed the freezer door. 'Gracie's getting married in June. I'm not going to be the maid of honor at that wedding, twenty-five pounds overweight and living like an old maid. I went back to my shrink.'

'This sounds like Sherman's march on Georgia,' Harlan said, looking pleased for her. This was exactly what she needed and had for years. He'd been losing hope for her recently. Her eating habits were as bad as ever, and her weight never changed. 'You go, girl! Let us know if there's anything we can do.'

'No more ice cream. No pizza. I'll do the treadmill. I'll go to the gym. Maybe Weight Watchers. A nutritionist. A hypnotist. Whatever it takes, I'll do it.'

'Who's Gracie marrying, by the way? Isn't she a little young? She just graduated last week.'

'She's way too young, and it's totally stupid. My father loves him because he's rich. It's the same guy she's been dating for four years.'

'That's too bad. But you never know. Maybe it'll work.'

'I hope so for her. She's going to give up her whole identity to marry him. But it's what she wants, or thinks she does.'

'It's a long way till June. A lot could happen by then.'

'That's true,' she said with a fierce light in her eye that he hadn't seen in years, maybe ever. She was on a holy mission. 'I'm counting on it. I have one year to get my life and body into shape.'

'You can do it,' Harlan said with conviction.

'I know I can,' she said, and finally believed it, wondering what had taken her so long. For twenty-nine years she had believed her parents, that she was ugly, fat, and doomed to failure because she was unlovable. And she suddenly realized that just because they said it, or thought so, didn't mean that it was true. She was bound and determined now to shed the shackles they had put on her. All she wanted now was to be free.

She signed up at Weight Watchers the next day, and came home with instructions and a scale for food. And she enrolled at a new gym the day after. They had beautiful machines, a weight room, a dance studio, a sauna, and a pool. Victoria went there every day. She jogged around the reservoir every morning. She followed her diet diligently, and went in to be weighed once a week. She talked to Gracie nearly every day about the wedding, and her mother more than she wanted to. It was all they thought about now. Victoria called it Wedding Fever. She had lost nine pounds by the first day of school, and she felt good. She was in shape. She still had a long way to go. She had reached a plateau, but she was determined not to get discouraged. She'd been there before. Many times. But this time she was not going to let go, and she was seeing her shrink regularly. They were talking about her parents, her hopes for her sister, and they were finally talking about what she wanted for herself. She had never done that before.

Her students felt the difference in her too. She was

stronger and more sure of herself. Helen and Carla told her they were proud of her.

Victoria was annoyed that her sister wasn't working and hadn't since graduation. She wasn't even looking for a job now that she was engaged, which Victoria didn't think was good for her, or her self-esteem. She said she had no time, but Victoria knew there was more to life than just planning a wedding, and being married to a wealthy man. Her shrink told her it wasn't her problem, and to concentrate on herself, so she was. But her concern for her sister troubled her too.

She only lost two pounds in September. But she had lost eleven in all, so she was halfway to her goal, and looking fit, when Gracie announced in October that she was coming for the weekend to look at wedding gowns, and pick bridesmaids' dresses, and she wanted Victoria's help. Victoria wasn't sure she was ready to do that, but Gracie was the baby sister she loved and could never deny anything to, so she agreed, despite a stack of papers she had to correct that weekend. Her shrink asked why she hadn't asked Gracie to come some other time. The wedding wasn't until June.

'I couldn't do that,' Victoria said honestly.

'Why not?'

'I'm not good at saying no to her. I never do.'

'Why don't you want her to come this weekend?' They were into total honesty.

'I have work to do,' Victoria said easily as the doctor looked at her and called her on it.

'Is that really the reason?'

'No. I haven't lost enough weight, and I'm scared she'll pick a bridesmaid dress I look awful in. All her friends are the same size she is. They're all a size two or four. They've never heard of a size fourteen.'

'You are you. You won't be a size fourteen by next June,' the doctor reassured her. Victoria hadn't wavered in her resolve.

'What if I am?' she said with a look of panic. Her dream was to be a size eight. But even a ten would have been thrilling if she could maintain that weight.

'Why do you think you won't succeed?'

'Because I'm afraid my father's right, and I'm a loser. Gracie just proved him right again. She's going to be married at twenty-two to the perfect guy. I'll be thirty by the time she gets married. I'm still not married. I don't even have a boyfriend, or a date. And I'm just a schoolteacher.'

'And a good one,' the doctor reminded her. 'You're the head of the English department at the best private high school in New York. That's not small potatoes.' Victoria smiled at what she said. 'Besides, you're the maid of honor. You can wear a variation or even something entirely different, if she picks something that won't look good on you. She's giving you a chance to choose.'

'No,' Victoria corrected her. She knew her baby sister. She might be willing to let Harry run the show, but she had her own ideas about some things. 'She's giving me a chance to watch *her* choose.'

'Then this is an opportunity to do things differently with her,' the therapist suggested.

'I'll try.' But Victoria didn't sound convinced.

Gracie arrived on Friday morning while Victoria was still at school, and she rushed back to the apartment to meet her as soon as she could. She had left the key under the mat outside the apartment, and Gracie was inside, waiting for her, walking at a brisk pace on the treadmill.

'This thing is pretty good,' she said as she grinned at her sister. She looked like an elf or a child on the big machine.

'It should be,' Victoria answered. 'It cost us a fortune.'

'You should try it sometime,' Gracie said as she hopped off.

'I have been,' Victoria said, proud of the weight she'd lost so far, and disappointed that Gracie didn't notice. Her head was totally into the wedding, as she hugged her older sister. She wanted to go downtown right away and start shopping. She had a list of stores she wanted to get to. Victoria had been at school all day and felt like a mess. She'd had to get there early for a department meeting. But she got ready in five minutes, and they left to go downtown. It was hard not to be distracted by the giant rock on her finger. 'Aren't you afraid you might get hit on the head wearing that thing?' She still worried about her. She would always be her baby sister, no different than the day she'd walked her into first grade.

'No one thinks it's real,' Gracie said nonchalantly as they got out of the cab at Bergdorf's.

They went upstairs to the wedding department and started looking at gowns. They had a dozen of them hanging on racks and spread out around them as Gracie looked around and shook her head. None of them looked right to her, although Victoria thought they were gorgeous. Gracie shifted gears then and asked to see bridesmaids' dresses. She had a list of designers and colors that she wanted to check out. And they brought everything they had to her. It was going to be a formal evening wedding. Harry was going to wear white tie, and the groomsmen black tie. And so far she was thinking of peach, pale blue, or champagne for the bridesmaids, all of them colors that Victoria could wear. She was so fair and had such pale skin that there were some colors she just couldn't get away with, like red, for instance, but Gracie assured her that she would never put her bridesmaids in red. She looked like a little general marshaling her troops as the saleswomen brought her things. Gracie was in full control, and planning what appeared to be a major national event, like a rock concert or a world's fair or a presidential campaign. This was her finest hour, and she was going to be the star of the show. Victoria couldn't help wondering how her mother was dealing with it. It was a little overwhelming at close range, and their father was sparing no expense. He wanted the Wilkeses to be impressed, and his favorite daughter to be proud. In the heat of her intense concentration on what she was doing, Gracie still hadn't noticed the weight Victoria had lost, which hurt her feelings, but she didn't want to be childish about it, and she paid attention to the gowns that Gracie was picking out. She had three maybes in mind when they left. And there were going to be ten bridesmaids. It occurred to Victoria, when Gracie told her, that if she had been getting married, she didn't even have ten friends. She would have had Gracie as her only attendant, and that was it. But Gracie had always been a golden child. And now she was the star, and loving every minute of it. She was becoming more like their parents than Victoria wanted to admit. She came from a family of stars, and Victoria felt like a meteor that had fallen to earth in a heap of ash.

They went to Barneys after that, and finally wound up at Saks. And for the following day Gracie had made an appointment with Vera Wang herself. She also wanted to see Oscar de la Renta, but hadn't had time to set it up. Victoria was beginning to realize just how big an event it was. And the Wilkeses were giving a black-tie rehearsal dinner that was going to be bigger and more elaborate than most weddings. So it was going to be a double header in terms of the dresses that they'd need. Gracie said that their mother had already decided to wear beige to the wedding, and emerald green to the rehearsal dinner the night before. She was all set. She had gone to Neiman Marcus, and the personal shopper had found the perfect dresses for her for both events. So Gracie could concentrate on herself.

She didn't like the bridal gowns at Saks either, and made it clear that she was looking for something extraordinary for her wedding. Gracie, the baby sister, had come into her own. Suddenly nothing was special enough for her. Victoria was a little shocked at how determined she was. And Gracie wasn't excited about the bridesmaids' dresses she saw either, and then she gave a gasp when she saw a gown.

'Oh my God,' she said with a look of amazement, as though she'd found the holy grail. 'That's it! I'd never have thought of that color!' It was without question a spectacular gown, although Victoria couldn't picture it at a wedding, particularly multiplied by ten. Brown was the color of the season going into the fall. It was softer than black, the saleswoman explained to them, and very 'warm.' The dress that had caught Gracie's attention was a heavy satin strapless gown, with tiny tucks close to the body to just below the hipline, and then it widened into a bell-shaped evening gown to the floor. The workmanship on it was exquisite, and it was a deep chocolate brown. The only trouble with it, from Victoria's perspective, was that only a tiny, wraithlike flat-chested woman could wear it. The place where it stopped hugging the body and flared at the hips would make Victoria's bottom look like the broad side of a barn. It was a dress that only a girl with Gracie's proportions could wear well, and most of her friends looked like her. The sample she was looking at would have been too big for her and was a size four. Victoria didn't want to imagine what it would look like on her even if she lost weight.

'Everyone's going to love it,' Gracie exclaimed with a delirious expression. 'They can wear it afterward to any black-tie event.' The dress was expensive, but it wasn't a problem for most of her bridesmaids, and her father had promised to cover the difference if she found a dress that some of her bridesmaids couldn't afford. The price wasn't the issue for Victoria, since her father was paying for it. The problem was that the dress would look hideous on her. Her breasts and hips were just too large for the style. And to add to her misery as she looked at it, it was the color of bittersweet chocolate, which Victoria just couldn't wear with her fair skin, blue eyes, and pale blond hair.

'I can't wear that dress,' she said reasonably to her sister. 'I'll look like a mountain of chocolate mousse, with either spelling. Even if I lost fifty pounds. Or maybe a hundred. My chest is too big. And I can't wear that color.' Her sister looked at her with imploring eyes.

'It's exactly what I wanted. I just didn't know it. It's a gorgeous gown.'

'Yes, it is,' Victoria readily agreed with her, 'but for someone your size. If you wear that, and I wear the wedding gown, it'll be perfect. That dress will be frightening on me. I'm sure it doesn't even come in my size.'

'You can order it in any size,' the saleswoman said helpfully. It was an expensive dress, and would have made a handsome sale.

'Can we get ten of them by June?' Gracie asked with a look of panic, totally ignoring her sister's pleas for mercy.

'I'm sure we can. We can probably have them for you by December, if you get me all the sizes.' Gracie looked relieved and Victoria near tears.

'Gracie, you can't do that to me. I'll look horrible in that dress.'

'No, you won't. You said you want to lose weight anyway.'

'I still couldn't wear it. I wear a double-D bra. You have to be built like you to wear that dress.' Gracie looked up at her with tears in her eyes, with the same look that had melted her older sister's heart since she was five.

'I'm only getting married once,' she said imploringly. 'I want everything to be perfect for Harry. I want this to be my dream wedding. Everyone has pink and blue and pastel colors. No one ever even thinks of brown for the bridesmaids. It'll be the most elegant wedding L.A. has ever seen.'

'With a maid of honor who looks like an elephant.'

'You'll lose weight by then, I know it. You always do when you try.'

'That's not the point. I'd have to have surgery to pull this one off.' And the tiny tucks of fabric all the way down the long-waisted bodice would only make it worse.

Gracie was already planning to have the bridesmaids carry brown orchids to go with the dress. Nothing was going to dissuade her from it, and she placed the order while Victoria stood by wanting to cry. Her sister had just ensured that she would look like a monster at the wedding, while all her tiny anorexic friends would look stylish in the brown strapless gowns. There was no question that the dress was beautiful, but not on Victoria. She gave up trying to dissuade her, and sat silently while Gracie gave the saleswoman the sizes for most of the gowns. They were almost all size fours, except for three size twos. She was going to confirm the rest of the sizes when she got home. She had a look of elation on her face when they left the store. She was almost dancing she was so excited, and Victoria sat in silence in the cab all the way uptown. They stopped at the deli on the way back to the apartment, and without thinking, Victoria put three pints of Häagen-Dazs on the counter. Gracie didn't even notice. She was used to Victoria buying ice cream. She had no idea that Victoria hadn't had any in four months. This was like a recovering alcoholic sidling up to the bar and ordering a vodka on the rocks.

They went back to the apartment, and Gracie called their mother while Victoria unpacked the groceries, just as Harlan walked in. He took one look at the ice cream, pointed at it as though it were on fire, and stared at Victoria in horror and disbelief.

'What's *that*?'

'She ordered strapless brown gowns for the brides-maids that I can't wear.'

'Then tell her you can't wear it, and to order you something else,' he said, taking the ice cream from Victoria's hand and dropping it in the trash. 'Maybe the dress isn't as bad as you think.'

'It's gorgeous. Just not on me. I can't even wear that color, let alone the shape.'

'Tell her,' he said firmly, sounding like her shrink.

'I did. She won't listen to me. This is her dream wedding. She's only planning to do it once, and it has to be perfect. For everyone but me.'

'She's a nice kid. Explain it to her.'

'She's a bride, on a mission. We must have looked at a hundred gowns today. This is going to be the event of the century.'

'It won't help anything to blow the diet now,' he said, trying to encourage her. It had upset him to see her with the ice cream in her hand. She had been so good until then. And he didn't want her to blow it now over a stupid gown.

Gracie was on the phone by then with all her friends,

telling them about the fabulous dress she'd ordered for all of them, and Victoria had a sense of hopelessness as she sat down in the kitchen. She felt like an invisible person again. Gracie wasn't hearing her. It was all about Gracie right now. It was hard to live with, and she was depressed about the dress. She didn't know what to do about it. It was clear that Gracie wasn't going to listen to her, no matter what.

They had dinner with John and Harlan in the kitchen that night, and Gracie told them all the details of the wedding. By the end of the meal, Victoria wanted to throw up.

'Maybe I'm just jealous,' she said to Harlan in a whisper after Gracie left the room to call Harry before she went to bed.

'I don't think you are. It's a little much. She's like a kid out of control. Your father is creating a monster, letting her do whatever she wants with the wedding.'

'He thinks it makes him look important,' Victoria said, still looking depressed. It was the first time in her life that she hadn't enjoyed Gracie's company. So far, the weekend was a catastrophe.

And the next day wasn't much better. Victoria went with her for her appointment with Vera Wang. They looked at a dozen wedding dress possibilities, and finally the designer offered to send her sketches based on what Gracie had said. She was thrilled.

It was afternoon by then, and they went to Serendipity for lunch. Gracie ordered a salad, and Victoria ordered the cheese ravioli, and a frozen mochaccino topped with whipped cream, and ate it all. Gracie saw nothing unusual in what her sister had ordered, because she was used to Victoria eating things like that. And blowing her diet depressed Victoria even more. By the time they got back to the apartment, she was exhausted, depressed, and felt as if she were about to explode. She hadn't eaten anything like that in months, and Harlan could see the guilt on her face.

'What did you do today?'

'I met Vera Wang,' she said vaguely.

'That's not what I meant, and you know it. What did you eat for lunch?'

'You don't want to know. I shot my diet all to hell,' she said, looking guilty.

'It's not worth it, Victoria,' he reminded her. 'You've worked too hard for this for the past four months. Don't fuck it up.'

'The wedding is making me nervous. I'm suicidal over the dress I have to wear. And my sister is turning into someone I don't know. She shouldn't even be marrying the guy, or anyone, at her age. And he's going to run her life just like my father does. She's marrying our father,' she said miserably.

'Let her, if that's what she wants. She's old enough to make her own choice, even if it's a mistake. You can't screw up your life on top of it. That's not going to change anything, except make you miserable. Just forget about the wedding. Wear whatever you have to, get drunk at the wedding, and come home.' She laughed at what he said.

'Maybe you have a point. And besides, it's eight months away. Even if the dress is wrong for me I could still lose a lot of weight by then and look good.'

'Not if you blow your diet.'

'I won't. I'll be good tonight. We're staying home. And she's going back to L.A. tomorrow. I'll be back on the wagon as soon as she leaves.'

'No. Now,' he reminded her, and went to his own room. Victoria got on the treadmill then, to atone for her sins. And Gracie ordered a pizza from the restaurant whose card was on the fridge. It arrived half an hour later, and was more than Victoria could resist. Gracie ate one piece. And her older sister finished the rest. She wanted to eat the box so Harlan wouldn't see it, but he did. He looked at her as though she had killed someone. And she had. Herself. She was consumed with guilt.

And they went out for lunch the next day before Gracie left. To thank her for her help, Gracie took her to the Carlyle for brunch, and Victoria had eggs Benedict, and when Gracie ordered hot chocolate and little cookies, she couldn't resist them.

Gracie thanked her profusely when she left for the airport, and they hugged each other tight. She said she had had a terrific time, and would keep her posted on the designs from Vera Wang and everything else. Victoria stood on the sidewalk waving to her as the cab pulled away, and as soon as it was out of sight, Victoria burst into tears. From her perspective, the weekend had been an utter and complete disaster, and she felt like a total failure at everything. And on top of it, she was going to look awful at the wedding. She went upstairs, let herself into the apartment, and went to bed, wishing she were dead.

Chapter 18

It was a relief for Victoria to go back to school on Monday. At least it was a world she understood, and where she had some control. She felt as though her sister Gracie was totally out of control with the wedding, and just being around her was depressing these days. And the effect on Victoria had been disastrous. She had gone totally berserk with everything she ate. She had an appointment with Dr. Watson that afternoon after school, and she told her about all of it and how depressed she was.

'I was like a crazy person,' she confessed, 'eating everything in sight. I haven't eaten like that in years. Or months anyway. I weighed myself this morning, and I put on three pounds.'

'You'll lose it again,' Dr. Watson reassured her. 'Why do you think it happened?' She looked interested and not panicked.

'I felt invisible again, like nothing I said mattered. She's turning into one of them.'

'Maybe she always was.'

'No, she wasn't. But the guy she's marrying is just like my father. I feel outnumbered now. And the dress she wants me to wear to the wedding will look awful on me.'

'Why didn't you speak up?'

'I tried. She wouldn't listen. She ordered it anyway. She's being a terrible brat at the moment.'

'That happens to brides sometimes. She sounds completely unreasonable.'

'She is. She wants her dream wedding. And she shouldn't be marrying this guy at all. She'll wind up like my mother, and I don't want that to happen to her.'

'You can't alter that,' the doctor reminded her. 'The only person you can control is yourself.' Victoria was beginning to understand that, but it was painful to watch Grace become just like their parents. Victoria felt better when she left the psychiatrist's office. She spent an hour on the treadmill when she got home, and then she went to the gym.

Victoria came back at eight o'clock, and she was so

exhausted, she went to bed. Gracie had sent her two texts that day, thanking her again. Victoria felt guilty about being so upset about the weekend. Although Gracie had thought it was fabulous, it hadn't been fun for her. She could hardly wait for the wedding to be over, so they could spend some decent time together again. It was going to be a long eight months.

The next day Victoria went to Weight Watchers before she went to work. She confessed her sins to one of the counselors and submitted to the weigh-in. She had already lost two of the pounds she'd gained on the weekend, which was a relief, and she was back on track again.

She taught three classes back to back before lunch, and she was just leaving her classroom and heading for her office, when she saw one of her students crying in the hall. The girl had a look of despair on her face, and she darted into the ladies' room when she saw Victoria coming, which worried her. She followed her inside and found her in the bathroom alone.

'Are you okay?' Victoria asked her cautiously. The girl's name was Amy Green, she was a good student, and Victoria knew from the grapevine that the girl's parents were getting divorced.

'Yeah, I'm fine,' Amy said, dissolving into tears again.

Victoria handed her several tissues, and Amy blew her nose and looked embarrassed.

'Is there anything I can do?' The girl shook her head, speechless with despair. 'Do you want to come to my office for a few minutes, or go for a walk?' Amy hesitated, and then nodded. Victoria had always been nice to her, and Amy thought she was 'cool.'

Her office was only a few doors away, and Amy followed her. Victoria closed the door as soon as Amy walked in, and she waved her to a chair. Victoria poured some bottled water into a glass and handed it to her, while Amy dissolved into uncontrollable sobs again. Things weren't looking good. Victoria sat quietly waiting for her to calm down. And then finally Amy looked at her in utter terror.

'I'm pregnant,' she sobbed. 'I didn't even know. I just found out yesterday.' And it was easy to guess who the boy was. She had been dating the same one for two years, and he was a nice kid. They were both graduating in June. It suddenly pushed all thoughts of her sister's wedding from Victoria's mind.

'Have you told your mom yet?' Victoria asked quietly, handing her more tissues.

'I can't. She'll kill me. She's upset about the divorce.' Her father had left for another woman, and Victoria had heard rumors about it. 'And now this. I don't know what to do.'

'Does Justin know?'

Amy nodded. 'We just went to the doctor. We used a condom, and it broke. And I stopped taking the Pill because it made me sick.'

'Shit,' Victoria said, and Amy laughed through her tears.

'You can say that again.'

'Okay, shit.' This time they both laughed, although it was no laughing matter. 'Do you know what you want to do about it?' It was a decision she would have to make with her parents, but Victoria could listen.

'I don't know. I'm too young to have a baby. But I don't want to have an abortion. Will they kick me out of school?' She looked panicked, and was suddenly sorry she had told her.

'I don't know,' Victoria said honestly. In her seven years at the school, she had never dealt with this before. She knew other students had gotten pregnant, and she had heard about it, but she had never been in the front lines or the first to know. Those things were usually handled by the counseling staff, the dean of students, or the headmaster. She was just an English teacher, even if she was the head of the department. But she was a woman and could relate to this young girl, although it had never happened to her. And she hated not to have Amy graduate. She had a real shot at Yale or Harvard, and all the first-rate schools she had applied to. 'Maybe we can work something out.' She knew they had never allowed a pregnant student to attend classes. 'I think you need to talk to your mom first.'

'It'll kill her.'

'No, it won't. Things like this happen, to lots of people. You just have to find the right solution, whatever that is. That's up to you and your mom. Do you want me to talk to her with you?'

'No. I think she'd be mad I told you first,' Amy said with a sigh, and took a sip of the water. She had calmed down. But she had some tough decisions to make. She was seventeen years old, and had a bright future ahead of her, without a baby. With one, it would be a lot harder. 'Justin said he'd talk to her with me. He wants me to keep it, and maybe we can get married one day.' She looked sad as she said it. She didn't feel ready for a baby, or marriage, but the alternative sounded worse to her.

Victoria jotted her cell phone number down on a piece of paper and handed it to her. 'Call me anytime, at any hour. I'll do anything I can to help. And if you talk to Mr. Walker, maybe I can help out there.' She didn't want her to get kicked out or suspended. She wanted her to finish school, which was what Amy wanted too.

They left her office together a few minutes later, and Victoria gave her a hug before Amy went to find Justin in the cafeteria. And she saw them leave school together after lunch. She hoped she was going home to see her mother. And the following day she didn't come to school. And then Amy called her. She said they were meeting with Mr. Walker that afternoon after school, and she asked Victoria to be there. She agreed to do it, and she was waiting outside his office when Amy and her mother arrived. Amy looked as if she'd been crying, and her mother looked bleak. Amy smiled as soon as she saw Victoria, and her mother thanked her for coming.

The headmaster was expecting them, and stood up as soon as they walked into the room. He looked surprised to see Victoria, and invited them all to sit down. He looked concerned. He hadn't heard of any problem Amy was having at school, and he had no idea why they were there. He assumed it was something to do with the divorce, and hoped she wasn't changing schools. She was an excellent student, and they would be sorry to lose her if she did. He looked startled when Mrs. Green told him that Amy was pregnant. He looked instantly sorry for her. It wasn't the first time this had happened, but it was

Danielle Steel

always a tough situation for the student and the school. Mrs. Green said the baby was due in May. And then she amazed Victoria and the headmaster by saying that Amy had decided to keep it. Her mother was going to take care of the baby when Amy went to college in the fall. She had applied to Barnard and NYU, and could stay home with the baby. Amy's mother was being very supportive about it, and Amy looked less upset than she had two days before.

'What we need to know,' Mrs. Green said as calmly as she could, 'is if Amy can stay at school here, or if we have to remove her from the school.' It was one of their biggest fears at the moment and would probably impact whether she went to college if her senior year were completely disrupted.

'Amy, how would you feel about being here?' the head-master asked her directly. 'Would that be too hard on you, with everyone talking and aware of your situation?'

'No. Since I'm keeping the baby anyway.' She smiled gratefully at her mother, and Victoria could see that it hadn't been an easy decision, but she thought they had made the right one. She thought having the baby and giving it up would be a huge mistake and much more traumatic to Amy than the adjustments she would have to make now. And if her mother was willing to help, she could go on with her life. 'I'd rather stay here,' Amy said honestly, and the headmaster nodded. He had never allowed a pregnant student to stay in school, but he didn't want to destroy her academic career either. He had a responsibility to her as well as the other students. He was trying to figure out how soon it would show.

'I could put you on independent study, but the college that accepts you might not like it. When is the baby due again?'

'The first of May,' Amy told him.

'We have a long break in April for spring vacation,' he said, thinking out loud. 'That will take us to the end of April. What if you stay until spring vacation, and stay home after that to have the baby? Then you can come back to school by the end of May to take final exams and graduate with your class in June. It won't disrupt you too badly academically, and I think we can make it work here. I've had students stay out longer with mono. And I don't want you to blow senior year. This will be a first for us, but we can live with it if you can,' he said, looking at both of them, and Amy nodded and started to cry again. She was so relieved. Victoria hadn't said a word, but she had been there to support her. Amy's mother thanked the headmaster profusely, and they left the room a few minutes later. Justin was waiting for them outside, looking worried. Amy smiled at him the minute they came out, and he put his arms around her as her mother and Victoria watched. He was very sweet to her and very protective, and Victoria was hopeful for them both. Maybe things would work out, with her mother's help.

'They're letting me stay,' Amy told Justin, beaming. 'Mr. Walker was really nice. I'll stay till spring vacation and come back after the baby for final exams and graduation.' Justin looked like a huge weight had been taken off his shoulders too. They were both really good kids, and everyone was committed to help them.

'Thank you,' Justin said to Victoria and Amy's mother.

'I didn't do anything,' Victoria corrected immediately, and Amy intervened.

'Yes, you did. You listened to me the other day, and helped me get up the courage to tell my mom. We went to see her right after I saw you.'

'I'm glad,' Victoria said quietly. 'I think you've all made some good decisions, and some very challenging ones, I'm sure.' There was no ideal resolution, but this was the best they could all do.

'Thank you for your support,' Amy's mother said to Victoria in a choked voice, and the three of them left the school a few minutes later to go home.

It made Victoria think of her sister. She was glad

nothing like that had ever happened to her. She knew it could happen to anyone. And Mrs. Green was being particularly understanding about it. Amy and Justin were handling it well too, and being very brave. She was still thinking about them when she went home that night. Amy came to Victoria's classroom to thank her again the next day. Justin was glued to her side, as he had been for two years, and Amy looked better than she had in days. It was going to be an interesting school year with a pregnant student in their midst. And as the headmaster had said, it was a first. Victoria couldn't help thinking that there was never a dull moment with kids.

Chapter 19

As she did every year, Victoria flew to L.A. for Thanksgiving. It was going to be different this year because Harry had agreed to join them. It was a prelude to what it would be like when he and Gracie were married. And when Victoria got to the house on Wednesday night, her mother was in a flap setting the table with their best linens and Gracie was nowhere to be seen. She and Harry were out having dinner with his sister, who was going to her in-laws' the next day. Their parents were away, so Harry was having Thanksgiving with the Dawsons instead. And her parents were acting as though a head of state was going to be with them. Their best everything was being used, which seemed silly to Victoria. But she helped her mother set the table as soon as she arrived. They were using her grandmother's linens and crystal, and Christine's own wedding plates.

'Gee, Mom, do we really have to go to all this trouble for him? I can't remember you ever using these plates before.'

'I haven't in twenty years,' she admitted sheepishly. 'Your father wants me to. He thinks Harry is used to only the finest, and he doesn't want him to think we don't have nice things.' It gave Victoria a sudden urge to turn Thanksgiving into a backyard barbecue and use paper plates. It seemed so pretentious to go to such lengths for a twenty-seven-year-old kid, who was about to be family after all. But her parents were showing off. Harry would probably have been just as happy with their everyday plates, which he had seen before, and were perfectly fine. It turned their holiday into a much bigger deal than it usually was.

Gracie came home at midnight and raved about how adorable Harry's sister was, and what a good time she'd had with them, although she'd met her before. But they were going to be sisters-in-law now. His sister supposedly had a nice husband and two children. And Victoria missed the days when Gracie talked about something other than the Wilkeses and the wedding. And she still hadn't accepted the fact that she had to wear the brown dress at the wedding. It was impossible to get Gracie's feet on the ground these days and talk about anything other than the wedding.

'Maybe you should get a job,' Victoria said sensibly. 'It would give you something else to think about till the wedding.'

'I don't think Harry wants me to,' Gracie said meekly about the job.

'She doesn't have time,' their mother added. 'She has too much to do for the wedding. We still have to order the invitations and pick out everything for her registry in three stores. Harry wants to find an apartment, and she has to help him with that. We're still waiting for the sketches from Vera Wang, and Oscar de la Renta is also doing some sketches of wedding gowns that would go with the bridesmaid dresses. She hasn't picked the cake. We have to meet with the caterer, the florist. We need a band. We're not sure about which church. And then she'll have to have fittings for the dress, be photographed in it. There will probably be counseling at the church. She doesn't have time for work. She'll be busy every day with the wedding.' Victoria was exhausted just listening to the list, and her mother looked it. It had become a full-time preoccupation for both of them, and seemed ridiculous to Victoria. Other people managed to work *and* get married. But not Gracie.

'This must be costing a fortune,' Victoria commented to her father the next morning while her mother was basting the turkey, wearing a white wool Chanel suit and an apron. They had gotten very fancy. Victoria was wearing gray wool slacks and a white sweater, which seemed like enough for their usual Thanksgiving. They didn't normally get this dressed up or make as much effort. But a new day had dawned ever since Gracie was engaged to Harry. Victoria thought it was absurd and inappropriate, and didn't want to join in.

'You're damn right it's costing a fortune,' her father confirmed. 'But they're a very important family. I don't want Gracie to be embarrassed. Don't expect something like this if you ever get married,' he warned her. 'If you find some guy to marry, you'd better elope. We couldn't do this again.' She felt as though he had slapped her. As usual, she was being informed that Gracie deserved a wedding fit for a princess, but if she ever married, which her father considered unlikely, she'd better plan on eloping, because they weren't giving her a wedding. How nice. And how clear. Welcome to second-class citizenship, again. The family was going first class, and she had to go steerage. They were always singling her out to be different and 'lesser than' everyone else, or a failure. She wondered why they didn't just put up a sign on the door to her room, 'We don't love you.' Her parents said it every way they could, and for a minute she was sorry she had come home. She could have had Thanksgiving with Harlan and John at her apartment. They were having friends over that day, and she was sure she'd have been more welcome than she was here. She couldn't have felt less welcome and less loved after what her father had just said. She didn't mention the wedding again. It was becoming a sore subject with her, even if it was the only thing her sister ever thought of now. And when Harry arrived at noon, it got worse.

Everyone got nervous and started running around. Her father served champagne instead of wine. Her mother was anxious about the turkey. Victoria was helping in the kitchen, and Harry and Gracie went outside and were whispering and giggling, while her parents made fools of themselves. And once they got to the table, her father and Harry talked politics. Harry told them what was wrong with the country and what should be done to fix it, and her father agreed. Every time Gracie started to say something, Harry cut her off, or finished the sentence for her. She had no voice and no opinions, and none were allowed about anything but the wedding. It was no wonder she talked about it all the time, it was the only thing Harry would let her talk about. Victoria had always found him annoying while they were dating, but he was insufferable now and pompous beyond belief. Between Harry and her father, she wanted to scream. Gracie played stupid all the time now, to please Harry, and her mother kept running back and forth to the kitchen. Victoria didn't have an intelligent conversation with anyone all afternoon. And she finally walked out into the backyard after the meal to get some air. She was horrified by what Gracie was getting herself into. And when she came outside to find Victoria, her older sister looked at her in despair.

'Baby, you're smarter than this. What are you doing? Harry doesn't even let you say anything. How can you be happy like this? There's life after the wedding. You can't be with a man who runs you over all the time and tells you what to think.'

'He doesn't do that,' Gracie said, looking upset by what her sister had said. 'He's wonderful to me.'

'I'm sure he is. But he treats you like a doll with no brain.' Gracie looked shocked, and she started to cry as Victoria tried to hug her, and Gracie wouldn't let her.

'How can you say something like that?'

'Because I love you, and I don't want you to screw up

your life.' It was as blunt and honest as she could be, and she thought it needed to be said.

'I'm not. I love him, and he loves me. And he makes me happy.'

'He's just like Dad. He doesn't listen to Mom either. None of us do. We just listen to him. And she goes out and plays bridge. Is that who you want to be when you grow up? You should have a job and something intelligent to do now. You're a smart girl, Gracie. I know that's a sin in this family. But in the real world, it's a good thing.'

'You're just jealous,' Gracie said angrily. 'And you're mad about the brown dress.' She sounded like a petulant child.

'I'm not mad. I'm disappointed you're making me wear something that I'll look awful in. But if it's important to you, I'll wear it. I just wish you'd have picked something I'll look good in too, not just your friends. It's your wedding, you call the shots. I just don't want you to give up your brain at the altar and trade it for a wedding ring. I think that would be a very bad trade.'

'I think you're being a bitch!' Gracie said, and stomped back inside, as Victoria stood outside and wondered how soon she could leave and fly back to New York. The next plane wouldn't be too soon for her. They were so busy showing off for Harry and trying to impress him that the holiday had been totally destroyed for her. She went back inside and had coffee with the others, and Victoria didn't say anything. Gracie was sitting on the couch next to Harry, and a few minutes later Victoria went out to the kitchen to help her mother do the dishes. They all had to be washed by hand, they were so delicate. Her father stayed in the living room to talk to Harry. It had been a hard day for Victoria. They felt even more like someone else's family now. Everyone had a place and a role here except her. Her role was that of misfit and outcast, and it wasn't one she enjoyed.

'The turkey was good, Mom,' she said as she dried the dishes.

'I thought it was too dry. I got nervous and left it in too long. I wanted everything to be perfect for Harry.' Victoria wanted to ask her why. What difference did it make, if he was going to be family? He wasn't a king or the pope. She had never seen so much fuss made for anyone who visited them before. 'He's used to all the finer things in life,' her mother added with a smile. 'Gracie will have a wonderful life with him.' Victoria wasn't so sure. In fact, she was sure Gracie wouldn't if he never let her finish a sentence or say a word. He was a handsome, intelligent man from a wealthy family, but Victoria would have preferred being alone forever to being married to him. She thought her sister was making a terrible mistake. He was insensitive, opinionated, domineering, full of himself, and he seemed to have no respect for Gracie as a person, just as a decoration or a toy. She was marrying their father, or maybe worse.

Victoria didn't say another word about it for the rest of the day and evening, and she tried to make peace with her sister the next day. They met for lunch at Fred Segal's, which had always been one of their favorite places, and Gracie still looked unhappy about what Victoria had said the day before. But she warmed up halfway through lunch. And Victoria was so upset, she ate a full plate of pesto pasta, and the entire basket of bread. She realized that being around her family was what made her eat excessive amounts, but she couldn't help herself.

'When are you going back?' Gracie asked her as Victoria paid the check. Gracie looked as though she had forgiven her by the end of lunch, which was something of a relief. She didn't want to leave on bad terms.

'I think I'll go back tomorrow,' Victoria said quietly. 'I have a lot of work to do.' Gracie didn't argue with her. She knew they were out of step with each other these days. Gracie thought it was just the pressure of the wedding, but Victoria knew it was deeper than that, and it made her sad. She felt as though she were losing her baby sister to 'them.' That had never happened before, and Harry had added his weight to theirs, and he was one of 'them' too. Victoria felt like an orphan as never before, and it was the loneliest feeling in the world. For once, food wouldn't dull the pain. She hadn't even eaten dessert on Thanksgiving, and she usually loved pumpkin pie with whipped cream. Her father didn't notice Victoria's abstinence, but if she had eaten dessert, he would have commented on that, and the size of the portion she took. There was no winning with them. It was hopeless.

She made a reservation for a flight on Saturday morning, and she had dinner with her parents on Friday night. Grace was at Harry's, and Victoria called her when she left. They all said they'd see her at Christmas, but she had made a decision. She wasn't coming back to L.A. for Christmas. She didn't tell them, but she knew there was no point. There was nothing for her to come back to. She'd be there for the wedding, and not before. She was going to spend Christmas with Harlan and John. That was her home now, not this. It was a major step for her. She felt like she had lost her little sister, who had been her only ally for years, and no longer was.

Her father took her to the airport, and Victoria kissed him goodbye. It was an empty feeling as she looked at him. He told her to take care of herself, and she knew he probably meant it. She thanked him, and walked toward security and didn't look back. She had never been as relieved in her life as when the flight took off and she left L.A. The plane headed toward New York, and she knew she was going home.

Chapter 20

The days between Thanksgiving and Christmas were always chaotic at school, but Victoria made sure she checked in at Weight Watchers every week, no matter how busy she was. No one was in the mood to work. Everyone was anxious to go on vacation, and once exams were over, all anyone talked about was what they were doing for the holidays. There were trips to the Bahamas, visits to grandmothers in Palm Beach, or relatives in other cities. There were ski trips to Aspen, Vail, Stowe, and a few who even went to Europe to ski in Gstaad, Val d'Isère, and Courchevel. They were definitely rich-kid vacations in fancy locations around the world. Victoria was startled to hear one of her students discuss her holiday plans. She was talking about it to two other girls as they packed up their things after class, and Victoria couldn't help overhearing. The girl's name was Marjorie Whitewater, and she blithely announced that she was having a breast reduction over Christmas. It was a gift from her father, and the other two girls were asking about it. One of them laughed and said she was having the opposite procedure. Her mother had promised her breast implants, as a graduation present next summer.

All three girls seemed to take their assorted surgical procedures in stride, and Victoria looked up with a start.

'Isn't that very painful?' Victoria couldn't resist asking about the breast reduction. It sounded awful to her, and she knew she wouldn't have had the courage to do it. And what if she didn't like the result? She had complained about the size of her breasts all her life, but getting rid of them, even in part, sounded like a major step to her. She had thought about it over the years, but never seriously enough to do it.

'It's not that bad,' Marjorie answered her. 'My cousin had it done last year. And she looks great.'

'I had a nose job when I was sixteen,' one of the other girls said. It was a serious medical discussion about the benefits of plastic surgery among teenagers. Victoria was startled by their nonchalance and knowledge about the various operations. 'It hurt,' she admitted about the nose job, 'but I love my new nose. Sometimes I forget it's not the one I was born with. I hated my old nose.' The other two laughed, and Victoria shyly spoke up.

'I hate my nose,' Victoria confessed to the three students. It was a fascinating conversation. She had happened into it accidentally, but she was part of it now. 'I always have.'

'Then you should change it and get a new one,' one of the girls said easily. 'It's not a big deal. My surgery wasn't too bad. My mom had a face-lift last year.' The others were impressed, and Victoria was mesmerized by what they said. It had never occurred to her to change her nose. She had said it jokingly, but she'd never actually considered it an option for her. She wondered how expensive it was, but she didn't want to ask the kids.

She said something to Harlan about it that night. 'Do you know any plastic surgeons?' she asked him casually, as they cooked dinner together. They were having vegetables and steamed fish, and she was being good about her diet, and she was beginning to shed the weight she had wanted to lose for so long.

'Not really. Why?'

'I'm thinking of getting a new nose.' She said it like a new hat or a pair of shoes, and he laughed.

'When did that happen? You've never mentioned that before.'

'I was listening to some of my students after class today. They're an absolute encyclopedia of surgical procedures. One got a new nose two years ago. Another one is having a breast reduction over Christmas, as a Christmas gift no less. And the other one is getting breast implants next summer, for graduation. I felt like I was the only one in school with my original parts. And these are just kids,' she said in amazement.

'*Rich* kids,' John added. 'None of my students get nose jobs and implants for Christmas.'

'Anyway, I don't know how expensive it is, but I was thinking of treating myself to a new nose over Christmas. I'm not going home, so I've got the time.'

'You're not?' Harlan was surprised to hear that she was staying in New York. 'When did you decide that?'

'At Thanksgiving. My family is too crazy these days with the wedding. And now that my sister's fiancé is part of it, I'm outnumbered. There are too many of "them" and only one of me. I'm not going back till the wedding.'

'Have you told them that?'

'Not yet. I thought I'd tell them closer to Christmas. I just thought I'd ask about the surgeon. I didn't want to ask the kids in school.'

Harlan didn't say anything, but he gave her three names of plastic surgeons the next day. He had gotten them from people he knew who said they were pleased with their work, and Victoria was thrilled. She called two of them the next day. One was leaving on vacation over the holidays. And the other one, a woman, gave her an appointment for the end of the week. They referred to it as rhinoplasty, and she told Harlan she felt like a rhinoceros going in to get her horn removed, and he laughed.

She went to see Dr. Carolyn Schwartz on Friday afternoon. She had a bright cheerful office on Park Avenue, not far from school, and Victoria walked over after her last class. It was a cold sunny day and a nice walk after being cooped up in school. Dr. Schwartz was pleasant and young. She explained the procedure to her and how much it cost. Victoria was impressed by how reasonable it was. She could actually afford it, and Dr. Schwartz said that she'd be pretty bruised for about a week, and then it would start to fade. She could cover it with makeup when she went back to school. She had an opening on her surgical calendar the day after Christmas, and Victoria looked at her for a long moment and then grinned.

'I'll take it. Let's do it. I want a new nose.' She hadn't been as excited about anything in years. The doctor showed her computer printouts of possible noses for her, after taking a photograph of her profile and full face.

Victoria said, after looking at all of them, that she wanted a variation of her sister's nose, so she'd look like part of the family. And the doctor suggested a modification of it to suit Victoria's face. Victoria said she would drop off a photograph of her sister the following week, after she went through some photographs she had at home. She had always thought that Gracie had a gorgeous nose, unlike hers, which made her look like a Cabbage Patch Doll, she said, and the doctor laughed. She assured her that it was a fine nose, but they could do better. With the help of the computer, she showed her several possibilities, and Victoria liked them all. Anything seemed better to her than the nose she had.

When Victoria left her office, she felt as if she were walking on air. The nose she had hated all her life, and that her father had made fun of, was about to go. So long, nose.

She told Harlan and John about it as soon as she got home. They were stunned that she had already made the decision and had an appointment to get it done. The only problem, she explained, was that she'd need someone to pick her up at the hospital after the surgery. She looked at them hopefully, and John said he'd be there, since he'd be on vacation too.

She had discussed liposuction with the surgeon too,

which sometimes seemed like an easier option than all her dieting, and a quick fix. But when Dr. Schwartz described it to her, it sounded more unpleasant than she'd thought, and she decided against it, and stuck with her plan for a new nose.

The last days of school were fraught with the usual tensions and preholiday excitement. She had to press her students to complete assignments and get them turned in. She urged them all to work on their college essays during vacation, and she knew some would, and most wouldn't, and then there would be a mad scramble in January to get them done before the deadline the colleges imposed.

And there was a major drama in the last week of classes, when one of the juniors was found using drugs at school. He was doing a line of coke in the bathroom, and one of the other kids turned him in. His parents had to be called, and he was suspended. The headmaster handled it, and the parents agreed to put their son in rehab for a month. Victoria was glad that it wasn't one of her students, and she didn't have to get involved. It sounded like a mess to her. She had her own students to worry about. She was keeping an eye on Amy Green, who was doing good work in school, and her pregnancy still didn't show, and probably wouldn't for a long time. And all was going well for her.

Victoria finally told her parents the week before Christmas that she was not coming home for the holidays. They said they were disappointed, but they didn't sound it to her. They were busy with Gracie and Harry, and they were planning to have dinner with the Wilkeses before they left for Aspen for the holidays.

Gracie called her and was genuinely upset that she wasn't coming, and to justify it, Victoria confessed that she was getting a new nose, and Gracie was shocked, but amused.

'You are? Why? That's so silly. I love your nose.'

'Well, I don't. I've been stuck with Dad's grandma's nose all my life, and I'm turning it in for a new one.'

'Whose nose are you getting?' Gracie asked her, still shocked, and disappointed that she wasn't coming home. But she understood it better now. Her sister didn't tell her that even without the rhinoplasty, she wouldn't have come. There was no need to say that.

'My own, kind of an individualized version of yours and Mom's,' Victoria said, and Gracie laughed. 'We picked it out on the computer, and it suits my face a lot better than the one I have.'

'Will it hurt a lot?' Gracie sounded worried for her, which touched Victoria. Gracie was the only one who ever cared about her, no matter what.

'I don't know,' Victoria said honestly. 'I'll be asleep.'

'I mean after.'

'They'll give me pain pills to take home, and she said I'll be pretty bruised for several weeks. And slightly swollen for many months, although most people won't see it. But I have nothing planned anyway, so this is a good time. I'm doing it the day after Christmas.'

'There goes your New Year's Eve,' Gracie said sympathetically, and Victoria laughed.

'I have no one to spend it with anyway. So I'll stay home. I think Harlan and John are going skiing in Vermont. I'll be fine. You can come keep me company if you want.'

'Harry and I are going to Mexico over New Year,' she said apologetically.

'Then I'm glad I'm staying here.'

'Send me a picture of your new nose. After it's not blue anymore.' They talked about it for a few more minutes, and afterward Victoria was in a good mood and decided to go to the gym. It was bitter cold outside, but she didn't want to get out of the routine. She was being very good, and using the treadmill at home too.

The doctor had told her that she wouldn't be able to exercise at first after surgery, so she wanted to do all she could beforehand. She didn't want to get out of shape while she was nursing her nose.

It was starting to snow when she got to the gym, and it looked like Christmas around the city. People had their trees up, and she was planning to get one with Harlan and John that weekend. They were having friends over to help them decorate it. And Victoria was thinking about it as she rode one of the Exercycles, and she noticed that the man on the one next to her was exceptionally rugged and good-looking, and he was talking to a beautiful girl on his other side. Victoria stared at them for a few minutes, mesmerized. They were an extremely handsome couple, they looked like they got along very well, and they laughed a lot. For a lonely moment, she couldn't help envying them the relationship they obviously shared. She was wearing her iPod so she couldn't hear what they were saying, but their faces as they looked at each other were warm and loving, and watching them tore at her heart. She couldn't even imagine having a man who looked like that in her life.

The man exercising next to her had piercing blue eyes and dark hair, and a square jaw and chin with a deep cleft in it. He had broad shoulders and long legs, and she noticed that he had nice hands. She was embarrassed when he turned and smiled at her. He had sensed her staring at him, so she looked away. And then she noticed him looking at her again, and admiring her legs when she

got off the bike. She was wearing leggings and a sweatshirt, and he was wearing a T-shirt and shorts. And she
thought that their relationship must be very secure for the
woman he was with not to get upset when he looked at
her like that. She seemed not to be bothered at all.
Victoria had smiled at him, and then left the gym to go
home. She could hardly wait for her vacation to get her
new nose. She hated to miss time at the gym, but she
promised herself to work twice as hard on her workout
program as soon as she could start again. With a newly
toned, slimmer body and a better nose, she could hardly
wait for her new life to begin. She was smiling to herself,
thinking about it and feeling hopeful as she left the gym
that night.

Chapter 21

Victoria spent a quiet Christmas with Harlan and John at the apartment, and although she missed Gracie, she was happy not to have to travel during the holidays, or deal with her family's hysteria over the wedding. It was still six months away, and everyone was already nuts, particularly her parents. It was the first time she hadn't gone home, and it felt strange, but peaceful.

She, Harlan, and John exchanged presents on Christmas Eve, as she did with her family usually, and they went to midnight mass afterward. The traditions hadn't changed, just the people and the venues. It was a beautiful mass at St. Patrick's Cathedral, and although none of them was particularly religious, they found it very moving, and they came home and had tea in the kitchen and went to bed. And she talked to Gracie several times the next day. She was shuttling back and forth between their parents' and the Wilkeses'. And Harry had given her diamond earrings for Christmas, which she told Victoria were gorgeous.

On Christmas night, Victoria was extremely nervous about what was going to happen the next day. They had given her pre-op instructions. She couldn't eat or drink after midnight, couldn't take aspirin. She had never had surgery before and didn't know what to expect, other than a nose that she loved at the end of it, or at least not one that she hated as much as she had her present one all her life. She couldn't wait for the change. She knew it wouldn't transform her and suddenly make her beautiful, but she knew she would feel different, and that a major irritant that had embarrassed her for years would be altered. She kept looking in the mirror and couldn't wait for it to be altered. She already felt different. She was shedding the things that had made her unhappy, or trying to, and she was proud of herself for not going home for Christmas, as she had every year. Thanksgiving had just been too awful. And the Christmas she spent in New York was easy and warm at least, with her roommates.

It was sad, but her parents were just too hard for her to be around. Their overt, covert, and subliminal message was always the same: 'We don't love you.' For years she had tried to turn that around, and she couldn't. Now she no longer wanted to try. It was her first step toward health. And the rhinoplasty was another. It had deep psychological meaning for her. She wasn't condemned to be ugly and ridiculed by them forever. She was taking control of her life.

Victoria got up early and walked around the apartment nervously before she left. The tree was sitting in a corner of the apartment, and she wondered how she'd feel when she got home. Not too bad, she hoped. She hoped she wouldn't be in terrible pain or feel sick. And she was scared to death when she took a cab to the hospital at six A.M. Had it been for anything else, she might have backed out and canceled. She was terrified when she walked through the double doors into the same day surgery unit. And from then on it was like being sucked into a well-oiled machine. People greeted her, had her sign papers, and put a plastic ID bracelet on her wrist. They drew blood, took her blood pressure, and listened to her heart. The anesthesiologist came to talk to her, and reassured her that she would feel nothing and be asleep. They wanted to know about any allergies she had, which she didn't. They weighed her, put her in a surgical gown, and had her put on elastic stockings to avoid blood clots, which seemed odd to her, since they were operating on her nose, not her knees or her feet, and the stockings felt funny and went from her toes to the top of her thighs. And she hated the weigh-in, because on their scale she had gained three pounds, even if she insisted on taking off her shoes to be weighed. The war for her weight was not won yet.

Nurses and technicians came and went, someone put an IV in her arm, and before she knew what had happened, she was on the operating table, and her surgeon was smiling at her and patting her hand, while the anesthesiologist talked to her, and seconds later she was asleep. Nothing happened after that, and she woke up feeling incredibly groggy while someone far, far away kept saying her name over and over again.

'Victoria . . . Victoria . . . Victoria? . . . Victoria . . .' She wanted them to be quiet and let her sleep.

'Hmm . . . what . . .' They kept waking her up as she tried to go back to sleep.

'Your surgery is over, Victoria,' a voice said. She fell asleep again, and then someone put a straw in her mouth and offered her a drink. She took a sip, and slowly she began to wake up. She could feel tape on her face, and it felt strange, but she wasn't in pain. They gave her oral pain-killers after she woke. She spent the day in and out of sleep. And they made sure she was warm enough. They finally told her that she had to wake up if she wanted to go home. They cranked up the bed and made her sit up, while she nodded off again. And then they gave her Jell-O, and she looked up and saw Harlan standing next to her bed. John had a cold, so he didn't come.

'Hi . . . what are you doing here?' She looked at him in surprise and felt drunk. 'Oh yeah . . . that's right. I'm going home . . . I'm kind of out of it,' she said apologetically, and he grinned.

'I'll say. I don't know what they're giving you, but I want some.' She laughed and felt a sharp twinge in her face when she did. He didn't tell her that the bandages on her face looked like a hockey mask. They'd been putting ice packs on her face all day. And a nurse came in to help her dress while Harlan waited outside. She was in a wheelchair still looking sleepy when he saw her again.

'How do I look? Is my nose pretty?' she asked him groggily.

'You look gorgeous,' Harlan said, exchanging a smile with the nurse. She was used to groggy patients. Victoria was wearing sweatpants and a top that opened down the front, which they had told her to do, so she didn't pull it over her head. The nurse had put Victoria's shoes and socks on, after taking the elastic stockings off, and her hair was disheveled and pulled back in an elastic band. And they had given her pills to take with her in case she was in pain when she got home. Harlan left her in the lobby with the nurse while he went to get a cab and was back in less than a minute. Victoria was shocked to see that it was dark outside. It was six o'clock, and she had been there for twelve hours. The nurse rolled the wheel-chair right out to the cab, and Harlan helped Victoria in, settled her on the seat, and thanked the nurse. He hoped Victoria hadn't heard her warn him that she was a big girl, so he didn't try to lift her. He knew how she hated that expression. It was one of the painful mantras of her childhood. She didn't want to be a 'big girl,' just a kid then, and a woman now.

'What did she say?' Victoria frowned as she looked at him.

'She said you look like you've been on a two-week drunk, and she wishes she had your legs.'

'Yeah,' Victoria nodded seriously, 'everyone says that . . . they want my legs . . . great legs .. . . fat ass though.' The driver smiled in the rearview mirror when he heard her, and Harlan gave him their address. It was a short drive home, and Victoria dozed with her chin on her chest, and once she snored. It was not a romantic vision, but Harlan loved her. She had become his best friend. He woke her when they got there.

'Okay, sleeping beauty. We're back at the castle. Get your gorgeous ass out of the cab.' He wished he had the wheelchair at the house, but she didn't need it. She was a little disoriented and woozy, but he got her in the elevator and into the apartment in minutes, and led her to the couch, so she could sit down while he took off his coat and her own. John came out of their bedroom in a bathrobe, and smiled when he saw her. She looked like an alien in the bandage that covered most of her face, with two holes for her eyes and a splint to protect her nose. She was quite a sight, but he made no comment about it to Victoria and hoped she wouldn't look in the mirror. There had been cotton packing in her nose all day, but very little bleeding. And the nurse had removed it before she left.

'Where do you want to be?' Harlan asked her gently. 'On the couch or in bed?' She thought about it for a long moment.

'Bed . . . I'm sleepy . . .'

'Are you hungry?'

'No, thirsty . . .' she said, running her tongue over her lips. The nurse had given her Vaseline to put on them. 'And cold,' she added. They had put warm blankets on her at the hospital all day, and she wished she had one now.

Harlan brought her a glass of apple juice with a straw, as they had told him to do. Victoria had several pages of post-op instructions for the coming days. And a few minutes later he led her to her room, helped her undress and put her pajamas on, and five minutes later she was sound asleep propped up on pillows in bed to elevate her head, and Harlan was back in the living room with John.

'Wow, she looks like a train wreck,' John whispered to Harlan, and he nodded.

'They told her to expect a lot of bruising and swelling. She's going to have two big shiners tomorrow. But she's happy, or she will be. She wanted a new nose, and she got one. It may not look like a big deal to us, but I think it's a big deal to her psychologically, so why not?' John agreed. They spent a quiet evening on the couch, watching two movies, and every so often Harlan would go in and check on Victoria. She was sound asleep and purring softly. And somewhere under the bandages she had the new nose she wanted. Santa Claus had brought it to her the day after Christmas. It was a gift she had wanted all her life.

The next day Victoria woke up feeling like she'd been in a rodeo all year. She ached, she was tired, she felt as though she had been drugged. There was a dull ache in her nose. She decided to have breakfast and take a pain pill, but she wanted to eat something first so it didn't make her sick. By sheer habit, she opened the freezer and was staring at the ice cream when Harlan walked in.

'I don't think so,' the voice of her conscience said right behind her when he saw what she was looking at. 'You have a fabulous new nose. Let's not go crazy with the ice cream, shall we?' He closed the freezer door, opened the fridge, and handed her the apple juice. 'How do you feel?'

'So-so, but not too bad. Kind of woozy. I'm a little sore. I'm just going to sleep today, and take the pain medicine.' She wanted to stay on top of it so it didn't get too bad. The swelling had gotten worse, which they had warned her would happen for the first few days.

'Good idea,' he said. He made some whole wheat toast, covered it with a low-fat synthetic dairy spread, and handed it to her. 'Do you want eggs?' She shook her head. She didn't want to lose track of her diet in the coming days, especially while she couldn't exercise.

'Thanks for taking care of me yesterday,' she said, trying to smile, but there was tape on her face and it felt odd. She felt like the man in the iron mask, and she couldn't wait to get the bandages off in a week. They were annoying, and she was afraid to look in the mirror. She had made a point of not doing so in her bedroom, or when she went to the bathroom. She didn't want to scare herself and knew she might, and you couldn't see her nose anyway. It was all covered up under the bandages and splint.

Victoria slept for the next two days and hung around the house after that. It was a quiet time, she had no plans, and she had done the surgery over the holidays so she could take it easy. Harlan brought her movies, and she watched TV a lot, although she had a headache for the first few days. She talked to Helen, but she didn't want to see anyone except John and Harlan. She didn't feel up to it and was afraid she looked too scary. And by New Year's Eve she was feeling pretty good and didn't need the pain pills. Harlan and John had gone skiing in Vermont by then, and she spent the evening alone watching TV and loving the idea that she had a new nose, even if she hadn't seen it yet. Gracie called her from Mexico that night. She was at the Palmilla Hotel in Cabo with Harry and some of his friends, and she said it was fabulous. As his fiancée and soon-to-be wife, she had a golden life now. Victoria didn't envy her, though, because she wouldn't have wanted to be there with him, but Gracie sounded ecstatic.

'So how's the new nose?' Gracie asked her. She had

called several times that week, and sent Victoria flowers, which was very sweet. Victoria had been touched by the gesture. Their parents knew nothing of the surgery, and Victoria didn't want them to. She was sure they would disapprove and make rude comments about it. Gracie had agreed to keep it secret.

'I haven't seen it yet,' Victoria admitted. 'They're taking the bandages off next week. Supposedly, except for the bruising and some swelling, it should look pretty good. They said I'd be back to normal, relatively, within a week or two, except that I'll still be tired. But I can cover the bruising with makeup.' They had told her that she would only have a Band-Aid on her nose after that, but all the bandages and stitches would be gone within a week or two. 'Are you having fun?' She suddenly missed her baby sister terribly.

'It's fantastic here. We have an incredible suite,' Gracie said, sounding happy.

'You're going to be one spoiled brat as Mrs. Wilkes,' Victoria teased her, but she didn't begrudge it to her. She liked her own life better in some ways, and her job. At least no one was telling her what to think, do, and say. She couldn't have stood it. Gracie didn't seem to care, as long as she had Harry. It was the same pact with the devil that their mother had made, and Victoria felt sorry for them both.

'I know,' Gracie tittered in answer to the remark about being spoiled. 'I love it. Well, let me know how the nose looks.'

'I'll call you immediately when I see it.'

'Your old one was fine,' Gracie said again. It wasn't hideous, just round.

'My new one will be better!' Victoria said, happy about it again. 'Have fun in Cabo. I love you . . . and Happy New Year!'

'You too. I hope it will be a good year for you too, Victoria.' Victoria knew she meant it, and wished the same for her. They hung up, and Victoria settled back to watch another movie from the couch. And at midnight she was sound asleep. It had been a quiet New Year's Eve for her, and she didn't mind at all.

Chapter 22

Dr. Schwartz took Victoria's bandages off eight days later and said she was very pleased with the result when she saw it. It was healing nicely. Victoria had been brave enough to see her face-mask bandages in the mirror by then, and she thought she looked ghoulish, though for a good cause. She didn't regret the surgery for a minute, and when she saw the result unveiled, she was thrilled, despite the bruising, and slight swelling. The doctor pointed out where the swelling was and where she could expect improvement, but all things considered, it looked great, and Victoria let out a squeal of delight. The surgeon had done a fantastic job. And the patient was ecstatic. She said she already felt like a new person.

The only shocking thing, and Victoria wasn't surprised, since she had been told to expect it, was the extent of the bruising, which was severe. She had two huge black eyes, and bluish discoloration that went down most of her face. But the doctor assured her that it would go away soon, was normal, and she could start covering it with makeup in a few days. She said she'd be quite presentable by the time she went back to school in another week. And it would continue to improve after that as the swelling went down and the bruising disappeared. It would continue to look even better over several months. She put a Band-Aid over the bridge of Victoria's nose and sent her home. She said she could go back to normal activity, within reason. No sky diving, water polo, or touch football, she teased her. No contact sports. She told her to be reasonable and not do anything where she might hit her nose, and when Victoria inquired, she said that she could go to the gym, but again be sensible about it and not overdo. No jogging, no strenuous exercise, no swimming, no extreme workouts, which Victoria didn't want to do anyway. It had been freezing outside all week. And the doctor added 'no sex,' which unfortunately wasn't an issue for her at the moment.

Victoria was so happy with the result that she bought a big Caesar salad on the way home, and ate it in the kitchen. She had lost a few pounds from not eating much while she was sleeping her way through her recovery, and the pain pills had killed her appetite. She hadn't even eaten ice cream, and just to be on the safe side, Harlan had thrown it away again. He called it her 'stash.' In the Chutes and Ladders of weight loss, it set her back at zero again every time.

She put on her gym clothes after she ate the salad, and walked the several blocks to the gym, in leggings, gym shorts, an old Northwestern sweatshirt, a parka, and a pair of beat-up old running shoes. Harlan and John were still skiing in Vermont, and the day was crisp and clear in New York despite predictions of snow.

She signed in at the gym, and decided to ride the exercise bike, and put it on the easiest setting since she hadn't exercised in a week and wanted to start slow. She put her iPod on and was listening to the music with her eyes closed as she pedaled rhythmically along. She didn't open them until she'd been on the bike for ten minutes, and was startled to see the same very good-looking man sitting next to her whom she'd seen there before Christmas. This time he was alone, without the beautiful woman who'd been with him, and he was looking at Victoria when she opened her eyes. She had forgotten what her face looked like after the surgery, with all the bruising, and she wondered why he was staring at her, and then she remembered and was embarrassed. He was looking sympathetic and pained for her. He said something and she took the iPod out of her ear. He had a light tan on his face as though he'd been skiing, and she was struck again by how handsome he was.

'What does the other guy look like?' he teased her lightly, and she smiled, suddenly acutely aware of the bruises on her face and remains of two black eyes. And she wondered if he had guessed why. He looked more serious then as he chatted with her. 'I'm sorry, I didn't mean to make a joke of it. It looks painful. It must have been a nasty accident. Car or ski?' he asked matter-of-factly. Victoria hesitated, with a look of confusion, and she didn't know what to say. *Nose job* sounded a lot worse to her, and would have made her feel foolish to a stranger.

'Car,' she said simply as they pedaled along.

'I figured. Did you have your seatbelt on, or was it the air bag? People don't realize how easily you can break your nose with an air bag. I know several people who have.' She nodded as a blanket yes and felt really stupid. 'I hope you sue the hell out of whoever hit you,' he said, still sympathetic, assuming immediately that it was the other guy's fault, not hers. 'Sorry. I'm a lawyer. I get litigious at the drop of a hat. There are so many drunk drivers on the road over the holidays, and bad ones, it's a wonder more people don't get killed. You were lucky.'

'Yes, I was.' Very. *I got a new nose*, she thought to herself, but didn't say it.

'I just came back from skiing in Vermont with my sister. She was with me the last time I saw you. The poor thing was minding her own business and got hit by a kid out of control on a snowboard and broke her shoulder. She came out from the Midwest to spend the holidays with me, and now she goes back with a broken shoulder. It's really painful. She was a good sport about it.' Victoria was staring at him, with the information that the beauty he'd had with him was his sister. So where was his wife? She checked, and he had no wedding ring on, but a lot of men didn't wear them, so that meant nothing. And even if he wasn't married or didn't have a girlfriend, she couldn't imagine him wanting her, even with her new nose. She was still a 'big girl,' even with a smaller, better nose.

He pointed to her sweatshirt then. 'Northwestern? My sister graduated from there.'

'Me too,' Victoria said in a hoarse croak, which had nothing to do with her surgery. She was too dazzled by him to speak.

'Great school. Shit weather though. I wanted to get out of the Midwest after growing up there, so I went to Duke.' It was in North Carolina and one of the best schools in the country, Victoria knew. She tried to help her students get in there all the time. 'My brother went to Harvard. My parents still brag about it. I couldn't get in,' he said modestly with a grin. 'I went to law school at NYU, which is how I wound up here. What about you? Native New Yorker or other?' He was chatting away as they rode the bikes, and it felt very surreal to her, riding along next to this gorgeous man who was telling her about his family, his education, where he came from, and asking about her. And he acted like her face was normal and not black and blue, and she didn't have two black eyes. He looked at her as though she was pretty, and she wondered if he was blind.

'I'm from L.A.,' she answered his question. 'I moved here after college. I teach at a private school.'

'That must be interesting,' he said pleasantly. 'Little kids or big ones?'

'High school seniors. English. They're a handful, but I love them.' She smiled, hoping she didn't look like a ghoul. But he didn't seem to think so, and didn't look bothered by it at all.

'That's a tough age, judging by myself anyway. I gave

my parents a tough time in high school. I stole my dad's car and totaled it twice. That's easy to do on black ice in Illinois. I was lucky I didn't get killed.' He mentioned after that that he had grown up in a suburb of Chicago, and she could guess that it was an affluent one. Despite the workout clothes, he looked well heeled, had a good haircut, was well spoken, polished, polite, and was wearing an expensive gold watch. She looked like a bum, and always went to the gym that way, and hadn't had a manicure in over a week. It was the one luxury she always indulged in, but she hadn't gone since the surgery. She didn't want to scare anyone, explain her bandages, and she wasn't going out anyway. Now here she was next to the most gorgeous man she'd ever seen, and she hadn't combed her hair and didn't even have nail polish on.

Their bikes stopped at almost the same time, and they both got off. He said he was going to the steam room, and with a warm smile he stuck out his hand.

'I'm Collin White, by the way.'

'Victoria Dawson.' They shook hands, and after a few inane words, she picked up her things and left, and he headed to the steam room, and stopped to chat with a man he knew along the way. Victoria was still thinking about him when she walked home. She felt good after some exercise at the gym, and he'd been nice to talk to. She hoped she would see him again.

Her doctor was right, and by the time she went back to school, she could cover most of what was left of the bruising with makeup. There was a faint shadow still around her eyes, but she looked pretty good, and the swelling had come down a lot around her nose. Not all the way, but close. And she loved her new nose. She felt like she had a whole new face. She couldn't wait to see her parents in June and watch their reaction, if they noticed. The difference seemed enormous to her.

She had just taught her last class of the day, after helping half a dozen students with the college essays they hadn't finished and were now panicked about, when three of the girls were lingering in the classroom, talking. One of them was the student who had had the breast reduction over Christmas, and the same threesome who had discussed it before. They were best friends. They went everywhere together at school.

'How did it go?' Victoria asked cautiously. She didn't want to be too intrusive. 'Not too painful, I hope.'

'It was great!' the girl said, pulling up her sweatshirt and exposing her bra, since there were no boys in the room at the time. 'I *love* my new boobs! I wish I'd done it sooner!' And then she looked at Victoria intently, as though seeing her for the first time, and in some ways she was, parts of her anyway. 'Omigod! You did it!' She was staring at the middle of Victoria's face, and the other two girls looked too. 'I love your new nose!' she said emphatically, and Victoria blushed to the roots of her hair.

'Can you tell?'

'Yes . . . no . . . I mean, you didn't look like Rudolf before. But it's a definite subtle difference. That's how it's supposed to be. People aren't supposed to shriek and know you did it. You're just supposed to look better and no one can figure out why. Your nose is great! Watch out though, it's addictive. My mom does something all the time. Chin implants, botox, new boobs, lipo. Now she wants to reduce her thighs and calves. I'm happy with my boobs,' the girl said, looking pleased.

'And I love my nose,' Victoria admitted happily, since they were all so much more sophisticated than she was, and familiar with the process. 'I actually decided to do it after talking to you. You made me feel brave. I'd never dared to do it before.'

'Well, you did good,' she congratulated her, and gave Victoria a high-five.

They all left the room together, and passed Amy Green

and Justin in the hall. She smiled broadly at Victoria. She hadn't admitted the pregnancy yet at school, and it still didn't show, although it would soon. She was young and her muscles were tight, and she was dressing carefully to conceal it. Justin was constantly with her protecting her like a security man guarding the Hope diamond. They were sweet to watch. 'He follows her around like a puppy,' one of the girls said, rolling her eyes as they walked by.

Victoria thanked the girls again for their good advice and went to her office to pick up some files she wanted to take home. She was touched by their praise of her new nose. She loved it too. She wondered for a minute then if she should have a breast reduction too, and then she remembered what the girls had said, that plastic surgery was addictive and some women didn't know where to stop. She was going to stop here, with her nose. She'd have to work the rest off the hard way, and she was working at it steadily. The wedding was five months away.

She ran into Collin White again that night at the gym, and they chatted easily as they rode the bikes. He told her what law firm he worked at on Wall Street and that he was a litigator. It was an important firm, and his job sounded interesting to her. And she told him where she taught. He had heard of the school. They talked about nothing in particular, and when they got off the bikes, he surprised her and asked her if she wanted to go for a drink across the street. She looked as big a mess as she had before, and couldn't believe that he'd ask her anywhere or want to be seen with her. He asked her again as though he really meant it, and she nodded, put on her coat, and followed him across the street, wondering why he'd want to have a drink with her.

They both ordered wine, and she asked how his sister's shoulder was after the snowboard accident.

'Painful, I think. Those things take a while, and you can't do much with a shoulder, except time. She was lucky she didn't need surgery when it happened.'

He asked more about the school where she worked then, and why she'd gone into teaching, and about her family. She told him she had a sister who was seven years younger, had just graduated from USC the previous June, and was getting married in five months.

'That's pretty young,' he commented, looking surprised. 'Especially these days.' He had told her he was thirty-six, and she said she was twenty-nine.

'I think so too. Our parents got married at that age, right out of college, but people did that more then. Nowadays, nobody gets married at twenty-three, which she will be in June. I was hoping she'd wait, but she won't. It's all about the wedding. My whole family is temporarily insane,' she said with a rueful grin. 'At least I hope it's temporary. They're driving me nuts.'

'Do you like the guy she's marrying?' he asked, looking at her closely, and Victoria hesitated for a long time, and then decided to be honest. 'Yes. Maybe. Well enough. But not for her. He's very domineering, and opinionated for a young guy. He doesn't let her open her mouth and thinks for her. I hate seeing her give up her personality and her independence just to be his wife.' She didn't say that he had a huge amount of money, and didn't think it appropriate to do so. And that wasn't the point. She wouldn't have liked Harry any better for Gracie if he'd been poor. The money made him pompous. But his own personality made him controlling, which was what Victoria didn't like about him. She wanted more for Gracie than that.

'My sister almost married a guy like that. She dated him for three years, and we all liked him, but not for her. They got engaged last year, she was thirty-four, and she's all wound up about getting married and having babies, and she's scared to death she'll miss the boat. She finally realized what she was getting herself into, and they broke up two weeks before the wedding. It was a mess. She was really upset, and my parents were great about it. I think she did the right thing. It's tough for women,' he said sympathetically, 'at a certain age, that time clock starts ticking like a bomb. And I think a lot of women make bad decisions because of it. I was proud of my sister for bailing out. You saw her here. She's thirty-five, and she'll find the right guy, hopefully in time to have kids. But she's better off alone than with the wrong guy. It's not easy to meet good people,' he said thoughtfully. Victoria had a hard time believing that a woman who looked like his sister didn't have ten men running behind her waving wedding rings, or at least wanting to date her. 'She hasn't met anyone since they broke up,' he added, 'but she's over it, and she says she won't go back to him. Thank God she woke up.'

'I wish my sister would,' Victoria said with a sigh. 'But she's a kid. She's twenty-two, and she's all excited about the dress and the wedding and the ring. She's lost sight of what's important, and I think she's too young to get it. And by the time she does, it'll be too late, and she'll be married to him and sorry as hell.'

'Have you said that to her?' He looked interested in what she said.

'Yes. She doesn't want to hear it and gets all upset. She thinks I'm jealous. And believe me, I'm not.' He believed her. 'And my parents are no help. They're big fans of the match, and they're impressed by who he is.' She looked pensive then. 'And he's a lot like my father. That's a tough one to fight.'

'You're swimming upstream on that one,' he said wisely. 'All you can do is say it and leave it at that. And maybe it'll work for her. You never know,' he said philosophically. 'People want different things and not always what we think they should have, or want for them.'

'I hope it works, but I doubt it,' Victoria added, looking sad for her sister.

'Are you two very different? Other than the age difference.' He got the feeling they were. Victoria appeared to be a smart, sensible woman with her feet on the ground and a good head on her shoulders. He could tell just by listening to her. And her younger sister sounded flighty, young, and spoiled to him, and maybe headstrong and impulsive too. He wasn't wrong.

'She's more like my parents,' Victoria said honestly. 'I've always been the odd man out. I don't look like them, think like them, or act like them, or want the same things. Sometimes it sounds like we didn't have the same parents. We didn't actually, because they treated us very differently, so her life experience and her childhood were completely different from mine.' He nodded as though he understood, and she had the feeling that what she was saying wasn't unfamiliar to him.

He looked at his watch then and asked for the check. 'I've enjoyed talking to you,' he told Victoria, as he paid it. 'Would you like to have dinner sometime?' he asked with a hopeful look as she stared at him. Was he crazy? Why would he want to go out with her? She thought he was much too good for her. 'Like next week?' he added more precisely. 'Just something easy, if you'd like that.' He didn't want to snow her with a fancy restaurant. She was a kind person and easy to talk to. He wanted to spend a real evening with her, getting to know her, not show off and try to impress her. He wanted to know more about who she was. He liked what he'd heard so far. And he liked her looks, even with her bruised face.

'Yes, of course, I'd like that,' she blurted out when he looked as if he expected an answer. She didn't add 'Why?' She could only assume that he wanted to be friends, and liked having someone to talk to. This was obviously not a date.

'How about Tuesday? I've got a partners' meeting Monday night.'

'Of course . . . yes . . . sure . . .' She felt like an idiot burbling at him.

'Could I have your number or your e-mail?' he asked politely, and she jotted them down and handed them to him. He put them directly into his phone, and slipped it back into his pocket with the piece of paper, and thanked her. 'I've really enjoyed meeting you, Victoria,' he said pleasantly, while she tried not to focus on how handsome he was. It was too unnerving.

'Me too,' she said weakly. This was very odd. She liked him, but she thought a man like him shouldn't even be talking to her. He should have been with some drop-dead-gorgeous beauty, like his sister, who had no dates. Go figure. The world was too strange.

They left each other in front of the gym, and she walked home, thinking about him and trying to figure out why he had asked her to dinner. She told Harlan about it when she got home, and explained that it wasn't really a date, he just wanted to be friends.

'How do you know that?' Harlan looked surprised by what she said. 'Did he say so?'

'Of course not. He's too polite. But it's obvious. You should see the guy. He looks like a movie star, or a business mogul, or an ad in GQ. And look at me.' She pointed to her workout clothes. 'Now you tell me, would he date a woman that looks like me?'

'And he was wearing black tie at the gym?'

'Very funny. No. But guys like him don't date women like me. This is friendly, not a date. Trust me. I know. I was there.'

'Sometimes romances start out that way. Don't rule it out. Besides, I don't trust your interpretation. You don't know shit. All you know is your parents telling you that you're not deserving, you're not worthy, and no one will ever want you. Believe me, tapes like that play so loud, you can't hear anything else. Even when it's clear otherwise. I'm telling you, if this guy has any brains at all and eyes in his head, he knows you're smart, funny, a good person, bright as hell, good looking, have fucking unbelievable legs, and he'd be the luckiest man in the world if he got you. So maybe this guy is no fool.'

'It's not a date,' she insisted again.

'I'll bet you five bucks it is,' Harlan said firmly.

'How will I know if it is?' She looked confused, while Harlan pondered the question.

'Good point, since your radar is out of whack and you have no decoding skills. If he kisses you, obviously it's a date, but he won't if he has any manners, on a first date. He sounds smarter than that. You'll just know. If he asks you out again. If he looks interested. If he makes nice little gestures, touches your hand, looks like he's enjoying you. Oh fuck, Victoria, just take me with you, and I'll tell you if it's a date.'

'I'll figure it out for myself,' she said primly. 'But it isn't.'

'Just remember, you owe me five bucks if it is, by any

of the aforementioned criteria. And no cheating. I need the money.'

'Then start saving, because you're going to owe me five bucks. It's not a date.' She was sure of it.

'Don't forget your new nose,' he teased her. 'That could swing the vote.'

'I hadn't thought of that,' she said, laughing. 'The second time he saw me, I had bruises all over my face and two shiners, and I wasn't wearing makeup.'

'Oh my God,' Harlan said, rolling his eyes. 'You're right. It's not a date. It's true love. Double the ante. Make it ten.'

'You're on. Start saving.' He gave her a brotherly shove as they both left the kitchen and went back to their rooms. She had a stack of papers to correct. And the mystery of whether Collin White had asked her for a date would be solved soon enough. They were having dinner in five days. He hadn't asked her out over the weekend, which made her wonder if he had a girlfriend. She had been through that with Jack Bailey, and hoped it wasn't another situation like that. But this was nothing. She was sure. Just dinner with a friend. And it was less scary that way anyway.

Chapter 23

Five days later, on the day Victoria was supposed to have dinner with Collin White, she had to do one of those painful duties that sometimes went with her work. The father of one of the students had died suddenly of a heart attack on a ski slope in New Hampshire, and she had to go to the funeral, along with the headmaster and several other teachers. The family was devastated, and the youngest son was one of her seniors. There were four children in the family, and all of them had gone to Madison. It was a family that everyone loved, and she went to the funeral as part of a group with Eric Walker and a number of other teachers. It was very sad, and the eulogies were extremely moving when each of the children got up to speak, and everyone cried. Victoria's heart went out to her student. She put her arms around him and hugged him afterward, when they all went back to the family's apartment on Fifth Avenue. She had taught his older brother and one of his sisters too, in her seven years at the school, and liked them all. The oldest sister had gone to Madison before Victoria got there, and she was married now with two kids. Their father had been relatively young and in good shape, and his sudden death had been a terrible shock to all, and most of all his children.

It was a sobering experience, and Victoria spent the rest of the day quietly, and she tried not to think about it when Collin came to pick her up at seven. But she told him about it anyway, and he said he had an uncle who had died suddenly. It had been terrible for the family, but he said it was a great way to go, healthy, in no pain, just gone, after a great life. He made a good point.

She met him downstairs, and they took a cab to a restaurant he knew and liked in the Village. She had heard of it and it was hard to get in. The Waverly Inn. It was lively, and the food was good, the atmosphere was wholesome, fun, and the food mostly American. They both ordered steaks, and she had to fight herself not to order the macaroni and cheese to go with it, which he said was great.

'I've been on a diet since I was born,' she confessed

when she ordered steamed spinach instead. 'My parents and sister are thin and can eat whatever they want. Apparently I inherited my great-grandmother's genes. She was a "big" woman, as they say. I've been fighting that battle all my life.' She found it surprisingly easy to be honest with him since she viewed him as just a friend. Her clothes were loose on her now, so she could talk about it, without the usual shame and guilt over what she'd eaten. She'd been good for months, and it showed. She was determined to get down to a size ten by the wedding, and she was close. And after that, she'd have to stay there, which was like circling in airspace with a 747.

'People are so obsessed with that these days. As long as you're healthy, what difference do a few pounds make? Crazy diets. Thirteen-year-old girls on magazine covers who wind up in hospitals because they're so anorexic. Real women don't look like that. And who wants them to? No one wants a woman who looks sick or like she's been liberated from a refugee camp. All through history, women are supposed to look like you,' Collin said simply, and he looked as though he meant it, and not like he was trying to butter her up. She stared at him in disbelief. Maybe he was crazy. Or liked big women. It made no sense to her.

They had an interesting conversation about art,

politics, history, architecture, the latest books they'd read, the music they liked, the foods they hated. Brussels sprouts for both, and cabbage. She said she had tried a cabbage soup diet with great results that reversed immediately. And then they talked about their families, and Victoria told him more than she meant to. She told him about being named after Queen Victoria because her father thought she was so ugly and it was a great joke, and she told him about the remark that she was the tester cake and Gracie the perfect recipe. Collin looked at her in horror when she said it.

'It's amazing you don't hate her,' he said, looking sympathetic.

'It's not her fault. It's them. And she looks just like them, so they think she's perfect. And she is gorgeous, I have to admit. She looks something like your sister, in a smaller version.' It was a standard of perfection Victoria had never achieved and knew she never would.

'Yeah, and my sister hasn't had a date in a year, so that's no guarantee of happiness either,' he reminded her. Victoria still found that hard to believe. 'People who say things like that to their kids shouldn't have them,' he said seriously.

'True. But they do anyway. Anyone can have kids, whether qualified or not, and many people aren't. My father thinks it's funny when he makes cracks about me. I did a couple of years of therapy a few years ago, and then I took two years off. I went back last summer. It makes a difference. Intellectually at least you get that it's about their being flawed, not you. But in your gut, you remember all those things they said when you were five and six and thirteen, and I think you hear it in your head forever. I tried to drown those voices in ice cream,' she confessed. 'It didn't work.' She had never been as honest with anyone in her life, and he seemed completely non-judgmental about it. She really liked him and hoped he was being sincere, although she was leery of everyone now after the experiences she had had with dishonest men, like Jack Bailey and a few others. Her dating life had not been a happy one thus far.

'I have a strange relationship with my parents too,' he admitted. 'I had an older brother who was the perfect son. Perfect athlete. Perfect student. Perfect everything. Harvard undergrad, captain of the football team, Yale Law School, top of his class. He was a fantastic kid and a great guy, and a wonderful brother. He was killed by a drunk driver on Long Island on the Fourth of July week-end, right after he found out he had passed the bar, the first time of course, with flying colors. It took me three times to pass it. And I kind of lumbered along in the middle of my class. Duke and NYU did not cut it with my parents, compared to Harvard and Yale. I'm not a jock and never have been. I keep in shape and play some tennis and squash, but that's about it. Blake was the golden boy. Everyone loved him. He was my older brother. I was always in his shadow as a kid. And the world stopped for my parents when he died. They never recovered, either of them. My father retired, and my mother kind of withered up. No one has ever measured up for them since. And I sure don't. My sister kind of skated under all that because she's a girl. But they figure I'm a bad trade for Blake. He wanted to go into politics eventually and probably would have done well. He was kind of Kennedyesque, with a huge amount of charisma and charm. I'm just a regular guy. I lived with someone a few years ago, and it didn't work out, so now they're wondering what's wrong with me that I'm not married. As far as they're concerned I've been kind of a poor second best all my life, or I don't qualify at all, compared to my brother. It's rough being around them and feeling like you never measure up. He was five years older than I, and he died fourteen years ago. I'd just graduated from college, and I've been a disappointment to them ever since.' He hadn't had the tough childhood she'd had, but he had had a hard road for fourteen years and she could see it in his eyes, that terrible feeling that you're not good enough to be loved by the people you love most, and eventually by anyone else. She knew it well. 'I'm not as ballsy as you are. I've never gone to therapy and I probably should. I just accepted the mantle my brother left behind. I tried to be him for a while, and I couldn't. I'm *not* him. I'm me. Which is never good enough for them. They're sad people.' And he wasn't, which was the good news. But he had lived with the same toxic messages she had, for different reasons. And from some of the self-help books she'd read, she thought he might have survivor guilt in some form.

'I always feel like my parents should be holding up a sign, "We don't love you." It would be more honest.' She smiled at him, and he laughed. The visual was so perfect, and exactly what he felt about his parents. Their life experiences were amazingly similar and dovetailed well. They had a lot in common, given difficult relationships with their parents, which they had striven to survive well, and remain healthy people. Both of them felt as though they had made important discoveries about each other by the time the evening ended. He put an arm around her on the way back in the cab, but he didn't try to kiss her, which was a plus for him. She hated being pawed by strangers who thought you owed it to them because they paid for dinner. He didn't do that, and she respected him for it. And before they got back to her building, he asked her if she'd like to have dinner again. He said he hoped she would, and apologized for broaching such serious subjects with her on a first date. But for both of them it was real life, and a relief to share it with someone who understood.

'I'd love to have dinner with you again,' she said sincerely, and he suggested that Saturday night, which in theory dispelled the worry that he had a weekend girl-friend, unless he was seeing her on Friday, Victoria reminded herself. Jack had done that. But Collin was not Jack. He was great.

He kissed her on the cheek and saw her to her elevator, and said he'd call her the next day. She was smiling when she walked into the apartment, and Harlan beamed from ear to ear when he saw her. John had already gone to bed.

'I owe you ten bucks,' she said as she walked in, and beat him to it.

'How do you know?' He looked intrigued.

'Fantastic conversations, great evening, great guy. Arm around me in cab on way home. Touched my hand twice at dinner. Doesn't care if I'm fat or not, he likes "real" women. And invited me to dinner Saturday night.' She was beaming, and he reached over and hugged her.

Harlan was always hugging and kissing her. John was always a little cooler with her, it was just his nature, and he was less comfortable with women. He had a horrible mother who used to beat him, and put him off females forever. Everyone has their scars.

'Shit,' Harlan said after he hugged her, 'you owe me fifty. Maybe a hundred. That's better than a date. It's a real guy. He sounds fantastic. When can I meet him? Before the wedding. Yours, I mean. Screw Gracie's.' They were both laughing, and she peeled a ten-dollar bill out of her wallet and handed it to him. She had a date! And with a terrific guy! He had been worth waiting nearly thirty years for, although it was much too soon to know what would happen. It might go nowhere, and even if it did, it might fall apart. Real life.

Collin called her right before she went to sleep that night and told her what a great time he'd had, and couldn't wait to see her again. She felt exactly the same way about him.

'Sweet dreams,' he said before he hung up, and she smiled as she lay in bed with the phone still in her hand after they did. Sweet dreams indeed.

Chapter 24

Victoria's second date with Collin was even better than the first. They went to a fish restaurant in Brooklyn and had fresh lobster wearing big paper bibs. The restaurant was noisy and fun, and they enjoyed each other. Their conversations were just as meaty as before, and they both felt comfortable talking about themselves and who they really were, and exposing themselves to each other. They started meeting at the gym in the evenings and talking about their day as they rode the bikes. They were totally at ease. He always hugged her and kissed her on the cheek, but it had gone no further and she was fine with that, and liked it.

For their third date, he took her to the ballet because she said she enjoyed it. They went to an exhibit at the

Met on a Sunday, and brunch after. He took her to the opening of a Broadway play. She was having a ball with him, and Collin was very creative about where he took her. It was always well thought out and something he thought she'd enjoy.

And after their night at the theater, he looked uncomfortable for the first time when he asked her to dinner. He warned her that it was an evening she might not like, and not likely to be exciting, but he wanted to ask her anyway.

'My parents are coming to town. I'd like you to meet them. But they're not a lot of fun. They're just not happy people, and they'll talk about my brother all night. But it would mean a lot to me if you met them. What do you think?'

'I think they've got to be a lot better than mine,' she said gently. She was touched and flattered that he wanted her to meet them.

And when she did, they were everything he had said and worse. They were good-looking, aristocratic people, and they were intelligent. But his mother looked depressed, and his father looked broken by life and the son he had lost. His shoulders drooped, and their faces and lives were colorless. It was as though they didn't even see Collin, and only the ghost of his brother. All subjects led back to him, and all mention of what Collin was doing led to an unfavorable comparison to his brother. Collin couldn't win. In their own way they were as bad as her parents, and just as depressing. She wanted to put her arms around Collin and kiss the hurt away after they dropped his parents off at their hotel, but he kissed her instead. It was the first time he had, and everything she felt for him poured out of her, all the compassion and sympathy and love. She wanted to heal all the old hurts he had suffered, and the loneliness of his parents' rejection of him. They talked for a long time afterward about how hurtful it was for him, and he was grateful for her support.

John and Harlan had already gone to bed when Victoria and Collin went back to her apartment and they talked and kissed for several hours. She disliked his parents almost as much as she did her own, although his had an excuse and hers didn't. Hers just didn't like her. His were mourning their son. But either way they had been unkind and unloving and rejecting to the point of being cruel, and in both cases had convinced their own children that they were unlovable. And both of them would carry the scars of it forever, as so many people did. To Victoria, it seemed like one of the worst crimes perpetrated by parents, to convince your own child not only that you didn't love them, but that they were unworthy of it, and no one else would ever love them either. It had been the curse of her life, and of Collin's too.

And that night they managed to give each other the love, comfort, and approval that they deserved and had needed for so long. It had been a meaningful evening for both of them. Very much so. And she was no longer telling Harlan everything that happened on their dates. She was developing an allegiance to Collin, which seemed right. And he felt the same way about her. He would only tell his sister so much whenever she called. He wanted to protect Victoria too, and the budding relationship they shared. They were both respectful and discreet.

The next dinner they shared after his parents' visit was an important one for both of them. It was silly and hokey, and Victoria was embarrassed that it meant so much to her, but it did, and Collin got that. It was Valentine's Day, and he took her to dinner at a small romantic French restaurant with delicious food, although she ate sensibly. The dinner was wonderful, and afterward they went back to his apartment, not hers. He had champagne for her, and a little gold bracelet with a small diamond heart on it that he put on her wrist, and then he kissed her, and it was the perfect time and place for both of them. She melted into his arms, and a moment later into his bed with him. Their clothes disappeared, and all the lonely years they had lived through until then without each other. And the one thing they both knew, when the evening ended, was how much they were loved. They felt worthy of it, and lovable at last.

From then on their life together took on an everyday quality. They went out to dinner, stayed home, did laundry together, went to the gym, spent nights at his apartment or hers, went to movies, and managed to blend two real lives into one. It all worked, better than either of them could ever have dreamed.

And it was Collin's idea to take a week off and go away with Victoria for spring break. Gracie was begging her to come to L.A., but Victoria didn't want to. She knew that her family would spoil it for them, and if they stayed together, he'd have to meet them soon enough. She dreaded introducing him to her parents, and had discussed it several times with her shrink, who was happy for her.

'Why are you afraid of having him meet your parents?' the psychiatrist asked, puzzled by her resistance. And the relationship was going so well. Better than Victoria had ever dreamed.

'What if my parents convince him of how unworthy

and unlovable I am, and he decides they're right?' She looked panicked as she blurted it out.

'Do you really think that's going to happen?' the doctor asked, looking her in the eye, and Victoria shook her head.

'No. But what if it does? They're so convincing.'

'No, they're not. The only one they've ever convinced is you. No one but their own child would believe them, which is why what they do is so cruel. No one else would buy into it or has. And Collin sounds a lot smarter than that.'

'He is. I just worry about what they'll say, and that they'll humiliate me in front of him.'

'They might. But if they do, I guarantee he won't like it, and will think even less of them. Have you invited him to your sister's wedding yet, by the way?' Victoria hadn't mentioned it.

'Not yet. But I'm going to. I don't want him to see me in that brown dress that looks so horrible on me. It's embarrassing.'

'You can still get her to let you wear something else. It's not too late,' the therapist reminded her.

'I tried. She won't let me. I just have to suck it up and wear it. But I hate for Collin to see me looking awful.'

'It sounds like he loves you anyway. The brown dress

won't matter to him.' The doctor was sorry Victoria wouldn't confront her sister about it.

Her sex life with Collin was also terrific, but she had been embarrassed about her weight at first. Even with her weight down she was bigger than she wanted to be, and there were plenty of extra rolls here and there and some jiggle. She didn't want him to see it, and always turned out the light. She kept covered up and ran to the bathroom in the dark, or wore a robe. Until one day he finally convinced her that he loved her body exactly the way it was, he reveled in it, he worshipped it, he loved every inch of her womanly body, and she actually believed him. He looked at her like a goddess whenever he saw her naked. He made her feel like the queen of sex and the high priestess of love. Nothing had ever been as exciting in her life, and once she began to realize how he felt about her, and believed him, they were in bed all the time. She had never had so much fun in her life, and the desperation came out of her diet. She ate sensibly, and she stayed away from ice cream and the really fattening stuff, and was diligent about going to Weight Watchers. But above all, she wanted to shout from the rooftops that Collin loved her. She was lovable after all. She had never been as happy in her life, and Collin felt the same way too. He basked in the warmth of Victoria's love, approval, and admiration, and thrived. It was all he had been missing in his life for years. Their life together was a watered garden where everything grew lavishly. The love they shared was a beautiful thing for both of them.

Just before spring break, Victoria had attended a baby shower for Amy Green. She was due to have the baby any minute, and would no longer be attending classes until after it was born. It had been touching to see her so big, with her mother hovering nearby. Amy looked happy, and the arrangement at school had worked well. And she'd be back after the baby, in a few weeks, to take final exams. She'd been accepted at Harvard and NYU. And she had decided to stay in the city, so she could be with her baby and her mother, who was going to help her. And Justin was going to NYU too. It had worked out perfectly for them. He had moved in with her and her mother for the last few months of the pregnancy, with his parents' approval, although they hadn't been thrilled at first. But Amy's family had been reasonable, and it was touching to see young people trying so hard to do the right thing. They had both just turned eighteen. And Victoria had told Collin about them. She loved sharing all aspects of her life with him, and he did the same about his work, and was anxious to introduce her to his friends. Together they were more than they each were alone. They didn't take away from each other, they added all that they were.

Collin surprised her with a wonderful old remodeled Connecticut farmhouse he had rented for them for spring break. It was private and lovely, and supremely comfortable. It was like playing house for both of them. It was next to a quaint village. They went for long walks, rented horses and rode through the countryside, cooked together at night, and made love all the time. They hated to give back the house when the time was up. It had been perfect.

Everything was going smoothly in both their lives, until a week after they came back from spring break. Victoria was at Collin's when the call came on her cell. It was Gracie, and she was crying so hard that Victoria couldn't understand a word she said. From her end of the conversation and the questions she was asking, Collin could tell that something was wrong, but neither of them knew what. She thought maybe one of her parents had died, or Harry. Gracie was incoherent, and Victoria was starting to panic.

'Gracie, calm down!' she shouted at her, and the sobbing continued, and then the story tumbled out.

'He chhh . . . chhheated on me,' she said, and then dissolved in floods of tears again.

'How do you know?' Victoria asked sharply, thinking that maybe it was a blessing if it kept her from marrying the wrong man. Maybe this was meant to be, and not such a bad thing, however devastating for Gracie.

'I saw him leaving a building with a woman. I was driving to Heather's house to show her sketches of my dress, and I saw him. He was walking out of the building with her, and he kissed her, and then they got in his car and drove away. He told me he had to meet with his father about some business, and he lied.' She was racked with sobs again. 'And he didn't go home last night. I called him and he didn't answer the phone.'

'Are you sure it was him?' Victoria asked sensibly.

'Positive. He didn't see me. My car window was open, and I could even hear them laughing, I was that close. She looked cheap, but I've seen her before. I think she's one of his father's secretaries.' Gracie was crying like a child.

'Did you tell him you saw him?'

'Yes. He said it's none of my business, we're not married yet, and he's still a free man. And if I bug him about it, he'll cancel the wedding. He said that's why my ring is so big, so I keep my mouth shut and stay off his back.' It was a horrible thing to say, and Victoria was shocked. It confirmed who she already thought Harry was, and worse.

'You can't marry him, Gracie. You can't marry a man who treats you like that. And he'll cheat on you again.' Collin had the drift by then, and sat down on the couch next to Victoria with a worried look. He hadn't met her younger sister, but he felt sorry for her already. She was just a kid.

'I don't know what to do,' Gracie said, sounding like a lost child.

'Cancel the wedding. You have no other choice. You can't marry a guy who's already cheating on you now, sleeping around, and tells you to keep your mouth shut because he gave you a big ring. He doesn't respect you.' Or himself apparently, Victoria thought to herself. And Collin was nodding approval of what she said. The guy sounded like a creep. He wouldn't have wanted his sister marrying him either.

'I don't want to cancel the wedding,' Gracie sobbed. 'I love him.'

'You can't let him treat you like that. Look, why don't you come to New York for a few days? We'll talk. Did you tell Dad?'

'Yes. He said men do that sometimes, it doesn't mean anything.'

'That's bullshit. Some men do. Decent men don't if they love their wives. I guess it can happen, but not like that, with some bimbo two months before your wedding. That's not a good sign.'

'I know.' She sounded devastated and lost.

'I'll get a ticket. I want you to come tomorrow.' It was too late that night.

'Okay.' Gracie sounded docile between hiccups, and was still crying when she hung up. Immediately after, Victoria called the airline, booked a ticket, and texted Gracie the information. She was willing to take a few days off school if she had to, to spend time with her sister. This was important. She couldn't marry Harry. There was no question about that. And Collin agreed with her when she told him what had happened.

'This is only the beginning. If he's already cheating on her now, he'll never stop. He probably has all along, and she just didn't know it,' Collin said, and Victoria agreed. He'd had plenty of opportunity, with his family, on trips to Europe, on bachelor party weekends. Collin was right, if Harry was a cheater, Gracie was in for a miserable life. They were still talking about it when they went to bed that night.

The next day Victoria waited till a decent hour to call her between classes. Gracie had just gotten up, after crying most of the night. She said Harry hadn't called, and the last time she had talked to him, he had again threatened to cancel the wedding, as though Gracie had done something wrong by calling him on his behavior and telling him what she'd seen.

'Let him,' Victoria said harshly. She hoped he would.

'I don't want him to cancel it,' Gracie said, weeping again, and Victoria was panicked. She couldn't marry this man. He hadn't even apologized for what he'd done, and showed no remorse, all of which were terrible signs. He was a badly behaved rich boy who did what he wanted, and was threatening his future wife instead of prostrating himself at her feet, begging her forgiveness, which would have been a start, and maybe still not enough. It wouldn't have been for Victoria.

'Just get on the plane. We'll talk about it here. Tell Mom and Dad you want to visit me. Besides, I want you to meet Collin.' She had told her all about him, although this didn't seem like a good time for them to meet.

'What if he gets madder because I go to New York?' She sounded panicked.

'Gracie, are you nuts? What if *he* gets madder? He cheated on you. You're the one who's supposed to be mad. Not him.'

'He said I was sneaking around, spying on him.'

'Were you?'

'No, I was going to see Heather to show her my dress sketches,' she explained again.

'Exactly, so he's full of shit. And a cheater. Come to New York.' She reminded her of the flight time, and Gracie had ample time to make it.

'Okay. I'll come. I'll see you later,' she said, sounding nervous, but she wasn't crying. Victoria had put her on a noon flight out of L.A., and it was due to land at JFK at eight P.M. New York time. Victoria was planning to go to the airport to get her. She was going to take a seven o'clock shuttle, which she had already booked. Her cell phone rang at six P.M., while she was at her apartment, getting organized for Gracie, and changing her sheets.

It was Gracie on the phone, and Victoria was confused. 'Where are you? Are you calling from the plane, or did you land early?'

'I'm in L.A.' She sounded upset and guilty. 'Harry just left. He said he'll forgive me and he won't cancel the wedding if I drop this whole thing, and don't do it again.' She sounded like a robot, and Victoria felt nuts.

'Do what again? Get cheated on? What is he talking about? What are you not supposed to do again?' Her voice was shaking out of anger and concern for her sister. Harry was turning the tables on Gracie and blaming her, when he was so blatantly at fault, not her sister.

'Spy on him, and accuse him of things.' She was crying, but Victoria couldn't hear it. 'He says I don't know what I'm talking about, and all he did was kiss her, and it's none of my fucking business anyway.'

'Is this who you want to marry?' Victoria was shouting. She was alone in the apartment and at her wits' end.

'Yes,' Gracie said sadly, and then started to sob. 'I do. I don't want to lose him. I love him.'

'You're never going to have him, except in name, if he's already cheating on you. That's not enough. He's blackmailing you into silence, Grace. He's telling you that if you call him on his shit, even if he's wrong, he'll abandon you. He's an asshole!' Gracie just cried harder.

'I don't care. I love him!' She was suddenly angry at her sister, instead of her future husband, for making her face the truth, which was too frightening for her to deal with. 'He says he won't cheat on me when we're married.'

'Do you believe him?'

'Yes! He wouldn't lie to me.'

'He just did,' Victoria pointed out in a tone of despair. 'He was out with another woman two nights ago. You saw him. And he didn't go home. You told me so yourself. Is that the life you want?'

'No, he won't do that. He said so. He's just having wedding jitters.'

'Wedding jitters don't make you a cheater, or they shouldn't. And if they do, there shouldn't be a wedding.'

'I don't care what you say,' Gracie said venomously. Victoria was dragging her into the light of truth, and she was doing everything to escape and take solace in Harry's lies. 'We love each other, and we're getting married. And he's not a cheater.'

'No, he's a great guy,' Victoria said caustically, 'This is disgusting, and you're the one who's going to pay the price.'

'No, I'm not,' Gracie said. 'It's going to be fine.' Victoria knew it wouldn't, and Gracie didn't want to hear it.

'Are you coming to New York?' Victoria asked in a dead voice.

'No. Harry doesn't want me to. He says I have too much to do here, and he'd miss me too much.' And he didn't want his naïve future wife influenced by her wiser older sister, who wasn't snowed by him. Victoria could figure that out easily.

'I'll bet. He just doesn't want you talking to me. Do whatever you want, Gracie. Just know that I'm here for you.' And she knew that sooner or later, her little sister would need her. It broke her heart. And she couldn't help wondering, as they hung up, if this had happened to her mother too. Maybe her father had cheated on her too at some point, and that was why he was willing to give Harry a pass. He shouldn't have otherwise, for his daughter's sake, money or not. Money wasn't going to give her happiness if Harry was a cheater or a bad guy. But he liked the prestige the alliance gave him by reflection.

Victoria thought about calling her father, but it seemed pointless. He wouldn't listen to her either. He was too invested in Gracie's marriage, for the wrong reasons. The three of them were in collusion to get her married to Harry Wilkes, come hell or high water. And it sounded like hell to Victoria. She called Collin and told him what had happened, and he was upset for her. He knew how much she cared about her sister, and this sounded like a bad situation to him.

'It's a shame your parents aren't being smarter than this.'

'They're fools, and they like his name. And she's a very foolish child. She thinks that if she loses him, there will never be anyone else like him. She's going to be miserable with him one day.' Collin didn't disagree. And she was depressed about it that night. She sent Gracie a text telling her that she loved her, but she didn't call her. There was nothing she could say, except the truth.

And Dr. Watson wasn't much help the next day. She said the same thing she had all along, even now, after Harry had cheated on Grace, or it looked that way.

'These are her decisions,' she reminded Victoria, 'and her life. I agree fully with what you're saying. He's blackmailing her, he's controlling, and he's probably dishonest. But she's the only one who can stand up to that and either change it or walk away. You have no part in this.' She was definite about it, and it made Victoria angry at her too. She felt helpless.

'So I have to sit by and watch?' Victoria had tears of rage and frustration in her eyes.

'No, you have to lead your own life. Concentrate on your life with Collin, and I'm glad it's going well. There is nothing you can or should do about your sister's life, or her marriage. This is entirely her choice, whether good or bad, and no matter what you think.'

'Even at twenty-two, when she doesn't know any better and needs guidance?' Victoria cringed at what Dr. Watson was saying, especially because it was true.

'That's right. She's not asking you for guidance. She's telling you to back off.' Victoria knew the therapist was right, which only made her fight harder.

'So she can buy into his lies?' She looked outraged.

'Yes, if that's what she wants to do, and apparently it is. I don't like it either, and hearing stories like this disturbs me too. But your hands are tied.'

'I hate this.' She was fiercely upset by Gracie's marrying him. But she didn't want to lose her relationship with her sister over this, and she knew she could. Harry had her sister blackmailed into silence, aided and abetted by her youth and neediness and their father's narcissism and greed. He wanted his daughter married to a Wilkes, at any price, so he could show off. And Gracie was afraid to lose Harry. Victoria was afraid her sister was about to lose herself, which was worse.

The next jolt after that was a call from Grace a week later. As maid of honor, she wanted Victoria to plan a 'destination bachelorette weekend' in Las Vegas for her, with all ten of her bridesmaids, including Victoria, which sounded hideous to her. When Victoria inquired, Gracie said everything was great with Harry and changed the subject. She had been threatened into the silence he wanted, even with her sister. If Gracie was worried, she wouldn't admit it. All she wanted was for Victoria to organize what sounded like a ghastly weekend to her. She really didn't want to organize it or go, and she didn't want to enable her marriage to a jerk, but she didn't have the guts to refuse either.

'Don't people just go out to dinner anymore for a bachelorette party? Who has time for a destination weekend?' Only people with a lot of money who didn't work, which was not the case for her.

'No, people do destinations now. Harry had his in St. Bart's last week. They went for five days,' Gracie said, and Victoria didn't want to imagine what had gone on there.

She sighed loudly, unhappy with the plan. 'Send me a list of what you want, and I'll see what I can do. Isn't there someone else who can do this? I work, Gracie, and I'm dealing with the time difference. You're all on the West Coast, and none of you work.' All of her bridesmaids were spoiled rich girls being supported by their parents, or still in school.

'You're the maid of honor, you're supposed to do it,' she said stubbornly, and Victoria felt guilty. The relationship as sisters was strained to the max these days over this wedding.

'When do you want to go?' Victoria asked, sounding discouraged.

'In May,' Gracie said happily, oblivious to her sister's discomfort.

'Okay. I'll take care of it. I love you,' Victoria said sadly, and hung up. Gracie had promised to send her all the names and details. And she said their father was paying for that too. He was shelling out big time for this alliance, and would have done none of it for Victoria, she knew. He had even said so to her and told her to elope if she ever found a husband.

Fortunately, in spite of all the stresses over the wedding, things were going well with Collin, but Victoria didn't consider it good news when she got a call from her mother, saying that her father had to see a client in New York and they were coming in for two days. That was all Victoria needed, and they knew about Collin, so she knew they'd want to meet him. And she had met his parents. She hated the things she knew her father would say about her. She told Collin that night.

'Will you have dinner with them with me?' she asked him with a woebegone look, and he smiled and kissed her.

'Of course.'

'And while we're on the subject, there's something I want to ask you.'

'The answer is yes,' he teased her. 'What's the question?' He knew how upset and anxious she was these days, and he felt sorry for her. She was worried for her sister, justifiably, from all he'd heard.

'Will you go to my sister's wedding with me?' she asked, and he smiled at her.

'I thought you'd never ask.'

'Everyone else looks gorgeous in the bridesmaid dress, and I look like shit in it. Be prepared. You won't be proud of me,' she said with tears in her eyes.

'I *will* be proud of you, and to be with you. And you couldn't look like shit if you tried. When are your parents coming, by the way?'

'In two days.' She made it sound like the end of the world, and it was to her. Her father would make a fool of her in front of the man she loved and prove how un-lovable she was. And what if Collin believed him? It didn't occur to her that it would make her father look bad and not her. Collin knew just how lovable she was.

She made the calls for Vegas the next day, although Dr. Watson reminded her that she could refuse to if she wanted to. But she didn't want to disappoint Gracie. She never did.

And her parents arrived in New York the day after. They were staying at the Carlyle, and invited her and Collin to the Bemelmans Bar for drinks. As it turned out, her parents had to dine with her father's client and didn't have time for dinner with them, which was a blessing. Drinks would be enough. She knew her father could destroy her in five minutes – he didn't need a whole evening to do it.

She could see immediately how impressed her father was with Collin, and how surprised he looked, as though he couldn't believe that Collin would be with someone like her. Victoria couldn't believe it either, but he wanted to be with her and had proven it abundantly for the last four months.

Everyone was on their best behavior, and they'd been chatting for half an hour when her father commented that he hoped she was watching what she ate so she'd fit into the maid of honor dress her sister had ordered for her. Victoria stiffened when he said it.

'I've lost weight, Dad,' she said quietly, 'and we go to the gym every day.'

'I'm sure you're a good influence on her,' he said, smiling broadly at Collin, who looked guarded as he waited to see what would come next. 'Watch out for the ice cream, though,' he said with the laughter she hated. Neither he nor her mother had noticed the weight she'd lost, nor her new nose, which Collin didn't know about either. She'd never told him. She didn't think he needed to know. He turned to Collin then and told him what a great guy Harry was, and how pleased they were about the marriage.

Victoria spoke up in a clear voice then. 'No, he's not a great guy, Dad. He cheated on her, and you know it.' Her father looked startled for a minute, to be called on it. He looked at Victoria intently.

'Just some harmless high jinks,' he said blithely. 'All boys do things like that before they get married. It takes the pressure off.' He winked at Collin, as though he would agree with him. Collin did not return the wink.

'How can you let her marry someone who is already cheating on her before the wedding?' Victoria said, looking upset, as her mother pretended not to hear her and sipped her drink, staring into space. She had checked out.

'Just a little lovers' quarrel, and a misunderstanding, I'm sure,' her father insisted, still smiling. Victoria wanted to blow a gasket, but she didn't. She knew there was no point arguing with him. He wasn't going to agree with her, and he fully approved of the marriage, no matter what Harry did. And Collin looked undismayed by the scene. He looked pleasant and strong, and his whole demeanor conveyed the fact that he was Victoria's ally and no one else's. Her father got the message that she had an ally now, and anyone who attacked or belittled her would be dealing with Collin too. It came across loud and clear, even without words. Her parents left shortly after, and told Collin it had been great to meet him.

'They weren't as bad as usual,' Victoria said as they left the Carlyle and walked toward her neighborhood. It was a balmy evening, and they were holding hands. She was stressed just from seeing her parents, and everything else that was happening these days, over which she had no control.

'They didn't fool me,' Collin said quietly. 'I heard him about the dress, the weight, the ice cream, and he doesn't give a damn if Harry cheats on your sister. He wants her married to a rich boy. He thinks it makes him look good. Just like my parents thought all of my brother's accomplishments made them look good, so they could brag about him, and mine were never good enough. I know exactly what these people are like,' he said as he looked at Victoria sympathetically. He could see what she had dealt with all her life, and the toll it took on her. She looked unhappy and uncomfortable in her own skin as they walked along. And she seemed tense and withdrawn when he kissed her on the way home. It was as though she was pulling away from him too. He could see it in her eyes. He stopped walking, and he looked at her.

'I'm not the enemy, they are. I hear them. You're not good enough so no one could ever love you. Come here,' he said, pulling her into his arms and looking into her huge blue eyes that were the same color as his own. 'I love you. You *are* lovable. They're idiots. And I love everything about you, just the way you are. Now that's my message to you. It's not theirs. It's mine. You are the most lovable woman I've ever known.' As he said it, he kissed her, and tears of relief slid down her cheeks, and she sobbed in his arms. He had just told her everything she had waited to hear all her life, and had never heard before.

Chapter 25

When Victoria got to school the next day, there was a huge bunch of blue balloons in the lobby that one of the students had brought in. There was a big sign up on the bulletin board. Amy Green had had her baby, a little boy. He weighed six pounds eight ounces, was nineteen inches long, and his name was Stephen William. Victoria was happy for her, and hoped it had gone well. She was sure she would hear all about it from some of the girls. The school was buzzing with the news all day.

Victoria heard later in one of her classes that Justin had been in the delivery room with Amy, with her mother. They hadn't known the baby's sex before, so that had been a surprise for them, and mother and baby were supposedly doing well, and going home in another day.

She was hoping to be back at school in two weeks, three at the most. The school had really made it work for her. Victoria was planning to go and visit her when Amy felt up to it. The girls who talked to her said she felt great, and the delivery hadn't been too bad. Victoria was relieved. They were young, but at least they were seniors, not freshmen. It was a long shot, but they had a chance at making it work, especially with Amy's mother's help and support.

During one of her breaks, Victoria had more calls to make on the Vegas trip, and she called her sister about it that weekend. Gracie sounded calmer than she had during the discovery of Harry's cheating. And it had been neatly swept under the rug, per Harry's wishes. Everyone was cooperating with him on that, especially the bride and her parents, which Victoria didn't think was the way it should be at all. But she was trying to detach from it. Collin and she went to the gym every morning, not because he was concerned about her weight, but because he said it would help her with stress, and it seemed to. She was feeling less anxious again, and she gave Gracie all the details she had arranged for the Vegas bachelorette weekend, which she still thought was a bad idea, or not one she'd enjoy anyway. She would have much preferred a quiet weekend in Santa Barbara with Gracie and her friends, at the Biltmore or the San Ysidro Ranch. But they were young, and they wanted to play.

She had booked rooms for all of them at the Bellaggio, two girls to a room, and the girls all had to give Gracie their credit card numbers. Victoria had made dinner reservations, and gotten tickets to Cirque du Soleil. She would be flying in from New York, and the others from L.A., arriving on Friday night and leaving on Sunday morning, when they checked out of the hotel. She had done her job as maid of honor, and her sister was happy with the plan, and apologized for putting pressure on her about it.

'It's okay. This is your big moment,' Victoria said, trying to be a good sport about it, which she always was. And in this case, doubly so, since she disliked Harry so much and was so worried about her sister. She felt as though she were leading her to her own execution, but it was what Gracie wanted. And Dr. Watson was right. It was Gracie's life.

'I'll do it for you one day,' Gracie said, sounding more like herself. Victoria knew she was under a lot of pressure, not just with the wedding, but from Harry, who was calling all the shots, and more so every day. A number of things had been changed to suit him. He was taking her to the South of France on their honeymoon. First to the

Hôtel du Cap in Cap d'Antibes, and then to St. Tropez, where he wanted to meet up with his friends, on his honeymoon with Grace.

'I hope you won't be doing it for me in Vegas,' Victoria laughed, relaxing a little.

'How's Collin?' Gracie was anxious to meet him, and she couldn't believe she hadn't seen her sister since Thanksgiving. It was the longest they had ever gone without seeing each other, and a lot was changing for both of them.

'Terrific.'

'Dad liked him,' Gracie commented, which surprised Victoria, since Collin had sat there like a vigilante protecting her, and had sent out a strong subliminal message to her father. Maybe he hadn't gotten it or pretended not to. 'He was surprised he was with you. He said he seems like a successful guy, and thought he was more likely to be with another lawyer, and not a schoolteacher. But he liked him.' The putdown was clear. She wasn't good enough for Collin. Now the messages were coming with Gracie. She was not only Harry's puppet, she was their father's.

'Maybe he likes me,' Victoria said quietly. She felt totally secure in his love now, and it was a great feeling.

'Mom says he's very good-looking.'

'Yes, he is. I'm sure that surprised Dad too. I'm sure he expects me to be dating someone he considers a loser like me.'

'He's not that bad. Don't be so hard on him.' Gracie defended their father, and Victoria wouldn't enter that conversation with her. She knew it was pointless. He was giving Gracie a big wedding and everything she wanted, and she was buying the party line, from him and her future husband. And he was the father who had always been nice to her and adored her. And if she was willing to be Harry's enabling handmaiden, she was willing to be her father's too. She and her mother had that in common now, and Victoria was at the opposite end of the spectrum. She was the freedom fighter taking a stand for the truths no one wanted to hear. And Collin was her ally now, not Gracie. Those days were over, and would never come again if she married Harry, and it looked like she would. Victoria missed the relationship she had once had with her sister and no longer did, and she was more grateful than ever to have Collin.

She finished up the details with Gracie for the Vegas trip, and then she spent a peaceful weekend with Collin. She was going to Las Vegas the following weekend. She wasn't looking forward to it. It wasn't her idea of a fun trip.

She went to visit Amy Green and her baby before she left. He was adorable and tiny, and Amy looked happy. She was nursing him, and was going to pump when she went back to school. It was only for a few weeks before summer vacation. Justin was there too, and looked like a proud papa as he held the baby while Amy chatted with Victoria. She had brought them a little blue sweater and booties, and Amy put them on him like a little doll. It was odd watching these two young kids as parents now. Babies having babies, but they both seemed mature and responsible with their son, and her mother was always hovering nearby to help them. It was an ideal situation for Amy and Justin, and had given her mother new life after the divorce. It looked like a blessing for all.

The next day Victoria flew to Las Vegas after school. She had promised to call Collin, and he knew how she was dreading the trip. She was sure Gracie's friends would drink a lot, play, gamble, go crazy, and pick up boys, since none of them were married. She felt like a chaperone on one of her senior school trips. They were a bunch of twenty-two- and twenty-three-year-olds prepared to go wild. And she felt like the old lady in the group, about to turn thirty.

The one nice thing about the trip was that Victoria got to see her sister, and Gracie threw herself into her arms when she arrived. She checked out Victoria's new nose and said she liked it.

The girls had started drinking before she got there, and some of them had already played the slot machines and won a little money. They all went out to dinner, and afterward they wandered through the casino, which was a strange, artificially lit world, full of bright lights, no windows, excited people, money changing hands, and girls in sexy costumes passing out free drinks. Some of it was wasted on the girls, but they loved the atmosphere and had already discovered that there was good shopping in all the hotels, particularly theirs, and lots of single men roaming around the casino and hotel.

Victoria felt as though she had to stay with them all evening, and she was exhausted and bored. They were mostly silly and had too much to drink, and flirted with the men they saw, except for Gracie, who behaved. Harry called her all night to check on her. It was two o'clock when Victoria finally got to her room. She was the only one who didn't have a roommate and didn't want one. Gracie was rooming with her best friend. And Victoria couldn't call Collin when she finally got to her room because it was too late in New York, although she had texted him several times and he had responded with encouraging messages to hang in. It was a marathon weekend, but she felt it her duty as maid of honor, and Gracie was visibly loving every minute of it. She was like a kid in Disneyland more than a bride.

The next day was chock-full with shopping, lunch, gambling, massages, manicures, pedicures, a swim in the pool, dinner at Le Cirque, Cirque du Soleil, which was a spectacular show, and finally back to the casino till three A.M. It was easy to lose track of time there, as there were no clocks and time seemed to stand still, which was what the casinos wanted. And some of the girls stayed up all night, and got blind drunk, but Gracie didn't. And Victoria slipped away at three and went back to her room to sleep.

They all met for a late brunch the next day, and then Victoria left the group to go back to New York. The others were leaving later, and she kissed Gracie before she left. Some of her friends had ferocious hangovers, but all of the girls said they'd had fun.

'You did a great job,' Gracie thanked her. 'I guess I won't see you till the wedding,' she said wistfully. 'I really miss you.'

'I'm coming out a few days early to help you,' Victoria reassured her. And then they hugged again, and Victoria left, grateful to be going home to New York. It had been a very long weekend. It hadn't been terrible, and there had been no mishaps, but she hadn't had fun either. Going to Las Vegas was not her idea of a good time. And Collin had told her several times how happy he was not to be there. She chatted with him on the phone, as she waited at the airport for her flight. He was going to meet her at his apartment, and he had promised her an early night. She needed it. And she had a big project at school the next day. It was the annual school play. They were doing *Annie*. It was a huge production, and she had promised to help backstage, with scenery and costumes, just as she had in high school. She had missed all the dress rehearsals that weekend. But she was sure someone would fill her in. From what she had seen so far, it was going to be great. And they had a final dress rehearsal on Monday morning. The big opening for parents and guests was Monday night. And one of her students was the star of the show, with a voice worthy of Broadway. Collin had said he'd try to come.

She had never been as happy to see anyone as she was to see him that night. She folded into his arms with relief. She had been anxious and felt as if she were on duty all weekend, trying to make everything go smoothly for her sister, and some of the girls weren't easy. They were spoiled young women who were used to getting their way. But in spite of that everything had gone well. And

Collin got into bed with her after they showered together. They made love, and five minutes later Victoria was asleep, as he tucked her in with a gentle smile. He had missed her.

They both left early the next morning. She had some things to do in her office before she went to the auditorium to start helping with the stage production. And she was there till noon while they set up, ran through all the musical numbers again, and Victoria was pushing scenery around with the students when she backed up, trying to make room for another big piece of scenery that was coming through. She stepped backward to avoid being knocked over, and before she could stop herself, she had fallen off the stage and lay flat on her back. There was a collective gasp as everyone saw it happen, and she was unconscious for a minute, and then she came to, and reassured everyone that she was fine. But she didn't look it. She was deathly pale, and when she tried to stand up, she couldn't. She had an excruciating pain in her leg, which was at an odd angle from her body. She insisted she'd be all right, but Helen went to get Mr. Walker and the school nurse, and they called 911. Victoria was mortally embarrassed when the paramedics walked in and put her on a stretcher. She had tried to get up, and she couldn't, and she had gotten a nasty bump on her head when she fell. And in the ambulance, they told her that it looked like her leg might be broken, and she told them that was impossible, she hadn't fallen that hard, but Helen, who had gone in the ambulance with her, said she had, and hit her head hard too. They wanted to do some X-rays and a CT scan of her head.

'This is so stupid,' she said, trying to be brave about it, but she felt nauseous and her blood pressure was low. And she called Collin and told him what had happened. He promised to meet her at the hospital right away. She told him he didn't have to.

'I know you think you're not worthy of it, you goof. But I love you, and I'm coming up. I'll find you when I get there.' She started to cry when he said it. She was scared, and relieved that he was coming, but she would never have asked him to.

He found her in the emergency room when he arrived. They had already seen on the X-ray that her leg was broken, although it was a simple fracture and didn't need surgery, just a cast, much to her relief. And she had a mild concussion, and all she needed for that was rest.

'Well, you did quite a morning's work, didn't you?' Collin said ruefully. He was worried about her, but relieved it wasn't worse, and she didn't say it, but she was thrilled she hadn't hurt her new nose. And after they set her leg and put the cast on it, Collin took her home and set her up on pillows on the couch. He brought her mushroom barley soup and a tuna fish sandwich to eat. She had crutches, and they told her they would take the cast off in four weeks, about ten days before Grace's wedding.

Collin had to go back downtown for a pretrial meeting at his office that he couldn't get out of, but he promised to be back as soon as he could. She thanked him, and he kissed her, and flew out the door, and then she called Harlan at work and told him what had happened.

'You klutz,' he teased her, and she laughed, but it hurt. They said it would for a few days. She called Gracie too, and she and Harry sent her flowers, and Harlan brought her a stack of magazines when he came home. And an hour later, Collin walked in with a cooked chicken and grilled vegetables from Citarella for all of them, and kissed his patient.

'Sorry. I came back as soon as I could. We're trying to settle the case.' She felt like a queen surrounded by her court as they all fussed over her, and Collin stayed with her that night. She was in a lot of pain, and he gave her the pain-killers and rubbed her back in bed.

'You're a good nurse,' she said, thanking him. 'I'm sorry. This is so stupid.'

'Yeah, I figured you did it on purpose.' He smiled at her. She had been sorry to miss the play, but she was in too much pain to go, and she was sorely disappointed. And she was annoyed that she'd have to be on crutches. At least the cast was due to come off before the wedding, if it healed well. It was a headache she didn't need. Her mother had called her that night too, and left a message on her voice mail that she was sorry to hear about her leg.

She hobbled into school the next day, and all the students helped her get around. Helen and Carla came to check on her in her classroom, and Eric Walker stopped by to say hello. Everyone was happy to see her back, and they said *Annie* had gone fabulously. And at the end of the day she was really tired, and took a cab home. She realized on her way back to the apartment that she was not going to be able to exercise for the next month, and she was terrified she would gain weight. She said as much to Harlan when he got home. Her vow to herself had been to lose twenty-five pounds by June, have a life, and a man she cared about. She had a life now, with Collin, and she had never been happier. She had lost eighteen pounds and looked great. But she had wanted to lose the last seven pounds before the wedding and it would be hard now, hobbling around on crutches, unable to exercise, and lying on the couch.

'You just have to be careful not to eat crazy,' Harlan warned her. 'No ice cream. No cookies. No pizza. No bagels. No cream cheese. Especially since you can't move around much.'

'I won't, I promise,' she said, although she had a small urge for ice cream that night when her leg hurt. But she didn't ask for any, and she didn't go near the freezer. But she had two helpings of pasta for dinner, which tasted great. And she vowed not to do it again. No comfort foods in the next month. Or she'd look like a blimp at the wedding, and prove her father right, that she was hopeless.

She shared her concerns with Collin, and he told her that whatever she gained while she was on crutches, she could lose again once she could exercise, and so what if she didn't.

'You don't need to worry about it. You're a beautiful woman, and one dress size is not a big deal, one way or another.'

'It is to me,' she said sadly. 'And I don't want to look like a brown cow in that dress.'

'That dress doesn't sound like you, no matter what size it is. I can't see you in brown,' he said cautiously, although women's fashions were not his area of expertise.

'You will soon,' she said unhappily, worrying about her

weight. She wanted to visualize herself into thinness. She had bought a pale blue chiffon dress for the rehearsal dinner, with a silver bolero and high-heeled silver sandals. It was very flattering and slimming, she was happy about that, but her dress for the wedding still upset her. It was a total no-win for her.

'We can have a ceremonial burning of the dress after the wedding,' Collin said with a sympathetic grin. 'I would love you in a burlap bag, so don't worry about it.' She smiled at him, and they kissed. They stayed at her apartment for a few days until she felt better, and then they went back to his, which was easier for him, and it was closer to his office.

He broached an interesting subject with her one Sunday afternoon at his place, two weeks after she'd broken her leg. 'What would you think about our getting a place together one of these days? We could look for it this summer.' Up till now they had been going back and forth between apartments. They had been dating for five months, and their relationship was so solid that they both felt ready to make the move, and then see what developed later. 'How does that sound to you?' Until then, when he was preparing a trial and working late, he stayed at his place. The rest of the time he stayed with her during the week, and she stayed with him most weekends.

'It sounds good,' she said peacefully, and leaned over and kissed him. He had signed her cast six times, and Harlan twice, and John added his name in red. And every kid in school had signed it at least once. Helen said it was the most decorated cast in New York, and looked like an art exhibit, or an example of graffiti. 'I like that idea a lot,' Victoria said about living with him.

'So do I. Will Harlan and John be upset?' he asked with a look of concern.

'No. I think they're both doing okay now, and can afford to keep the apartment without me. They might like the space.' He nodded. And they were in no hurry to find their own place. Collin wanted to start looking at the end of June, early July.

They told Harlan and John a few days later, when they went back to the apartment. Harlan said he wasn't surprised. He had been expecting something like that, or an announcement of their engagement, he said with a mischievous look at Collin, who just laughed and smiled at Victoria. They hadn't talked about it yet, but it had crossed his mind. His sister had said the same thing, and she wanted to meet Victoria that summer. There was time. There was no need for them to do anything in a hurry. They were enjoying what they had. They had both waited a lifetime for it, and were savoring every moment.

And his sister had just met someone too. Collin hadn't met him yet, but he sounded perfect for her. He was a widowed doctor with two young kids, and his sister said they were really cute. Five and seven. Life had a way of working out. The lid-for-every-pot theory seemed to work, if you waited long enough and were patient. Victoria was now a firm believer in it. They agreed to start looking for an apartment together after her sister's wedding, when she was no longer in a cast and on crutches and could get around. He had a lull between trials, and she'd be out of school then. She could hardly wait.

Victoria got her cast taken off three days after school closed for the summer. The leg felt a little weak and wobbly, but she had to do physical therapy and exercise, and they said that would strengthen it. And in the meantime, she had to be on her feet for the wedding. She could put her full weight on her leg, but it didn't feel strong. And she couldn't overdo at the gym yet. She had to do therapy first.

She didn't say anything to anyone, but the day she got the cast off, she walked into her bathroom and weighed herself, and as soon as she did, she sat down on the edge of the tub and burst into tears. She had been careful, but not totally. There had been some pasta on bad nights when her leg hurt and she needed comfort food, a couple of pizzas, the occasional ice cream, cheese and crackers, and there had been mashed potatoes and some delicious meat loaf Harlan had brought home from the deli. And it all added up. It spelled out that, immobilized as she had been and unable to exercise at the gym, she had gained back seven of the eighteen pounds she'd lost. So instead of losing twenty-five pounds for the wedding, she'd lost eleven. She knew she might be able to knock off another three or four if she tried hard and did a regime of special herbal teas before the wedding. So now she was going to be wearing an unflattering dress that didn't suit her, and she'd be fat. She sat there and cried, and as she did, Collin walked into the bathroom.

'What happened?' He looked worried. 'Is your leg hurting?'

'No, my ass is,' she said, looking angry at herself. 'I gained seven pounds with my stupid broken leg.' She was embarrassed to admit it to him, but he could see that she was crying, so she'd told him.

'You'll lose it, and who cares,' he said, and then he had an idea. 'I'm throwing your scale away. I don't want your whole life dictated by what you weigh. You look great. I love you. And if you gain five pounds or lose ten, who gives a fuck? I don't.'

'I do,' she said unhappily, and blew her nose in a tissue, still sitting on the edge of the tub.

'That's different,' Collin said. 'Then do it for you, don't do it for me. I don't care. I love you the way you are, whatever size you happen to be.' She looked at him with a smile.

'How did I get lucky enough to find you? You're the best thing that's ever happened to me at a gym,' she said.

'We earned each other, by being miserable for a long time. We deserve to be happy,' Collin said, and leaned down to kiss her.

'And loved,' she added, and then he kissed her again, and she stood up and he took her in his arms.

'When are you leaving for L.A., by the way?' He knew it was soon, now that she had her cast off. That was what she had been waiting for, and the green light from her doctor. And now she had it.

'In two days. I hate to leave before you do,' Victoria said with a sigh, 'but Gracie says she needs me.'

'Just watch out for your parents. They bite,' he warned her, and she laughed. He was right. 'It's a little bit like swimming with the sharks. And I'll be out on the Thursday before the wedding. I tried to come out earlier, but I can't. I've got to try and settle this case if I can before I come out.'

'I'll be fine,' she said bravely, and he kissed her again.

In the end, Victoria spent the weekend with him in New York, and she left on Monday for L.A. Collin was due to arrive three days later. She assured him confidently that she could deal with her family on her own for three days – she'd been coexisting with them for nearly thirty years.

Gracie met her at the airport and drove her back to the house. She said that all her bridesmaids were in town. The dresses had been altered and tried on and were perfect. The caterer was organized. The florist was on track. They had picked their music for the church and the reception, and hired the band. She loved her dress, and Vera Wang had done it in the end. She went down her whole checklist, and everything was fine, and then she remembered that her sister hadn't tried her dress yet.

'You should try it when we get back to the house,' Gracie said, with a worried look. 'Do you think you'll need it altered?' she asked, glancing over at Victoria next to her in the car. She looked about the same to her, but you couldn't always tell.

'No, I'm not much thinner than I was,' Victoria said, looking discouraged.

'I meant bigger,' Gracie said hesitantly, and Victoria shook her head. That was how they all thought of her, as an ever-growing mountain that never got smaller, only bigger. She'd lost a pound since she took off the cast, but no more than that. She wasn't exercising enough to make a difference, even without carbs.

And when they got there, their mother was at the house, checking gifts off a list. There were piles of silver and crystal in fancy boxes. They had turned their dining room into a warehouse.

Her father was at the office, and Victoria didn't see him till that night. When she did, he hugged her and commented that she looked well. With him, *healthy* and well were always synonyms for *bigger* and *fatter*. She thanked him, said he did too, and walked into the other room. She hadn't seen him since he met Collin in New York. And she remembered Collin's comment about sharks and steered clear.

She managed to tread water for three days until Collin arrived. They had a family dinner that night, for both families, which was fairly benign. And the rehearsal dinner was the next day at the Wilkeses' country club. The wedding reception was being held at the Dawsons' swim and tennis club in a huge garden, under an enormous 'crystal' tent that had cost a fortune. Five hundred and forty guests had accepted.

The morning that Collin was due to arrive, Victoria

got a few minutes alone with her sister and asked her once and for all if she wanted to go through with this and if she was sure about Harry. And if so, she promised to forever hold her peace. Gracie looked at her solemnly and said that she was sure.

'Are you happy?' she asked her. She didn't look it. She looked terribly stressed, and whenever Harry was around she was jumping through hoops to please him. If she married him, that was what her life was going to be like from now on. It was what he thought he deserved. Victoria hated it for Gracie.

'Yes, I am happy,' Gracie answered, and then Victoria sighed and nodded her head.

'Okay. I'm on board. That's all I want for you. And you can tell him from me that if he ever makes you unhappy, I will personally kick his ass,' Victoria said, and Gracie laughed nervously. She was afraid her sister meant it.

'He won't,' Gracie said seriously. 'I know he won't!' She sounded like she was trying to convince herself.

'I hope you're right.'

Victoria didn't bring it up again after that, and she was relieved when Collin arrived. Harry went to considerable lengths to impress him and charm him, and Collin was polite and went along with it, but Victoria could see that Collin didn't like him. And she didn't either. But they were stuck with him now. For better or worse.

The rehearsal dinner was a monumental affair, done by the fanciest caterer in L.A., with all the most important people there. The Wilkeses were extremely gracious, and they made an effort to make all the Dawsons feel at home, and they said all the nicest things about Gracie. She was young, of course, but they said they thought she was the perfect wife for their son. And Jim Dawson went on and on ad nauseam about how much he loved Harry. And there were endless speeches at dinner, some of them clever, and most of them very boring. Victoria was going to have to say a few words too, but she was doing it at the wedding, as older sister and maid of honor.

Victoria was looking beautiful in the pale blue chiffon gown she had bought for the occasion. And Collin had complimented her several times. Her father had had quite a few drinks, when he came over to Victoria and Collin after the rehearsal dinner started to break up and people were milling around. He had on his hale-and-hearty voice, which Victoria knew was usually a bad sign, and when he was most likely to take potshots at her. She wanted to warn Collin as her father walked over, but she didn't have time. He was standing on top of them before she could say a word.

'So,' he said, looking at Collin as though he were

fourteen and had just shown up to take Victoria out for the first time, 'you've made a good choice here. Victoria is our smart one. Gracie's our beauty. Smart women are always interesting to have around.' It was his first shark attack of the night. She hadn't seen him talk to Collin till then. And there was blood in the water. As usual, it was hers. Collin looked at him pleasantly as he put an arm around Victoria's shoulders and pulled her close to him. She could feel his strength as he held her, and his protection. And for once in her life, she felt safe. She always did with him. And loved.

'I'm afraid I don't agree with you, sir,' Collin said politely.

'About smart women?' He looked surprised. Usually, his opinions were never challenged, no matter how outrageous, inaccurate, or insulting. No one ever bothered.

'No, about your family beauty and brain. I'd say Victoria is both, beauty and brain. You underestimate her. Don't you agree?' Her father stammered for a minute, and then nodded, not sure how to respond. Victoria almost laughed, and she squeezed Collin's hand in silent thanks. But her father wasn't willing to let it go at that. He didn't like being contradicted or interfered with while belittling his daughter.

He gave a hollow laugh, which was another bad and

familiar sign. 'It's amazing how genes skip generations, isn't it? Victoria looks exactly like my grandmother, she always has, and nothing like us. She even has my grandmother's build, coloring, and nose.' He was hoping to embarrass her, because he knew how much she had hated her nose all her life. It was his revenge for the protection Collin provided her. Innocently, Collin leaned closer and studied Victoria's nose, and turned to her father with a puzzled expression.

'It looks very much like her mother and sister's nose to me,' Collin said honestly. And of course it did, thanks to Dr. Schwartz, but Collin didn't know that, as Victoria blushed. Her father looked annoyed and looked closer himself, and he had to admit, to himself if not to Collin, it did look like Gracie and her mother's nose.

'Strange, it used to look just like my grandmother's,' he muttered. 'She's a big girl like my grandmother though,' he said with a malevolent glint in his eye. It was the description she had loathed since she was a child.

'Do you mean tall?' Collin asked with a smile.

'Yes, of course.' Her father recanted for the first time ever, and then without further comment, he slunk off into the crowd. His barbs had been as sharp as ever, but this time they had missed their mark. It was obvious to her father that Victoria didn't care, and even more so that

Collin loved her. Her father had lost the target of his jokes and putdowns forever. Victoria sighed as she watched him find her mother and tell her it was time to go.

'Thank you,' Victoria said quietly to Collin. She would have liked to confront her father herself, but she was still afraid to. There was too much water behind that dam. Maybe one day, but not now.

Collin had an arm around her as they walked to where the valet parkers had the cars and limousines. 'I can't believe the shit he says about you,' he said, looking annoyed. 'What's with the nose?' he asked looking puzzled, and she burst out laughing as they waited for the car and driver Collin had hired for the night.

'I had a nose job during Christmas vacation. That was the car accident when I met you,' she said, looking embarrassed at having kept it from him out of vanity until then. But she didn't want any secrets from him, now or ever; so she made a clean breast of it, and was relieved. 'I hated my nose, and he always made cracks about it. So I fixed it. I never told them, just Gracie. Neither he nor my mom noticed when I saw them in New York, or now.' Collin couldn't help smiling at her admission.

'That was a nose job when I met you?' He looked amazed. 'I thought it was a horrible accident.'

'It was my new nose,' she said, looking half proud and half shy.

He studied it for a minute with a grin. He had had a fair amount to drink too, or he wouldn't have taken on her father. He didn't usually do that. But his putdowns of Victoria irritated Collin beyond belief. 'It's an extremely cute nose.' He complimented her. 'I love it.'

'I think you're drunk,' she said with a laugh. She had enjoyed watching him subtly take apart her father.

'Actually, I am drunk. But not dangerously so.' He stopped to kiss her, and then their car and driver showed up and they got in. He was staying at the house with her, so they were bound to run into her father again, but they went into her room quickly when they got back. And Collin was so tired, he was asleep in five minutes. Victoria lay with him for a while, and then she went to find Gracie in her room.

She poked her head in the door, and Gracie was sitting on her bed and looking a little lost. Victoria went in and sat down next to her, as she used to when they were kids. 'Are you okay?'

'Yeah. Nervous about tomorrow. I feel like I'm going to his family and losing ours,' she said, looking anxious. Victoria wouldn't have considered it a loss, except for

Gracie, but she knew Gracie did. She loved her parents. And they loved her.

'You won't lose me,' Victoria reassured her. 'You'll never lose me.' Gracie hugged her without saying a word. Gracie looked like she was about to cry, but she didn't. Victoria couldn't help wondering if she was having second thoughts about Harry. She should. But she didn't admit it if she did. 'The wedding will be fine,' Victoria said soothingly. But sadly, the marriage would not, or at least Victoria doubted it.

'I like Collin,' Gracie said, to change the subject. 'He's really nice, and I think he loves you a lot.' It was easy to see, he took wonderful care of her, and looked at her adoringly like he was the luckiest man in the world.

'I love him a lot too,' she said happily.

'Do you think you'll marry him?' It looked that way to her, and Victoria smiled.

'I don't know. He hasn't asked. It's too soon. We're happy like this for now. We're going to get an apartment together this summer.' They were moving slowly, but Gracie was about to become a real married woman in a few hours. She seemed much too young to her sister to take such a big step, especially to Harry, who was going to control every aspect of her thought and life. It made Victoria sad for her. But this was what she said she wanted, and the price she was willing to pay to be with him.

'I'm sorry about the brown dress,' Gracie said suddenly, with a guilty look. 'I should have picked something that suits you better. I just liked the dress. But I should have thought about you.' Victoria was touched that Gracie realized it and told her, as she gave her a forgiving hug.

'It's okay. I'll get even with you when I get married. I'll pick something you look like shit in.' They both laughed and chatted for a while, and then Victoria hugged her and went back to her room. She felt sorry for her little sister. She had the feeling she wasn't going to have an easy life. A moneyed one for sure, but not necessarily a good one. All she could do now was hope for the best for her sister. They were each responsible for their own lives.

Victoria got into bed next to Collin, smiled at him, and then cuddled up with him and went to sleep. For the first time in her life, she felt safe in her parents' house.

Chapter 26

On the morning of the wedding, the house was bustling with excitement and activity from the moment everyone got up. There was breakfast laid out in the kitchen so people could help themselves. Collin and Victoria took theirs out to the garden so they didn't get in anyone's way. Gracie was having a manicure and pedicure in her room. The hairdresser came to do all the women in the house. All Victoria wanted was a simple French twist, so she went first.

The wedding was set for seven o'clock that night, but people came and went all day. All the bridesmaids were there from lunchtime on, and Victoria couldn't get near her sister, so she left them alone, and did whatever she could to help her mother. But everything seemed in surprisingly good control. And Gracie's wedding gown was laid out in her mother's room. Her father had been relegated to the guest room to dress, and everyone seemed to have something to do. There were a million phone calls and deliveries, and Collin volunteered to man the doors and phones. Victoria's father disappeared for a while, and then came back, but he never said a word to Victoria all day, nor to Collin. He had gotten a dose of his own medicine the night before, and Victoria was glad. It was about time. And Collin had done it well, with style and finesse. With his protection, her father would think twice before attacking her again.

And by five o'clock the countdown had begun. The hairdresser did Gracie's hair. All the bridesmaids had been done. And at six o'clock they all slipped into their dresses. Victoria took a deep breath and put hers on, and one of the bridesmaids zipped it up, while another one held it closed, and Victoria held her breath. She didn't look in the mirror. She could feel how it looked. She could hardly breathe, even with the weight she'd lost, and her breasts were tightly compressed and poured out of the strapless dress. It was excruciatingly tight, and the zipper almost didn't close. And she knew just how ugly it looked on her, but she really didn't care. Collin loved her, and if it wasn't the best dress for her, it wasn't important. She had found brown satin shoes to match and slipped them on. The heels were high, and she suddenly looked like a very tall woman. But a good-looking woman. She felt like she had come into her own in the last year, not just because of Collin, but the efforts she'd made to free herself of the past and the damage it had done. Collin had happened because she was ready for him. She had made the changes, and he had arrived – the changes weren't because of him. She felt sure of herself suddenly even in the dress that didn't suit her. She looked beautiful, and shone from within. She put on a little more blush, and the color of the dress didn't look quite so bad with her pale skin.

She went in to her sister, and her mother was just slipping the elaborate white lace gown over Gracie's head. Her mother was dressed in a dark beige taffeta gown with a jacket, and she looked elegant and demure. She was still a beautiful woman. Sometimes Victoria forgot that. And the minute the enormous white lace dress fell over Gracie's tiny body, she looked like a princess. She was wearing her engagement ring that looked like a headlight, and the diamond earrings Harry had given her. And his mother had given her a string of large pearls with a diamond clasp as a wedding gift. She seemed much too young to be wearing all that jewelry, and Victoria was reminded of when they played dress-up when they were children, but Gracie looked lovely. She was the perfect bride, and when her father walked in a few minutes later, he started to cry. He was overwhelmed by the vision of her in her wedding gown. She had always been his baby. And she always would be. And she was Victoria's baby too. Gracie looked around the room at her family, and she was about to cry too, but her mother warned her not to ruin her makeup. Gracie felt as though she were leaving them all forever and setting out in the world, on unfamiliar waters. It was a scary feeling, especially for such a young girl. She appeared vulnerable and fragile and childlike in the dress, as her mother settled the long veil on her head.

Victoria and her mother helped her down the stairs and carried her train. And then she was getting into the car with her father to go to the church to marry Harry. Her father came unglued as they drove away, and Gracie leaned over and kissed him. She had a father that Victoria had never known, and would have loved to have. But now she had Collin instead.

And then Victoria and her mother got into the town car waiting to take them to the church. Collin had left a while before and she would see him there.

And once at the church, everything happened in good

order. Harry was waiting at the altar. The bridesmaids preceded Grace in the elegant brown dresses, and Victoria walked down the aisle right before Gracie. Her eye caught Collin's as she glided past him, and he smiled, looking proud. And their father walked Gracie down the aisle in solemn, measured steps.

They exchanged their vows, and Harry put a diamond band on Gracie's finger, and then they were pronounced man and wife. They kissed as Victoria cried, and they walked back down the aisle beaming. It had happened. It was over. The wedding that had driven them all crazy for a year was under way. And the reception was as spectacular as her parents had wanted, and Gracie had dreamed of. She came to kiss Victoria as the reception began, after the photographs and the receiving line. She just wanted a minute with her big sister.

'I just want to tell you that I love you. Thank you for everything you've done for me all my life. You always take care of me, even when I'm a brat, or I'm stupid . . . thank you . . . I love you . . . you're the best sister in the world.'

'So are you, and I'll always be here for you. I love you, baby . . . I hope you'll be happy.'

'So do I,' she said softly, and she didn't look as sure as Victoria would have wanted. But if it didn't work out, they'd deal with it and know what to do. Sometimes you just couldn't figure it out beforehand, no matter how hard you tried.

Collin sat next to Victoria at the reception, at a long table with all the bridesmaids and groomsmen. Victoria made her speech, and everyone applauded. She and Collin danced all night. Harry and Gracie cut the cake. And Victoria even danced with her father once. He looked dignified and handsome in his dinner jacket and black tie. And for once he made no ugly comments about her – they just danced as he spun her around the floor, and then he turned her over to Collin again. It was a beautiful wedding. And Gracie was an exquisite bride. And much to Victoria's relief, for tonight at least, and maybe forever if they were lucky, Gracie and Harry looked happy. There was no way of knowing if it would last, for them or anyone. All you could do was your best.

She was dancing with Collin when they announced that Gracie was going to throw the bouquet, and asked all the single women to assemble on the dance floor. Grace stood on a chair, waiting to do it, and all the single women started to approach. Victoria's mother glided past Victoria as she was about to join them and gave her a reproving look.

'Let them have it, dear, they're all younger than you are. They'll all get married one day. You don't even know if you ever will.' In a single sentence, she had dismissed Collin as a real possibility, and told her that not only was she likely to be a spinster but she really didn't deserve the bouquet. She was undeserving again, and unlikely to be loved since they never had. Victoria could feel herself shrink back to the edge of the crowd, as Gracie tried to wave her forward, but her mother's message had been a powerful one. Collin had seen her mother say something to her, and the look on her face afterward, but he was too far from her now to have heard what was said. Whatever it was, he could tell that it had devastated her, and he could see her collapse inwardly, as she stood with her arms down, as Gracie got ready to toss the bouquet. She was watching her older sister as she did, and she took careful aim with an arm like a pitcher, and the bouquet flew through the crowd like a missile heading straight for Victoria, but her mother's words had hit her too hard. Victoria felt frozen and couldn't lift her arm, and Collin stood there, watching her, as did Gracie, willing her to reach out and grab it. All she had to do was hold out her hand and catch it, if she only believed she deserved it. Collin felt a searing pain at the agony he sensed that she felt, and he said the words aloud that he was thinking. 'You're lovable!' he said to Victoria, even though she couldn't hear him. And as though she had, her face broke into a smile, and in a split second she reached out and grabbed it. She held it aloft and everyone cheered, and Collin loudest of all. Victoria looked over at him at that moment, and he gave her a thumbs-up with both thumbs, just as Harry lifted his wife from the chair and they went upstairs to change. They were leaving for Paris on his father's plane that night.

Collin made his way through the crowd to Victoria, and she was beaming at him when he got there. He still didn't know what her mother had said to her, but he knew it was hurtful, and this time he didn't want to know. All he wanted to do was shield her from those wounds forever. She was still holding the bouquet.

'We'll put that to good use one of these days,' he said, gently taking it from her, and setting it down at their table, and then he swept her onto the dance floor and held her in his arms as they danced away. She was a beautiful woman. She always had been. She just didn't know it, and now she did. And as she looked up at him, she knew just how much she was loved.

Turn the page for a sneak preview of

Danielle Steel's wonderful new novel,

44 CHARLES STREET . . .

Chapter 1

Francesca Thayer sat at her desk until the figures started to blur before her eyes. She had been over them a thousand times in the past two months – and had just spent the entire weekend trying to crunch numbers. They always came out the same. It was three o'clock in the morning and her long wavy blond hair was a tangled mess as she unconsciously ran her hands through it again. She was trying to save her business and her house, and so far she hadn't been able to come up with a solution. Her stomach turned over as she thought of losing both.

She and Todd had started the business together four years ago. They'd opened an art gallery in New York's West Village where they specialized in showing the work of emerging artists at extremely reasonable prices. She had a deep commitment to the artists she represented. Her experience in the art world had been extensive, although Todd had none at all. Before that, she had run two other galleries, one uptown after she graduated, and the other in Tribeca. But this gallery that they had started together was her dream.

She had a degree in fine arts, her father was a well-known artist who had become very successful in recent years, and the gallery she shared with Todd had gotten excellent reviews. Todd was an avid collector of contemporary work, and he thought that helping her start the gallery would be fun. At the time, Todd was tired of his own career on Wall Street as an attorney. He had a considerable amount of money saved and figured he could coast for a few years. The business plan he had developed for them showed them making money within three years. He hadn't counted on Francesca's passion for less expensive work by entirely unknown artists, helping them whenever possible, nor had he realized that her main goal was showcasing the work, but not necessarily making a lot of money at it. Her hunger for financial success was far more limited than his. She was as much a patron of the arts as a gallerist. Todd was in it to make money. He thought it would be exciting and a welcome change of career for him after years of doing tax and estate work for an important law firm. But now he said he was tired of listening to their bleeding-heart artists, watching his nest egg dwindle to next to nothing, and being poor. As far as Todd was concerned, this was no longer fun. He was forty years old, and wanted to make real money again. When he talked to her about it he had already lined up a job at a Wall Street firm. They were promising him a partnership within a year. As far as selling art was concerned, he was done.

Francesca wanted to stick with it and make the gallery a

success, whatever it took. And unlike Todd, she didn't mind being broke. But in the past year, their relationship had begun to unravel, which made their business even less appealing to him. They argued about everything, what they did, who they saw, what to do about the gallery. She found the artists, worked with them, and curated the shows. Todd handled the money end of things and paid the bills.

The worst of it was that their relationship was over now too. They had been together for five years. Francesca had just turned thirty when she met him, and Todd was thirty-five.

It was hard for her to believe that a relationship that had seemed so solid could fall apart so totally in a year. They had never wanted to get married and now they disagreed about that too. When Todd hit forty, he suddenly decided he wanted a conventional life. Marriage was sounding good to him and he didn't want to wait much longer to have kids. At thirty-five, she still wanted what she had when they met five years before. They had talked about maybe having kids one day, but she wanted to turn their gallery into a success first. Francesca had been very honest with him about marriage when they met, that she had an aversion to it. She had had a front-row seat all her life to her mother's obsession with getting married – and she watched her screw it up five times. Francesca had spent her entire life trying not to make the same mistakes. Her mother had always been an embarrassment to her. And she had no desire whatsoever to start emulating her now.

Francesca's parents had gotten divorced when she was six. She had also watched her extremely handsome, charming, irresponsible father drift in and out of relationships, usually with very young girls who never lasted in his life for more than six months. That, combined with her mother's fetish for marriage, had made Francesca commitment-phobic until she met Todd. His parents' own bitter divorce when he was fourteen had made him skittish about marriage too. They had had that in common, but now he had begun to think that marriage made sense. He told her he was tired of their bohemian lifestyle where people lived together and thought it was fine to have kids without getting married. As soon as Todd blew out the candles on his fortieth birthday cake, it was as if a switch were turned on, and without any warning, he turned traditional on her. Francesca preferred things exactly as they were and had always been.

Now suddenly, in recent months, all of Todd's friends seemed to live uptown. He complained about the West Village where they lived, and which she loved. He thought the neighborhood and people in it looked scuzzy. To complicate matters further, not long after they opened the gallery, they had fallen in love with a house that was in serious disrepair. They had discovered it on a snowy December afternoon and were instantly excited, and had gotten it at a great price because of the condition it was in. They restored it together, doing most of the work themselves. If they weren't working in the gallery, they were busy with the house, and within a year everything in it gleamed. They bought furniture at garage sales, and little by little they had turned it into a home they loved. Now Todd claimed that he had spent all of the last four years lying under a leaky sink, or making repairs. He wanted an easy modern condominium where someone else did all the work. Francesca was desperately fighting for the life of their business and the house. Despite the failure of the relationship, she wanted to keep both, and didn't see how she could. It was bad enough losing Todd without losing the gallery and her home too.

They had both tried everything they could to save the relationship, to no avail. They had gone to couples counseling and individual therapy. They had taken a two-month break. They had talked and communicated until they were blue in the face. They had compromised on everything they could. But he wanted to close or sell the gallery, which would have broken her heart. And he wanted to get married and have kids and she didn't, or at least not yet – and maybe never. The idea of marriage still made her cringe, even to a man she loved. She thought his new friends were dreary beyond belief. He thought their old ones were limited and trite. He said he was tired of vegans, starving artists, and what he considered left-wing ideals. She had no idea how they had grown so far apart in a few short years, but they had.

They had spent last summer apart, doing different things. Instead of sailing in Maine as they usually did, she spent three weeks in an artists' colony, while he went to Europe and traveled with friends and went to the

Hamptons on weekends. By September, a year after the fighting had begun, they both knew it was hopeless and agreed to give up. What they couldn't agree on was what to do about the gallery and the house. She had put everything she had and could scrape up into her half of the house, and now if she wanted to keep it, he expected her to buy him out, or agree to sell it. They had less invested in the business, and what he wanted from her was fair. The problem was that she just didn't have it. He was giving her time to figure it out. Now it was November, and she was no closer to a solution than she had been two months before. He was waiting for her to get sensible and finally give up.

Todd wanted to sell the house by the end of the year, or recoup his share. And he wanted to be out of the business by then too. He was still helping her on weekends when he had time, but his heart was no longer in it, and it was becoming increasingly stressful for both of them to live under one roof in a relationship that was dead. They hadn't slept with each other in months, and whenever possible he spent the weekend with friends. It was sad for both of them. Francesca was upset about ending the relationship, but she was equally stressed about the gallery and the house. She had the bitter taste of defeat in her mouth, and she hated everything about it. It was bad enough that their relationship had failed – five years seemed like a long time to wind up at ground zero in her life again. Closing the gallery, or selling it, and losing the house was just more than she could bear. But as she sat staring at the numbers, in an old sweatshirt and jeans, she could find no magic there. No matter how she added, subtracted, or multiplied, she just didn't have the money to buy him out. Tears rolled down her cheeks as she looked at the amounts again.

She knew exactly what her mother was going to say. She had been vehemently opposed to Francesca going into business and buying a house with a man she loved but didn't intend to marry. She thought it was the worst possible combination of investment and romance. 'And what happens when you break up?' her mother had asked, assuming it was inevitable, since all of her own relationships had ended in divorce. 'How will you work that out, with no alimony and no settlement?' Her mother thought that all relationships had to start with a prenup and end with spousal support.

'We'd work it out just like your divorces, Mom,' Francesca had answered, annoyed by the suggestion, as she was by most of what her mother said. 'With good lawyers, and as much love for each other as we can muster at that point, if that happens, and good manners and respect.'

All of her mother's divorces had been on decent terms, and she was friendly with all her former husbands, and they still adored her. Thalia Hamish Anders Thayer Johnson di San Giovane was beautiful, chic, spoiled, self-centered, larger than life, glamorous, and a little crazy by most people's standards. Francesca referred to her as 'colorful' when she was trying to be nice about her. But in fact, her mother had been an agonizing humiliation for her all her life. She had married three Americans and two Europeans.

Both of her European husbands, one British and one Italian, had titles. She had been divorced four times, and widowed the last time. Her husbands had been a very successful writer, Francesca's father – the artist, the scion of a famous British banking family, a Texas land developer who left her comfortable with a big settlement and two shopping malls, which in turn had allowed her to marry a penniless but extremely charming Italian count, who died eight months later in a terrible car accident in Rome in his Ferrari.

As far as Francesca was concerned, her mother came from another planet. The two women had nothing in common. And now of course she would say 'I told you so' when Francesca told her that the relationship was over, which Francesca hadn't had the guts to do yet. She didn't want to hear what she would have to say about it.

Her mother hadn't offered to help her when Francesca bought the house and opened the gallery, and she knew she wouldn't help her now. She thought the house a foolhardy investment and didn't like the neighborhood, and like Todd, she would advise Francesca to sell it. If they did, they would both make a profit. But Francesca didn't want the money, she wanted to stay in the house, and she was convinced there was a way to do it. She just hadn't found it yet. And her mother would be no help with that. She never was. Francesca's mother wasn't a practical woman. She had relied on men all her life, and used the alimony and settlements they gave her to support her jet-set lifestyle. She had never made a penny on her own, only by getting married or divorced, which seemed like prostitution to Francesca.

Francesca was totally independent and wanted to stay that way. Watching her mother's life had made her determined never to rely on anyone – and particularly not a man. She was an only child. Her father, Henry Thayer, was no more sensible than her mother. He had been a starving artist for years, a charming flake and a womanizer, until, eleven years ago, he had the incredible good fortune to meet Avery Willis, when he was fifty-four. He had hired her as an attorney to help him with a lawsuit, which she won for him, against an art dealer who had cheated him out of money. She then helped him invest it instead of letting him spend it on women. And with the only genius he had ever shown, in Francesca's opinion, he had married Avery a year later, she for the first time at fifty, and in ten years she had helped him build a solid fortune, with an investment portfolio and some excellent real estate. She talked him into buying a building in SoHo, where he and Avery still lived and he still painted. They also had a weekend house in Connecticut now. Avery had become his agent and his prices had skyrocketed along with his financial affairs. And for the first time in his life he had been smart enough to be faithful. Henry thought his wife walked on water – he adored her. Other than Francesca's mother, she was the only woman he'd committed to by marrying her. Avery was as different from Thalia as two women could ever get.

Avery had a respectable career as a lawyer, and never had

to be dependent on a man. Her husband was her only client now. She wasn't glamorous, although she was good-looking, and she was a solid, practical person with an excellent mind. She and Francesca had been crazy about each other from the first time they met. She was old enough to be Francesca's mother, but didn't want to be one. She had no children of her own, and until she got married she had the same distrust of marriage that Francesca did. She also had what she referred to as crazy parents. Francesca and her stepmother had been close friends for the last ten years. At sixty, Avery still looked natural and youthful. She was only two years younger than Francesca's mother, but Thalia was an entirely different breed.

All Thalia wanted now at sixty-two was to find another husband. She was convinced that her sixth would be her final and best one. Francesca wasn't as sure, and hoped she'd have the brains not to do it again. She was sure that her mother's determined search for number six had frightened all possible candidates away. It was hard to believe she had been widowed and unmarried for sixteen years now, despite a flurry of affairs. And she was still a pretty woman. Her mother had had five husbands by the time she was forty-five. She always said wistfully that she wished she were fifty again, which she felt would have given her a better chance to find another husband than at the age she was now.

Avery was totally happy just as she was, married to a man she adored, and whose quirks she tolerated with good humor. She had no illusions about how badly behaved her husband had been before her. He had slept with hundreds of women on both coasts and throughout Europe. He liked to say he'd been a 'bad boy' before he met Avery, and Francesca knew how right he was. He had been bad, in terms of how irresponsible he had been, and a lousy husband and father, and he would be a 'boy' till the day he died, even if he lived to be ninety. Her father was a child, despite his enormous artistic talent, and her mother wasn't much better, only she didn't have the talent.

Avery was the only sensible person in Francesca's life, with both feet on the ground. And she had been a huge blessing to Francesca's father, and to her as well. She wanted Avery's advice now, but hadn't had the guts to call her yet either. It was so hard admitting she had failed on every front. In her relationship, and in her struggling business, particularly if she had to close it or sell it. She couldn't even keep the house she loved on Charles Street unless she could find the money to pay Todd. And how the hell was she going to do that? Bottom line, she just didn't have the money. And even Avery couldn't work magic with that.

Francesca finally turned off the light in her office next to her bedroom. She started to head downstairs to the kitchen to make a cup of warm milk to help her sleep, and as she did, she heard a persistent dripping sound, and saw that there was a small leak coming from the skylight. The water was hitting the banister and running slowly down it. It was a leak they'd had before, which Todd had tried to fix several times, but it had started again in the hard November rains, and he wasn't there that night to fix it. He kept telling her that she'd never be able to maintain the house by herself, and maybe he was right. But she wanted to try. She didn't care if the roof leaked, or the house came down around her. Whatever it took, whatever she had to do, Francesca wasn't ready to give up.

With a determined look, she headed down to the kitchen. On her way back up, she put a towel on the banister to absorb the leak. There was nothing else she could do until she told Todd about it in the morning. He was away for the weekend with friends, but he could deal with it when he got home. It was exactly why he wanted to sell the house. He was tired of coping with the problems, and if they weren't going to live there together, he didn't want to own it. He wanted out. And if she could find a way to pay him, the problems were going to be all hers, on her own. With a sigh, Francesca walked back upstairs to her bedroom, and promised herself she'd call her stepmother in the morning. Maybe she could think of something that Francesca hadn't. It was her only hope. She wanted her leaky house and her struggling gallery with its fifteen emerging artists. She had invested four years in both, and no matter what Todd and her mother thought, she refused to give up her dream or her home.

Read the complete book – available now

44 Charles Street

Danielle Steel

What makes a house . . . a home?

Everything is falling to pieces for Francesca Thayer. Her beautiful, old house is full of leaks and in need of total restoration. Then her relationship with lawyer Todd collapses and he moves out. As the owner of a struggling art gallery she can't possibly manage the mortgage alone, so she is forced to do the one thing she never imagined she would: she advertises for lodgers.

First arrives **Eileen** – a young, attractive schoolteacher who has just moved from LA.

Then comes **Chris**, a newly-divorced father struggling with a difficult ex-wife and the challenges of parenting his seven-year-old son who visits every other weekend.

Last to arrive is **Marya** – a famous cookery author who is hoping to rebuild her life after the death of her husband.

And so Francesca finds that her house has become a whole new world – and as things begin to turn around, she realises that her accidental tenants have become the most important people in her life. Over their year together, the house at 44 Charles Street fills with laughter, hope and heartbreak.

And Francesca discovers that she might be able to open her heart again after all . . .

9780593063040

Family Ties

Danielle Steel

A life of devotion. An empty nest. A new beginning . . .

Annie Ferguson – a bright, talented young Manhattan architect – had the world in the palm of her hand . . . until a single phone call altered the course of her life forever. Overnight, she became the mother to her sister's three orphaned children. Suddenly, her own life seemed indefinitely on hold.

Years later, she is as independent as ever, with a satisfying career and a family that means everything to her. Annie is comfortable being single and staying that way, but with her nephew and nieces now young adults, with careers as diverse as fashion editor, law student and rebellious artist, she is facing the empty nest with some trepidation. Then a chance encounter of her own changes Annie's life yet again.

From Manhattan to Paris and all the way to Tehran, *Family Ties* is a novel that reminds us how challenging and unpredictable life can be, and that the powerful bonds of family are the strongest of all.